SOME PLACE BETTER THAN HERE

A NOVEL

LANDEN WAKIL

◆ FriesenPress

Suite 300 - 990 Fort St
Victoria, BC, V8V 3K2
Canada

www.friesenpress.com

Author portrait photograph by Diego Mora

ISBN
978-1-5255-0609-3 (Hardcover)
978-1-5255-0610-9 (Paperback)
978-1-5255-0611-6 (eBook)

1. YOUNG ADULT FICTION

Distributed to the trade by The Ingram Book Company

Praise for Some Place Better Than Here

"SPBTH needs a warning label: Do not read as a distraught teenager. It fills your head with idealistic notions of finding love, discovering yourself, and mending a broken past."

—*Wattpad User, reLaX646*

"This story broke me."

—*Wattpad User, onehundreddays*

"This is definitely one of those books that I'm probably going to contemplate about forever. Thank you for that."

—*Wattpad User, TheEccentricArtist*

"I loved the book simply because it reflects reality."

—*Wattpad User, reislust*

"I love and hate you so much for your beautiful words and metaphors and characters because I'm crying my eyes out and up way too late."

—*Wattpad User, roguehopes*

SOME PLACE BETTER THAN HERE

LANDEN WAKIL

This story is dedicated to those who had lived it.

Act I.

1

I've Just Seen a Face

DANNY

It was the seventeenth of too many summers spent in that dumpy little town when everything life-changing happened. The intolerability of living in that town reached its peak when, during the fifteenth summer, I had my bike stolen from the beach and had to walk two hours home in a melting puddle of sweat. I needed a car.

Things did get better, however, when months before starting the sixteenth summer, after aceing parallel parking in one shot on the exam, I got my full-blown license and no longer needed Mom in the passenger seat to drive.

So that day I finally got my license, got in a car, and got to drive anywhere my heart oh-so-wanted to go, felt like the first day my life truly began. Even something about the way I listened to music changed when the sound came blasting (always blasting) out of the speakers of a car. From then on, freedom only went withheld by where I didn't steer the wheel. But mind you, that freedom was still limited to the streets of that shit town. My license was only a hall-pass from the prison of my dreams. Because, if I'm going to start being honest with you—the only thing I had ever really dreamt of doing, was running away.

So, all that being said, it half-killed me that morning when my mom had to drive me to work.

"And what did I say?"

"Seriously? Mom——"

"Do not take his car out. Drive it home. Clean it. And leave it at home."

She was talking about my boss's Porsche. Do you get why this sounds stupid now? But I'll continue to regurgitate.

"Yes, Mother," I said. "I get it. He trusts and respects me, and I need that job." Which was a complete and utter lie. I didn't really need that job. Mom and I were soon moving to California.

"Wow. Congratulations, Danny! Something got through your thick skull!" Mom said, scratching my head with her knuckles as we pulled up into the driveway of Superior Carwash.

"Mom. Mom. Whoa. My hair."

"Danny—you're going to a carwash. Come on. See you later. Love you."

"Loveyoutoo," I said as I grabbed my bag, shut the car door, and then went on to trudge through the open garage of Superior Carwash. In my imaginative little noggin, where most of my life played itself out, good ol' Superior was some sort of retro Ford Motors assembly plant.

Geez, now that I think of it, maybe I did have some sort of mental disability that at my then elderly age of seventeen-going-on-eighteen I was still playing in my head.

But, I guess I had nothing to truly fear, because for as long as I can remember, I always made up stories and scenarios in my head. Such as the time when I was in the fifth-grade, nursing a stupidly major crush on class hottie, Julie Holdaway, and had just discovered the religion I would soon become a devote adherer of: The Beatles.

My then growing obsession with The Beatles—in particular the song "I've Just Seen A Face"—led me to the point where I began living my life through the lyrics. It got so bad that at recess, I made sure to "look the right way" at Julie on the tetherball court, because "had it been another day, I might have looked the other way" to the basketball nets.

"Danny!"

The voice of my carwash manager, Rob, boomed as I walked into the garage, my rubber soles squeaking on the wet concrete floor. Inside the carwash, a conveyor-belt stretched through the rectangular building that shotgunned all the way back in a long open tunnel.

"Nice of ya to show up today, buddy," he remarked. Now, Rob was your typical American-Italian guy with a cropped goatee who always *remarked*. Always something dumb though, such as: "You're looking bigger" or, "you're looking smaller" or, "your hair's too long" or, "your pants are too low," "you look tired," etc. Rob was also one of those guys who wore white cargo shorts. But I never made that remark.

And then as I said, "Yeah, yeah. Thought I'd do you guys a favor today," he held out his fist for a bump. Rob was hip.

"I hope you showered this morning," he then said, shifting into all seriousness. "I know what you're up to, man. *Banging* all these chicks. Believe me. I was your age once too. I know you're getting blowies left and right!"

Now, that is where I tended to freeze up. As I never really knew if I *should* respond to Guy Talk with my forty-year-old boss. I just awkwardly smiled and went: "Ha ha yeah…."

Rob went on to tell me that it was alright. Healthy even.

"I just don't want you smelling like pussy hopping in these cars, buddy. You're gonna give the old guys a heart attack!" He then spun around to attend the cash register.

For some inexplicable reason, all the guys at Superior Carwash were under this belief that I was like this major Playboy. Possibly due to the rumors Rob spread about my sex life. Which at that point was, well, virtually nonexistent. Why? No reason in particular.

It was rather simple: the girls at my high school sucked, and like, I don't know? Where does one four years shy of legally entering bars seek out girls to have sex with? How other guys my age found these girls was well beyond me. Certainly, they were not to be found within the confines of Superior Carwash.

But then in the instant that Rob turned from the register, I ceased being a delinquent and entered the world of Responsibility as he clasped the keys to the universe in my hands. Telling me, "Don't lose these," as I looked down at the glinting gold emblem and read the inscribed word: **PORSCHE.**

Rob warned me about what would happen if I lost them, which turned out to be a faux backhand to the face. He got a big kick out of my flinching. Guys like that are always getting a *riot* out of somebody flinching.

It was just then that the dryer fired up and quickly consumed all other noise in its vacuum; a car was coming down the assembly line.

Rob then did something totally unexpected.

He smacked my ass and said: "Hop in!"

I drive out cars. That's normal. It was the whole smacking my ass thing that was a little strange. Anyhow, I quickly slung my bag up on the hooks, snatched a pair of rags, hopped in the little Fiat (the steering wheel was practically sitting on my lap I was so cramped in there), slapped the gearshift into drive, and pulled out of the garage like an asshole clown in an asshole clown car onto the driveway where my buddy Max was drying down an Acura.

"Danny-O!"

"Maxwell!" I hollered back, returning the exaggeration.

After somehow managing to free my legs, I proceeded to basically flop out of the clown car and saw an old guy staring at me. Thank God I didn't smell like pussy, or I probably would've given that geezer a heart attack.

I whipped out the rags stuffed in the back pockets of my jeans and began wiping down the clown car.

"Rob give you his Porsche or what?" Max asked after the owner of the Acura got in and drove away.

I yanked the Porsche key out of my pocket and dangled it around my index finger, as I, using my other hand, slid the rags over the hood.

"Suh-weet!" Max said, "I love it when Old Robbie Boy goes to Fort Lauderdale for the weekend!"

For your greater comprehension of events, that was the first time Rob had ever gone to Fort Lauderdale.

While crouching down to clean the rims, I said back, "Yeah, but, dude, we can't. He paid me like, fifty bucks and everything."

"Shit! We take that fifty and buy beers, bro. They'll totally think we're legal when we pull up in that beast."

It did not occur to Max that that was rather illogical, but his absent rationale made much more sense a couple minutes later when we were back inside folding rags.

"Dude," I deadpanned mid-fold. "Were you smoking weed?"

Slanty-eyed and grinning larger than his face, Max snickered, "No."

He reeked terribly.

"Are you an idiot? Rob's going to know you're high."

"Danny. Man. You got to chill, dude. Old Robbie Boy burns all the time. He gets the gange, man. Trust."

Never trust someone who's high; advice I wish I'd taken a little further ahead in life. But I rolled along with it and did not doubt the fact that practically everyone who worked at Superior Carwash got stoned and went to work. I may have been the only one who didn't. Because, you know, hugs not drugs.

Stoned Max and I continued our duties folding the rags coming hot out of the dryer on this cheap wooden worktable that faced a window like a glass portal to the bright and green world outside the carwash.

"Dude," Max blurted out after we went through a silent folding sprint. "Concert's gonna be ill."

With my hands methodically at work, laying each rag precisely in line with the edge of the last, I made an agreeing mumble and then said, "For sure, man."

Suddenly from behind us Rob shouted, "Hey! What did I say about talking?"

At the exact same time, Max and I wheeled our heads around to look at Rob jutting his stocky finger out from across the conveyor belt.

"Dude—I swear that guy has ears like a cat."

"I know, he's like Miss Bergmann."

"She was such a bitch."

"Oh, she was a huge bitch."

Rob boomed Max's name again, and once more we both turned around to see that stocky finger floating in space.

"Max—" Rob said, his voice back at ease. "Go to the back with Joey, seeing as you girls can't shut up."

My automated sarcasm was obliged to remark on Rob's sexism. But, ah. Whatever.

"Dude. Literally Miss Bergmann," Max said as he threw his half-folded rag onto the counter and dragged his feet across a puddle to the back of the garage.

Work was dead to the point where I was able to wash, dry, and fold an entire new collection of rags before another car hovered down the assembly line.

Keeping up with my folding duties, expecting Rob to race up to the register booth, I ignored the woman waiting at the vacant window. But when realizing that the fans were getting louder, and Rob wasn't showing, I soon became aware that I was the only one up front, and so I lunged over the conveyor belt and despite my mathematical limitations, did the dirty work.

With the calculator close at hand, I cashed the woman out (without losing Superior any money...I think), and watched as her van rolled along the assembly line into the digestive system of the carwash.

From the register booth, the woman smiled and said, "My kids wanted to go for the ride."

In my head, I was imagining them going nuts over the brightly colored soap splashing against the windows. And then screaming in harmony after the older boy decided that with the whirling brushes lashing against their car, they were to meet their end.

I suppose that's because that was the game my brother and I used to play when we went through the carwash. It's the funnest thing in the world when you're a kid. My brother used to tell me that we were being digested in the belly of the carwash monster, and although the bright square of daylight shone before us, with the promise of Freezies awaiting at our next stop, the 7/11, we would together, in unison, let out a loud shrilling scream until it was over. There wasn't much else that he ever taught me. But I guess that was the most important. Imagination.

Me: "Y'all had a gud time there?"

I said as I popped into the driver's seat and guided the van outside onto the driveway.

The One Kid: "Yeah! It's like a spaceship!"

The Other Kid: "Yeah, yeah, like Star Wars!"

When in the midst of doing the dry-down on the van, their mom came up to the car, and so I ran over to open the driver's door like an excellent valet runner.

Their mom: "Thank you very much."

Me: "You's a very welcome, ma'a—miss."

(Trick: Older Women lose their minds if you call them miss.)

She patted my arm and smiled. It felt awkward. Probably more awkward that I was in East-Central New Jersey and had an Oklahoman accent.

When I was bored at work, I would change my accent up from

car to car. Knowing I was on the money when I'd get asked, "Oh, so where are you from?" One time, Max and I had even successfully convinced an Australian couple that we were indeed Australian exchange students on working visas. Why? No reason other than shits and gigs. Plus I was always doing that, character voices and stuff. My best character voice was Rob.

But I never told him that.

It was after the family blasted off in their spaceship down the driveway onto Ridgeway Avenue, and then pulled into the grocery store next door, that another voice booming, "Rock Star!" grabbed my attention.

Rob's second in command, Miller, marched up from the back of the carwash.

"Stop wasting your time, holding doors open an' shit. Drive. Dry. Done," he said, puffing out his lower lip and shaking his head, staring at me with mindless eyes. My neck twitched nodding. Miller stared at me for a second longer. Then mumbled "Christ," under his breath before he turned to walk away.

In my opinion, Miller had no valid reason for getting all fidgety. I swear I had only thought: "What did I do wrong now?" but it turned out that I said it out loud.

"What did you do wrong?" Miller repeated, skidding around on his heels. "Rock Star, buddy." He lumbered towards me. "We're not one of your fancy rich places. We're not paid enough to do that kinda work."

With my eyes skimming side to side, not quite looking down at the ground or at his face, but somewhere in the middle, I asked, "What kind of work?" And readjusted my feet so I was one foot in, and one foot out of the garage.

"Rock Star? Are you getting mouthy with me?" Miller said, adjusting his posture to look at my chin, I guess. "All I'm saying is that I don't think Rob likes it too much. 'Cause then we gotta be doing that fancy shit all the time. You understand?"

I nodded. Though, there must have been something about my nod that did not please him because Miller jolted suddenly forward, completely invading my personal space, hovering his face inches away from mine.

(Coffee Breath. Bad Coffee Breath.)

"And what the hell have you been doing all day?" he barked, continuing his power-jaunt. "This place looks like shit!" Miller then broke away, walked up to the worktable, picked up a neatly folded rag. Studied it. And then threw it at my face. "Clean up a bit will ya, Bon Jovi?"

Triggers exist everywhere. And if you're like me, anything, at any second, can and will blow your head off. All you have to do is pay attention.

"*Rock Star!*" I squeaked to myself in my Miller-imitation voice as I pushed out the sudsy backwater using a squeegee into a drain on the driveway. "You lazy piece of shit. Clean up a bit, will ya?"

"What do you expect, Miller?!" Rob replied. "They're goddamn girls!"

One trigger. Boom. Two triggers. Bang!

Suddenly I was on high alert. On edge. Panicking. Afraid that just one more stupid thing would happen and a third trigger would fire back, driving me to some subversive anguish.

But that was when on the trail of the breeze, I heard what sounded like a river rolling over stones. And then leaning my weight against the handle of the squeegee, I looked up at the trees swaying ever so slightly on the opposite side of the street. The invisible wind rippled the leaves so that the shaded sidewalk danced in a beautiful patchwork of sunlight and shadow.

The tilted mid-afternoon sun beaming down transformed the color of my bangs from brown to gold, and pierced through the leaves. Playing with the illusion of being phosphorescently illuminated from within.

The sublime simplicity momentarily allowed me to forget. Forget that I was at work and in the same vicinity as the trigger holders. And that's why I whipped the handle of the squeegee against the brick wall. It fell and smacked the pavement.

What the hell am I doing with my life? I wondered, looking out onto Ridgeway Avenue. Confused as to why I held onto that crummy job, and why, when I was at home, with plenty of time spent alone, the desire for wanderlust never arose. But when I had to be locked in somewhere (practically every day of my life from the first one of pre-school to the last of twelfth) all I wanted to do was participate in the sunlight and discover how it re-energized the dull colors of the world.

The way that I undeniably knew how, that just down the road on the beach, the sunlight was bringing to life the tanned and toned body of a girl baking in the heat. How she was there ready for me to meet. With the tipping of her sunglasses and the split of an endearing yet cautious smile, I would see that her eyes were already a solar phenomenon.

What I had allowed my imagination to convince me I was missing out on infuriated me. There was an internal surge of angst matched with the never-ending urgency I felt for freedom. Then, in an alarming moment as all of my muscles aggressively tensed, I realized I was very well holding my own third trigger. The barrel aimed right at my head. In the seconds right before I tightened the fatal grip, I heard some birds sing. The tension that strapped my body eased and seemed to dissolve with the heat of the sunlight shining on my face. And with the sweet sounds of the birds chirping, I let the third trigger go. Other than the faint smell of a burning cigarette, blowing in from somewhere, I had found some sort of peace. I would be okay.

But in accordance to How Life Works, my bliss was disturbed and my peace instantly forgotten when the sound of a car grinding its over-exhausted engine, and blaring a bass-heavy song too loud for the speakers to handle, devoured the world. The birds' wings flashed white in sudden flight.

Of course, I heard it before I saw it, but I wasn't any less surprised when a black Chevrolet came racing in a zigzag down the road, and then stomping on the brakes, screeched in a sharp turn up into the driveway next door. The man driving rifled out of the car, slammed back the door, and chased a girl inside the grocery store. I couldn't quite tell if she had been in the car, but there was, in fact, a girl, and in the second that I turned to watch the action, I saw the long trail of her hair as she fled inside.

Alert with energy and adrenaline running high, my first instinct was to charge off after them. Something inside of us all intuitively knows when something just doesn't look or feel right. I dashed forward, but then my feet fell like concrete blocks. Not out of the fear of any danger—God knows that it didn't even cross my mind—but my comfort zone kicked in and kept me paralyzed. But I guess I was driven crazy by my hero's complex because, when I crooked my head inside the car wash, and neither Rob or Miller were anywhere in sight, I ran off in a sprint.

Nerves crept up, but I pushed them down and pushed my feet forward to the grocery store. What inspired me to find out what Chevy guy was up to?

Couldn't tell ya.

Either my intervention was going to save someone—again, hero's complex—or I was going to stumble upon a scenario I could write a song about.

I already had the opening verse composed in my mind by the time I twisted the blotched golden handle on the door and crept inside.

MARY

My sloppy, done-on-the-fly side braid kept falling apart about every two friggin' seconds. And well, at work, especially when you are bagging someone's groceries, playing with your hair isn't one of the more socially acceptable things to be doing. Like really, I wouldn't want some long scraggly strand of brown hair wrapped around my bunch of cauliflower either.

"Thank you for shopping," I said, doing my best telephone operator impersonation, waving goodbye to a customer.

There was no one next in line, so I had a chance to fix my braid. I undid my hair band and let my impossibly thick mane fall over my shoulder, then took it in three parts and started weaving. While using my faint reflection in the window to, y'know, make sure I wasn't making a disaster outta myself, I saw this mother and her two dumb kids get out of a van. The frumpy looking mother had one of those short haircuts women get when the reality of parenting had finally strangled that whole "losing the pregnancy weight" dream. And out from the trunk popped a stroller that the littlest of snots got to ride in, even though the dumb kid looked bigger than the actual stroller itself. This amazing stroller that I am spending way too much time rambling on about was seriously pimped out though. It had chrome rims with spinners and hydraulics, heated seats, satellite radio, everything.

Gotta love the shit rich people spend their money on! Jim would've said.

I then felt a sharp tug against my scalp as I wounded my hair too tightly while zoning out, examining this family. Goodness Lord. I couldn't even imagine being responsible for two human lives when I can't even get my hair in a proper braid.

Every Basic Bitch other than me could do this. I was always super envious of those girls who could just throw their hair in a bun or ponytail and still make it look cute. I mean, I'm often throwing my hair in a quick bun or pony too—I just don't think it looks cute. It's just convenient.

The electronic sensor beeped as the doors scrolled open and the stroller family walked into Wright Bros. I'm pretty sure the actual Wright Brothers were the dudes who invented the airplane. What's the correlation between aviation and locally jarred jam? That I have yet to figure out. But it wasn't until I wound down my weaving that it happened. I started craving a cigarette.

I know I shouldn't. I know in grade school all that was drilled into our impressionable (and vulnerable) young minds, aside from the multiplication tables (which I surprisingly still remember), was the fact that *smoking will kill you!*

Wanna know how it started? Doesn't matter. I'm gonna tell you anyways. I was fourteen and dating my first high school boyfriend, Simon Jenkins. It was kinda hilarious when we were together cuz I was a good two inches taller than him. But anywho—he would always smoke when we hung out, and believe me, back then I was grossed out. Especially when we kissed; I could literally taste the burnt nicotine on his tongue. But I joined the Dark Side when, one day, after this major fight I had with Jim, Simon offered me a cigarette and, well, I sort of liked it. And then Emmanuel, the dude who worked at the Chevron by my house, never ID'd me when I went to buy smokes, so, that's how he got fired, and how my addiction began.

On the stroller family's way out of the store, as the bowl-cut mom grabbed her grocery bags, the poor little turd who had to walk was babbling on and on to the stroller snot about the carwash being like a spaceship tunnel or something.

Kids. Can't stand 'em.

And, because you're sexist, you're assuming that, like most girls, my ovaries are exploding into overdrive at the sight of children, and then the next you thing you know, I'm poking holes in the next available condom so I can name my kid Xavier and post pictures of him wearing dumb outfits on the internet all for the thrill of a few extra followers. But after bearing witness to those dumb kids, I was just tempted to get my tubes tied and call it mission accomplished. Don't judge me. Did you see that bowl cut? And I thought the shitty blonde dye-job on the end of my hair was bad.

"Mary!" my manager, Linda, barked the second the family walked out. "Take your fifteen."

My inner philosopher was curious as to why this fat bitch had supreme control over my freedom, but the inner nicotine-addict was overjoyed as hell that I could finally go out for that smoke. Yes, I get it. It looks trashy as hell. Every damn middle-aged bitch that waltzes into my checkout line reminds me of it. Then, of course, there are the old creeps telling me, "You're too pretty to smoke!" and dumb shit like that. And then, when the regular customers catch me in the act, they forever have this slanted weariness when approaching conversation, and then, when my head's turned for a second, they begin sniffing like crazy as if they're gonna find me out. It's like, I can hear you whiffing like a dog, you senile idiot.

Sorry. I am a nice person. Really.

While sitting outside on the curb underneath the shade of the tethered yellow canopy, holding my smoke between my middle and ring fingers (because it just looks sexy) I got lost in my thoughts. Panicking over all the shit I had to do. Such as the cell phone bill that I'd been gloriously ignoring as it crept up. Life enjoyed compacting bullshit on top of the teenage-girl problems I already possessed, like period cramps and boys.

The canopy began flapping in the breeze that rolled through and redirected the fumes pooling out of the tip of my cigarette into my eye. After wincing and then rapidly blinking to water out my stinging eye, I turned my head away from the smoke and heard something smack the pavement.

A guy from the carwash next door was staring out at the road, looking at something. And as I began staring too, trying to see what he was looking at, from the same direction I saw it.

Charging in at a speed too fast for the engine, and blaring a rap song at a volume too heavy for the speakers, a banged up, black, 2006 Chevrolet Impala came screeching into the parking lot. I only know it's a 2006 Chevrolet Impala because it belongs to my—ex— boyfriend, Tanner. But I mostly know that it was his car because he would never shut up about that 2006 Chevrolet Impala and its custom spoiler.

He whipped to a stop in front of me and stomped out of the car, leaving me just enough time to jump up, toss my smoke (which wasn't yet finished), and march for the doors. Tanner chased after me, following me inside, and hollered my name.

"Mary!"

2

Lost in the Supermarket

DANNY

After tugging back the handle on the front door of the grocery store, a pair of glass doors grumbled open in front of me. The sensor beeped. Not quite the stealth entrance I had in mind, but I was already there and walking in like a stalker.

Standing at the door, staring out at the five aisles that made up the entire store and trying to decide which one would keep me best undetected, I heard two voices bickering from the back. Scooting down the aisle closest to the bakery section, silently landing my feet as I took careful steps, the voices grew louder, but not much clearer. Then, while reading the labels on the shelf, getting myself into the character of a curious shopper, one of the voices shouted. I snapped upright. My leg drew back, sliding my foot across the ground. The floor squeaked as I stunted my step. My position was given away.

Maybe this is totally a bad idea, I came to realize. *I've totally intruded on something personal.*

Suddenly feeling incredibly stupid, I resumed my role of scanning the shelves, looking for something to buy to justify my spying. Despite looking stale, the aroma of bread made my stomach growl.

Truly, I would've been the world's worst spy. I got mad at myself.

A voice then boomed. It sounded like a girl's. I stopped. Then things got quiet again. There was only more grumbling from behind the tarp that divided the storage room from the rest of the store, and grumbling from my stomach. A clock on the wall was ticking. And so did mine.

Rockstar was playing air-guitar with the squeegee, and then, in a dramatic Townshend-like exit, smashed the squeegee against the ground and left it there. I had to get back to work, fast.

Declaring to myself that this was pointless—I didn't know these people—and that at any second I was going to get in mega trouble with Miller, I spun around, thoughtless to how loud my feet squeaked, and ran to the front of the store.

But right as I made it to the end of the aisle, someone hollered: "TANNER LEAVE!"

Off the shelf beside me, I snatched a loaf of bagels and took a giant, casual lunge to the checkout line. Then crossing my hands behind my back, I curled my lips in a failed attempt to whistle. God, what goes through my head?

With a forceful whoosh, I heard the tarp bash forward. I jerked my head down the aisle. The driver of the black Chevy was stomping directly toward me. Then suddenly, spinning around, he shouted back towards the direction of the vinyl tarp waving in place.

"Whatever! It's your life, you stupid bitch!"

Just beyond the sideway bill of his baseball hat, I saw a hand swipe back the tarp, and once more heard the girl scream for him to leave. The Chevy driver spun around again, walking backwards towards me, and screamed in response, calling her a dumb bitch this time.

Absorbed by the action, I had hardly noticed that he and I were on an inevitable collision course. And in the second it took to realize that—and in the half second I had to react—it was too late.

We crashed. And upon recoil made direct, dead on, eye contact.

Anticipating a fist to the face, I flinched as his arm swung out—quickly thought of Rob—but then was surprised when his hand landed not on my nose, but on his own shoulder exposed in a baggy Devils Jersey. He snarled, cursed, and then charged past me. Making sure to smack every pack of gum off the racks on his way out. The sliding doors closed behind him. The sensor beeped.

That could've been bad, I thought, while rubbing my own shoulder that pleasantly did not appear to be fractured or dislocated or something. I flexed to shrink the throbbing.

Slight Shot
Head Shot
High Speed / Collision

I attempted to make some rhyme out of the scenario as I collected the last of the scattered gum packages off the floor, and then slotted them in their spots back above the celebrity tabloid magazines on the display rack.

At this point, I felt stupidly out of place. I knew I was going to get in trouble for ditching work, and I felt exposed. Like I had made an enemy. I didn't know what I was; I had tried pretending I was something. I thought of a bunch of things I could've been: a superhero in hiding, an Australian exchange student, stoned like Max, unaware and out of his senses. Maybe I'd caught some of his second-hand smoke? But nothing plausible came to me. I looked to my feet for the answer, which didn't help. All I could pay attention to was how the leather toes of my workboots were carved down like a rash. My mind blanked of lyrics—how could I blank of lyrics? I was always thinking of lyrics.

But when I looked up on the sound of the tarp flopping, lyrics didn't seem to matter anymore.

Actually, nothing really seemed to matter when the whole world apparently stopped so the sexiest brunette that I had ever seen could strut on through from behind the tarp.

Her every stride swung in slow motion. The way she wrapped her honey-dipped hair in a ponytail, a complete act of seduction. The sway and rocking of her hips, a more than polite introduction.

God Damn, I can sure rhyme, and curves will kill you if you're not careful.

When my too dry lips peeled apart, I realized I had become that guy. Totally forgetting that this amazingly hot girl was just involved in a shouting match about ten seconds prior to my being captivated by her hotness. Reality refilled when she stepped behind the register counter and let out a huge sigh.

I plopped the bagels horizontally on the white countertop. She kept on fixing her hair. I glanced down at the bagels, then glanced back at her, still fixing her hair. I wasn't sure if I should keep waiting until she stepped out of her bubble, or if I should say something, but clearly she knew someone was standing there, so....

"Are you okay?" I blurted.

"Uh. Yeah?" she said, looking down, still trying to make her hair work. "You heard that? Well, duh, of course you heard that. I shouted. We shouted. He shouted. My boyfriend shouted. Um, I mean, God, my, uh, ex-boyfriend, a douchebag who's not important anymore, shouted."

"Oh."

When it appeared as though she had mastered whatever variation of ponytail she was aiming for, she grabbed a red apron wrapped in a messy bundle off the counter and tied it below her plush chest, emphasizing the obvious arch from her stomach to breasts.

Though it wasn't until she finally looked up at me, making awkward customer service eye contact, and I saw how her silver nose-ring gleamed in the light, that I realized this girl wasn't hot.

My God, she was fucking gorgeous.

MARY

I stormed straight for the storage room. I knew exactly why Tanner had showed up. A stroke of brilliance must have forged somewhere in the silly-putty sufficing for his gray matter that, for literally the millionth time, like a door-to-door Jehovah's Witness, he would try to convince me that I needed him in my life. Eff that shit. I've done everything without even God so far, so why in the name of life would I need Tanner?

I made a fist and bashed back the tarp, and then as it flushed behind me, I heard Tanner bash through it, and without any shame in his game, follow me into the storage room squawking.

"Can you stop PMSing and just talk to me?"

(Because, you know, telling a girl to stop PMSing is a fabulous way to make her talk to you, right? Seriously, guys, go out and try it. That shit works, like, legit.)

"What do you want?" I shouted in his face, my voice echoing.

I felt the eyes of the non-English-speaking kitchen staff fall on us. All was silent. Then one brave soul split open a head of iceberg lettuce with a knife, and the insistent tack of dicing vegetables resumed.

"Seriously, Tanner," I yelled at the top of my whisper. "You cannot do this here!"

"If you wouldn't lob me every single time I tried figuring shit out with you, I wouldn't have to!"

I couldn't help but notice his gross blonde goatee flicker when he spoke.

And then, just as I thought of how easy it would be to snatch the knife out of José's hand if he took one step closer, Tanner grabbed my wrist. When I yanked back, my body twisted and my eyes fell on Nenita, one of the Hispanic, non-English-speaking kitchen staff in the midst of an iceberg lettuce chop, just staring at us. Eff off, Nenita.

Only Jehovah can judge me.

Before he opened his mouth again, I cut him off.

"Tanner, I am not kidding! I need this job. You can not and will *not* do this while I'm working!"

His mouth hung open like an idiot. I strongly resisted the temptation to punch him.

"This shit job? What, you're making minimum wage——"

And that's when I yelled at the top of my cigarette-tar black lungs for him to leave. Somehow he got the hint, and bolted from the storage room.

"Whatever!" he yelled as he pushed through the tarp. "It's your life, you stupid bitch!"

Thanks Tanner. Thanks for calling me a stupid bitch.

Supervising his exit, I yanked back the tarp right as he persisted in calling me a "dumb bitch," and then, a split-second later, watched him crash directly into a customer. Tanner then proceeded to smack every single pack of gum off the shelf before bolting out the door. I was going to puke.

White-Girl-With-Emotional-Baggage lures Douchebag Ex-Boyfriend in a 2006 Chevrolet Impala into dinky old Wright Bros to start a yelling match, vandalize the place, and practically beat up a customer? Great. I thought for sure I'd now have to go straight to Ashley's to print off resumes and start handing that shit out like herpes.

My body tensed with anxiety. The crawling nervousness, the pounding head, the runny pits; I needed Advil. And just as I thought things couldn't get worse, I felt something brush my shoulder and lightly tap the floor. My elastic had fallen out.

I was going to lose it.

"Okay, Mary, pick yourself up," I whispered soundlessly to myself as I forced every fiber in my body to bend over and scoop that stupid elastic up off the floor. I then wedged my hair into a side-ponytail (a decision made for practicality rather than the previous over-complicated braid choice) before walking over to my till. I heard the 2006 Chevrolet Impala squeal and burn away outside.

"Are you okay?" the broken-armed customer asked.

"Uh, yeah?" I winced, tugging too tightly on my hair. "You heard that? Well duh. Of course you heard that. I shouted. We shouted. He shouted. My boyfriend shouted. Um, I mean, God, my, uh, ex-boyfriend, a douchebag who's not important anymore, shouted."

"Oh," he uttered.

My fingers ached for that unfinished cigarette. With my eyes down on the bagels lying across the counter (and suddenly displeased with my dry knuckles as I went to grab them), I noticed that the gum packages were magically no longer on the floor. Sucker saved me the effort of cleaning. I grabbed the scanner thingy off its stand thingy, and then, as I scanned the loaf of bagels, I connected the dots.

First I recognized him by the rich tan of his arm, and then, as my eyes shot up, it was confirmed by the bangs fanned over his forehead that he was the Squeegee Boy from next door.

"Is this all?" I asked, The Bitch Voice slipping out.

"Yeah."

$4.32, including tax, calculated on the screen.

"I work next door."

"I know," I blurted.

"You know?"

"Well, like. Uh."

"Oh."

I resisted saying I recognized him squeegeeing. Because I know if someone said to me, "I saw you squeegeeing," I'd feel really gay. The poor kid probably didn't need any more homosexual accusations.

"I'm Danny," he said and held his hand out.

My hand, carrying the corpse of nicotine, reached for his.

I practically pinched his fingers and pulled away. Yes, I self-declare that that was the world's wimpiest handshake. My feminist membership card was surely going to be revoked for that girly shit.

"Your total is four thirty-two."

"Keep the change," he said, flicking his fingers. My eyelids fluttered as if I were epileptic.

Trash, I thought, sliding the change into the tip jar, each coin pelting the glass as they fell one by one. I caught an inhalation of my own greasy smoke.

"Thanks, Mary," he said. I stared up at him, probably with an accidental Bitch Face. "Your nametag," he quickly added.

"I totally didn't introduce myself."

"No!" his voice cracked. He covered his mouth. "No," he repeated, "that's okay. I can read."

Forcing a smile, I said, "I'm Mary," and wondered if my teeth looked yellow.

"I know."

"Nametag. Right." I felt stupid. "Okay, bye, D— uhh..."

"Danny."

"Danny," I repeated.

"It's okay. I don't have a nametag."

"Bye, Danny."

"Bye, Mary."

He almost forgot to take his bagels, but then spun around at the last second to grab them before running out of the store.

DANNY

"Is this all?" she asked, snapping me out of my daze.

"Yeah," I answered.

She scanned the barcode of the bagels.

"I work next door," I said, and must have thought that was a really interesting thing to tell this girl with a nose-ring.

"I know."

"You know?"

She started mumbling, "Well, like, uh," and then pushed her cheeks out in an unsure smile.

"Oh."

My incredibly small window of talking to this girl was almost closed. So I quickly eyed the racks of replaced gum—which she had yet to comment on—and floss and stuff to see if there was anything I could tack onto my order. But there wasn't.

"I'm Danny." I held my hand out, hoping that, somehow, it would lead me to a world of apron-less breasts or, at the very least, that conversation somewhere.

"Hi, Danny."

She shook my hand for a millisecond, as though she were morally obligated to because she was at work.

The antiqued green-digits-on-a-black-screen calculated the bagel's numerical value.

"Your total's four thirty-two," she recited.

I reached into my left, then my right pocket, and found a five-dollar bill to hand her.

The cash register sprang open. And as Mary's hand fled to tally up the amount of change, thinking that my indifference to pennies would impress her, I told her to keep it. She frowned. Then with the dirtiest look on her face said, "Oh, okay?" and I concluded that no matter what brilliant act of suaveness I produced, she would not be impressed. While wondering why all pretty girls, every single last damn one of 'em, had to be stamped with an attitude, I noticed that, from out of her trembling fingertips, from which the coins dropped into the tip-jar, how chipped her black nails were.

Then to get rid of me, she said, "Have a nice day," through a forced smile.

Whatever, I thought. *She's just some girl.*

"Thanks, Mary."

Chk—Chk—BANG!

She could not have looked more unimpressed. I think I (accidentally) creeped her out.

"Your—name tag," I quickly said, redeeming my potential stalker status.

"I totally didn't introduce myself," she said.

"No, that's okay. I can read," I said, making her laugh.

"I'm Mary."

"I know."

"Name tag. Right," she said, sort of remorsefully. "Okay, bye, D— uhh…."

"Danny."

"Danny," she repeated.

"It's okay. I don't have a nametag."

"Bye, Danny," Mary said, rolling her eyes.

I took a few steps towards the door, and then turned around to catch her goodbye smile. The crescents in her cheeks detonated an atomic bomb, blowing me apart.

I started to get the hell out of there, realized I had forgotten the bagels, ran back to the till, and then got the hell out of there.

The atomic radiation set my nerves on fire as I walked back over to the carwash, swinging the bag of what I had only realized later were sesame-seed bagels. Picking up the squeegee and returning it inside made me inexplicably jittery; clearly that atomic radiation was doing a real number on me because I was *glad* to be back at work.

I peered down into the long garage. There was still no one in sight.

What were they doing all day, was the real question to ask Miller. I shifted through the long shotgun tunnel, alongside the droning carwash machinery, towards Rob's office. I knocked on the door. Miller opened it only so slightly enough to tell me that I could take off for the day. Sweet.

After grabbing my bag off the hooks, I went around back and saw Max. Leaning up on one leg against the cinderblock wall, and sporting a pair of yellow, dollar-store bought Ray-Bans.

"Danny-O!" he sung.

It took me a second to clue in, but Max had a cigarette tucked in the center of his lips.

"Dude—you're smoking cigarettes now too?"

Max tried answering with the smoke in his mouth, but just ended up dropping it from his lips and chasing it as it rolled along the pavement.

After successfully capturing his rolling smoke, Max asked, "You ready to go to the show?" and poked the cigarette back in.

I knew what being "ready to go" meant. I looked over at Rob's silver Porsche stuffed amongst all the other cars in the parking lot. A speckled white light reflected on the hood, and the windshield beamed back a green mirage from the trees.

"Did Miller let you off too?" I asked, squinting in the yellow light of the late afternoon sun. My skin shivered in the heat.

"Yeah, man. They said I could take off. We're taking Rob's car. Obviously?"

In all actuality, there was nothing divine about having Rob's car. I was just supposed to clean it. I even suggested to Rob that he just leave his car in the parking lot. But Rob was under this impression that if he left his prized possession with the detail garage guys, his car would explode or something. Though the irony was that we had countless luxury cars, far more exquisite and expensive than Rob's, in Superior's care all throughout the summer. But out of all the staff, Rob trusted me most. So by then, the margin of time had vanished. The day was at a standstill and I had to make a choice: was I to take Rob's car, or not? I knew I shouldn't. Every voice of reason and logic—and the fear of Karma—told me not to. But then again, how much longer did I have to be stupid and seventeen? Not very much longer.

"Of course, we are," I said.

"Suh-weet!"

And that was it. The words were spoken and the seal had been shut. T's were crossed and I's dotted. The contract was forged. There was no going back now. I prided myself on being a man of my word—though I wasn't sure if at seventeen you were technically a man, but boy sounds condescending—and Rob never told me: *Don't take my car out with your idiot friend Max.* So, I had no other word but the one I gave Max to go back on.

With a shaking nervousness and the hollow folding-in of my stomach, I felt the thrill of breaking the rules. With every passing second, the shaking foreboding eases, and then the wild one can relax into the thrall of his criminality. We were stealing a car, baby.

3

Summertime Sadness

MARY

I didn't get fired. Thanks Jehovah, I owe ya.

But unvaryingly, I was rather disappointed with Wright Bros after they got me all psyched with that action. Squeegee Boy and Tanner really spiced things up. Ya dig? For the rest of the afternoon, work was boring, but it did deserve a Jehovah-level thanks because it gave me the fifteen minutes (yes, a whole fifteen minutes) required to get my hair in the PERFECT BRAID.

No one said anything about the shouting thing, and I guessed as long as Squeegee Boy didn't sue for a fractured collarbone, or something pussy like that, we're all good in da Wright Bros hood.

But the real deal was what I was going to do with my first Friday off in like, forever. I was scheduled to work every weekend. I was even scheduled to work during exams. Which was super gutless of Linda. She probably realized my scholastic career was a waste of time anyway. But yes, what to do on Friday night?

My friend Ashley, the A-1 regular smoker, was lovedrunk on her new hookup and wanted to be a committed side-hoe and go to his band's show.

Don't you hate those friends that don't take your amazing

advice? Like, I'm *basically* Oprah Winfrey, and Ashley still thinks that "dating" (swap that for any other verb, my darling freaks) another nineteen-year-old college dropout who plays bass in a band is a good idea.

Sparing all the boring details, I'll summarize our texts back and forth on the longest bus ride home of my life: I agreed to go. I owed Ash one for letting me squat at her place the week before, and she needed a wing-woman.

Call me the Wright Sister.

After Mary and The Caravan of People Too Poor To Afford Cars, (cuz let's be honest, only poor people in Gilmore Park took the bus) got stuck in Ridgeway Avenue's rush hour traffic, and then got delayed further by roadwork on Lockport, the longest bus ride of my life came to an end. Giving me like, no time to get ready. For the sake of other humans subjected to being around me, I wanted to shower, you feel? Like, a long day at work gets you all greasy-feeling. And believe it or not, I wanted to look half-decent for the boardwalk.

There could've been hot guys there. How was I supposed to know? But let's be honest, every male in Gilmore Park is like, *repulsive*.

So I got pretty because, well, there's beef between Ashley and I. Which is ironic because Ash is a vegetarian. But like, one of those "I'll gorge on fries and frappuccinos" kind of vegetarians. But, well, like. Okay. I'll say it. I'm the pretty one. Now, most Basics would sell their soul to the Devil for beauty; I'd tell that ol' horny bastard to take his vanity and shove it up his ass. Because gorgeous or not, c'mon hunny, you know he'll do you as long as you spread your legs. You know how many ratchets get laid? But I'd gladly offer my soul like poker chips to Ol' Lucy any night if it meant looking better than Ash.

I had just enough time to do all the necessary means of Adriana Lima-ing myself. So yes, you betcha I plastered on that eyeliner and spoke just enough dirty Brazilian to turn myself on, and then I tried finding something to wear.

My closet stared me dead in the face and laughed for a solid minute and thirty-two seconds as I mentally composed about one hundred outfits. All of them heart-wrenching. My go-to shopping habit was thrifting, then coming home and realizing what I got was hideous, and then further realizing that one cannot simply just cut the sleeves off and make it look like a $79.99 dress from Urban Outfitters.

The laundry basket was sympathetic though; it knew I wanted to get laid. It coughed up my go-to: black jean shorts, my gray crop top (that when pit-checked, didn't smell like Mary after a long day at Wright Bros), and my Yankees snapback.

Why are you giving me that dirty look, you ugly bastard? Of course I was going for the whole Lana Del Rey thing. She's the most perfect person on planet Earth and she pretty much sings my life and I don't really buy into the whole celebrity worship thing, but she's worth all the worship. God, would I go lesbian for her. Did I mention she's perfect?

After getting ready in world-record-breaking time, I went to the kitchen and saw that the alcohol cabinet was left open, as if inviting me to fall into the footsteps of the generational alcoholism running through my veins.

Landing on my knees after I had pushed myself up onto the tiled-stove counter, I accidentally knocked over the empty boxes of Mac 'N' Cheese, and then looked through the alcohol cabinet. And yes, I did check the stove-pot; only the crust of burnt cheese brimmed the bottom.

The cabinet door bounced back on the hinges and hit my shoulder as I pushed through the empty bottles all the way to the back, searching for my Sourpuss Vodka that the magical Booze Fairy must have downed in the middle of the night. It was gone. I searched the fridge for my Vexes. Gone. I scavenged for the Holiday Bailey's pack Ash got me for Christmas. Gone. For Ol' Lucy's sake.

Finally, in an act of desperate measures, I resorted to my ninth-grade tactics and filled an empty water bottle with one of his off-limits bottles of vodka, and then filled the rest of the vodka bottle back up with tap water. Call it an act of revenge. I may or may not have also swiped a cigarette (or two) out of a pack of his Indian Reserves in the drawer. Call that an act of charity. Charity just like the Welfare Fraud Warning letter left haplessly amongst all the other unopened mail on the counter by the front door.

Ashley needed to hurry up.

When I finished lacing up my scuffed white Converse All-Stars, I secured my possessions for the night, and pushed through the cringing screen door onto the front porch. Out on my way to please my cigarette-aching lungs across the street.

Typically, on my way down the porch, I would stop and tell this old damn rusted barbecue, that Jim profoundly refused to get rid of, to "go die," for it only contributed to the clutter and the neighborhood reputation.

A little ways down and across the street from my house, at the end of Seadrift Drop, where the road ended in, well, a straight drop into the waters of Danae's Bay, sat a rusted yellow guardrail. It was my sorta go-to spot when I needed to get out of the house, or smoke a joint.

As I sucked back the cigarette, I watched a seagull glide under the shadow of a giant willow tree that the sunset had backed onto the pink ocean. That stupid seagull escaped Danae's Bay until it became nothing more than a speck far south down the coast. From the crest of the bay, I could easily see the Carraway Beach boardwalk, and the lighthouse in the distance already blinking with the oncoming of night.

My phone vibrated. Ash claimed, via text, that she was here. I looked back around to the street.

Hmm. No, you're not.

I replied telling her to meet me at the corner of my street and

Seadrift. Not long after, I saw the yellow sign reading: DEAD END (ha, isn't that ironic) light up in the glow of the headlights, and then, as I turned to look behind me, I saw a blue van speeding down Seadrift and swerve onto my street.

And not even in the mood to conjure up annoyance at Ashley for ignoring my instructions, I marched over.

"Hey, hey, hey! Gurrl, whaddup?" Was the exact way Ash greeted me when she rolled down the window and waved her hand with a cigarette clutched between her unsexy fingers, fanning out the ashes.

"Hey, Ash! Let's go!" I said, as Ashley like, struggled, to get out of the van idling on the gravelly slab of my driveway. The stones crunched beneath her feet as she ran up to hug me.

"My nigguh, Mary. Whoop! Whoop!"

I burst out laughing. I'll grant Ash that at least. She could make me laugh like nobody else. No, I am not that big of a bitch. She made me laugh cuz she was crazy. I wasn't laughing at her, not then, anyways.

" 'Kay, let me go find my straightener," Ashley said.

"Ash…" I gazed toward the street. "Can I bring it to you later?" I said, and then through gestures tried leading us back towards the van.

"Mary, I need my straightener."

(FYI, Ash had, like, pin-straight hair. She really didn't need to fry her dyed blonde split-ends any further.)

"Ashley, can this wait?"

"It'll take me like, two seconds," she said and pushed past me, scattering the stones as she dragged her feet up to the porch steps.

"Ashley," I ran to her. "Please."

My pleas were really all for her sake because her mug looked like my dirty foot based on the stank-face she was giving me. Ash stared real hard, but my inner bitch was much more fierce and gave her evil eyes until she got it and backed off from my house.

Oh no, don't get me wrong, she was not impressed or expressing any sympathy or something the way I would have. She just rolled her eyes, said "whatever," and waltzed back to the van.

Can't blame her——she just wanted to look hotter than me.

So, with my super duper Friday night off to a great start, I followed behind Ash, checking out her flat scrawny ass all the way to the van. And as I pulled on the handle of the back door, it slid open in my face with an intense blast of weed. Faint circles of smoke lingered in the air around the dudes sitting in the back.

From the passenger seat, Ashley announced: "This is my friend, Mary," as the dudes in the back slid over to make room for my ass. A bong sat between the legs of the bro next to me, vapor still swirled in the base.

Well, apparently I'm breathtaking (duh), because they all just sorta nudged their heads in my direction as I said Hi.

When Ashley specifically introduced me to Cody, her bass-playing hookup, he hardly had as much of a "hey" to say to me. Real personable bunch. Now, I could see how Ashley found Cody attractive; there was something sexy about him, but he wasn't my type. He really didn't even look like a true musician. He seemed like the kind of guy who, since discovering pot in the eighth grade, just resumed the role of being a bass player because it fit the whole stoner gig and justified the Bob Marley posters in his room.

"Mar," Ash said, turning around to face me as the van rolled down my driveway.

"Yeah?"

"Do you have a dart?" she asked.

No, I don't have an extra dart you can have. But I will graciously, out of the goodness of my heart, give you one because you're my friend, and I am a nice person.

"Sure," I said.

The van jerked on the brakes, then pulled forward as I pulled the pack of smokes out of my purse and handed Ash one of Jim's cheap Indian Reserve cigarettes.

"Thanks, Mar!" Ashley handed the cigarette to Cody.

Screw you, Ashley.

As the van whipped through the narrow streets of my neighbor-hood and approached the main road, I noticed that the dude sitting next to me, who I assumed (purely by the stench) was the drummer, kept looking down at the nearly indistinguishable outline of what barely deserves to be described as my tits.

Like, dude! I am not even showing a fraction of any cleave, I'm like a B cup. WHAT can be so sexy about two barely visible lumps on my chest, THROUGH A SWEATER. God. Damn. Boy.

I safely assumed my role this evening was that stupid friend that they all tried to finger on the basement couch as Ashley and Cody went off to bang. Great.

"I'm Nick," Drummer Boy said in the *stoner voice*. I think he knew I noticed him checking out my twelve-year-old-girl chest.

"Hi, Nick," I replied in the *stoner voice*. Then nudging my head back into the headrest, I looked down at the bong and said, "Let me take a rip of that."

Without hesitation, Nick handed me the bong, fished a lighter out of his pocket, and I went to take my hit. The glass bottle grew hot as I held the light and slurped up the smoke. I then felt imme-diately dizzy, on the brink of death. My throat closed, raw, heavy with smog. I coughed; they laughed. The dizziness faded, and so did my mind. Just like that, I was cooked to perfection. Call me an Easy Bake oven.

DANNY

Summer can be quite oppressive to those of us not participating in its multitude of activities. Forget single loaded barrel guns. That whole goddamn town was like a row of machine-gun armed guerilla soldiers led by Che Guevera, thirsty to kill anybody even curious about participating in a rebellion. Wanna play rock 'n roll music? Freak.

Unbeknownst to me at the time, I carried the rebel flag nailed through my flesh on my back. My existence hosted a rebellion, a coup d'état against the Gilmore Park mentality. Which was that you're supposed to drive a pickup truck, enter the same trade as your father, drink away the day's burdens at the plaza pub, watch your kid do the same thing. Then die. But what else could've been expected from an abandoned factory town with a boardwalk tourist scene hobbling on its last peg leg? One hurricane, or dip in the economy away from the sea swelling up and swallowing it whole like Atlantis.

As Max and I drove in Rob's Porsche, I found the sixties satellite radio station which was God's gift to me. '60s on 6, '70s on 7, '80s on 8. Hell, even when Max and I jammed out to "Hip Hop Hurray" on '90s on 9, I kinda had fun.

While pretending to be a Formula 1 driver, surrendering to the demand of Atlantic Way as it swung over Lake Heeley in a bridge shaped like an S, I caught in the air the smell of a simmering barbecue——the signature scent of an early summer eve. And out past my elbow hanging over the ledge of the window, the sun was slowly relaxing its way towards the horizon. Its setting light, like a skimboard, skipped pastel colors eastwards onto the lake, and in the distance, the Atlantic Ocean.

"Dude," Max sparked up outta nowhere. "Change this shit,"

he said, turning off "I've Just Seen a Face." "We're gonna look like fags."

Max then scrolled through a thousand stations until he found something cool. Shortly after the Lake Heeley Bridge, Atlantic Way whipped around downtown Carraway Beach.

Carraway Beach, like many other coastal communities, considered itself its own township within Gilmore Park, though the only properties actually addressed "Carraway Beach" were the shops on the boardwalk and the downtown area. The downtown was nothing much more than a single block of nineteenth-century buildings built upon a hill that rolled up from the coast, and then continued to roll on all the way north into Danae's Bay. The storefronts wrapping the perimeter of the downtown block consisted of coffee shops, two-cent restaurants, a retro candy store that everybody loved, maybe a junky swim and surf stop, and old people bars. But the heartbeat of downtown was an alleyway that cut through the block and followed the roll of the slope until it reached the road. The locals had simply called this alleyway: The Alley. Lining The Alley were bars that redefined the meaning of bar-hopping, where the bands could be heard playing all night long.

"This is my shit," Max said, cranking the volume up on a song he found just as we wound up stuck on Atlantic Way in the God-Awful bumper-to-bumper traffic that Gilmore Park seemed to have a fetish for. That, and traffic lights. Lots of traffic lights. And one-way streets. Pretty much the whole goddamn catalog was a sham.

"Dude," Max piped up, bobbing his head to the beat, "all these girls are so ugly."

Out past my window, where the chrome on the Harleys lined up outside the biker bar, Gypsies, gleamed in the sun, I saw that the sidewalk had become a runway of thin-legged girls pretending to be in California. Strutting around in their bright tank tops, sheltering all the wonders in the world that were only the drop of a strap, or the snap of a pant away.

"It's gonna be ill when you have the house to yourself," Max said, as we inched a little bit forward in traffic. "We're gonna bring back so many bitches."

I made a noise in agreement. Out on the street, the charade of people matched the charade of music blasting from every available speaker. Everyone had a different idea of what a summer evening sounded like and imposed their soundtrack onto the traffic jam.

Jukebox Doo-Wop sang out sweetly in all its four-chord captivation and desperate lovesick melodies from the candy store, Gypsies thought the beachside scene called for AC/DC, and down by the sailboats reggae blared; Max and I obviously thought Demon King's "Bitch City" went melodically with the setting sun.

"I, uh, actually," I began incoherently saying as I crawled the car slightly forward in traffic, bringing the shafts of the setting sunlight into direct confrontation with my vision. I reached up and swatted the sunvisor down. "I think, I'm, um, going. Actually."

"Wait—what?"

"Yeah, man. Well, you know how my mom was really against it and everything. And, well, my late application got accepted, so yeah, I think I'm going…"

"Fuck, man. Danny-O. My main-man, Danny-O. Fuckin' Cali cooch. I love it, bro."

"Yeah."

Max cranked up the volume on "Bitch City."

It was the crosswalk of The Alley and Atlantic Way that caused the traffic holdup. And additional foot-traffic was produced because, next to downtown, beside where the old Gilmore Bowling Alley stood proud, a carnival was setup. These things began with the Fourth of July and did not end until September. The mechanical questionability added suspense to every ride. You never knew when it could be your last.

Max lowered the volume on the song. "Dude, I'm gonna get

out here."

Max got out of the Porsche, feeling more important than ever before in his life, and disappeared into the bustle of downtown. At that point, I couldn't have cared less as to ask why. I skimmed through the radio, back to my sixties——keeping the volume low so I wouldn't look like a fag.

Now, don't get me wrong. It's not that I hate modern music; I don't have some ensconced bias because I need to validate my resistance against the mainstream and wear my hipster badge with pride. Not at all.

It just matter-of-factly sucks.

There have been a few good bands that have cropped up in recent years. Such as The Killers, Arcade Fire, Kings of Leon, the 1975, The Strokes—to name a few. But exactly, where are the *bands*? The bands! Where did the bands go? Where are the voices as ugly as the guys who were singing? The guys with their freaky clothes and freaky hair? Gimme some crudeness and some crass. Some slop and slosh. A voice wailing outta key least is real; not every vocal inflection filtered through auto-tune. I want to see the scars in the pick-guards, thrashed through thousands of hours of practice, the drum-kits beaten 'til they're bruised. Please, treat my soul to the electric guitar solos setting the soundwaves ablaze, making my body move in ways that I'm terrified by. I want something loud, something screeching at supersonic speed, something to shred inhibition to ribbons. Bringing down the entire house in a red hot meteor crash, exploding onto the stage with a blast of smoke that swarms the lead guitarist like a Rock 'n Roll Resurrection of Christ. Best part apart about it? No Gucci required.

Have you ever listened to "All Along The Watchtower"? How about "Jumpin' Jack Flash"? It should be mandatory to listen to "Purple Rain" from start to finish.

And it ain't just all about rock. I love Pop from mostly every era. "I Want To Hold Your Hand" made me fall in love with The

Beatles after all. Rock 'n Roll's Daddy, Elvis Presley, was the first Popstar, and Michael Jackson was the King Of.

Hell, even crank up the volume on Taylor Swift.

The problem is not in the music; it's in the production. I can hear it. I call it Flying Saucer Sound. Smooth. Flat. Repetitively spinning around. I do try to like new music. I really do. I give every new Pop hit on the radio a chance. But music nowadays just doesn't move, doesn't soar. It can't set a fire in your soul 'cause there's nothing gritty about the sound to strike the match. The blood's all drained; the color's all been taken out, the nuances and details lost in the mixing. And lyrics have lost their integrity, where's the storytelling?

The dynamic range of the instruments is being compressed to nothing until its just one garbled cacophony that can be cranked up loud enough to come out clean and smooth and soulless through your speakers.

Completely stalled in the traffic-jam and wondering why I was the friend who had to drive, I watched summer be herself in full-throttle beyond the tinted windows, and saw how people were staring at me. Thinking for sure it was because I was listening to Elton John's "Crocodile Rock."

A wake of courage then hauled upon me. It might've been because "Get Off of My Cloud," came on the radio next, so I blasted the volume and punched up the bass. Now people stared harder. I didn't care. Gilmore Park should've awarded me, or at the very least, given me one of those keys to the city or something for teaching these people about good music. I knew the old guys at Gypsies would think I was hot stuff.

Oh yeah! they'd think. *This young guy's got some real muscle. Let's invite him for a drink!*

And I'd go over to Gypsies, where Bill and The Boys would buy me beers as I delighted them with my knowledge of classic rock, specifically how the Gibson guitar defined Woodstock. They needn't know I'm personally a Fender guy.

But no. Neither Billy, nor Ricky, nor Ricky's sister, nor Tommy or Timmy (old cats always have names like that) looked my way.

Eventually, the crossing guard gave me his blessing to go on through the crosswalk and so I floored the pedal like James Dean in his Porsche Spyder, and thought of how tragedy glorified the damned.

I rode the circuit of Atlantic Way and Dalhousie Street several times, keeping an eye out for a convenient parking spot. Considering I had nothing better to do than that, and wait for a text.

It's true. There was a girl. For the sake of time, let's just recall her name as—Jess. A fine gal, a swell gal, whatever kinda gal Jess was, I remember her telling me once in a passing conversation, that she liked The Broken Lyre. You might have even been fooled into thinking that Jess was a cool girl. She posted black and white pictures, avoided Top 40, and dressed as a fashionably recognized hipster. I had actually texted her before I left the carwash. But I kept that a secret.

After circling through the parking lot a few hundred times, a spot eventually became available. So, as I sat in the parking lot that fringed upon the boardwalk for a text I knew was hopeless to wait for, I did the worst thing one with my disease could do. Scroll through social media. Before long, I was plagued with photos of everyone I knew having sun-induced fun. The Hamptons. We ♥ NYC. Girls that looked unrealistically good pulling up the straps of their bikini bottoms, melting in the sun as displayed on the internet.

Then, after sitting in the car for so long, looking at the real world in all its online glory, I was convinced my body had sagged into the leather seat.

Then suddenly determined to get out of the car and be a part of the summer, I pushed open the door, swung my legs out, and then was laughed at. When I walked around to the trunk, these two blondes standing across the fence were laughing. I was certain it was at me. So, I checked my reflection in the tinted rear window.

Do I look like a psychopath? Did they hear my music?

There is no worse humiliation in this world than being subjected to an attractive girl's sneer. But, what did I honestly care? From out of my bag, I slid out my Lyric Book, threw my jean jacket on—despite the heat—and went for the boardwalk. Out of all the freaks that migrated to the beach, what was I doing that was so laughable?

"Hun'ner!" I then heard somebody screech as I crossed the sand. "Stahp yer cryin' and be a good big brother." Someone with breasts that should not have been so carelessly exposed said, scolding her child (whose name I pieced together as Hunter). The other one with breasts, though flatter and with hairs growing out of the faded blue eagle tattoo, sat with a burning cigarette in the driver's seat of their car.

The sunlight slanting through the thin haze in the sky blinded me as I observed the whole family affair, squinting like a patched-eye pirate.

Hunter was putting up a fit. He didn't wanna leave the beach or something. His mother—the nipples on her unappealing breasts cutting through her shirt—started yelling at him. And then she cursed. Which I hated.

Stop it, I should have said.

Whaddafug? The hairier and flatter-chested one would've answered.

He's just a kid. Let him be.

Who da fug are you t' tell me how t' raise ma boy?

He just wants to play for a little bit longer. Let him be a kid.

Then I would slash open the back door of the car, freeing Hunter and his sisters from the smoky backseat. And then the wind coming in curls over the beach, like the hair of a golden goddess, would cleanse them of the smoke while I built them the biggest and best sandcastle ever. Like with a moat and everything.

But as I was weirdly watching, I made eye contact with the starchy-nippled one, still all squinty like Patchy the Pirate, and kept on my way.

Turning onto the pier after walking down the boardwalk, I looked down to the sand and observed the familiar sights of Carraway Beach. A pink bikini top cradled a pair of tits like a hammock. Laughter radiated from the drunk thirty-year-olds playing volleyball and listening to crappy music overlaid with AM static. An old tanned cat, pumped like Tarzan, proud of the salt and pepper patch of chest-hair that matched his mustache, stood at the shoreline with his hands on his hips, letting the waves break against his shins. All the characters I saw inspired me to yank out the black wire-ringed notebook I kept shoved in my left butt-pocket. Then, taking a seat on a bench, resting my Lyric Book on my thighs, I slipped the cap off my pen and spewed cheap rhymes. Awash in the golden-orange light of the sinking sun, I masked myself behind the impatience of the pen as ink bled out, hiding from the world as I wrote out the lyrical fantasies it inspired.

4

Here Comes My Baby /
There Goes My Baby

DANNY

Max's face dropped with drop-dead concern. But I couldn't hear what he was saying over the thrash of music.

When I asked him again, he shouted: "HER ASS."

The table of art-scene-looking girls next to us looked as if they were about to write a vicious blog-post about Max and his patriarchal privilege.

"Ugh, I didn't really get to see."

"Okay. Uh. Well, how were her tits?"

"Decent. Hard to tell under her apron."

"An apron?"

"Yeah. You know, like what people wear when they cook."

"She was cooking?" he asked.

"What? No?"

"Then—why was she wearing an apron?"

"I don't know, man. It's part of her uniform? I dunno."

I leaned on the table, and Max's end wobbled up. *Goddamn*, I thought. *It's one of those tables.* We scooted the table over a couple inches, bringing us closer to the stage. It didn't make a difference. We established fixed elbow positions to prevent the insistent wobbling, pretending it didn't exist.

I looked up at the unlit patio lights that swung across the sky. According to local legend, back in the seventies a boardwalk band known as The Tycoons played a legendary gig at The Mansion Club and actually blew the roof right off that pop stand. Ridiculous, right? In actuality, it wasn't much more than a summertime patio bar, but locals loved to indulge and hassle tourists about the myth.

The drummer in the band did some ill-timed lick to close the song. To the untrained ear, it would've been impressive. The crowd, which was as wild as a piece of paper, applauded, and then the lead singer declared that the next song was their last.

"Okay, so finish telling me about this rocket you met, AKA Grocery Store Girl. Like, did you get her number?"

I wasn't expecting that question. It just occurred to me that I had no way of contacting her. Instinctively I reached for my phone, and then suddenly realized that when I got thinking about Mary and her smile like an atomic bomb, I couldn't give a crap about Jess.

"Uh—no. I don't know. It was weird, man. How was I supposed to get her number?"

I had girl—friends. I've had my fair share of drunken make-outs at school dances, and I've been on a few movie dates with some unfortunately uninteresting girls whom I had no chemistry with. You know, the usual. Whenever I talked to girls (for the most part), they were just inbox messages. I never actually asked a girl for her number, you know, like in person.

"Dude, can't believe you didn't get her number," Max scoffed as if he was absolutely peeved with my inability to approach a member of the opposite sex (successfully). But as long as I've known him, he's never taken a girl out, and I've known Max forever. He moved into a foster home at the opposite end of our school district when we were in the second grade. Around the same time it was just Mom and I.

"You at least got her name, right?"

"Well yeah, she had her nametag on."

"You got her name through her nametag?"

"Yeah?"

"Oh Christ." He smacked his forehead to his fist and shook his head.

The neon glow from a Budweiser sign nailed onto the nearby wooden fence turned the clumps of his uncombed hair a pinkish-red. I didn't tell Max the whole story of what happened at the grocery store; I left out the part about the douchebag ex-boyfriend.

"I told you, man, it was weird," I said and Max looked up, the red neon glow now shining on the side of his face. "When I got there, she had this super douche ex-boyfriend harassing her and causing a scene. So, by the time we started talking, she was already in a bad mood. I didn't want to bother her more. You know how females are."

"Run the other way, bro."

"Why?"

"Crazy, super douche ex-boyfriend? You're asking to get your ass kicked, man."

"I'd fight him back."

"Danny." Max raised his brow. "No, you wouldn't."

"Okay, yeah, realistically not," I admitted. I lifted a few dumb-bells now and then, and I think I'm decently strong, but I'd never been in a fight my entire life, and I was planning on keeping it that way.

With a crash of cymbals and a fading reverb effect on the guitar, the band that sucked had finished their set.

"Thank you, beautiful people!" the lead singer, who was really drunk, shouted into the mic. A sharp metallic screech pierced through the speakers. I always cringe when I hear that. The bar applauded for them. Max and I joined in. It was the polite thing to do.

"Give it up for my boys," the lead-singer shouted excitedly into the mic, "Crystal Prism! Comin' up next."

The Mansion Club—or Mansion for short—was full of people, which was common in those days when The Alley sprang to life every weekend night between Memorial and Labor Day. It was an uproarious, unregulated, non-stop hurrah that started as soon as the workday let out Thursdays at five, and went on all weekend long until the first light of Monday's dawn. Heck, even by Monday's noon you could catch some strung-out rioter still asleep on the boardwalk.

Not that I personally knew the intoxicated delight of what The Alley had to offer. Only from the outside did I ever see within. Typically, it was when Max and I tried hanging out with some group on the boardwalk.

In the pre-car days, when a boy only had his bike and had to physically exert calories, stoking his already rampant appetite, to get anywhere, we'd bike from the South End all the way to Carraway Beach, lock up on any available steel railing we could find, and then go out in search for any mischief and adventure that the night had to offer. Max and I would loiter up and down the boardwalk, around downtown, back to the boardwalk, and repeat the pattern until we found a group. Any bunch of guys we might have vaguely knew from high school that were indifferent to having a few extra rag-tags would do. Max would try to impress whomever with loud-mouthed ranting of beers he didn't consume and blowjobs he never received. I can't clearly remember, but I think I would find a place in the huddle and nod along and yap in agreement with whatever the popular opinion was.

Between the lies of my kill count in Call of Duty or how hot I thought some girl I never met was, out of the corner of my eye, I was looking for love. I kid you not. Throughout any normal day in Gilmore Park, beautiful women held the same mythic status as the unicorn or the Jersey Devil. But my God, I don't know where they came out of hiding, but hot girls—anything blonde wearing eyeliner with hiked up jean shorts was apparently good enough to fit the bill—entered the dimension on those hot summer eves. One of them had to be interested in a guy like me. But they were always like a scorching mirage, out of reach. Always fenced in by some hotshot guy or disappearing behind the bouncer's guard into the bars.

The Beatles (those bastards) filled my young, dumb, teenage mind with notions that these things were to come casually. That I was just going to see her standing there, waiting for some charming guy to sweep her off her feet into the cool breeze of an endless summer night. Unfortunately, and much to my silent embarrassment, projecting the personality of a 1960s Liverpool girl onto the millennials always left me astonished to discover that they were more interested in dropping down and twerking like shawty to some computer produced beat.

But that night was going to be different. I had accepted The Beatles were liars, and I was finally that older bastard on the opposite side of the bar's gate. Well, sort of. For the concert, the doors to Mansion were opened to All Ages, so tonight was my first crack at it. I was going to drink. And since bartenders can't spot out a fake as well as bouncers can—that was my theory anyway—I busted out my fake ID.

"Dude, I'm gonna run to the bar and see if my fake works," I said, flashing the ID to Max.

"Michael…Macdonald? Born…nineteen eighty-nine…. Quebec City?" He said, lifting an eyebrow for a very good reason. "I was half expecting this thing to say McLovin' on it. Good luck."

I got up from our table, rattling the fixed position, and was about four steps away when Max piped up: "Wait, dude. You're super anal about drinking and driving and shit. What are you going to do about the car?"

"Uh… not drive it."

"Danny! We need the car, man. If you're going to be gay about drinking, don't."

If sobriety was a part of some sort of conversion practice, I guess I would have to not drink.

"Well, do you want the beer if it works?" I asked.

"Hell yeah. Bring on the brews."

Max was always looking for any excuse to get drunk. When we were thirteen, for some reason, we thought it would be a brilliant idea to steal an entire two-four of beer that some college kids playing football in the snow left by the side of Charles Demore High School. So what do thirteen-year-old Max and I do? Each grab a handle on this thing and made a break for the woods. We didn't even drink the beer. We just, like, opened one, took a sip each, dumped it, and left the case of beer there. Why? Because we were mischievous little shitheads who were invincible and couldn't die.

It was just as I crossed underneath the lights laced across the open patio sky that they illuminated to life. I paused, and for a second dismantled the blockade that was my over-active mind, and allowed myself to take in the magic of the sight.

The newly sparked lights growing brighter as they absorbed the modestly retreating colors of twilight.

Mind you, to frame the picture I had to shuffle a tad to the left, turn halfway around, and then look up. Just so I didn't have to see any fools. The glow from the pale red Budweiser sign sort of ruined the shot, but that was okay. It wasn't until a guy backed into me, with a shock of beer erupting from his pint, missing me by an inch, that my little magic moment got completely ruined. He got mad. Guys like that are always getting sensitive about a waste of beer.

"Your house beer," I ordered at the bar like Clint Eastwood. I had no clue what Mansion's house beer was, or if house beers were even a thing. Seriously. I've never drank at that place. Mom was always ordering the house wine wherever she went; I figured it was a safe bet.

When the bartender hesitantly asked, "Can I see some ID?" I was in disbelief that he dared question Clint Eastwood. I figured Michael Macdonald could gamble his better luck. So I offered his identification to the gentleman appropriately skeptical of the monsieur's legality after Michael answered with, "Oui."

Under a beard that looked quizzically itchy, the bartender was one of those bastards who had pretty eyes. Seriously. Pinching the faux ID in his sausage-like fingers, he looked up, scowling at me. He then asked, "What's your date of birth?"

And just then, all thirty-five seconds spent memorizing Michael MacDonald's life lost all and any relevance. Because beyond the opposite side of the bar, leaning against a brick wall covered in pearlescent, watt-powered orbs streaming across it like vines, looking impossibly beautiful, and impossibly bored, stood Mary.

Unintentionally, she was doing all the right things to knock me off my feet. When Mary bowed her head back, parting the curtain of hair over her wide-set eyes—that were so bright they pushed back the night—I knew she wouldn't be staying. That place could never capture her. No place could. That's just the thing with the beautiful ones. They're too beautiful to stay in one place for very long.

"Date of birth?" the bartender asked again.

But nothing mattered anymore. Not even that house beer. Propped up on my toes, I lifted my head to see over the crowd, to see what kind of people Mary hung with, wondering if there was room for me. I saw that Mary was standing next to some blonde wrapped under the arm of the last band's bassist, and figured she was the kind of girl who liked boys who played in bands.

Just as I, in my head, played out a scenario where I'd confidently walk up like Eastwood, and we'd bond over the beauty of the pearlescent lights overlapping and zigzagging across the sky—because she would be impressed with my sensitive artistry or something unlikely like that—and then we would somehow go on to live happily ever after——she walked out of the bar.

And then just as the bartender commanded, "I am not going to ask again. Date. Of. Birth?" the speakers by the stage screeched with the anticipation of rock 'n roll.

"It's fine, I'm seventeen," I said and split from the bar, taking off for the front gate as the entire bar roared on the avalanche of drumming. People gave me hell when I put effort into politely pardoning my way through the crowd. I was sworn at, and I think, even spat at. And an elbow jabbed into my ribs when I slid through a near impassable clump of bodies. With one damp shoulder of beer later, I trudged through the bar swept over with ovation, slipped between the bodies hovering around the gate, and made it out onto The Alley.

I spun around in a circle.

Mary was nowhere to be seen. I swear beautiful girls can walk to and from the Fourth Dimension at will.

> We boardwalk boys / Losin' our minds
> Over them Boardwalk Angels / Stealing our hearts
> Hey, uh, Mister Audition Man
> I read for Romeo / Do I get to play the part?

I composed in the Lyric Book Of My Mind as I fled down the slope of The Alley, staggering my fast falling feet in sideways steps.

A car then jerked on the brakes and blared the horn as I darted through the crosswalk on Atlantic Way. I swear, people hated me everywhere I went. Whatever. Mary was the only thing on my mind, and my first bet was that she was on the boardwalk.

Mary was nowhere to be seen on the boardwalk.

I raced back to the street. When I came flying back out onto the road, I saw her and The Blonde Friend coiled up in what appeared to be a fight.

All it took was catching one good glimpse of her face, and my fearless ambition suddenly shrunk into nervousness. Maybe that wasn't the greatest time to just walk up and be like, *Hey! It's the guy who read your nametag earlier!*

My chest expanded rapidly against my T-shirt; all that sprinting left me winded. Sweat collected at my temples and slipped down my face as I stopped to catch my breath. Then looking up, I noticed that, by then, all the warm colors had faded from the sky, save the jet trail brushed pink in the sun's last ditch effort.

Car horns began blasting. During their exchange of words, The Blonde Friend kept gesticulating towards the van that held up traffic, and after what seemed like a not-so-pleasant final dis, The Blonde Friend got in the van and drove away. The pile of cars backlogged in the jam quickly resumed what would have been their respective distance on the road. And in the clarity of the newly emerged vacancy, the ambiance of the carnival sprang back to life. Another result of the post-traffic conundrum was that Mary, head down at her phone, was left all alone.

Her friends ditched her. Mary's by herself. This is perfect!

She then began walking in the opposite direction. I contemplated running after her. But then I figured she would need a ride, and well, it would've been rude of me not to offer her a ride. Right?

My feet practically grew mini wings as I raced to the parking lot. Like a runner with the Olympic torch, I held the Porsche key to the sky, jamming my thumb onto the alarm button a thousand times until I heard the little gray bug going off like a maniac in the corner. I snapped open the door, jumped into the beige leather seat, patiently waited as a merry-sweet couple took their jolly time passing behind the car, and then finally reversed, screeching out of the spot with a twist.

I whipped out of the parking lot and bolted down Atlantic Way, driving past the Carnival and the old Meadow Theatre, towards where the boardwalk ended and the beach houses took over.

The heavier my foot weighed down on the pedal, the faster I closed the distance between us, and the speck she had become down the road got larger. The whipping wind lashed my bangs into my face and pricked my eyes. They watered. I clamped my hair down and sucked it up.

Then something happened. A Pontiac Sunfire spun in front of me, cutting me off. Forcing me to stomp on the brake. The momentum whipped me against the seatbelt. The strap sliced into my chest before throwing me back against the seat.

All of the worst-case scenarios came to my mind as the Pontiac Sunfire stopped directly beside Mary at the Penelope Street crosswalk—the worse one of them all being that her ride had arrived. The Pontiac sat low to the road as if it were an actual professional racecar and not just some Jersey Junkies' imagining of one. Hardly a second later, Mary's middle finger flashed in the air and I heard only the faintest syllable of the eff word over the pipsqueak throttle of the Pontiac as it peeled down the rest of Atlantic Way, the taillights flashing as it had to brake behind another car soon after. Mary turned right onto Penelope Street.

So I slapped up the right indicator, spun the steering wheel, declared myself a stalker, imagined the police knocking down my door with a Mary-Ordered restraining order, and just before I checked back into reality, Mary was staring dead on at me as I idled alongside her.

I patted my hair back down flat as I blurted, "Hi, Mary?" and to my relief, that was just a bad dream. Because I wouldn't have so stupidly said her name as a question had it been for real.

Mary stared at me. I was bound to wake up any second. An unlit cigarette sat still in the perfect arch of her lips. She plucked the smoke out, said, "Hi," poked the smoke back in her mouth and went to light it.

"I swear I'm not stalking you!"

"Okay."

By that point, yeah, all hope of my words being the result of a dream mistreating me was gone. Morning couldn't save me now.

Mary turned back around and kept on walking, flicking the lighter again.

"Are you okay?"

Continuing to trot along the curbside, outright ignoring my question in favor of consistently jolting the lighter's spark wheel, scratching then sparking, yet failing to light each time she flicked it, Mary finally said, "Yeah, I'm fine."

"Are you walking for fun?" I asked, keeping my foot steady on the brake pedal as I inched beside her, moving down the street.

Mary kept clicking her lighter, making subtle grunting sounds as her frustration with the lighter increased, and well, probably with me too. The streetlights along the quiet residential neighborhood beamed to life. The weight of the dipping sun pulled a navy curtain over the sky.

"Sorry, not my place to ask," I said, then thought of something quick and sly. "Where are ya heading?"

Clutching the cigarette using her middle and ring fingers, Mary slid it out of her mouth, and told me in two short words that she was walking to the "North End."

Damn the word count, I was happy I got a reply.

"Well, you realize from here it's about a two-hour walk."

"That's good exercise," she said, still trying to get that spark to catch a flame, and I guess I was doing the same thing.

"You want a ride?"

"No."

Out of nowhere, I heard clicking. Something vibrating. I looked for my phone, mute in the cup-holder, then looked up to see Mary clawing through her purse and yank out hers.

"Ashley?" she said into her phone.

The voice on the other end started shouting: "You know you actually ruined my whole night…" then faded into a near inaudible garble when Mary repeatedly clicked the button on her phone to lower the volume.

Turning her back to me, Mary tried getting through to the person on the other end. "Whatever…it's fine, Ashley…Ashley… just keep it."

The other voice kept ranting. By the really loud and constant rambling of the garbled phone voice, it sounded as though this Ashley chick was drunk. And amidst her babbling, which went on for so long, Mary actually held her phone away from her ear and gave me a look. Which was totally awesome because it was like we were on the same team. Major points for Danny.

By the end of Ashley's long-winded rant and rave, the only intelligible word I could make out in English, was the word *parents*.

Mary put the phone back up to her ear. "Tell your parents, thanks." And hung up.

I really wish I had some clue as to what was going on with her. From the impression I got, and Ashley's bitch fest, it didn't seem too good. As she struggled to slide her phone back into the pocket of her tight jean shorts—which generously showcased her figure—she struck her lighter, and yet again, it didn't catch flame.

"Stupid thing!" Mary yelled and whipped the lighter against the ground. And as if I weren't idling beside her in Rob's Porsche, she jolted her neck back, looking upwards at the sky, and dramatically moaned.

I looked up too. A few ambitious stars were trying to transcend the gradient sheet of blues.

"How long of a drive is it to Danae's Bay?" she asked.

"Is that in the North End?"

"Yeah."

"About fifteen minutes, tops."

"Can you—would you—mind giving me a ride?"

"N-no. Not at all."

5

Stuck in the Middle With You

DANNY

Ever been on a date with a mute? Me neither. But I am sure it would be something very similar to being stuck in the car with Mary. A black dome lowered over the sky to enter the world into the obverse and oversee the activities of the night. The sun had been swapped for the moon, and on the streets, the drivers behind the passing windshields lost their identities to the shape and shine of their headlights.

Nothing on the radio seemed to impress Mary. And making conversation through the radio was my backup plan, hoping that a song I landed on would be one that she liked and we could talk about—a girl's taste in music can reveal a lot of her heart. But Mary's radical indifference to all the amazing tunes I stopped for a second on revealed that she was clearly heartless. Or deaf.

I forgave her though. Something on her phone must have been very pressing in that it demanded all of her attention. The light cast from her phone was really distracting to my driving, and so was the annoyance of her being on her phone, but I used it as a good excuse to check her out.

Mary's face shone pale blue in its glow. And when I looked

down at her phone, sitting atop the shredded denim strings on her thighs—thighs—I wanted to do everything from crash the car to make out with her.

"What band were you at Mansion to see?" I eventually asked her.

Mary grumbled, her body turned away from me, her eyes now fixated on the suburbs that sprawled over the streets the further north we drove.

"None of them."

And asking her about The Broken Lyre proved just as pointless, as in seeing she had "never heard of them."

Despite "Let's Live For Today" by The Grass Roots on the '60s on 6, I didn't dare suggest she stop rolling through the stations. Yes, she seized the dial without asking. The speaker grilles rattled with a hard pounding bass beat when Mary landed on a song that's lyrics had something to do with: cutting your head off, and your mom's too.

The digital green writing on the audio deck read: "Dirty Ridin' Niggas" by a fellow named Nukka. I wondered who I would be if I lived my life through Nukka lyrics.

My mind was taken off the radio for a second as I slowed the car for a red light. Baffled that Mary liked that sort of music—as, you know, she did not flip it off like the other hundred more bearable song choices—I looked over at her.

"This is Tanner's favorite rapper," she said, eyes glued to the dashboard.

Before I answered, I asked which way to turn at the intersection of Lockport Road and Ocean Avenue. "Right," she said, just as the light blinked green.

"Tanner?" I asked, resuming the topic, knowing damn well who he was, remembering her shouting at him in Wright Bros, but for the sake of creating something like conversation between us, I asked anyways.

"The guy from the grocery store," she said.

"Oh, ex-boyfriend, Tanner."

Out of the corner of my eye, I saw Mary shoot up an eyebrow. "Yeah, the ex-boyfriend who almost broke your arm, Tanner." She went back to her phone.

Over the speakers, Nukka was informing me that I was having a far lesser amount of sex than he was.

Then, while we were caught at the next red light, my eyes drifted back over to her and unfortunately had to notice the clear distinction the seatbelt made strapped between her breasts. I caught a whiff of her perfume and immediately stiffened in my seat.

"That's a nice smelling perfume," I said, eyes chain-locked to the road. Realizing stupidity cannot be unspoken, I followed it up with, "What's its scent?"

"Its scent? Uh, some shit I get called Beach Baby."

"Ah. Cool."

The light blinked green, and I raced through the intersection. Hoping to leave my embarrassment on the road behind.

At first, I wasn't quite sure where Mary was leading me. My first guess was that she lived further west by the Winston Woods park, but she told me to keep straight, and then hang another left into what locals argued was not Gilmore Park, but in fact Danae's Bay. Very much like Carraway Beach, it was another tiny coastal-township that demanded its own identity despite not being much larger than a suburb of old Dockworker's houses and half-renovated mansions, which was, to a greater or lesser extent, the dichotomy of New Jersey.

Cruising down the narrow streets connected by telephone wires draped from wooden-posts, latched and connected to each home as if fired from a harpoon, I glided to a halt for a stop sign on a street called Fisherman's Alley.

"Stop here," she said.

"Well, no duh. It's a stop sign."

Now, Mary had this look that can only be best described—in what she later told me was a genetic mutation at birth—as The Bitch Face. Mary gave me The Bitch Face, popped out the door of the Porsche, and ran off down Fisherman's Alley. From out the windshield, I watched Mary scurry down the road, look back to see if I was watching, although I'm sure I was invisible behind the tinted glass, and then spin to the left and saunter down another street. While contemplating whether I'd been ditched or not—in an attempt to understand Mary a little better—I tried to make out what sort of neighborhood Danae's Bay was. Fisherman's wasn't a terrible street. Other than the shack with the baby blue roof on a slant and the outhouse with the same blue trim, it at least looked like a South End street.

The night felt suddenly large and empty. The first, maybe thirty seconds, didn't feel that obscure. But as my fun little game of listening to a song from each decade-dedicated radio station got to the eighties, I felt that nervous lump in my chest. Mary had played me like the lust-struck fool I was and ditched me.

I imagined Mary had gotten me to drop her off at the house of some guy who listened to Nukka and somehow knew the magical words that got her talking. Clearly a talent lost on me. My mind fell into its familiar habit of over-thinking and over-imagining what happened. I even considered that maybe she'd gotten kidnapped. Alien Abduction was a solid runner-up theory, but when I didn't see a flying saucer, or the ray of a tractor-beam shooting out from the sky, I ignited my car, preparing to leave. Because the most realistic conclusion I could come up with was that I was simply some stupid boy, not worth a girl like Mary's time.

Then out of the black came three knocks on my window. Mary was back.

"What's up?" I asked as I began to roll down the window.

"Do you want to take me on a date?"

"Um. What?"

"Come on. Let's go on a date. Impress me. Who were they? The Brokers?"

"The Broken Lyre," I corrected her, surrendering to the indisputable.

Okay, I began thinking to myself as we drove in Morning Mass-like silence back down south to Carraway Beach. *Someway, somehow, I've managed to be out on a date with Mary. Wait—was she serious when she called it a date? Or is this a 'hangout'? Does a 'hangout' mean I've been definitely Friend Zoned? Why was she all of a sudden interested in going out with me? Does she think I'm attractive? She's really attractive. Her personality sucks so far, though.*

Like majorly sucks.

All those "10 Ways To Ace Your Date" Men's Lifestyle articles I'd read seemed to have been totally pointless. They never explained what to do if she wasn't talking to you at all. I hadn't even had a chance, as per expert suggestion, to "say her name often."

When nearing Carraway Beach, where the gas stations and plazas lit up the night, the traffic light in front of us jumped from green to yellow. The temptation to run it ran hard, but I'd already tempted fate one too many times that night, so responsibly, I slammed on the brakes. The seatbelt struck against my chest, and when the bop shot Mary back into her seat, with a long strand of hair coiled up around her fingers, she reckoned, "You could have made that."

"Yeah?"

Mary rolled her eyes from the windshield to me. Stared. And mouthed, "Yeah."

A hot-orange neon sign advertising *Drive-Thru 24 Hrs.* glowed through the window behind her. And out on the Broadway stage of the sidewalk, a brigade of lost boys shuffled a cigarette back and forth as the leader strutted ahead with his arm wrapped around his girl's waist and walking a mile apart.

Then not more than a second later, a current of cars from the Friday night rat race rushed up all around us. Left. Right. Behind. In the silver Porsche, we were gridlocked front and center.

The entrancing beat of a pop song, high with bright yellow and hot pink notes, came soaring in from the right, accompanied with the singing-along of teenagers in an overpacked, red, doorless Jeep. Behind it, a souped-up, emblem-stripped, 1970-something Challenger cruised in with a guttural roar. Its diesel stinking the street. And piercing blue headlights appeared with a low black Cadillac that crept up from behind. The air thumped loudly with a reverberating pattern. The night grew thick with exhaust and steaming engine heat. Our common desire to put away the pavement was all but temporarily put on hold by a yellow box with a condescending red orb.

"Okay," I began saying, all too aware of the rumbling engine dying to explode with speed. "You drive someone's expensive car and see what you do, Mary."

Stopping mid-hair twirl, she asked, "Is this not your car?"

Beside us to the left, an engine revved a triad. "N-no," I answered, reaching for the radio dial. "I mean, no, it is my car."

The engine revved three more times.

"Cool." The twirling continued. Someone from next door made a sound. I turned the radio up. Nukka again.

A muddle of shouting sprang up over the next series of revs, so I looked over and saw the illest squad you've ever seen in a Blue Rimmed Honda taunting me to race. I believe I overheard something about the dimensions of my penis and something about a "bitch's car!"

Rob was not a bitch, thank you. I rolled the window up and flipped to another song.

"You're just gonna let them talk about your car like that?"

I kept flipping through the radio, passed the sixties—ha, forget Classic Vinyl, no matter how great listening to "Baba O'Riley" would've been right then.

Then landing on the same trendy Pop Girl's hit single that the red, roofless Jeep was blaring, just at a different time in the song, I said, "This song's kinda overplayed, huh?"

It was following a comment from the Blue Rimmed Heroes next door about the status of my virginity when Mary asked, "How old are you?"

I was naturally offended.

"No," she said. "Like, don't give me that look. I'm seriously curious."

"Seventeen."

"So you're still in high school?"

"My birthday's August. So, like, yeah. I mean, I graduated, but I'm not eighteen yet."

"When in August?" Mary asked. I told her—the twenty-eighth—and asked her about herself. "Yeah," Mary uttered, gazing towards the car full of bros who were now enthusiastically telling Mary about their penises. She looked back at me. "I'm a December baby, so yeah, seventeen still. Oh my God, will those dickholes shut up already?"

I jolted my head back towards the car full of guys all sporting similar haircuts, all of who were getting a real bang out of each other's jokes. To be honest, I was far more taken aback by Mary's rather dramatic noun than by anything the Blue Rimmed Bros had to say.

(I think the word pussy was used about two and a half dozen times. I really am not a cat. I know it may be hard to believe, due to my giant whiskers, but I really am not. Thank you.) If this were The Wild West, I would have shot each one dead.

"Just ignore them," I said.

Mary made a sound as if she were about to rant, but held her breath in. According to our friends, I was now: a female dog, a cat, and a committed Catholic.

To distract myself from pulling out my Smith & Wesson and galloping off to the nearest saloon, I asked Mary some more stupid small-talk questions. Turns out she went to Saint Maria Goretti's; I told her I went to Thomas Jefferson High, answering her similar inquiry back. I asked if she knew a guy I knew, Nick Savignano, who went to Saint Maria Goretti's.

"Yeah, I know him. It was, like, super weird. He was in my English class, like, every year up until last year. How do you know him?"

"Oh. I met him at the mall once, like back in eighth grade." Nick Savignano was one of the guys a part of the few groups Max and I would frequently run into and tag along with for our exploits on those Carraway Beach nights.

Mary made an approving sound. And my conversation with Mary began and ended with Nick Savignano. *I should call him up and thank him,* I thought, hiccupping a laugh. Mary looked over at me like I was weird. With these clowns to the left of me, and Mary, a real joker, to my right, I thought of Stealers Wheel, you know, those poor guys whose song everyone mistakes for being Bob Dylan's.

Then, with the flash of the traffic light, all of our hoods turned green and the Blue Rimmed Boys screeched off, making sure to call me a female dog one more time on their way out. The light at the next intersection ahead flashed red. And so to avoid another confrontation, I signaled my way right, opposite of where I wanted to go, which was back to the concert, and went down the residential streets. Maybe the boardwalk wasn't the best idea. When I suggested Oceanside Park instead—maybe I could get this girl some ice cream there or something—Mary didn't put up a fight.

MARY

Earlier, Squeegee Boy was strapped like the tar on my black lungs about seeing The Brokers, and then suddenly, after we were on our way, he drove randomly to Oceanside Park. Kinda weird. I mean, I wasn't like, marching in the streets against the idea. I didn't really care what I did to waste time, but still, it was kinda weird.

But Squeegee Boy was like a puppy. Puppies don't rape. Speaking of the R-word, Jim told me that no matter what them leftists were saying, he was gonna buy me a gun so I can shoot any rapist in the ballsack.

Oceanside Park was Gilmore Park's wretched hive of stoners and nightcrawlers. Back in, like, the 1800s, there was a concert hall and a mini-put course and a rollercoaster that touched the sky, but now all that was left was one dinky little carousel that even kids found rather sad. And in place of where all those rides that provided entertainment for the pre-technology age, was just a big empty field wrapped inside a sidewalk that led to the beach. During the day, families who wanted away from the tourist scene of Carraway still came to enjoy the beach, and old people still came to limp on the sidewalk. But at night, Oceanside Park was for drunk teenagers and drug deals. Which conveniently worked in my favor, because when we got there, I smelled pot, and like the police dog I am, followed my nose to the stoners and borrowed their lighter, which worked. Thank God.

After I lit my smoke and we began walking, out of nowhere, Danny said, "I don't want to smell."

Rather pretentiously, in my opinion, but anywho, when I looked up from my phone, I saw that he was walking on the opposite side of the sidewalk, right on the edge of the beach, away from me.

Must suck to get sand in your shoes. We continued walking in awkward silence as I smoked my precious, making myself smell. After a while, curiosity got the best of me. My eyes glided from the light of my phone to him, to see, you know, what was up (like if Squeegee Boy was getting sand in his shoes) and noticed that he was too wearing white Converse.

God, we were matching.

Our cute little elderly stroll led us past the old pavilion, which, if you thought too long and hard about the size of the spiders in the corners, it would give you nightmares for years, and then we heard the dramatization of drunk ninth graders. Danny walked by fast.

Further down the sidewalk, right about the same time the cheap Indian Reserve cigarette started canoeing due to the inconsistent ocean wind, we approached the carousel spinning around red and alive. Some kids rode on it, making the ancient old crapper look like a cheery delight while their bored parents watched. Most likely with the regret that they didn't take the contraceptive lesson in Sex-Ed a little more seriously, or wishing that they would have just bought their dumb kids iPads instead. Squeegee Boy proposed that he wanted to sit down cuz he was short of breath or something. So without agreeing or disagreeing (as I didn't really care), I took a seat on the park bench he gestured to. Squeegee Boy blinked as he stared down at me, and then took a cushion on a lumpy rock, again, on the opposite side of the sidewalk.

As I sat looking down at my phone, with the cigarette in my other hand growing warmer as it neared its last breath, I opened the Tumblr app and took a drag at the same time. Though unconscious of how hard I sucked on the filter, unused to smoking such shitty cigarettes, I took in a deep drag of thick and ashy Indian Reserve smoke that scraped my throat, constricted my lungs, and then burst in a harsh cough and a cloud of smoke like an exorcism. Tears bled from my eyes, taking swabs of mascara with them as they rolled down my cheeks.

Squeegee Boy, sitting across from me on the rock, dared ask why I smoked. I told him that I was eager to see what hell was like.

"Well, that's stupid."

"Did I ask for your opinion?" I said, wiping a black tear away with the broad side of my hand. I then untangled my earphones and celebrated the unevent that was Tumblr. There really are only so many cat pictures on the internet.

For what seemed like minutes, or at least a Lana Del Rey song, I sat there on my phone until I heard a grunt, and decided that I hadn't looked at stupid pictures of pugs in a long time. Then I heard another grunt.

When I peeled half the song away with the tug of my earphone, I heard Danny say my name. Which, for the record, is a sin. You never pull out an earphone on a Lana song.

"Hmmm, what's up?"

"Do you want ice-cream?"

"Um, no?"

He looked disappointed. "What are we doing?"

And right as I was about to explain that we were on a date, I saw a picture of a pug in a tutu and laughed, almost half-snorting. Now, I'm not that terrible, I felt one-hundo for S.B. (Squeegee Boy), but clearly, a boy will always assume something else is gonna happen when a girl trotting along a solemn roadside willingly gets in his car. That's called prostitution. I ain't 'bout that life. God, that pug was so freaking cute.

"I don't want to miss The Broken Lyre."

I looked up in surprise at hearing a low voice. It was as if puberty and all its bliss had hit him at once. Somehow, I guess, his statement confused me. Is he asking me or telling me he wants to go?

As I was thinking of something to say, he jammed his fists in his pockets, and something about such an aggressive gesture wiped any interest I might have had away, and just grossed me out. Uncomfortably stirred, disgusted, I shut down Squeegee Boy's entire little fantasy. "Okay, you can go." And then I put back in my earphone.

Believe me, darlings, I know guys like the back of my pale and freckled hand—the freckles being all their bullshit.

It never occurred to me why Squeegee Boy wanted to take me to Oceanside Park if he was so constipated about seeing The Broken Lyre, until the voice over the loudspeaker at the carousel declared they were closing after one more ride.

"I'm gonna ride the carousel," he said and got up from his lumpy rock.

While watching Squeegee Boy saunter across the field, feeling all sorry for himself, hanging his head down, I ashed my smoke and screeched when a cinder burnt my wrist. I flew my stinging hand to my lips, and when I looked up, I saw him from across the field looking back at me. His golden-brown hair was swept up off his forehead, emphasizing the arch of his brow, which, until then, had been concealed by his floppy bangs. So while smothering lipgloss all over my hand like a horny adolescent, I flashed him a peace sign, gangsta style, and returned to the wonderful world of internet pugs.

Then, underneath the volume of Lana's "Video Games," I heard my name blasted over the intercom, followed by a request that I kindly get on the carousel. And then my phone vibrated, clattering all the shit in my bag, with another text from Ashley reminding me that I was a shitty friend.

The intercom gurgled out my name a second time, so I looked over and saw Danny standing beside the ride attendant he was harassing. Poor guy. There he was, dying to get home from his shitty job at the carousel, and Danny starts harassing him to get on the intercom. Out of sympathy for the carousel guy, I quickly checked the selfie-cam, and then got up and went over to the carousel.

6

On a Carousel

DANNY

She was a bitch. It was an inarguable fact that Mary was a bitch. I didn't get why she was legit mean. I don't recall coming across particularly obnoxious or threatening or something. To be honest, it was heartbreaking. It shouldn't have been, because I hardly knew her, but it was. I convinced myself that she wasn't even pretty anymore.

Bargaining with the guy operating the carousel was no easy task either. First he said calling Mary on the intercom was against their rules. So I said I wouldn't tattle on him. He thought about it, and then still insisted no. So I slipped him a five and he called Mary on the intercom.

If anybody actually pinched themselves when they couldn't believe what was going on, I would've done just that when I saw Mary get up from the park bench. I began to wish that she hadn't gotten up when I watched her drag herself over, effortlessly launch the cigarette from her fingertips, and then cross her arms. I quickly fled to the closest pony, a poor little brown fella with a pole impaled through his tummy, as Mary stepped onto the carousel plate and climbed on the pony behind me.

Of course, she climbed on the one behind me. Of course. What else would make sense?

I didn't expect anything from her that didn't imply she simply wished I would die. The saddle was rather small and quite unkind to my crotch, and on top of that, we weren't speaking. I could feel her staring at my back. It was awful. Fed up and sure I was just going to drop her off at her house after the dumb ride, I called her out on her bullshit.

"I'm glad you're easy to get along with," I said, turning my torso, straining my back to face her.

"I am a people person," she said, in an almost not mean tone.

But before I could say anything else, something heavy sounding crunched as an accordion jingle crackled on the speakers. The plate then hammered through a few jerks before spinning smoothly beneath our hooves. The song sounded like it was from a music box; a tune that kids from an era not terrified of clowns, or the general overall idea of the circus, would've found amusing. I looked up at the dusty mirror wrapping the ceiling, and watched as the rusted cranking rod spun on its axis, carrying the ponies (and the occasional lion or zebra) off the ground and into the air.

Light bulbs reminding me of an old Hollywood theater lined the brim of the carousel canopy, and on the inner walls hung nineteenth-century influenced paintings of an establishing Americana Frontier. Mind you, they were rather controversial paintings by today's standards. One painting depicted now nearly extinct animals hunted by men in hunting coats and coonskin caps. Another exhibited a very racist portrait of Indjins chasing unsuspected bison. For a second, I fancied myself the cowboy mounted on his steed somewhere on the rocky frontier. Yet there I was, on a carousel pony.

"If this is honestly an absolutely terrible experience for you—" I began to say while starting the horrible process of once more turning my body around. "—I'm sure there's a party or some bar we could hit up."

"There's no way you go to bars."

"What do you mean?"

Then ignoring me, in typical Mary fashion, she just said back, "And I don't really party."

"Yeah right," I scoffed, shimmying my torso to kick my left leg over the saddle, and then looked up at her to claim my rightness. I had imagined Mary to be the White Girl Wasted type.

"I mean, I like drink, and stuff. But I don't party."

"Oh. That works because I don't either—party, I mean," I said, being truthful. Unlike her. I didn't party because, well, I never really got invited to parties.

The painting of my cowboy took me away for a second, but I snapped back to the conversation when Mary began laughing.

"Come on, Danny, have some game," she said, her cheeks rising all rosy red. "You realize—you don't need to agree with the girl all the time, you know?"

"What? That I don't party? I don't. And I'm about to disagree with you, that I'm not agreeing with you."

"That was pretty clever," she applauded. "You're quite the wordsmith."

"Oh, I prefer lyricist."

"You write lyrics?"

"Yeah. Christian Rap."

Mary puffed out air then began laughing. "That's funny. Good job. Though I must say, you totally struck me as a dubstep kinda guy."

"Ah, good attempt. But a little outdated of a reference, no?"

"A little outdated? Hunny-boo. Let's get one thing straight here, I'm always on time. And well," Mary eyed me up and down. "At least I'm not the one stuck in the nineties."

"Stuck in the nineties—*what?*"

Mary started laughing like that was the funniest thing in the world, though it made *zero* sense.

"What do you mean, nineties?"

"Do you play music?" Mary asked.

"Ugh—no. But what do you mean, *stuck in the nineties?*"

"Homeboy, chill. I'm kidding. You see? It's a joke. You're dressed just fine."

"Wait, you're saying I dress like I'm from the nineties? How am I dressed like the nineties?"

"Relax," she sizzled the word as she spoke it. "I just mean you don't dress like most guys. Most guys wear, like, snapbacks and clunky skateboard shoes and name brand stuff. You're dressed just fine, sweetie. God, you're difficult."

I wanted to instantly hate her for calling me sweetie, but hating her soon became impossible when her smile inflated her cheeks like ninety-nine luft balloons. Instead I wanted to jump off a cliff.

"Well, I just don't dress like I listen to Nukka," I came back with.

"So, nineties?"

"Oh My Gosh. No. Like anything played with real instruments, performed by real people, with real talent. Before words like shawty ever came into existence."

"So you like oldies and stuff?" Mary said in her raspy voice, not making it clear as to whether the answer to that question would lead to something good or bad.

"Yeah," I uttered. "Is there anything wrong with that?"

"No, that's uh." She tossed her brows. "Dope."

"Dope?"

"For sure. Old music is sick. The last CD I bought was Spice World, and after that, I knew nothing could ever compare."

Not quite the old music I had in mind, but it still beat shawty. Mary then professed her affinity for Lana Del Rey, Kanye, 'Queen Bey,' and some underground R&B artists whose names all kinda sounded the same.

"Other than that, I'm a nineties girl. Kurt Cobain is a God. So yeah, believe me, your jean jacket is just fine." Then in a thin voice, Mary began rapping TLC's "Waterfalls," getting as far as the bridge where it says something about: "Is it because my life is ten shades of gray / I pray all ten fade away..."

And that was when my face actually hurt. No really. Your face will actually hurt from smiling too much. I kinda wished she would go back to being a bitch for a second, just to let my face chill.

I took a deep breath and looked up at the dusty ceiling mirror mimicking us; miming our every move. Then I turned my gaze to the stream of Old Hollywood theater-like lights, spinning round and round in rapid bright flashes, an endless afterimage of the moon. I then flinched when my sight shifted back to the mirror and saw Mary, in her reflection, sticking her tongue out at me. By the time our dizzy gazes traveled downward from the mirror and met, blushing overlapped the conversation.

Mary ended the staring contest—which had divided itself into pocket glances—by asking me if I liked sixties music. I've never heard a dumber question. Mary said she wished it were the sixties so it would be socially acceptable to walk around naked in a hippie commune and drop acid while rocking an Indian headdress. One of the paintings on the carousel wall depicted a Chieftain rocking a headdress. My version of the sixties consisted more of a poet with an Abbey Road haircut sitting under a willow tree preaching peace and love for all mankind, but Mary naked in a headdress worked too. We agreed that liking Bob Dylan had become a cliché (though his lyrics are still great), and I told her that I loved anything and everything British Invasion, and that The Beatles were the only band that had ever really mattered.

Amidst my rambling, Mary scrunched her cheek against the pole streaming through the white pony she sat on, and then let out a giant moan as she gripped the pole tighter.

"I love Jim Morrison. He's like *sex*."

And something about the way she rolled her eyes left me convinced she truly meant that.

"Uh, yeah?"

Mary then said, totally non-sexually, "Yeah."

Lost in the moment, I repeated the phrase like a moron. Mary's lips splurged with another soft Yeah as her eyes scanned mine. She had the kind of eyes that were always scheming, confessing more than she knew. Eyes designed with the capability to mold you to her needs. They were eyes that pierced through yours and reminded you that something in your chest was alive and playing the drums. My face really hurt by that point.

Seconds later, the operation dragged, stuttered, and then ground to a halt as the music wound down to a silent, buzzing static over the speakers. The Carousel hadn't been as suave as it used to be.

We got off our ponies and walked by the now impatient operating guy. I thanked him. Legit. Wholeheartedly, I thanked him because we were getting along so well all because he "Violated His Terms" and called Mary over the intercom.

While preoccupied, struggling to find a way to talk about something after we'd just sorta stopped, the tips of my fingers touched the arch of her thumb. I quickly wedged my fingers in my pocket. Neither of us acknowledged that very forward sexual advancement. Avoiding awkwardness, I cocked (not in a phallic way) my head at the sidewalk that diverged from the Carousel grounds towards the path that led back to the beach. Mary gave a nod thing to confirm. We silently began walking. Insects competed on opposite sides of the looming sidewalk for a spot in the Cricket Choral Choir, binaurally shrilling their songs from deep within the bushes and shrubs.

But it was when I looked over at the deserted playground designed like a pirate ship that we synchronously blurted:

"Do you want to—"   "Let's —"

And I never found out where that "Let's—" led to because we were both taken aback by a loud POP. A fireball hurled across the sky. Then several muffled-sounding cannonball shots boomed from the dark, and we watched a polychromatic series of spherical explosions somersault upwards from the beach.

Mary insisted on checking it out, so we checked it out, and saw a group of college-aged kids in a Roman Candle fight having a grand old time. Mary wanted to approach them, and despite my reluctance—as I wanted to get back into the groove of our conversation—she went ahead and did it anyway.

"Mary!" someone shouted.

One of the random guys recognized her. It was some dude with shorts and a backward baseball cap. Naturally, I hate the idea of Mary recognizing any thirty-year-old-looking guy, but he was one of those sorry bastards that—either through extensive insecurity, or stupidity—was super eager to shake my hand. I could only imagine how many hands he shook in a day.

"Great to meet ya, pal!" the fellow, who had introduced himself as Justin, said on the impact of our handshake.

His crew, who were surprisingly all very normal guys and gals, offered us a Roman Candle.

"Like this!" Mary said, lacing her hands around mine on the firework. She sparked the fuse with the tip of a cigarette she had lit, and then, with a rumble in our grip, a pink orb shot out and dispersed in the sand. She jostled our hands up and we watched one, two, three, four, five, six more shots disintegrate into the moonlit night.

Justin suggested we all divide into teams and have a "fight." I liked the idea of this; it sounded dangerous and fun, and I undoubtedly thought that this could finally be the beginning of an Endless Summer Night. We all grabbed fireworks; Mary went on Justin's team, which was okay because some gal who looked like an Environmental Studies major was, I think, flirting with me.

It felt better wielding my own candle, and all of us, relatively all at once, blasted a spectrum of colors across the silver beach. After leaving a wake of smoke above the sand, Mary came back laughing and smacked my ass.

"That wasn't so bad, was it, kiddo?"

What's up with people smacking my ass?

Somehow, accidentally, I told Mary that I liked firing what felt like laser blasts out of my hands—revealing far too much of my inner-fourteen-year-old geek.

Frowning, Mary said, "Yeah, Danny. I like that, too."

The vapor, caught and densified by the rays of the moon, began to evaporate from the beach when Justin came up and invited us to join them back at "Ryan's for beers."

"We have a concert to make," Mary said.

Justin told me that he hoped to see me around and that we should go for beers. Being (decreasingly) below the legal drinking-age, and not knowing him other than a semi-drunk firework fight on the beach, didn't seem to matter. He insisted. I guess he *really* wanted to go for beers. Mary gave Justin one of those impartial hugs "bye," and I grabbed a Roman Candle (or two, maybe three) for Max. I thought he would be less pissed about my leaving him if I came back bearing explosives.

"Do you seriously want to go back for The Broken Lyre show?"

"Is that what your band is called?

"Yes."

And without a second's hesitation, Mary exclaimed, "Then yeah! Let's go!"

And so we went.

A miracle must have aligned a runway of green lights on the city streets, banishing all the boundaries in our way, setting the speed of the Porsche free. In the thrall of that speed, we whipped back down south to Carraway Beach, soaring past all the hotshots in their summertime machines crammed on the lanes of Atlantic Way. We glided down and around the curvature of the hill and circled downtown. My eyes were alert, scanning for any space to stop the car. When passing the outlet of The Alley at the crosswalk of Atlantic Way, I heard a pocket of The Broken Lyre's music drowned amongst the clatter and melodic murmuring of the street. Driven with a new eagerness—irked I missed the beginning of the set—and desperately chasing down whatever time we had left, I veered the car into a parking lot across the street and spun into a not-so-legal space. Diagonal white lines did mark down the ground, but I figured they were mere suggestions.

I bolted out of the car, and in the blank space following the slam of the door, I heard in the distance the crash of drumming. Sonically, the pattern felt right in my ear, and albeit clarity of the words or notes, I knew my favorite song, a famous set-closer, was halfway over.

"Ah, crap!" I exclaimed. "They're almost done!" Dwelling on how far Mansion was from the end of The Alley.

But before anything else entered my mind, before I could make any move, I felt something slender and smooth collide with and then clasp tight around the spaces between my fingers.

Confused, I looked down. Mary's hand was in mine. And then, leaning into me, her body so warm against the cool of the night, Mary's lips grazed my earlobes when they split with a smile.

"Then let's run," she whispered.

Her breath, those words, drove a shiver down my spine, and then with the bend of my wrist and the tug of my shoulder, I was being dragged by the hand, running across the street.

Suddenly, I had an urge to stop midstride. "Do you think my car will be all right?"

We glanced back as the right headlight winked in the beam of a passing car.

"Yeah," she said. "Should be."

And so, for a second time, we fled with the wind at our feet.

With our hands woven tight, we dodged piles of people streaming from the carnival and the boardwalk and the beach. Then, out of nowhere, this brave little gunslinger holding an orange balloon froze in our path. Our arms like an umbrella, inflated with our fingers twisted and tied, upheld an archway as we ran forward and the little tyke scooted underneath. Afterward, as if this were all a rehearsed ballet, with the spin of my fingers, Mary twirled into my arms and fell against me. Then we tripped. Her body caved into mine as I backpedaled, holding her up by the hips. And then spiraling up to stand on her feet, Mary blossomed her fingers around my face, and with her nails brushing up and scratching my cheeks, she kissed me.

First a moment, then a breath, and then re-awoken with the spark of her laugh, I fluttered my eyes open just enough to see our two stark shadows entwined in the pink and green and blue bath of neon lights.

The Alley sprung back to life. First with the rumbling and the chatter, and then with the synchronized screams from the regretful passengers on the Ring of Fire; peering out from the skyline of the bars. And then, like an electrocution, the shriek of a screaming guitar solo jolted the impulse at our feet and we continued our flight.

Heads turned from the patio of every bar we passed, and again as we glided into the gates of Mansion. We presented the backside of our fists to the bouncer. Underneath his flashlight, our black-lighted stamps shone. He nodded. We were in.

Without regard for concert convention (which doesn't really exist, does it?) we plunged through the crowd that was groovin' and boppin' and grindin' and slippin', all encouraged by the excess of alcohol and the summertime heat, and maneuvered our way to the center of the dance floor. Enshrouded by the crowd, convinced by the kick-pedal, and with our dignity defended by the night's status quo, I grabbed Mary's hand and we danced to the bop of the very last beat.

When the encore was over, the entire bar roared in whistles and applause. But it felt like they were cheering for me, because when the stage lights flashed on like a sudden blinding sun, I looked over at Mary, already smiling at me.

7

The Blitzkrieg Bop

MARY

He grabbed my hand and smiled back. It then took about two seconds for Danny to get hormonal as hell and start blushing like crazy. He tried fighting it back by clamping down his mouth. But that only lent to strengthening the corners of his jaw, sending his pressed lips into a diagonal smile, emphasizing his high cheekbones. Despite the commotion of the now stirred, rummaging crowd, as the tight mass of bodies tried inching their way out of the bar, all I could find myself paying attention to was the boldness and unexpected manliness in his eyes. It should have left the impression that he was nothing but confident, yet they still quavered nervously as they searched mine. And I'll admit, the sharpness of his brows was piercing; stunning, really. He was stupid to his own ability to seduce. But I wouldn't give in. I would never give in. Danny's eyes then abruptly left mine. Something above my head had caught his attention.

"Max!" Squeegee Boy (Danny) shouted.

A boy, who weirdly looked a lot like Danny, just shorter and a little rougher, popped up through the rushing crowd. Danny dropped his mouth and began rambling as Max (with red, glazed-over eyes) halted right in front of him.

"Where were you, bro?"

Danny froze. It was only a second that they stared at each other without saying anything; Danny, dumbfounded; Max, disinterested (but there was an air of something unsettling in that second).

Max then broke his straight-faced skit and laughed. He smelled of pot and I immediately wanted to befriend him. Max looked at me, gurgled, and his eyes lit up.

"Grocery Store Girl?"

I looked at Danny. "Grocery Store Girl?"

"Grocery Store Girl," Danny confirmed.

"I'm sorry," Max said. "You're not wearing a nametag. I'll need an introduction."

"Mary."

"Max, Danny's best friend. Charmed to meet ya, Mary," he said, swiping for my hand.

Max and I spoke the same gang sign-language and did a Gilmore Park Ghetto shake. Swipe. Swipe. Bump. Bump. Up. Down. Pound; explode: "BITCH!"

Max, if maybe he exfoliated his face once in a while, was actually kinda hot.

Our squad stood by the stage and talked until the populace of the bar had filed out. We all agreed that it was not worth struggling with the crowd, and even worse, according to Danny, the parking lot.

"Dude," Max exclaimed once we were all finally walking up to Danny's Porsche. "Not a scratch, aye?"

The hood glimmered under the streetlight, showing off the sparkling metallic texture.

I then yelled, "SHOTTY!" And raced to the passenger side to grab the front seat.

"So where'd you guys go?" Max asked, getting into the back. "You missed, like, the *illest* show." And flicked his wrist against

Danny's shoulder.

My torso snapped, twisting in my seat to face Danny. "Wait. Danny. Did you just leave your friend here?"

"Max," Danny said, ignoring my question, as we were all clicking in our seatbelts. "Check under my seat."

Max shuffled around behind us. "Dude. A Roman Candle? That's the nicest thing you could have done for me—after leaving me for two hours, dickface." Max had a snarky kinda laugh. "You owe me some serious McDick's munchies, bro."

"Oh! Danny! Yes! We need McDick's!" I exclaimed as Danny turned the key in the ignition and the car came on with the radio blasting at the volume we'd left it on at.

In the wake of Danny spinning the volume down, Max said, "Man, you're lucky she's hot, or I woulda totally been cheesed you ditched me."

I slowly turned around, harnessing all the stank possible in a Bitch Face. His open palms flew up beside him in mock surrender.

"I'm totally just kidding, Mary. I would've thought your nose ring was super gnarly—even if you weren't a total rocket."

I tilted my chin down, applauding his obedience. Boy knew who wore the crown around here. Yeah, me. Queen Vicious, muthafucka.

While crawling out of the parking lot (which Danny had been right about, it was slow as hell) me and Max annoyed him to the point where he gave into our artery-clogging cravings and drove us to the McDick's on Lockport. Seriously, when the munchies call and you're craving McDick's—that's no laughing matter.

So, yes, it was pathetic and lame, and very small-town, but for everyone from tweens getting out of the movies, to drunk college kids leaving the bar, McD's was thee place to be. It's where the after-party was at. It was a thing of beauty, let me tell ya. Fights. Hookups. Breakups. Occasionally getting booted out by security. All the kind of shit that gets talked about Monday morning.

McDick's was McJammed packed, and we all saw people we

knew from high school. When I'm out, Drunk Bitches always want to be my friend. A group of 'em came up and tried kissing my ass, always, y'know, making sure to remind me of how pretty I am and wanting to hang out. Some skateboard-looking stoner dudes walked off with Max to the bathroom, but no one (from what I saw) talked to Danny.

"I'm not gonna have anything," Dan the Man said defensively, after the Drunk Bitches left me alone and I asked him if he wanted a Big Mac.

I ordered him one anyway and he ended up devouring the whole bastard. More and more kids poured in, all rowdy and drunk as hell, making all the staff fear a terrorist attack. Eventually some random dudes did say Hi to Danny as we picked at our fries in silence. Our schools didn't really party (at Saint Maria Goretti's we pretty much stayed with the North End kids) so there was a lot of Jefferson people I didn't know. Yes, my earlier accusation did, in fact, stand correct: all guys in Gilmore Park *are* repulsive.

"Beg my pardon, sweetie," I said, leaving Danny confused as hell when I went to con cigarettes off some stoner lacrosse dudes I knew.

Chad Stevenson and Blair Bouche. Both of them, way back in the ninth grade, tried making out with me at the Halloween dance. While I was with Chad and Blair, some gross bitch got a boner over Squeegee Boy and ran up to smother him while he was stuffing his face with fries. The cigarettes practically slid outta Blair's pockets when I started rubbing his arm, reminding him to text me with a cell phone number I no longer used.

The fries were picked down to salt and crumbs by the time Max got back from the bathroom, and that was right when the drama started. It was pretty exciting. This couple was in a major fight. What I was able to pick up on, from their shouting, was that the guy in the Aeropostale polo shirt kissed his ex-girlfriend at the bar, and her best friend saw and took a picture and showed the girl who was now crying hysterically and punching Aeropostale polo shirt guy. Harsh.

But then things got real when some white guy apparently called a black guy the N word. Immediately they both started threatening to kill each other. Seriously, McDick's is a blast! Me and Danny were standing at the door, ready to leave, but had to wait for Max to casually order nuggets around the same time the white guy was claiming his 'boys' were gonna show. Then the black guy claimed that his 'boys' were gonna show. Why don't they ever call up their 'girls'? We're realistically crazier and more likely to get out of any police trouble. Like, they're really gonna believe that this five foot four white chick punched a six foot something black dude? Max got his nuggets and we left before anyone's 'boys' showed.

"I'm gonna take a pee out back," Danny said as we swung through the doors of McDick's, and then left to go behind the McDonald's dumpster to take his piss.

Max asked if I wanted to burn as he held a thin, freshly rolled, and delicious-smelling little joint in his fingers. Of course, I was tempted, but I politely refused.

"Danny'll have a fit," I said, and held out my Blair-acquired cigarettes instead, offering Max one in return for his charitable offer.

He gladly accepted. Then slipping the cigarettes out of my fingers, he took to lighting them by stacking both in his mouth, and then sparking with his lighter one long flame that encircled both the tips and inhaled. He rolled his lips as so the top cigarette fell, and then stretched them to the corners of his mouth. I clipped the cigarette to the left using my sexy fingers.

"Do you like 'im?" he asked, the remaining smoke flopping in his lips as I moved my hand away.

"Uh. Yeah." I wasn't prepared to answer that question, because I didn't know if I liked Danny. Like, he was annoying. "He's a cool guy," I said, brushing it off.

"He is a cool guy." Max lifted the cigarette to his mouth for another drag. And then in a smoke-clouded voice, said, "Danny and I are practically brothers," and coughed.

Before I could say anything back, Danny returned from behind the dumpster and told us that we were both disgusting. I blew smoke in his face as he walked past us to his car. I don't think he was impressed. I tossed my dart before it was finished. Only because I didn't want to smell.

Max weaseled his way into the backseat, with his smoke still in hand.

"Max!" Danny yelled, "Don't be a dick, put that out!"

Personally, I thought it was kinda funny. But Danny wasn't all that impressed.

"Oh come on, old sport!" Max jabbed his elbow into Danny's shoulder. "Y'all tired or—"

But he never finished his thought because, just then, the night's McDick's race riot suddenly got ushered out onto the street by a security guard.

The smoke from Max's cigarette filled the car.

"Dude, seriously! What the hell? Throw your cigarette out!" Danny yelled again, his eyes shifting between Max and the action broadcasted outside the windshield.

Max caved into Danny's whining and chucked his smoke out the window. I prayed a little prayer for the waste of two such good cigarettes.

Then as Danny turned the ignition and the car rumbled to life, I rolled down the window, discreetly attempting to catch a peek of the fight and instantly heard the slap and the crack of a fist to the face. Fights were nothing new to me. Growing up with Jim there was always UFC on TV, and there was practically a fight every other week at Saint Maria Goretti's. But no matter how many I'd seen, there's nothing worse than watching two guys ruthlessly beat each other. Yes, feminists, I said "guys" cuz catfights are just hilarious. The crowd, now amassed in a ring, raved and roared for the fight to go on. What the hell was that, blacks and whites fighting? A historical re-enactment? Progress in America is a lie.

The screaming and singing of police sirens like the Star Spangled Banner got louder from somewhere around the corner as we, in the getaway mobile, pulled out onto Lockport, away from the brawl. The array of red and blue lights bedazzled throughout the interior of the car in the reflection of the rearview mirrors. I spun around and saw two cop cars pull into the McDick's parking lot, and when I turned forward again, coming from the opposite direction, a vaguely familiar vehicular shape drew closer.

The discoloring of the poorly installed headlights were unmistakably those belonging to a particular 2006 Chevrolet Impala. My heart spasmed. Even though there was no reason why Danny or Tanner would recognize each other (or their passing cars) in the dark. And although I was concealed in the passenger seat, stupidly, as the cars slung by each other (both boys for that split-second divided by a mere few feet), I looked into Tanner's car.

Danny and Tanner were unaware, and normally they would be very disinterested in the other, but I sat somewhere in the middle. The common denominator in their mutuality was me. The encounter was dramatized in my mind, because before I could overthink it some more, it had gone by. In the side-mirror, I saw the 2006 Chevrolet Impala zip into the McDick's. For sure Tanner was one of the white dude's boys; as I would imagine his street-cred was a tiny bit insufficient for that of a black thug. But I was still racked up about the whole thing, because, for that second that zoomed by, someone in the backseat of Tanner's car looked directly at me. It wouldn't be long until his crew went on an egging spree of every Porsche Boxster in the city.

"So, y'all tired?" Max popped up, revisiting his words from earlier. "Danny, we should totally make Mary a fire on the beach."

And as the boys bantered about making a fire: where, whose firewood (Danny's), which beach, etc., some act of intuition (more likely a result of my overthinking apparatus) inspired me to click open the glovebox. And as it fell down over my thighs, I discovered what I goddamn knew.

"Oh, so your car won't be egged."

The boys' reactions were stalled, their eyes wide as if knowing they were busted.

"Danny—what's this?" I asked, holding up a convenient owner-ship paper. "Unless you're a master of grand theft auto, or you're secretly a forty-five-year-old Italian man named Rob Perrucci, you have some serious explaining to do."

Now, Max just thought that was plain hysterical and laughed to the point where it was unrealistic. Like, it wasn't that funny. There's nothing funny about lying. My inner CIA agent interrogated Danny over the vehicular-identity affair. He kept silent by saying that he Pleads the Fifth.

"So, what else did you lie about?"

"That he likes dick," Max snickered.

"Well, I like girls. So what?"

"Wait, you're lesbo?" Max asked, without any effort to hide he was hard as a rock. For real, you'd think I was the Second Cumming of Christ. Why do guys even think lesbians are hot? Leave us be. The whole point is to avoid dick.

The smell of grease seared the air as Max tore open his McDick's bag and started casually munching on his nuggets. That is where Max and I found common ground despite his immature sexism; the smell was heaven. Danny, on the other hand, scrunched his nose. He was such a rich kid.

"Mahn," Max said, chomping on a nugget. "Damn cats outta za bag. You'll be cleanin' this beaut' for Old Robbie Boy anyways. Come on, let's make a fire before Mary throws a fit."

Squeegee Boy looked at me, as if he were a kid needing a parent's approval. A fire it was.

We signaled left onto Ridgeway Avenue and took the highway

onramp onto Route 306, en route to the South End of Gilmore Park to Danny's. When all agreed that we wanted to see the power of the Porsche, Danny floored the pedal, and with a bolstering thrust, we slid back against the seats. From out the windshield, the hood of the car broke against the night. Taking Exit 33, we then crawled through the city to the South End.

Beyond the tall trees that's branches stretched out across the street, sheltering the road in an infrequent archway of leaves, loomed massive houses with long, pesticide-protected, and manicured front yards. Moderately expensive cars filled the driveways, and energy conserving lights lit the professionally landscaped gardens. American flags seemed to poke out of the side of every home (it made ya feel very patriotic) it was such a typical rich kid neighborhood. Jim told me that the South End was the part of Gilmore Park where the people who owned our lives, lived theirs.

The Porsche swung onto a street named Eneleda Crescent. The homes there were smaller, and about eight houses down we disembarked onto the curb right outside what I assumed was Danny's house. It was this generic, ol' white American jalopy, the cliché kind, in the sense that it looked like what kids drew when they needed to draw the typical house. A blonde light from the garden spilled onto the siding of his house, enlarging and creating funky shapes out of the shadows of the flowers.

As the boys walked in front of me to collect firewood from the garage, I slowed my pace, taking a moment to really observe Danny's rich-kid house. I guess you can say I have a weird thing for other people's houses, the cages containing their lives. Maybe, unlike the others on his street, his house seemed less rich kid and tended only enough to ward off the appearance of neglect.

The boys stood at the garage door next to a basketball net with a worn mesh dangling from the rim and, together, yanked it up and opened Danny's garage, and that's when I saw it.

Next to Danny, bent over, sticking his ass up in the air, jeans slipping down just enough for me to read the label on the waist-band of his underwear (Fruit of the Loom, by the way), collecting firewood and handing it over to Max, sat the *dopest* retro car.

"Danny!" I squealed. He jerked up. "This is so sick! Why didn't you tell me you drove… whatever this is?"

Jim was a retro car junkie. Back when I was a kid, every May when they closed off downtown for the car show, the old man used to take me, and I'd get bored as hell when he'd get talking to old dudes with white hair about carburetors, and V6 and V8 and fuel, and whatever guys that don't really know a lot about cars talk about.

"Oh yeah? You like it?" Danny asked as he handed another stack of firewood off to Max.

I hummed in agreement, circling the car. The paint was a deep red, almost maroon, and below the black and white racing stripes across the bottom of the doors, bold white letters read: SVO.

"What's SVO stand for?"

"Mustang SVO," he said (which didn't tell me much).

"Danny, I'm trippin'," I murmured, mostly to myself, peering in through the window at the leather and cloth interior. "It's so tacky." A blue air-freshener dangled from the rearview mirror. "I love it."

"Well, it's not really my car. It's my dad's. But thanks."

Maybe I was so impressed because in my head, I was expecting a 2006 Chevrolet Impala. Maybe. But this baby was straight from, like, the *nineties*.

"Can we take this sweet sex pistol out? Like, will your dad care?"

"N-no. He won't."

Danny snatched the keys from a hook in the garage and fired his baby up. The engine mumbled first with anticipation, and then burst to life with a galactic tremor, impossibly loud in the tiny garage. Then the taillights blinked and the canvas of the headlights melted off the wall of the garage as he reversed onto his driveway. The air stunk with the nostril stuffing and head-numbing smell of fuel that we all secretly love.

"God," I said, as I squeaked in through the door of the coupe into the back seat. "This makes you such a hipster."

Defensively, Danny began denying the hipster accusation, and then the car shook as Max slammed the trunk of firewood closed.

"It smells musky as hell in here," I said.

Danny scrunched his nose in his own version of The Bitch Face.

"I love it! I swear. I'm not making fun."

Max got in the passenger seat as Danny, facing forward, uttered, "Fine then." And then abruptly swung his hand out—Max quickly ducked—to swap the sunvisors down. He then cranked a latch on both sides, and pressed a button next to the lights. The roof let go of its grip on the windshield, and the electric motor whined as the soft-top fell back, clicking in fanfolds and exposing us, inch by inch, to the atmosphere of the night. Though it only took a matter of seconds, the anticipation stretched out time, and when the final fold fell back into the crevice behind the backseat headrest, like two pieces of a locket snapped in place, the night felt complete.

The boys had decided that the fire would take place at Carraway Beach. Having long since chilled out from the beach-day bullshit of earlier, Carraway was now a lot quieter; only the college kids still going strong in The Alley elicited a noise complaint. As we trekked down the boardwalk, the child-molesting sounds of an organ grew louder. The boys informed me that it was none other than Lunatic Larry (a Danny-original nickname). Apparently, he was some cracked-out old guy (Max's words), who set up his organ every night (never said Hi), and played creepy old carnival songs 'til dawn.

After a few failed attempts at lighting a fire that burned through all of our McDonald's garbage, Max ran to a recycling dumpster and brought back an unnecessary amount of newspaper. He was very particular about setting up our fire Teepee style.

Having kicked off my shoes, my bare feet exposed, I sat next to Danny on the deck of a lifeguard tower, digging my toes into the sand, and watched as Max attempted to tame the roaring pile of flaming newspaper. After reaching some level of embarrassing failure, he announced that he was going to fire off his Roman Candle. Leaving Danny and I alone. We both watched Max cross the beach, and then climb a nearby pile of rocks that the waves crashed against and then exploded into mist.

We sat in what shortly became a familiar silence. Me and Danny hadn't talked, alone, since before the concert, before we ran through The Alley. He nudged closer to my seat. The crest of the fire spun with an abrupt change in the wind, igniting a piece of wood to spontaneously burst into crackling sparks. After a shared, "Whoa!" at the sudden shock, I could feel his eyes looking to connect with mine. I consciously ignored this. I could feel the burning in his cheeks, the heavy ringing in his chest, so as he began rolling through the words, "So earlier—"

I injected: "Yeah! That shit at McDick's was cray!"

"Uh, yeah. But, um—" He was cut off by the sound of a long whistle, like a scream, as the first green fireball shot from Max's firework into the sea. Next, a pink blast tore through the sky, its reflection streaking the rippling black waves below. Max jumped back with each burst like he was shooting a rifle. Danny took the second between the blasts to say, "What I was going to say was—"

"Oh! Our fire's dying!" I cried, jumping to my feet.

Another whistle from the rocks—a blue shot went soaring over the water and Max yelled something indistinguishable. I grabbed a stack of flyers from the pile sitting on the sand and chucked them into the fire. A loose page on fire flapped open in the wind. I shrieked and skidded back to my seat next to Danny. He tried talking again, but another firework cut him off, and I told him I was cold to shut him up. What Squeegee Boy did next was ridiculous. He took off his nineties jean jacket and began wrapping it around my shoulders like a blanket.

"Danny, you don't—"

A pink blast screamed across the sea as he waved his hand in front of my face, which somehow silenced me, and also made me kind of want to punch him. He leaned his lips into my face. I flinched. But he only came up to my ear to whisper: "Look who's stuck in the nineties now."

If there is one thing I hate with guys, it's cheeseball. But Danny was just so cheeseball it wasn't even worth arguing with. So, I reached for the lapels and snugged his jacket closer around me. What? It was warm.

Squeegee Boy gave up trying to talk. Substituting conversation for silence, we alternated between watching the colorful waves roll in, and watching the fireworks scorch the black sky. While watching the pretty colors, my head nodding up and then down, I could feel his unsure glances falling on and off of me. But I kept my gaze fixed on the pyrotechnic show happening before my eyes. The frequency and volume of the blasts shut out the idea of talking. He wanted answers, I know, I know, but I didn't want to give them.

With one final blue burst above us, Max's arsenal of fireworks was finally emptied. A dense brownish smoke hung in a thin cloud above the ocean, which now sounded comparably softer than before. Then, out of nowhere, Danny decided he could force conversation out of me by saying the gayest thing of all.

"The stars are nice."

"Are they?" I laughed. I could tell behind his eyes, in his artsy little mind, he was trying to capture me.

"What do you think of the stars?" he pressed.

"What do I think of the stars?"

"No, no. Don't make fun."

"I'm not making fun. Just, like, what do you mean?"

He paused, and then tilted his cheek cupped in his hand. "I'm not really sure. Tell me anything."

He shifted his eyes down, locking with mine.

"I'm not too sure either," I answered. "I don't really think about that sort of thing. Don't all of our horoscopes, and, like, mood swings and chances of winning the lottery and shit, have to do with the stars? Like, the app on my phone is freakishly accurate. It's never let me down. So, like, something must be legit?"

"Oh, come on. I'm not talking about a stupid phone app!"

And like our fire that grew immense and hot as it scorched through the flyers, and then dissolved and quickly died, so burnt out our conversation about stars. And I, for one, didn't really care. Like, what the actual hell. Who actually talked like that? No one that I knew of, that's for sure. I could so tell Danny was just trying to relive, reinterpret, some scene from a cheesy-ass movie where the broad sucks his dick right after he points out some life-changing, hippie-crap thing about the stars.

Something in me needed to tear him apart for trying to pull that bullshit on me. Anyone who's just so whimsical about life and shit annoys the living hell out of me.

I kept grinding my shoulder along its blade, trying to massage out the tension that seemed to strap my back the angrier I got, waiting for him to say one more stupid thing so I could ridicule and rip him and his stupid beliefs apart. But he stayed silent.

Eventually I peeked over. He twisted his body away from mine as if he were disgusted.

"Okay let me check the app," I said. "Let's see what these fuckers—" I glanced up at the sky, "—have to say. Let's see if we're compatible."

I whipped out my phone and read aloud what I typed.

"Okay. Sagittarius woman…Virgo man…."

But as I clicked to find out if Danny would get a second kiss or not, Max came skidding up the beach, kicking sand everywhere, smelling like gunpowder.

"Dude, that was *sick*."

I clicked my phone off.

From within the pile of burnt flakes and dimming embers, another super-fire came ablaze when Danny and Max dumped in the rest of the recycling paper. Each of us sat on unused blocks of wood that we'd brought closer to the super-fire to stay warm, and found things to continually talk and laugh about. At one point, I even asked Danny if he wanted his jacket back. With his arms crossed, he shook his head No.

"Umm, Hysterical Girlfriend and Aeropostale Polo Shirt are having makeup sex right now," Danny said, as we all went around, telling our version of what happened to the McDick's fights. "And realistically, the cops broke up the N-word brawl, and all of their 'boys' were busy doing other things so no one showed and they just went home."

"I don't think so, dude," Max piped up. "I betcha like four of 'em got shot and now there's like a major gang war."

"No way." I corrected both of those idiots. "Hysterical Girlfriend totally ended up getting revenge and hooked up with her ex. And the cops got there and tried breaking up the creed of the street, so the gangs joined forces and are now warring with the cops," I said, then took a swig of my water bottle.

"That's really cute, Mary," Max mocked.

So I shot him the finger.

Max lit a cigarette of his own and offered me one. I looked at Danny for approval. He shrugged, so I took the smoke. The drag felt a little underwhelming, lacking the fulfillment my lungs ached for. But it was when I took another hard drag, burning through half the smoke, that from out of nowhere Danny lunged his arm out.

"Let me try that." He grabbed the cigarette out of my hand without approval, clipped it like a joint, and took a drag. He ended up coughing until he gagged, spitting out a giant wad of saliva.

"Pussy," Max said.

"Screw you," he croaked.

Max went on about some gossip he heard concerning some

investor people, who were talking to the city about buying downtown Carraway Beach and the boardwalk, so that they could demolish it to build a condo and some beach club or some shopping thing.

"Oh, that's ridiculous," Danny said. "They're not—no. There's no way they could demolish The Alley."

"Yeah, Max," I piped in, and took another drink outta my water bottle. "Like, the boardwalk is lame as hell, but Gilmore Park would literally be nothing without it."

Which was true. Gilmore Park is Carraway Beach. Without it, the entire city would just be plazas, used car dealerships, and, like, random stretches of gravel parking lots. And tons of drifting crackheads.

Danny, then kicking an outcast piece of wood deeper into the fire, said, "Yeah, like, The Alley's awesome. It's like, the only actual cool thing around here. Wouldn't even be fair if they ripped it out before we're twenty-one."

A glob of spit was drooling out from Max's lips when he blurted, "Oh, pfft—don't gimme that." The red and glowing bud of his cigarette swung through the dark as he went to take a drag. "Danny, you gon be in Cali, bro. What the hell do you care what happens to this shithole?"

"Wait," I interrupted. "I'm confused. Danny, you're going to California?"

Then Max butting in, said, "Yeah don't worry, Mary. I just found out too."

"Oh, Danny, that's sick. Yeah?"

Expressionless and looking down at the sand, Danny said, "Yeah. But, um, yeah—I don't think Carraway Beach is gonna get torn down."

From under the shadow of the firelight crossing Max's eyes, he looked up at Danny. "It's true man." He resumed poking the burnt flakes of newspaper with a stick. "They're gonna bulldoze this whole place. Just you won't be here to see."

The flames crackled. A block of wood fell and crashed in a small firework of embers. I took a swig of my water bottle.

Gradually, the heavy air that settled on our squad lifted, blown completely over when one of the boys made a joke about their manager at work, and the flow of our relentless conversation resumed. Max got up and claimed that now he had to "piss" (boys, I swear—) and in that brief absence, Danny asked for my number. By pure accident, I automatically recited the number I currently used, not that inactive one.

Max returned and we talked until the fire burnt out. I kept my eye on the last flame until it dipped out of sight and arose in a twirling smoke from out of the ashes. Since it had taken us so long just to start the fire, we didn't bother putting out the embers. It was fine.

The Mustang whipped back down Route 306, exited onto Brigham Road in the South End, and then drove through the suburbs to Max's townhouse complex.

Throughout my simplistic, welfare-stricken life, I had only really come across two sorts of people in Gilmore Park: rich and poor. And if you weren't in one of those distinct categories, you got away best with a bungalow that maybe lucked out with a flower garden. So when Danny's Horsy (cuz a Mustang's a horse, right? Oh, better yet, it's a pony) —So when Danny's Pretty Pony came in loud and thrumming into Max's townhouse complex, there wasn't a contest in deciding what category Max fell into. If Gilmore had a ghetto, we were in it. Not that I'm judging or anything, cuz I'm like, Queen Ghetto, after all.

The Pretty Pony crawled over what felt like an endless series of speed bumps before coming to a halt beside Max's driveway at the end of the street.

"Dude," Max said, leaning in from the backseat, his hands gripping the headrests. "See ya tomorrow?"

"Yeah, man. I'll call you."

Max got out of the car by hopping over the open convertible side, and when he landed, turned to me and said, "Later, alligator."

Cuz I'm Queen Vicious, I guess? I responded fashionably with, "In a while, crocodile."

Max ran up the driveway, took the stairs in one leap, and disappeared into his house. Teenage boys just fascinate me. They're so strange.

"He's a cool guy, Danny."

"You think so?"

"Yeah."

Danny then asked me if I wanted to go home. I checked the time, and told him not quite yet. "That's good," he followed up with, a half-smile slipped on his lips. You could tell he thought he was so smooth. Using his fingers, Squeegee Boy combed the underside of his bangs to fan them out, and then drove away.

As we crossed back over the speed bump that anchored the entranceway of Max's semi, we got in a little squabble about what to do next.

"*Gawd*, Danny, why do I always have to come up with the brilliant ideas?" I complained while he flicked the indicator, looking left then right. "Let's just go on a drive? Actually, yes. Let's do that. You know what, actually? Play me some of your favorite music and just drive."

Knowing that would light Squeegee Boy up like a Sears flyer set on fire. Without any hesitation, he plugged his phone into the dashboard's auxiliary and put on his Oldies playlist; he liked a lot of the same music as Jim.

Not long after we began driving, the gaslight blinked. I bugged him about getting us stranded. After crossing over the Delaware Road Bridge in the South End, we passed a Mobil gas station.

"Why aren't you stopping there?" I asked.

"Because there's a cheaper gas station that my mom wants me to use."

"Your mom pays for your gas?"

"Yeah. My mom gives me this Emergency Credit Card for gas."

"Your mom gives you a credit card?"

I'd never heard anything so ridiculous in my life. Danny defended his spoiled life by claiming that the 'Emergency Credit Card' was only for gas and, well, emergencies. We got on the 306 at the Lockport on-ramp, and escaped north out of town. Some miles later, we got off the highway and drove to County Line 55. Silhouettes of indistinguishable farmland lay on both sides of the long, dark, and relatively deserted road. And in the distance, a brightly illuminated gas station stood out like a beacon in the night.

The Mustang rolled into the gravel parking lot (I told you it's all gravel lots) and Danny told me to wait in the car as he paid with the ECC (Emergency Credit Card, for those of you who are a tad slow and didn't pick up on my brilliantly crafted acronym).

Bored as hell, waiting for Danny to remember his pin, I began reading all the writing on the fuel pump, and once I educated myself on the prices of fuel, I looked out to the bank of the road and read the sign staked into the grass:

Express Route 16 to I-67 West.

Obedient to New Jersey gas laws, the gas station attendant walked out with Danny, filled the Mustang up, grunted for a tip, and then we bolted back onto the road, rerouting our drive, opting out of the highway in favor of the scenic route that hugged the coast.

The southbound excursion back to Gilmore Park took us through a brief detour of the swampy Jersey Meadowlands. The marshes growing out of the deep ditches were so tall it nearly convinced me that Squeegee Boy had driven us straight into the mud. And as we drove, relentlessly chasing the glowing tunnel the highbeams cut on the lane and on the high reeds around us, the rolling wind swarmed the roofless car. Playing with the blowing ends of my hair that tickled my face. But it was when I pulled the elastic band from around my wrist to prevent my hair from becoming a disastrous mess, and funneled it between my hands, that Danny reached over and touched my arm.

"Just try it," he said.

And before I could even ask what he meant, Danny tilted his head back outside the door of the car. The force of the wind blasted the hair off of his forehead, revealing his hidden face again. So, as we drove through the swampy and winding road, where the crickets were louder than the music Danny played, my head fell back between the headrest and the door, and I let the wind blow back my hair. Having lived a lifetime with a lioness's mass of a mane, there was such an unfamiliar weightlessness I felt in that moment. And sealing my eyes shut against the wind seemed to enhance my other senses. Suddenly the wallowing mask of the racing breeze was all I could hear, and the balmy aquatic air was all I could smell.

Danny didn't exist. Neither did his music. Or his Mustang. Call it an out-of-body experience, maybe, but that's what it felt like.

Something then inspired me to open my eyes to the night sky, to the blue and white stars shining fiercely above. My long hair lashed out and upwards as if trying to touch them.

With the Meadowlands coming to an end at the county line, I could see in the distance where the coast swallowed in at Danae's Bay. The moonlight threw a vague path onto the water that flowed into the inlet. It really amazed me to see how much more there was to the shore that rolled on south for countless miles. I looked down to the rushing road and watched as the right headlamp devoured the white road line. And thought about how my whole world, the neighborhood streets, the encased homes, the patches in the pavement, could all be driven by on the highway in a second.

DANNY

The night had long since crawled over the threshold of midnight and into the infant hours of morning. By then, the after-hour pursuers, the drunkards, and the agents of speed had all cleared the roads. We owned the city, we owned the night. Our only adversary, the occasional red light. I had driven down those streets a hundred times before, and would a hundred times again, but there must have been something in the air that night that made them feel brand new. If I had to guess, some invisible mist composed of diesel and stardust put a spell on those dumpy streets. Making me, for the first time in my life, sort of glad I was from Gilmore Park, New Jersey.

I was all too aware that I never really participated in the moment that was happening. My mind was always reconstructing the past, imagining the future, or rendering the present to what I dreamed. People and places were always losing themselves to the fictional abstractions I fabricated them to be. Losing their true identities so that they could elaborate the story I wanted to tell. Such as that night had. That night must have held something in its hands that Mary and I were both secretly looking for—and maybe it didn't really matter who was beside us in that car. Maybe it only mattered that we were both not alone.

I'm not sure who decided the night was over, maybe neither of us did; maybe I was too eager to go home to lose her to lyrics and chords on the guitar.

Continual shadows from the telephone wires rolled over the dashboard as we drove through the narrow streets of Danae's Bay. Again, Mary guided me through the maze of one-way streets and fire lanes. And again, as I pushed down the brake pedal at the Fisherman's Alley stop sign, she told me to stop the car.

"Can I walk you to your door?"

The pleasant expression on Mary's face dropped back down to that of The Bitch Face.

"Why would you do that?"

"Oh. I dunno."

Mary tilted her head back against the headrest, highlighting the roundness of her cheek all the way down to the narrow dip of her chin before looking at me. "You can open my door, if you'd like."

Taking every opportunity to fulfill any romantic expectation— anything to reaffirm that the night was more than just a drive around town—I got out of the car. As I circled the hood to her door, I could smell under the breeze of the salty air the faint sweetness from a flower garden nearby. As Mary stepped out of the car, the line of her shin caught the same light that colored the tops of the rustling leaves.

Mary clutched my jean jacket tighter around her shoulders, and then rolling in her lips like how waves roll back to sea, her eyes dipped with the colors of the midnight sun fell large and black and bewildering on mine. For the first time, I was able to look at Mary without any words, without any interruptions. Her beauty struck me as something new, all over again. The composition of her face concurred with a set of rules symmetry recognized, blossoming a rare harmony; a quintessence typically reserved for the glory of nature.

"So," I said, stretching my thumbs around my belt loops. "Earlier—"

"Yeah! Your car is awesome."

"Mary, I'm not talking about my car."

"Okay."

"I'm talking about—"

"Danny, I'm glad I met you. You're a great friend," Mary said with a smile and then ran off through the ringed beam of the orange streetlight, disappearing around the corner, vanishing into the night.

"Hey, Mary, wait!" I yelled down Fisherman's Alley, listening, waiting for her reply. But this time, Mary did not come back.

Act II.

8

Please Mr. Postman

DANNY

The brightness of the sun beamed off the hood of Rob's Porsche Boxster into my eyes like needles into my retinas. Perhaps I didn't need to use that much wax. Aside from the obvious years behind the machine, when all washed up and waxed, it looked pretty sharp. Despite the growing heat of noon roasting the back of my hair and neck, provoking a patch of sweat, I was feeling a little sulky and cold. No, it wasn't Rob's car that was depressing me, it was…well, I kept checking my phone for a response that by noon, I was positive would never come.

Karma had been kind last night and sought mercy on my love-struck soul, leading Rob's Porsche peacefully through the night without a single scratch. About time my life dispelled those ridiculous Murphy's Law rumors. Even though by the time I rolled in on home it was three in the morning, I woke up unconventionally early and got a sunrise start to my Porsche duties. I let Superior do the bulk of the wash. When I got there, Miller and the boys got a real hoot outta calling me Rob Jr. Which was annoying. Still, believe it or not, I played along with it, and they all died at my Rob impression.

Miller kept saying, "That's jokes, Bon Jovi!"

And then I came back home to do all the precise work, like scrubbing the corners with a toothbrush. In an alternate universe, I filed some Child Slave Labor lawsuit. Working with a toothbrush. Who actually works with a toothbrush?

So, as I slaved away, driving the toothbrush in between the crease of the gearshift and the center console, I grabbed my phone to see if it was yet the Perfect Time. The time on my phone read 10:07am when I clicked it on—not too early, not too late—and so I typed in two consonants, one vowel, and two improperly placed punctuation devices, sending:

Hey :)

Then chucked my phone into the backseat. Giddier than ever, my heart raced with anticipation for Mary's reply. The seconds felt like hours. After such an amazing night, anything other than her and I rolling into a procession of crystallized summer scenes—slow walks on the beach, cracking open bottled Coca-Cola's at Seaside Shack Candies, catching the double-feature at Americaviews Drive-In—seemed impossible.

Though, no matter how badly I didn't want to check my phone, about every twenty seconds I would dig for it wherever I threw it last and click it on to see nothing but the clock add on minutes and pack on hours. Completely submerging myself into whatever cleaning task was next at hand did not serve as the distraction I wished it would be. She consumed every inch of movement. A thick square had wedged itself in my chest. And more than the emotional distress, I felt stupid because it was the kind of day where the smell of fresh-cut lawn sweetened the air, and the sun was shining high and bright in the pure blue sky, printing the colorless reflection of the crosshatch of leaves onto the street. Even my microcosmic daydream of being the kind of guy who works on a car while listening to sixties music on the radio—alternating between the 1961 Marvelettes version of "Please Mr. Postman" and the 1963 version by The Beatles—was plucked away from me. All because of a girl and her silly, torturous mind games.

MARY

"**Y**ou really can't reactivate my phone?" I said, plopping on my bed, cushioning my butt into the mattress.

"No sorry, miss. Your account has been indefinitely suspended due to continuous missed payments," the cell phone customer service guy said.

"What? This is bullshit. I had to help my dad pay for shit."

If my vicious cat claws were properly manicured, I would have reached through the receiver and clawed his face off.

"Again, I am personally sorry—"

"I sure as shit bet you are because you've had the shittiest customer service, and I'm glad this call was recorded for ensuring quality purposes because your quality has been shit. Bye."

I smacked the phone back on the receiver. Congratulations. You caught me being a red-hot liar already. I actually smacked the phone down on the brim of the receiver, so I lifted it up again and then smacked it dead on. God, how annoying.

Scattered in shapeless piles on my bed were all Jim's depressing bills and bank statements. Jim's a freaking gorilla when it comes to money, and we're like a quadrillion dollars in debt. So, like the teenage girl I am, I dramatically threw myself down on my bed, and cuz my mattress is a wobbly piece of crap, all the papers bounced up and drifted onto the floor, scattering half underneath my bed and half underneath my dresser. I snatched the pillow next to me and screamed burying my face into it.

My Goodness Lord. The test results came in and told me that no civilized human can survive thirty (freaking thirty) days without a phone.

Thank Jesus I'm a bitch from Venus.

While mulling over the death of my already non-existent social life, my OCD got the best of me and told me to start cleaning my room. Cleaning's like crack. Try it. Not crack, cleaning. Except, this sweeping motivation I had to suddenly become a maid died a swift, painless death when I dragged my wooden vanity chair across the carpet and saw Danny's jean jacket. When I picked it up, wanting to know what size Danny wore (medium, for the record), his scent immediately rolled into my nose. I tossed it on the floor. After all, it was just going to Goodwill. What do those bums care?

The rest of the shit on the floor, such as all those awful outfits I tried making look like they were purchased at Urban Outfitters, were on their way to the Laundromat. So while snatching up my mess and shoving it in the laundry bag, I thought of how Danny probably had maids to do this. Or at least a woman to do the domestic shit. It bothered me that I was expending innocent brain cells even thinking of him.

I don't even know why I "forgot" to give him his jacket back. Worse than my negligence, why didn't Squeegee Boy ask for it back?

Boys confuse the hell out of me. It was irking me that I couldn't place what goddamn scent that was on his jacket, so I picked it up again to decipher. Most likely it was deodorant. Now, whether it came from his chest or his pits, it was a tolerable boy smell. Most boys don't smell good, like at all.

Slipping a tank over, like, the only bra I ever wore (owning other bras is entirely pointless) I got changed to leave my house. Really all because (not to complain or anything, but I *am* just as deep in debt as Jim is, except my bad credit lies with Karma) I'd end up, like, missing my period or something stupid if I didn't return Danny's jacket.

DANNY

By two in the afternoon, I declared it was all over. The entire night—the carousel, the fireworks on the beach, the endless midnight country drive when the rest of the world was asleep—had all been a fluke.

"Danny!"

Mom yelled for me. I turned around to see her standing on top of the three cement steps that led up to the front door. While looking up at our house from the driveway, especially given the stark contrast with Mom's slender figure, our house looked and felt impractically large.

"Do you want lunch?" she asked.

Do I want lunch? Hah.

Our home at 21 Eneleda Crescent had been transforming. No, not any renovations or anything, but all that had been hidden away, pushed back in closets and stuffed in drawers for years, had recently coughed up all over the place. Boxes began piling on boxes, starting from the front foyer at the base of the stairs, down the hallway, and all the way into the kitchen. Mom had begun her crazy packing ritual.

"How was your night?" Mom asked as I walked into the kitchen, the tile floor felt cool beneath my feet.

"Good. Good."

I sat down at the kitchen counter and checked my phone again for stupid Mary's response. It didn't make sense. The ache had actually slipped away for two seconds when I forgot about it. Stupidity backslapped me.

"Did you take Rob's car out?" Mom asked.

I rebutted the outrageous claim as I picked up the plate of quesadillas to bring them outside.

"Oh, yeah right, Danny," Mom said as I walked down the hall. "I was seventeen when I stole your grandma's Stingray to see U2. The Broken Lyre was good? You know, I sort of miss when you used to always invite me to go to their shows."

My mother, a lot like me, is a goddamn fabulous storyteller. I never used to *always* invite Mom. She's only been with me, like, one or two times. When she's being a brat, I would never admit it, but I was somewhat grateful that out of all the potential mothers one could be brought into this world through, that I had been brought in by my mom. Considering everything the old gal has gone through, Mom still looked relatively good, a tolerable kind of pretty for a mom.

Mom went on to tell me that she had called LACM's (Los Angeles College of Music) submissions office after they had reopened from the Fourth of July long weekend, and that she wanted me to call myself and speak with the friendly counselor she had spoken to on the phone.

As soon as I could, I dismissed the conversation as I was not in the mood to talk about California—or anything really—and that conversation would only make me all the more upset.

For God's sake, she KISSED me.

And with the quesadilla plate in hand, I began walking back to my child labor when, through a clear trash bag on the ground, I saw something that would make Mary's non-reply feel outlandishly insignificant.

"Mom!" I yelled from the hallway. "What's my Tiny Tigers Tee Ball Mitt doing in a garbage bag?"

I marched back into the kitchen. The china glasses stacked in their designated cabinet shook in tiny clinking tremors with my steps. Behind the white marble counter, Mom was on her phone sending a text, rigorously ignoring me.

"Mom?"

"Sorry, sorry, Danny. Just figuring out a work license thing." Her fingers clicked away.

Goddamn, it would be nice if Mary could text me that fast.

"But, yeah, Danny, when was the last time you looked at that thing? And besides, that glove wouldn't even fit you anymore."

"Yeah, but, Mom, I wanted to keep that."

"Okay. Then you can keep it!" Mom got off her phone.

I went back to the hallway, dropped the quesadilla plate on the stairs, and shoved the boxes out of the way and rummaged through the plastic bag stuffed with board games, sing-along cassettes, and everything else that was shoved in the back laundry-room closet—and pulled out the mitt. The leather smelled stale, and the thumb cracked when I drew it back. I tossed the mitt inside the bag, grabbed my plate, and marched up the stairs with the entire bag in hand.

On my way up I yelled, "Mom! Can you please check with me before you throw anything else away?"

"Okay! I promise I will!"

By the tone and inflection of her voice, I could tell Mom was back on her phone.

The bag found space between my dresser and acoustic guitar-stand, right over the untamed etches of magic marker on the hardwood floor. Mickey Mouse's smiling face on an old board game met my frowning one when, out of the corner of my eye, I saw something move on the driveway. I jumped up to the window and saw Mary power-walking up to my house. I darted down the stairs and pushed through the front door.

"M-Mary!"

On the edge of my driveway, wearing a tight pale orange tank top, straddling the frame of an old rickety white bike, with her flip-flopped feet planted on the road, stood Mary. She turned around and just vaguely pointed at me. It took me a second to clue in that I should turn around. A Wright Bros shopping bag was slung on the hooks of my mailbox.

"Your jacket," she said.

"Oh. Thank you."

"You were beginning to look too much like this decade."

I wanted to laugh, sincerely I did want to, but the teenage girl locked within my soul was still all bent out of shape over the whole text message fiasco.

Mary began to peddle off.

"Wait!"

The bike jerked. The brakes screeched.

"Don't go. I mean, unless you have to go. But, um," I said, starting to walk down the steps.

"I have to go," she said.

I stalled for a second, staring at her. She looked unjustly perfect sitting on that bike. Reminding me of a black and white photograph of Audrey Hepburn I'd seen long ago. I was so mesmerized by the way the sunlight slipped in through the shadows of the leaves dancing across her body, and how the pattern resumed to fall on the grass behind her.

"Did you get my text?" I asked.

"Text? Oh. Uh, yeah," Mary began saying. Air wheezed through the tubes of her bike as she clutched the handbrakes and rolled towards me. "Funny enough, I dropped my phone right after you dropped me off. Giant crack in the screen. It won't turn on."

"Oh! Oh. Yeah. Shit." I stopped yammering when I saw how, as she slid forward from out of the shade, the glow of the midday sun shimmered upon her cheeks.

Up until then, I hadn't noticed all the freckles Mary had sprawled along the horizon of her tanned face. Being of the male gender, I couldn't quite place my finger on it, but she almost looked *better* than she had the day before. Her cheeks and nose were charred red, and she had on less of that black shit girls smother around their eyes. With the way her hair waved and sprung up in places she would've been embarrassed about, she looked like some gorgeous surfer girl who spent her summers down on the shore.

Mary gestured in the direction of the Porsche. "Your car looks good."

"Ha Ha. Funny."

Mary asked where (what she believed she was entitled to call) "her baby" was at. Mary clearly didn't understand the rules of car ownership and I wanted to call her out on her ignorance, but I didn't bother.

"Well, my baby's in the garage."

"Tell 'er I say Hi. Yeah. Okay, well, I just wanted to make sure you got your jacket back, it's supposed to be cold tonight."

I wanted to argue that all the weather reports called for an oncoming heat wave, but I didn't bother. Instead, I asked, "Do you want to hang out?"

"And do what?"

"Well, I dunno. Are you hungry?"

"Uh, yeah. I could eat."

Mary stretched her leg over the frame of the bike and with her foot, swept out the kickstand.

"Let me grab that," I said, taking the bike by the handles and then guided it up my driveway. While laying Mary's bike against the side of my garage, my pocket started vibrating. I reached into my shorts and pulled out my phone. Jess had replied:

Heyy ! No I couldnt make it :(boo. How was it???

I looked down my driveway at Mary swinging her head, throwing her hair back, using her fingers to brush out the kinks. And above, I heard whistling and the flap of wings as two birds flirted in song. I slipped my phone back in my pocket.

9

Peace Train

DANNY

We got in my Mustang, and before we were even backed out of the driveway, Mary asked if she had a name. I had to remind Mary that guys don't do things like nickname their masculine cars. Without my consultation, she dubbed my Mustang "The Stang," and somehow it stuck. I condemned Mary for her unoriginality. She applauded herself for embracing a cliché, which, somehow, in Mary logic, rendered it truly counter-culture.

So, like typical teenagers, we were indecisive as all hell and couldn't figure out where to eat. After what I think was our first disagreement—Mary wanted Thai, I voted pizza—we ended up going to a Shawarma place downtown. Which should not be confused with downtown Carraway Beach. Downtown Gilmore Park was an entirely different beast. To put it bluntly, downtown had seen better days. Nowadays, it lucked out with half a dozen tattoo parlors and bars that had, at most, a two-year lifespan (Yes, we had two bar scenes in town because Gilmore was a population of raging alcoholics).

So believe it or not, acquiring matching tattoos was not what we went to do downtown. There was a record store I wanted to take her to.

Cosmic Records smelled like mold, potential asbestos, and pot. Actually, mostly pot. And I'm also pretty sure the guy who worked there, who wore the same denim shirt every single day (as I've never seen him wear anything else), slept in the back behind the counter. But hey, they probably had every single record ever produced from Jermaine Jackson's solo career, to Irish Folk Songs for Children, and everything in between.

I was looking for a particular Cat Stevens album while Mary flipped through the nineties hip-hop bin and found Biggie Smalls. It slowly began to dawn on me that she was the one stuck in the nineties.

"I wish I could've told him he was beautiful when he was black," Mary said, looking at a wavering holographic poster of Michael Jackson from his BAD era.

She didn't really explain why and I left it at that. Mary then demanded that I had to choose one retro artist (male or female) that I would have sex with. Without even giving me a second to formulate a thought, she told me she would bone Steven Tyler and then quickly returned the question my way. After some good solid pestering, I professed my attraction to Debbie Harry.

"Debba—who?"

"You know, like, Blondie."

Mary got a hoot outta that and wouldn't let it go for the rest of the day. Whenever I asked her a question, she would scrunch up the blonde in her hair and then draw out her answer in a ditzy voice. It didn't matter how much I pleaded that Debbie Harry was a punk-rock chick, she would still do the ditz voice. For a girl who knew so much about pop culture, that surprised me.

Later, after walking around Downtown all afternoon, we hiked our way to the river basking at the bottom of the ravine that broke off from the street. While sitting, talking on the riverbank, listening to the rush of cars on the 306 hidden by the foliage of the trees, Mary asked me, "Why that one?" about my choice in record.

"Some of Cat's lyrics are like my gospel," I said, grabbing the album from the plastic bag and pulling out the lyric sheet. "Like this right here, the first track on the A-Side:

> Well you roll on roads / Over fresh green grass.
> For your lorryloads / Pumping petrol gas
> When you crack the sky / Scrapers fill the air.
> Will you keep on building higher /
> 'Til there's no more room up there?
> I know we've come a long way / We're changing day to day
> But tell me / Where Do The Children Play?"

A light swell of wind bent the top corner of the page, taking Cat's words away with the following silence. I looked up at Mary; her eyes suggested her mind was elsewhere. I kicked my foot into the dirt.

"Like, tell me——who, WHO, writes like that nowadays? Who actually cares? No one."

Mary just looked at me and started spinning a twig in her hands until it split, and I caught myself getting pissed that she didn't jump on board the ol' Peace Train and instantly agree with me.

"What is your religion?" Mary asked, out of nowhere, and then went scrounging for another twig and started spinning it.

"Cat Stevens and John Lennon. But if you want a technical answer: Catholic by Baptism and agnostic upon education. You?"

"I don't believe in anything," Mary answered. "What's the word for that?"

"Uh, Atheist."

"So, yeah, I'm an Atheist, I guess."

She stopped herself there and professed that she didn't want to accidentally offend my beliefs. I reminded her I wasn't all that convinced myself on the whole Church thing, so she continued.

"Okay. Well, like. Okay." Mary plucked another twig out from the assortment of fallen pinecones and yellowed-out locust leaves. "If there is a God sitting on his throne in cloud city, why does this world suck? Why do bad things happen to good people? Like, Danny, everything you read out literally says how shitty everything is. You'd think God would send down another Jesus or something by now."

"Well, wasn't that the point the first time around? That God sent His Son down to die for our sins and we were supposed to learn from His sacrifice to go out and spread the Good word?"

My voice drifted while looking out towards the thunderous rapids of the river. The unfortunate thing about this stupid river was that it wasn't a real river. Well, not anymore anyways. They used it to generate power, or something, and installed a bunch of turbines so it was constantly roaring like there's a Biblical storm. Which, at times, was quite a moving force to admire. At the very least, I could pretend that the powerful current was the result of an endlessly raging sea.

"What do you mean?" Mary asked, bringing the conversation back to God's parenting decisions.

I bobbed my head left then right in hesitation. "I don't totally like to bash religion," I answered at last, and then paused.

Something light tickled my forearm. When I looked down, I saw—and admired—the stealth of a ladybug as it crossed over the hurdles of my arm-hair.

"I mean, the story of JC himself is kinda cool. He was the original nineteen-sixties," I said, and then whistled silently onto my arm, sending the ladybug flying. "I only heard the bass line! Well, didn't you pay attention to the piano? The rhythm guitar progression was catchier than the harmony!

"Well, at the end of the day it's all in the key of G. It's all the same sound, you know? Like, it doesn't matter who you worship or what, or even if you don't believe in anything. The core of all religion is really just: Be a good person. I guess that's how I make sense of it all. For a band to sound good, everybody's gotta play along. It shouldn't matter what the lyrics of the song are."

I had noticed that I fluttered my eyes away from hers as I spoke, looking back out towards the rapids of the river. I didn't know how to say what I felt I understood on a deeper level. Half because I was terrified that, while rambling on to discover the right words, I'd sound crazy, and half because, at times, I doubted everything I had ever put spiritual faith in.

"Saint Maria's is a Catholic school, right?" I asked.

A tonally pleasing hum answered my question. Then she said, "Knowing that God disapproved of how I lived was sort of shitty. To be honest. And I guess making out in front of statues of the Virgin Mary was a little weird, now that I think about it."

"You were making out?"

The unfiltered question slipped from my tongue so fast that only by the time I chopped through the last syllable on "*out*" did I curl my lips, trying to take it back.

Mary frowned. "Yeah? Duh. It was high school. Obviously."

Obviously, right? It was only obvious that Mary and I were not making out right now. Deflecting my angst, I told Mary I was disappointed with the Catholic Youth, and she went on to tell me that the entire student-body was rather apathetic. Including her. The only thing she ever got out of attending Catholic school, and sitting through the bi-annual assemblies of boring Catholic-aimed rhetoric, was the story of Saint Maria Goretti herself.

Long story short: Maria Goretti was an eleven-year-old girl who was almost raped and stabbed to death for refusing to have sex (pleasant, I know), but upon her deathbed, forgave her attacker. Her only dying prayer was for him to see the light and someday join her in Heaven. After being released from prison, the attacker ended up devoting the rest of his life to the church.

"Originally when I first heard that," Mary said, "I was like, *super* pissed. Like, why is this poor eleven-year-old forgiving a rapist? And because of it, we make her a saint? Like, okay cool. Man rapes a kid but as long as it means getting a guaranteed ticket to Heaven, just forgive the prick? It's seriously so messed up. But I guess it was pretty noble of the bitch. Like, her devotion to God and faith and stuff was noble. And now she's the saint for rape victims, so I like that."

Telling Mary she was a weird-smart didn't go over as well as I had hoped. No matter how many times I backtracked, telling her it was a compliment, Mary tousled her hair, put on her "Blondie" voice, and kept reciting how deep and wise Danny was. So that was the end of the religion topic. We went on to talk about something else that I quickly forgot about while I traced the roots traveling up to the tree tops that had just let go of a new series of fluttering locust leaves.

MARY

Squeegee Boy distracted me from getting my laundry done. So, as expected, I smelled like shit. Just kidding. I sweat Chanel no. 5. But he did waste my time. He pretty much forced me to go downtown with him to this record store, then pretty much forced me to go to his house after to listen to that record. Whatta smooth criminal. Chastity belt on lock doe.

I had never been in a house as big, or as nice, as Danny's before. Most of the people I knew, figuratively speaking, lived in cardboard boxes. But Danny's house had a basement and an upstairs and, like, rooms that just had chairs and books in them. It was huge. Danny gave me the lowdown on the mess, blaming his mom, and took two steps up the stairs. Over in a room to my left, past two fanned open, windowed doors, sat a black grand piano. Danny told me that it was his mom who played when I asked him, and nudged me again to go up the stairs. For whatever reason, seeing that piano in someone's house amazed me. Tightening my chastity belt, I followed Danny up the stairs.

The stairway was pretty much a gallery of family photos. I couldn't figure out who Danny lived with. In some pictures on the wall, I saw two very similar, but different looking young boys. The pudgy baby, I instantly recognized as Danny. He still looked, like, exactly the same. But the older looking boy in the pictures I just assumed was his brother. Maybe? There weren't any new looking pictures on the wall either, which might be normal. Who really wants a framed portrait of some gawky fifteen-year-old on the family photo wall?

Danny twisted the handle and opened the door to his bedroom.

"Danny," I said, and he turned around to blink at me. "What the hell?" Two guitars, a wooden one and another plugged into a speaker, sat on stands in the corner of his room. "You totally play music."

Not much fazes me. A perk of being a Bitch from Venus is that you're born without a heart. So just like the time Tanner began selling weed and religiously lied to me that he was driving for a covert illegal cab company, Danny lied to me about playing music. Don't get me wrong, I honestly don't care that he lied. I just don't like being lied to.

"Why'd you lie about *not* being able to play music?" I asked.

Danny's verbal reflex game was on point, cuz he dodged every question with some sort of stupid sarcastic answer. Gotta hand it to him, the kid had wit.

"I'm not entirely sure," Danny finally broke, after my interrogation. "I didn't feel like it. Come on, let's just listen to our records."

I told him that, since he lied, he had to play Biggie first. So while Liar Liar Pants On Fire went to do that, my eyes swept over the rows of albums stuffed in the long rectangular shelf beneath his record player, and spotted the spine of a notebook popping out.

"Is this where I can find all your Christian Rap verses?" I asked, bending over and pulling the notebook out. My thumb swept through the pages just as Danny dropped the needle on Biggie and lost his mind.

"NO. No! Don't look through it!"

Danny took a giant lunge towards me, and all I saw was ten out-stretched fingers flying at my face. I swooped out of the way, and as Biggie began rapping over the speakers, I flipped to a random page and read:

> "She rocks her head to an out of tune lullaby.
> Waiting for a knight in—shimming—shining—armor
> To stop the tears from her lonely eyes—"

"Hey!" Danny grabbed for his book, but again I stepped out of the way, running in circles around his dirty laundry while holding (let's face it) his diary, open above my head. Then I tripped on this random plastic garbage bag. I caught my landing just in time and jumped up on his bed, flopping onto my tummy as I flipped to another page.

> "Oh forget what you think you understand!
> Live tonight and let that pretty stranger take your hand!"

"Danny! These are some straight up ghetto rhymes yo!"

"Those are all from, like, the seventh grade," he said (very defensively, I may add). "I write much better now."

The room seemed to ripple with his jitters. Boy oh boy was I grinding Squeegee Boy's gears.

"Yo. These are actually pretty good," I said, flipping through a few more blue-lined pages, and then looked up at him and added: "For seventh grade."

He didn't say anything. When I turned around, I saw that Danny's face, highlighted with the shaft of light coming in through the window to my left, was bright red. "I'm being serious, Danny! Like, you one sens'tive seventh grade nigguh. Were you like the Drake of middle-school?"

"No comment."

I guess if there's one way to really invade a man's privacy, you skim his diary. See, I never kept diaries and shit like that around, because that's just leaving behind cold-hard evidence of all the weird shit you don't want people ever knowing. Which is exactly what happened.

My fingers rapidly shifted through the book, scanning the unfettered bursts of blue ink along the pages. The markings of his relentless imagination. The indelible scribbles in the top margins when the pen must have dried out. Words and entire sentences scratched out completely in thick, repeated dashes, eliminating certain confessions from existence. Danny's humiliation grew hotter with the building momentum of my fingers flipping the pages, my giddy snickering each time I read something dorky. With my face burning from the inherited embarrassment radiating hot off of Squeegee Boy, I looked up at him, rolling his eyes, and then fluttered my gaze to the next page and went stone cold. The corners of my mouth throbbed. Consciously, I flexed the muscles in my face to keep smiling, pretending to still laugh.

Written without any regard to the boundaries of the blue lines, in hacked and staggered ink, was the beginning of a sentence I should've never seen. My heart felt frail, guilty, for unknowingly communicating with a dark thought that he must have only written down to leave its burden behind. The gravity of the room condensed to the size of a pinprick on my forehead.

I quickly struck through a hundred or so pages, hiding away the sentence, and instead read aloud the first thing I saw that was written coherently on another blue line:

> "Well now you've got me and won my heart,
> What more could you want?!"

Oh boy! That was hilarious.

Danny snatched the notebook out of my hands and threw it across the room. "Okay, that's enough out of you."

Biggie fired up a new verse and killed it.

Posters tacked up in a multicolored checkered pattern hugged the corner between the two walls behind him. Trying to name all the posters became a game of trivia, like naming all the celebrities on the Sgt. Pepper album cover, which was the first poster that caught my eye.

"What are you thinking about?" Danny asked.

"Oh, nothin'." Which wasn't true. As I mentally probed about every last square inch of his room, I wondered if Squeegee Boy was embarrassed about bringing me (or anyone, really) into his bedroom, because half of it was still like a little kid's.

"Is there something wrong?" he asked.

"No, Danny."

Taped unevenly up on the wall across from his posters, were shitty little kid drawings done in marker with like Pokémon and Dragonball Z shit on them. And next to the night table, he had stickers of the GameCube logo and like, Animal Crossing, peeling at the corners off the wall.

"Ooh!" I jumped to my feet. "Danny likes dem titties!" I said, walking towards his closet door that crept slightly open.

"What?"

Hung up on the inside of the door was a poster of some, like, seventies pin-up babe. "So these are the kinda girls you like! She's hot as hell." Checking out the poster of the gloriously divine goddess with a mass of curled hair hanging over her tits, I was secretly pleased to see that photoshop couldn't do nuthin' to those 1970s stretch marks. "She looks like Lana Del Rey."

"I think it's more accurate to say Lana Del Rey looks like Raquel Welch."

"Aren't you defensive of your—what? What would she be now? Like, ninety-year-old crush?"

"She was a good singer."

"Does she help you sleep at night? You know?" I said, wrapping my hand around and shaking an invisible banana.

"Screw off."

Seventies sex-kittens and Pokémon. Danny was a strange kid.

After making a mental note to find out if Raquel Welch aged like shit (which, no, unfortunately not), I gazed back to his array of instruments. "Play me your guitar," I ordered.

"No."

"Oh, come on. Please? Pretty please?"

"No way. Not after that bullshit."

"Just picture me in my underwear."

"WHAT."

"Or what? You'd rather me drape my hair over my tits?" I crossed my hands back behind my head, mocking the poster. "But isn't that what you're supposed to do? Picture your audience in their underwear if you're nervous?"

And even after prostituting myself to his imagination, Danny still stayed all stiff.

"Come on, Ringo," I said. "Just one Beatles song."

"Really? You gave me Ringo?"

"Yeah. I'd screw Ringo."

Danny started dying of laughter. With the way Danny's hair fell, he could've been a Beatle.

"What's wrong with saying I'd bone Ringo?" I continued.

"George kicked the can, and I mean he's a Beatle after all. So, c'mon, final offer for the underwear deal."

"You'd actually strip down to your underwear?"

"Promise you'll play?"

"Yup."

Someone then started knocking on the door. And I felt that my slutty bargain had been heard by the entire world. Yay for bringing home sluts!

"Danny?" A woman's voice questioned as the door nudged open. "Is that Biggie Smalls?"

Obviously, the woman was his mother. So, due to my lousy upbringing (absent of manners and respect for my elders—and all that), I answered, "Hell yeah it is!" Then wrapped my hands over my mouth.

What else would a random older woman be doing in Danny's house? You know, unless he was into that sorta thing. But their resemblance was crazy. It was made most obvious by the high, shapely cheekbones that protruded above their defined jaws. A.K.A Danny was a momma's boy, if that wasn't already obvious.

His mom just gave an approving murmur about Biggie and nodded. "Danny, I thought you might've had a friend over."

"Oh yeah, Mom, this is my uh friend…"

"Hi. I'm Mary," I chimed in. I thought I would be generous and help the kid out, because I am a nice person.

"It's nice to meet you, Mary."

"Okay! Cool!" Danny exclaimed. "We're all acquainted! Bye, Mom—"

"Why does your mother have to leave, Danny?"

"Yeah, Danny?" his mom joined in. "I like Mary. She has cool taste in music. Maybe we both want to rock out to Biggie?"

"Hell yeah, Danny's mom." It just slipped out accidentally again.

"Hell yeah, Danny's friend, Mary," she said, tossing me a wink. "See? I don't get why you're so embarrassed of me. You should be nicer to me in front of your friends. Don't you agree, Mary?"

"I totally agree. But you see, Mrs. Danny's mom, that's the problem. Danny doesn't know if we're—" I quoted my fingers "—friends or not. He's having a difficult time with his feelings."

"Bye, Mom."

She closed the door halfway. "Love you too, Danny." And then looking over at me while still speaking to him, said, "I hope you figure your feelings out. Oh. Danny, you didn't eat the quesadillas?"

Danny told her that his stomach was sore. His mom shrugged and closed the door. Some gunshots clicked off before The Notorious spat his next verse.

"Your mom is so cool."

Danny just grumbled and went to pick his notebook up off the floor. I harassed him about playing guitar again, but all I could think of was that notebook. What I had read, or started to have read anyways, wasn't okay. I honestly didn't know how to feel about it. All I knew was, that for whatever sadistic reasons of mine, that I burned to find out what exaggeration of suffering could make this spoiled rich-kid driving his own car, and living with his cooking and cleaning mom, want (I quote): "To die."

10

Mr. Tambourine Man

DANNY

As the late afternoon waned to early evening, with the sun dropping and changing the angle and color of the light being broadcast into my room, Mary and I spun through at least a quarter of my entire record collection and talked. Though I would put our ongoing conversation on hold during the important instrumentals or lyrics. Not to be rude or anything, just my music was an extension of me. Particularly during Bob Dylan's "Mr. Tambourine Man."

Mary and I could talk about anything and everything. And we did. Music, pseudo-intellectual points about society, ancient aliens, childhood memories, and stories about people from our different high schools that, when mentioned, couldn't be placed to a face, but were talked about anyways. Mary did, though, have this unmatched talent of cutting me off. Like hands building one on top of the other in a team huddle, so did our conversations. Important thoughts, opinions, and questions had to be de-layered and traced back. More often than not, the once so important point got lost completely.

And to think the night before I thought she was a mute.

At times when Mary was speaking, I would be so mesmerized

by the motion of her mouth, how certain words blossomed on her lips, that all I could think about was our kiss in The Alley. Screw me, right?

I had probably plotted a hundred different ways Mary and I would kiss again. Something like, I would tell her she had an eyelash on her face and then go in for it. But I thought better of it. It was probably stupid, really.

Mom even came in at one point and offered us reheated veggie chili. Mary claimed that it was the "best thing" she'd ever tasted. Personally, I believe Mary was just trying to kiss ass to Mom. And by the way, how the heck did Mom even know who Biggie Smalls was?

Before we knew it, it was dark out and already a quarter past nine. And right when Peter, Paul, or Mary started plucking the guitar on "500 Miles" from their (Ten) Years Together album, Mary (the one sitting in my bedroom) insisted she had to get going. I didn't want her to leave, not yet; there were so many important lyrics on that record.

If you miss the train I am on / You will know that I am gone.

While on the drive to Mary's house as my car—The Stang— crawled through the back streets of Danae's Bay, my hands could barely find the strength to hold onto the steering wheel. Having thrown myself back against the seat, my fingers slid and clutched at the leather of the wheel for dear life as we died of laughter.

"Tha—Tha—" I stammered, fighting the folding-in of my entire body as I gasped for air. "That's so mean but so horribly true! She's *totally* a dare!"

Unapologetically, we were laughing our heads off about a girl I went to high school with, who, according to her social media, was hanging out with the New Jersey Devils. Although in Mary's opinion, was more likely the team's dare at last bar call.

For a second, before the laugh attacked again, as I gasped in embarrassingly high-pitched bursts, I blinked the tears out of my eyes and looked over at Mary—to you know, make sure she was actually laughing too. And sure enough, she was gasping in silent heaves. Her face pink and brighter than the concealer under her eyes. And as her mouth stretched wide, I noticed her crooked bottom teeth.

Through a deep exhale I managed, "I'll grab your bike for you."

When I flipped the headlights off, the blackness of the night quickly refilled the space where the light drove it out. And yet again, as I compressed the brake for the stop sign at Fisherman's Alley and Seadrift Drop, Mary told me to wait. She scooted out of my car, ran right down Seadrift through the streetlight, and disappeared out of sight. All I could hear was the flip and flop of her feet echoing through the night that had otherwise remained courteously quiet for the choir of crickets.

I pictured all those little bastards, the crickets and the frogs and the mosquitos, organizing a symphony. The frog bulging his throat, dropping the beat. The rest joining in as a grasshopper pinched a weed and conducted the choral. I should've written Silly Symphonies or something. God, I am sorta weird. The ambiance of the coastline at night began to overwhelm the sound of the fading, echoing footsteps until she couldn't be heard at all.

As promised, I began to unstrap the bungee cords that held Mary's bike in place in my trunk—Mustangs really aren't the greatest means of bicycle transportation. Her bike was possibly older than my car; I noticed, as I lifted it up and onto the road, that foam sprouted from the tear in the maroon leather seat.

It was probably only a minute, maybe two, but it felt like Mary was gone for about seven hours. The whole routine of dropping Mary off on Fisherman's was getting repetitive and annoying, and I was never a big fan of mysteries. Above the buzz of the crickets, from a distance I heard the eerie chant of an owl.

Fed up, and terrified of the owl, I kicked my leg over the frame of Mary's bike, steered the handle, and pedaled down Seadrift, assuming that my roofless car would be all right amidst the sleeping streets.

Barricaded by a yellow steel divide, Seadrift ended at a cliff overlooking the ocean. I rode right up to the dead-end and looked down at the crest of the bay. *A quick and easy passage to Heaven*, I thought.

I hollered Mary's name. All I heard in response was the frog's bass line. Mary had literally vanished like she had the night before. The waft of seaweed and salt carried through on the wind smelled familiar, almost purifying. It didn't matter that from where I lived, I was only a ten-minute car ride to the beach. The myriad of oceanic elements never lost their novelty. The sea possesses an unmatched charm of captivation; I could've sat and watched the steady crest of the waves drift in and out with the tide all night.

While pedaling my way back to my car, assuming she had to re-enter this dimension at some point to claim her bike, I looked to my right down a street named Bayview Avenue. Several houses down on the left, exposed in the wash of a stern yellow light, a girl in a pale orange tank top jerked a doorknob, tugging on it with all her strength, before pausing and trying again. Unsuccessful once more, she took a seat on the top step of her porch.

I biked down Bayview.

Bayview Avenue was a funny street. To my right, the side backing onto the ocean, stood marvelous homes of East Coast heritage and post-modern design. Gardened with all the expectations of the million-dollar mansions that ornamented the Jersey Shore.

And then, to my left, a makeshift collection of homes were compacted tightly together. Gravelly driveways stretched out of some. Others were kept enclosed by rusted fences. Signs forewarned Beware of Dog. From what I knew of Gilmore Park's history, Danae's Bay was the neighborhood for the dockworkers at the old, now closed, Carraway's Port, before it became a beachside "resort."

Two different worlds were brought together on Bayview and

were divided by the asphalt that paved the lane between them.

"Mary?" I said, rolling up to her house and clasping the handbrakes.

"Danny?" She jumped to her feet. "What the hell? I told you to wait." Mary marched down the steps. "Go back to the car. Go."

"Are you okay?"

"Yeah. I'm great," she said, walking my way. "Go back to your car. I'll be two seconds. Ashley has my house key."

"Oh, Ashley lives with you?"

"No? Er—yes. I'm waiting for her."

"Did I drop you off at Ashley's?"

"No."

"Then where are we?"

"Fuck off."

Mary stomped back up the steps.

With her back turned to me, her head tilted against the wooden-beam, she said, "Thanks for my bike or whatever. Have a good night."

From where I stood, leaning on the handles of Mary's bike, her head blocked out the yellow porch light. Silhouetting her in its gleam. Past her head, bronzed numbers read 22.

22 Bayview Avenue.

It had the typical look of a dockworker's house: a raised bungalow in need of a major renovation, or straight-up demolition. Brown crud and algae splodged the white vinyl siding that was weather-worn and splintering. Lichen and all other stuff of the sort made frequent appearances on the front porch that matched the size of the house. And the white paint, which I had imagined stood clean and bold when freshly coated, had long since withered away. Like the face of a once snow-white girl now wrinkled with age.

"Are you locked out?" I asked, after a long while of just staring at her back.

"I'm just waiting for my dad to get home with the key."

When I asked if there was a back door, she told me that she had already tried it. We were thwarted into peril. Before, all my wits and sly remarks were just for charm, for show. Right then, I had a chance to be something more than a Nice Funny Guy. I wanted to be able to do something of importance. I wanted to be the someone who, if she fell, would be there standing strong to hold her.

As Mary leaned against her porch with her skinny back facing me, staring at the screen door—as if anticipating some ghost to come open it—I realized I was losing her. Up until then, I was a gum-collector off the supermarket floor, a last-minute ride home, a jean jacket in the cold. Now I was just another loser unable to offer her anything when it really mattered.

"Mary."

She turned around to look at me. She seemed suddenly older, more tired. Her eyes that usually spiraled with life and light were drifting, dark. Disengaged. The harmonious crickets continued to sing as the rest of the night held her breath.

Then, out of nowhere, I suggested, "Do you want to stay at my place?"

Mary's eyes were locked elsewhere. On a thought, or on a twinkling star shining above the mansions dominating the bay. Maybe she was staring up at a light from a window across the street.

"I swear I'll be wearing my onesie all night," I promised, voluntarily launching myself into a permanent position in the Friend Zone. "I couldn't get outta that thing if I tried."

Her hair swung over her chest as she broke with a laugh. "Are you sure? Like, would that be okay with your mom?"

"Oh yeah," I said. "My mom always wished she had another girl in the house." Because Mom did wish that. But I still got the impression Mary wasn't convinced.

Regardless of whether she believed me or not, Mary removed her hand from the screen door and let it slam shut. I leaned her bike against the mailbox nailed haphazardly onto the railing, and started walking back to my car. Mary walked down the porch steps, glanced up at her house one last time, and then followed.

So, for the second time that day, Mary and I somehow ended up on the bed in my room, huddled in for the night and talking. Mary was flabbergasted that, when I intruded on my poor mother reading some book about California, she not only agreed to let Mary stay the night, but also made an offering of a toothbrush and some face wash. From my closet I pulled out a baggy sleeping tee for her, the classic Rolling Stones lips and tongue.

Speaking of lip and tongue, I didn't get any of that.

Mary was persistent about reading more of my lyrics, but that case was long closed. She'd ruined her chances. Instead, I rifled through the bookshelves across from my bed and pulled out a sketchbook. Some silly, childish doodles drawn in marker took up the first few pages. Drawing was never really my thing. But Mary took up the pencil, said, "Me first," and went at it.

"You're surprisingly good, Mary," I said, looking down at the pencil in her hand as she cross-shaded the rings of a lead-designed eye. "I haven't drawn in forever."

Etching in a precise detail, head down in the transfixed state of an artist at work, it was a moment before Mary answered, "I like to draw."

I found the constant sound of the sketching pencil soothing. My lamp flushing its golden light out from underneath the shade added an intimacy to my room and threw an obtuse form of our shadows against the wall. For a while, and without even getting bored, I watched her go at it. Mary took to the task with the intensity that made me think of a little kid. A juvenile artisan discovering for the first time that what's seen in her mind can flow unconsciously into her hand. Mary would be pinching the tip of the pencil, scribbling in the shading, and then pull her hand away. The shadow of her forearm would cross the page as she studied it. Make a decision. And the shadow would shrink as she went back at it. All of that, to be free to openly admire her as she got lost in her art; then to get lost wondering what she was wondering, felt like an accomplishment.

Whatever filled the air, be it her sunscreen, shampoo, or Beach Baby perfume, intoxicated me. At one point Mary's shoulder fell against mine. I'd never been so aware of the nerves her warmth evoked under my bare skin. I could feel her muscles play as she sketched. My body raced with a physical anticipation that I couldn't quite acknowledge or, for that matter, ignore. I had to hold her, kiss her, something, or I would die.

"Danny," she said, putting her pencil down and moving her shoulder away from mine.

My heart skipped a beat. She knew what I was thinking, desiring. Through the thin ends of my hair, I watched her eyes study mine. Mary stared right through them, right into my ambitious mind. Maybe she wanted what I wanted too?

I prepared for a kiss. If there was ever going to be a perfect moment, it was right now and it was mine. When her fingers grazed my temple, I began to float my hand up to hold her cheek. She then brushed my hair off my face.

"There," she said and backed away.

"Uh," I dove my floating hand counterclockwise behind my ear to scratch a nonexistent itch. "Why'd you do that?"

"Your hair wasn't bad. It was cute. But it's a shame because you have such a handsome face."

Using her fingers, she lifted a few stray ends. The graze of her nails against my scalp felt like heaven. Mary then pouted, as if extremely embarrassed, and went back to her art. After a few wordless minutes she said, "Maybe if you're lucky, I'll do your eyebrows next."

Eventually we turned out the light, and from a sleeping bag on the floor, I whispered, "Goodnight."

11

California Dreamin'

DANNY

She was standin' by the water / Oh, the Moon was growin' hotter
Neon Signs lit up The Night
Turn it Down / Your Music's Too Loud
So we Ran from the Crowd
They're gonna call us liars
When we say
We Caught a Spark Brighter than those Broken Lighters

I wrote down in my Lyric Book and started strumming through the chords I liked; listening for the internal melody of the words hidden within the music. Then, all of a sudden, Mom came barging into my room.

"Can you sing and play that again? What you just played?" she asked (and was met with a blunt no).

Mom loved when I played guitar but knew I hated having an audience. She would embarrassingly stand outside of my door while I practiced and then start applauding when I finished. The thought of performing in front of anybody made me super uncomfortable and self-conscious, so Mom didn't nag the idea very often.

But today she nagged.

"How do you ever plan on becoming a famous rock star if you can't even sing for your mom?"

"Mom, please don't ever use the term rock star. They call me that at work, and it's annoying. And exactly, I'd be playing for a bunch of random people who voluntarily bought tickets. Not my mother intruding while I write."

"Are you writing about Mary?"

Mom, at times, was just as much—if not more—immature than I was. I took off my sock and threw it at her. Before it could hit her, Mom shielded herself by tugging the door halfway back, and then picked up my sock and threw it back at me. Bulls-eye right in the head.

"Remember, I was an athlete in my prime. Anyway, before you attacked me, I was coming to tell you that I'm going to drop off some stuff I'm giving away to the Gagliardis', and then I'm going to the post office to ship some stuff to California. Want to come?"

"The Gagliardi's house smells funky."

"It doesn't smell—it doesn't smell that funky."

I told her I was in a good writing flow and didn't want to interrupt my vibe, and that I was going to hang out with Mary soon. Mom graciously reminded me to call the Los Angeles College of Music, and then continued to harass me about writing about Mary, so I threw my other sock and she evaded it again by closing the door on time. And of course, the minute Mom left, I lost the good writing flow I'd been in.

"Froo Froo!" Mary inexplicably answered the phone when I called her a couple hours later to confirm our "hangout" later that evening. I didn't really know what response Froo Froo called for, so I improvised.

"G'day, Mildred!"

Mildred sounds like the type of chick who would call someone

Froo Froo. Mary rebutted that it was cute of her and that I should like that she called me Froo Froo. Which I felt was pretty ironic, because the conjoined words of Froo and Froo made me feel like a spoiled British poodle. And nothing about that is cute.

"Watcha doin', sugah?"

"Are you high?"

"On life. Yeah. Whaddup, foo'?"

I guess the abbreviation of "fool" was a step up from Froo².

"Just writing some stuff on my guitar. Yourself?" I didn't bother tacking on some slang because I knew it would sound awful.

"Ooh!" Mary exclaimed through the speaker. "What have you written about me so far?"

"How do you know I've written anything about you?"

"Because you're a romantic, artsy kinda guy who's falling in love and is good at writing. So you've written something about me by now."

Her self-indulgence could've been off-putting, and I didn't even want to figure out what her very bold claims about my attraction to her meant—but she said I was a good writer, so yeah.

"Yeah, Mary. This is the most romantic shit I've written yet, I hope you like it." I started making up words on the spot:

"She got an ASS, oh yeah, she got an ASS. If it's flat—we give it a PASS—oh yeah, she got an ASS!"

"That was marvelous."

I murmured in agreement. "Yeah, your personality has really won me over, if you can't tell."

Mary was fabulous at the idea of flirting. While on the phone, all I could think about were the highlights of Mary's eccentric mood-swings. One day a kiss. The next, I'm told to "eff off." And then an hour after that, when she randomly combs my hair, I'm suddenly handsome?

Then she claims I'm falling in love.

At one point in our phone conversation Mary told me to "hold on," and the line went flat. She picked up and asked if we could transfer our hangout to the next night. Naturally, there was a dip in my mood, but I played it cool. With my vibrant social life and having to do things like call LACM, I was so busy.

"You slept with her?" Max's voice jumped a thousand decibels in the midst of folding rags the next day at work.

"Shh!"

"Okay. Okay." He descended into a shout-whisper. "You slept with Mary?"

"I did not sleep with her. She slept over."

"In your room?"

"Yes."

"In your bed?"

"Yes."

"You're telling me that Mary slept in your bed, and you did not sleep with her?" Max's bafflement at my lack of sexual lasciviousness was equal to mine.

I felt almost stupid when he worded it like that, so I rolled my eyes.

"Well, yeah. I want to respect her and take it slow." Which was mostly true, anyway. Max dropped his hands, mid-fold, onto the plywood countertop with a loud thud that sounded like it snapped something important holding the table together.

"Take it slow? Dude. She willingly crawled into your masturbated cum and pube-filled sheets. Believe me. She was not in the business of taking it slow. Whatever taking it slow means."

I let Max rave on about how sexually clueless I was. What Max didn't know was that she was locked out of her house and that I'd insisted on giving her the bed, with clean sheets. Thank you very much. Even when I started to tune Max out, focusing all of my attention on the task of folding the steaming mountain of rags that had begun to fog the window portal to the bright and green world outside, I couldn't help but wonder—*What was I to Mary?*

To avoid sounding like a girl—and inviting harassment from Max—I did not tell him that Mary and I did, in fact, kiss the night before, in The Alley. That Goddamn kiss. Maybe Mary did like me? And then somehow, in the measly forty-eight hours that I had known her, I did something wrong? Mary was a mood pendulum. One moment, yes, the next, no. And wouldn't making a move on a girl I offered refuge to in my house be considered rape? With everything classified as sexual harassment nowadays—I wasn't really sure, as a guy, if you're even allowed to make a move on a girl. Jesus, Mom had gotten more intimate with Mary when she hugged her bye.

Team Nice Guy finishes last again.

"Wanna come drink with me and Stephen Belanger tonight?" Max asked, interrupting my thoughts. "Yesterday we climbed on top of St. Andrews, you know, the elementary school by my house? We wanna go back and make a fire. It's sick, man. There's this corner that you can't see from the street, so it's totally safe."

"Max. The last thing that sounds safe is drinking and making a fire on the roof of an elementary school."

"Well, dude, we're gonna burn too."

And that is why sometimes Max really pisses me off. He rips me for not taking advantage of a girl who's locked out of her house, yet finds no fault in possibly burning down a grade school. In all fairness to Max, it wasn't that long ago that, I too, belonged to the fellowship of pyromaniacs. Back when we were kids, in the summertime, we'd ride our bikes to the edge of the ravine, secure them to tree trunks that were just the right size, and then venture down to the creek to build fires and blow up aerosol spray cans. Axe cans, Mom's hairspray, air fresheners, Febreze. You name it, we blew it to smithereens.

"Dude, it's brick," Max protested. "It can't burn. Have you ever tried burning a brick?"

But now, I was all a little too aware of the repercussions of exploding things in modern-day America. Let alone scorching your face off.

I was about to answer before I was interrupted.

"Rock Star!"

I turned to see Rob hollering at me from the opposite end of the garage. "It's three. You can take off."

From the open garage door behind Rob, there wasn't a single car in line. Max had just gotten in an hour before, but I'd been working all morning, so I ditched rag duty and grabbed my car keys.

"So, dude, you gonna come with us or what?" Max asked me on my way out.

"Nah, man. I've got plans with Mary tonight."

Max reminded me to wash my sheets. I pretended not to hear him and walked out of the wash, determined to make tonight the night I got to kiss her again. Yes, tonight, Danny, like a battering ram, was going to break out of the Friend Zone.

The mall food court smelled arguably worse than the Gagliardi house. (Mary and I had made plans to see a movie—not quite the date at the Americanview Drive-In that I imagined, but teenage dating was defined by the cheap comedy movie date, because sex was elicited by the infamous Arm Around The Girl in the seats). The smell of grease simmered in the air, thanks to the semi-circle of one-off Chinese takeout cuisines, a McDonald's, and the JFC— yes, Jersey Fried Chicken—surrounding me. The smell was only occasionally beaten back by the reek of highly-potent cleaning solutions. I watched some middle-schoolers get a real kick out of sliding the plastic food tray with their JFC boxes in the trashcan. We were probably attending the same screening, and I realized I was bordering pathetic. I started tapping my fingers on the table. Looked around. Made awkward eye contact with the old man sitting next to me. Kept tapping my fingers. Checked my phone: 7:03pm.

Okay. Okay. Only three minutes late, no problem.

I checked my phone again.

Okay, only seven minutes late.

I then brushed off ten minutes. Excused fifteen. Got anxious at twenty. Doubtful at twenty-five. Angry at thirty. And gave up hope at fifty.

Mary stood me up, I declared to myself. *I can't frickin' believe this. Mary stood me up.*

Those middle-schoolers met up with some middle-school girls—heck, even the old man's coffee date arrived. And there I was, more pathetic than those acne-prone twerps, sitting by myself in the greasy food court. So I did the only logical thing: called her. I dialed the number Mary told me to call for her house phone. At first, it was silent and static, and then it rang twice, followed by the sound of a phone unhinging from a receiver only to be slammed back down. The line beeped.

What a bitch.What a cruel, mean, heartless bitch. All the worse possible scenarios came to mind. I considered giving her the benefit of the doubt and then scrapped that, concluding that she was probably hooking up with her ex-boyfriend, screwing in the backseat of that Chevrolet Impala. So I whipped out my phone and tried searching her name on all the popular contemporary forms of social media so I could message her. Nothing. I tried pretty much everything and couldn't find her.

Is she just a figment of my imagination? Why is she not anywhere on the internet?

I tried spelling different variations of her name. Mare-ee, Merry, Marrie, Mareigh. Nothing. I decided I was getting a little too obsessed with this online crusade when I began scrolling through Nick Savignano's followers.

Screw her, I thought, shoving my phone back into my pocket. I stood up to leave the smelly mall's food court. *You don't need her cockiness and tobaccoy breath and nose ring and romantic lyrical assumptions and white girl semi-racist Ebonic speech,* I told myself. *Screw Mary.*

And to make it all sweeter, I didn't talk to Mary for another two days.

On the second day of absence, I got a call from an unknown number. My heart leaped when I went to answer it, only to find out that an overly energetic woman had revealed that I'd WON a FREE tropical cruise.

I was in an irrevocable bad mood. Mom, during a dinner congested with her typical California soliloquy, interrupted herself to ask me what was wrong.

Where to begin?

In an epic beyond epic conversation Mom and I had that previous Fall, when all high school seniors must decide the fate of their careers amongst the days of changing leaves and football games, Mom proposed California.

Mom had a cousin out there who had convinced her that Cali was the Promised Land. Mom, a lot like me, hated the winter and the snow, and unlike many Northerners rejected the idea of skiing. So, Mom asked me what I thought about moving out there. Ironic, ain't it? That a guy who insisted that all he dreamt of doing was running away, instead mumbled in thought, and then shook his head.

"No."

For the rest of the year, there were arguments and guilt trips and—shit, Mom, I just didn't want to go. Why couldn't you understand? But, when I finally realized why Mom's eyes changed when she talked about moving, and slowly came to perceive the unspoken forces that drove her yearning—that it was much more than just palm trees and having a 9021—something zip code—I agreed to go. I mean, I always hated Gilmore Park and I'd always imagined that any place had to be better than that dumpy one. Although still reluctant, little by little, I became fond of California.

But what sealed the deal for me opened my mind like a Holy Enlightenment. Mom mentioned how many opportunities I would have for my music out there.

True.

The New Jersey music scene was rustier than the carousel, and New York was an impenetrable, stupidly over-expensive island.

But to be in Southern California with Hollywood around the corner? The possibilities would be endless.

The Troubadour. The Roxy. The Viper Room. Whisky a Go-Go. Sunset's House of Blues. And hell, who knew which drunken record-exec might just be in the crowd on any given night, and might just be impressed with the long-haired kid making lightning with his Telecaster. I was sure I could finally join a band that wanted to play something other than screamo.

The endless-summer weather. The California girls. Cruising down the PCH blaring The Ramones with the Mustang top down, convincing the world that James Dean never died. Getting to start over as anyone that I wanted to be. It would all be perfect. In my mind, I built a utopic fantasy of what life on the West Coast would be like, and I began to love it. God knows it was the only thing that carried me through the rest of high school, and made me—*sorta*—care about my grades.

The forefathers of adventure were calling. "Go West, Young man!" And I was the next eager disciple in line, ready to embark on that unknown road and travel out west. No one other than me and Tom Joad (ok, and maybe Will Smith in Fresh Prince), packin' up and participating in America's greatest tradition: moving out West. Smell ya later, Jersey.

"Danny?"

"Nothing, Mom," I barked. "Nothing, nothing is wrong. Really. Just a long day at work." (I called in sick that day). I knew just one sign of my emotional fragility would be detrimental to Mom. Her conscience needed to be kept clear from any ill during the Cali transition. Receding my feelings, I deluded Mom into believing I was just fine. I couldn't bother her with my drama.

Later on, in my bedroom, trying my best not to think about Mary and working through a few lead guitar riffs I came up with, during a moment of silence between the sting of the notes and the grainy feedback from my practice amp, I heard my phone vibrate on my bed. Mary.

I jumped up, laid my Telecaster down, and swiped for my phone. By the time I held it in my hand and looked at the screen, it had stopped ringing, but the screen flashed with a missed call notification from Max. I swiped the screen to call him back. It rang only once before it was answered with a long, gasping breath.

"Danny. Danny, dude, where are you?"

"At home, you okay?"

"I'm having one of those nights."

"Okay, stay calm. I'll get you."

It had never been medically diagnosed, but Max suffered from depression. In my ignorance, I did not feel it was clinical by any means. Unlike a splintered broken arm, you cannot see a splintered broken mind. But more often than not, Max let the slightest, smallest thing upset him, and then beat himself up with it until he was mentally bruised and emotionally exhausted. Never had I suspected that there was actually something inside of him, something deep in that intangible part of the spirit, that was broken. I mistook his depression as an elixir of his own eccentricities and teenage angst. Nothing devastating had ever occurred, just simple lapses. Much like me, Max was prone to the triggers in his own world. Though the difference may have been that, whereas I was hunted down by the guerilla soldiers, Max stood against the firing wall.

Do you need that? I thought as Max breathed a cloud of pot around his head while we sat at the boardwalk's edge.

Max shriveled into a hunched posture, incessantly shivering. The guy never wore a jacket.

"Man, I just need to get really high," he said as if reading my mind.

Maybe I outwardly projected my dislike for his smoking a lot more than I was aware. Sitting, waiting for him to reach his desired state of mind, I felt my phone vibrate from within the pocket of my nineties jean jacket. False alarm—it was just an email notification from damn LACM about July campus tour dates.

In three quick, saliva slurping inhales that sizzled the burning tip of the embrowned joint, Max folded his shoulders in towards his chest and threw what was left of his roach in the ocean. I turned around, looking to see if there were any trashcans close by. The night sat on the edge of eleven-thirty; at the moment, the boardwalk was deserted. Lunatic Larry was only half an hour away from setting up, and so I figured we would wait for him. The night was strangely foggy. The haze had thickened since we sat down and grown dense enough to expand the glow of the lamplights.

"Bro, I feel so good."

"Yeah?"

He turned to me, rocking his head. "Yeah, man. This world is fucked, Danny."

I wasn't so much in a world-hating mood. Well, I wasn't until I checked my blank phone again.

"This town, man, it sucks the life out of you," he continued. "It's a death trap. It's so depressing."

Although all I could think about was how Max was trying to suck the life out of me. For the first time in a while, I didn't feel depressed. But perhaps the only reason I wasn't all anti-Gilmore Park that very second was because I was still coming off of some Mary high—I'm not sure.

"Dude," he said. "I'm gonna fall into the water."

"No, you're not," I answered, irritated at his nonsensical doped delusions.

"Danny, man, the waters like coming at my face. Holy shit! It's like rising!" Max exclaimed through an excited, paranoid laugh.

I suggested that we walk a bit.

On our sobering stroll down the boardwalk, we passed soundless strangers sitting on a bench facing the water, as well as a couple chitchatting while their Doberman panted around. Only a few lonely stragglers passed us coming the other way. A man wearing a lifeguard vest, swerving on a bicycle weighed down with plastic shopping bags, preached loudly to the sea. In arrhythmic flaps, the gears of a flagpole clinked against the steel mast in the faint ocean breeze.

"Bro!"

"What?"

"Am I tripping? Or do you hear that? Like a trumpet or some shit?"

To my surprise, Max wasn't tripping. A low-blasting horn was coming from somewhere. To my ear's best guess, the brass hum was coming from the end of the pier. Deciding to check it out, we sauntered to the pier, where the saxophone sound grew louder, but its player remained masked in the fog—someone was trying to show-up Lunatic Larry. Walking nearer, the outline of the sax man slowly grew bolder, emerging out of the mist.

"Sick sax, man," Max said as we passed him.

I realized that the Sax Man, capped in a fedora, standing out on the sea's edge, was communicating in some accord with God, so I just nodded. I didn't want—or get—recognition back. I was convinced he was the most spiritual man I'd ever come across. Something deeper told me that once he packed up his horn and transcended through the thick of the fog, he would not emerge back on the boardwalk. He'd walk through the abyss straight up a misty stairway to heaven; he had reached some otherworldly enlightenment. Standing at the very end of the pier, standing on the edge of the World, my Sax Man sought a voyager ship to take him to new ones. Lunatic Larry, alone in the ruins of yesteryear past, would stay in the old one. Thinking like that was why I didn't need drugs; my mind was already so warped. If I smoked a joint or something, I would turn into electric rings of flashing light, spiralling atop the sea.

In a high, squeaky voice, Max started repeating: "Cannabis, puts me in a bliss... cannabis, puts me in a bliss... cannabis, puts me in a bliss." Then, shouting in his regular voice: "I FEEL SO GOOD! FUCK GILMORE PARK!"

Embarrassed as all hell, since I secretly longed to be as stoic as the Sax Man, I glanced back in his direction. Maybe to give him a look that told him, "That ain't me," but by the time I turned around, I saw he had already begun his pilgrimage to the celestial realms.

"Eight-teen, man," Max said to me, or himself—hard to say which. "Danny, you know what happens to me at eighteen?"

Before I could respond, as if that's what Max was looking for, he swung his leg, booting his foot off the ground, launching his shoe over the ocean. It submerged deep into the water with a loud plop.

"Shit! Shit, Danny!" Max's jovial attitude flashed in that second to genuine disparity. "My shoe! Goddamn!"

"Max. What was wrong? Why did you even call me?"

"My shoe, Danny! Fuck!"

He called me because he needed an outlet for his angst, I realized. For a couple minutes, Max volleyed himself into hysteria, no different than how he took a simple gesture and devoured himself into depression. An onlooker would be convinced that his life depended on that shoe.

After his initial exasperation, Max fell silent. He stared out at the space on the ocean where his shoe fell. The skin around his eyes suddenly wrinkled as if he were going to cry. Then slamming his shoed-foot down, he regained his composure. The waves lapped gently against the pier.

Quiet, in thought, he let out a single scoffing laugh. "Guess same thing happens to you at eighteen," he said, swinging his hands up in front of him and then looped his thumbs around one another and fluttered the forefingers. "You get to fly away like a *leetle* bird. Tweet, tweet." Max raised his hands up above his head and then unlatched his fingers. When he turned to watch for my reaction, I saw that the whites of his eyes were red.

"Hey Danny."

"What?"

"Did you—" he snickered "—bang Mary?"

"No. No, man. I didn't." Reminding me to yet again look at my phone and see nothing but the time displayed.

"Fuck girls, man."

"I agree."

"That Roxanne broad stopped texting me," he said.

"Oh, shit, man. Why?"

"Says she don't want to be serious or shit cuz she's going to college." He dragged the remaining shoe against the pavement. "Probably just wants to go to college to be a whore."

"Did you ever steal that street sign?"

"Told her I would and everything. She didn't give a shit. Stupid broad told me last week how romantic that would be and shit. I told her it could be something to hang in her dorm room. But she didn't give a shit."

The low-whirl of a jet plane with red and white blinking lights crossed the sky, and then quickly passed out of sight and sound.

"I had it all planned too, man. Been dicing up my tips to pay Stephen's older brother to drive me out to the sign so I could steal the fucking thing. And then the night I was gonna give it to her, I was gonna take the stupid broad to the beach house."

Max bent his neck out toward to the beach—down in the

direction of the private estates where, what I preferred to call, The Old Abandoned Beach House was.

"I even broke-in with Stephen last night and left some candles and sleeping bags to set it all up. Like to surprise her, y'know? Be all romantic and shit," Max continued. "Hookup and stuff looking out at the waves. Would've been the realest thing."

Instantly struck by the lightning bolt of my rebellious streak, I suggested: "Wanna go steal it?"

"Dude, it's like, all the way in North Brunswick or something. I Google Maps'd it, and it's like, an hour drive."

"Screw it. I've got nothing to do. Let's get it, leave it at her doorstep, then she can take it to college with her and hang it in her dorm room, and stupid Roxanne can be reminded of how great of a guy you were when she's with all those college pricks."

One-shoe Max and I trekked back down the pier, and unlike The Sax Man, we must've had lessons still to learn in this world, because we did not disintegrate into particles indistinguishable from the mist and merge with new ones. Back on the boardwalk, we heard Lunatic Larry play on.

In my car, we gunned out of Carraway Beach, taking the NJ-18 North all the way to North Brunswick, somewhere all the way out in the Middlesex County. The GPS on my phone led us through the suburbs until we arrived at Roxanne Court.

Now, we had not thought so far in advance as to how we would steal the street sign. Bringing neither a foot ladder to even reach the damn thing, let alone the proper tools to take it off the post.

We drove down the small circle and made a U-turn in front of the big gray house at the end. Parking on the opposite side of the street, I surveyed our terrain. We were on a mission. Two spies. Two vigilantes. Trained to scope the objective, relying on luck and intuition for the mission's success.

"Shit, man," I said under my breath. Thinking that we might

have just blown an hour's drive for nothing.

But a light bulb went off when I looked over at the bungalow next to us and saw a pile of empty trashcans sitting by the edge of the garage. Max agreed that was our best bet.

We got out of my car, and as stealthily possible, quieter than midnight, we approached the house. Taking the lead, Max following in his socked feet behind, we hunched over and placed soundless steps up the driveway. Looking back, our invisibility confirmed, we then snatched a trashcan each and booked it down the road.

Mid-stride, I flipped my trashcan down, planting it on the ground in front of the post. I then grabbed Max's, topping it over the first one. I held it still for support as Max lunged up, wobbled on the small surface, and then snatched my shoulder to keep from falling, nearly making me fall. It took a second, but he regained his balance. Slowly, and with precision this time, he lightly landed his other foot atop the doubled-up circular base, and then leaped upwards. The sign we wanted was harnessed to another; Max's fingers grazed the bottom one, and both signs shifted. Neither were secured to the post. They could be lifted off. Max checked in with me, I confirmed, and then in an explosive jump, he pushed the signs off the post. Sunny Terrace and Roxanne Court both crashed to the ground.

The trashcans kicked back with his momentum, banging and echoing as they hit the concrete. Max landed screaming, "Ow!", picked up the still secured together signs, now chipped at the corners, and we ran for our lives. Our pavement-smacking feet were the loudest noise in the universe. I flung my hands to the latch of the trunk, ripped it open for Max to drop the signs in, and then, in perfect unison, we jumped over the convertible sides of my car and gunned off. Bolting out of North Brunswick as if the cops were in hot pursuit.

Max read out the directions on my phone and, with only one mistake in navigation later, we launched onto the highway. Speeding down the freeway, we cranked up our victory anthems. Max blasted "Straight Outta Compton," condemning the world with the power of street knowledge, screaming, "Fuck you, Roxanne!" out the side of the car.

I let him have his moment, but the race back to Gilmore Park ended with my preference of The Clash's "I Fought the Law."

After dropping Max off, sometime after two in the morning, Mary finally called.

"Hello?" I answered the unrecognizable series of digits while lying on my bed, hopelessly inventing poetry in my Lyric Book, unable to sleep.

"Danny. Hey," she said, as if her voice did not require declaration.

I did not ask, nor did she tell, where she had disappeared. Mary, like all females, was an assembly of non-convention, or rather, a reflection of the paradoxical heart. The heart in its never-ending quest for acceptance yearns for companionship, yet shies away when companionship is presented. We long to have our hearts captured by someone, but the human arc has notoriously always been about freedom.

"Yo," she said.

"What?"

"Sorry."

12

Drop It Like It's Hot

DANNY

"Okay," Mary began. "This is the plan, Daniel." I wasn't even going to bother correcting her despite my name legally being: Danny.

"You're going to put on this—" Mary pulled out a rolled-up Snoop Dog T-shirt from her purse. "Waltz your cute little ass in there, grab a twenty-sixer of Absolut Vodka, and casually, without saying something stupid, walk up to the counter, hand the person working the till whatever the total comes to, accept the change, and walk out."

"Thank you, Mary. I know how to buy something at a store. But I can't do vodka. I'll puke."

Mary rolled her eyes. "Fine. Okay, so walk into the aisle that says whiskey, and pluck out a bottle of Jack. But you can't walk into the wrong aisle, or you're gonna look like you have no idea what you're doing."

I told her that whiskey would be worse. She told me I was impossible and said to just buy a thing of red wine; it didn't matter what kind, so long as it was red and under fifteen bucks.

During our phone call the night before, after a long static silence, Mary apologized for standing me up at the mall and said she would "make it up" to me. I had not yet received any clear explanation behind her vanishing act. The conversation had gone something like this:

"Oh, come on. Soften up on poor misfortunate little me. I'll make it up to you. Okay, Froo Froo?"

"Froo Froo does not in the slightest bit make me feel any better."

"We'll do something far more exciting than going to our shitty mall."

"Yeah. The mall's even shittier when you're stood up."

"Cry me a river, Froo Froo. Do you have a fake ID?"

"Yes. I have a fake ID. Are we going to be participating in illegal activity?"

"Is anything that's fun in life not illegal?"

So little did I know that her intention for my fake ID would bring us to Lockport Malts and Liquors the following day.

In the car, Mary continued to go on about her exorbitantly thorough outline of how to get away with buying booze. The mission was planned down to the very last detail, including, but not limited to, where I should look when I'm up at the counter, and what hand I should reach for my wallet with. I told her she was overthinking, and she told me that at least one of us thinks. And just as I got out of the car, it hit me.

"I totally lost my fake ID."

"You did what?"

"That night. At The Broken Lyre concert. I totally forgot my fake at the bar."

"Danny! You idiot! How could you forget your fake ID! That was our lifeline for my amazingly planned evening!"

"Hey, I left it at the bar to catch up to you."

"Well, what good is that doin' us now?"

Mary scolded me for my lack of responsibility overseeing illegal activity, and after declaring that this was "a woman's job anyhow," marched into Lockport Malts and Liquors. For some reason, she did not need to wear the Snoop Dog shirt to have the plan succeed.

Just as Mary pulled open the door, my phone began ringing. "Hello?"

"Danny—Rob. What are you doing right now?"

Whenever Rob spontaneously called, it was to coax me into a last-minute shift.

"I'm helping my Mom with some moving stuff. Why?"

"Shit. Shit. Miller called in sick. I need an extra guy. Shit. Say Hi to your mom for me," Rob said and hung up the phone.

A minute later, Mary walked back out empty-handed and absolutely bewildered by the vagary. Blaming her failure on reaching for her wallet with her left hand.

"Why don't we just take booze from my house?"

"Wait, we can do that?" Mary seemed so dumbfounded by the concept of taking one of my mom's bottles of wine. I told her it really wasn't a big deal, but she was getting weirdly paranoid.

"This shit's like a hundred bucks!" Mary gushed while analyzing the random bottle of wine I had pulled out of Mom's wine cabinet.

"Oh," I mumbled, "is it?"

"Yeah, Danny! I only drink the ten-dollar shit. I don't drink this fancy shit. Your mom's gonna lose her shit!"

"I promise you she won't," I reassured Mary. I was a little perplexed that Mary was so nonchalant over illegally buying booze, yet was freaking out that my mom would get mad at me for taking a bottle of red wine. So to shut Mary up, I called Mom on speakerphone so she could hear the entire conversation.

"Mom, do you care if I take…" I paused to read the label. "A bottle of Tillard's Estate Wine?"

"Are you going to drive after you drink?"

"Why would you even say that?"

"Okay, sorry. Then yeah, I don't care. Just don't be an idiot and BE SAFE."

Just as I clicked the button to hang up, Mary said, "I'm like shitting myself."

"That's a really gross visual."

"I just can't freakin' believe that your mom literally does not care that we're taking a hundred-dollar bottle of wine. That's like—crazy!"

Before we left my house, Mary was gung-ho on seeing if I had a particular record in my bedroom. When I asked her what album, she didn't say. And just as I walked out the front door, it dawned on me that maybe she wanted to bang?

But it was when stepping out of the front door; going back to my car, that Mary dropped the surprise bomb on me.

"Okay. Can you drop me off at work?"

"Wait, Mary, you have to go to work?"

"Yeah?" she dragged out the word as she walked to the passenger side door, looking at me from out the corner of her eye. I stood, frozen, on the front steps.

"What's the big deal?" she said. "I only work until seven tonight. Come pick me up then, if you're not going to stand with your mouth open like an idiot for the rest of the afternoon, Daniel."

All I could think about was Rob, understaffed and overwhelmed at the carwash.

MARY

"Apples? Check. Two-dozen bottles of Heinz Ketchup? Check. Patterson Family Farm jarred fruit jam? Check." I read and repeated out loud as I did inventory at work. Needless to say, Wright Bros was dead. Linda was so bored that she sent me to the back with a red sharpie to overview and check off the imports from the week. I flipped through the clipboard and saw I had one last sheet and row of boxes in storage to strike a giant red X through.

As I finished marking off that final row of imports, Linda hollered for me to go ring through a customer up front. She was yapping to some gal-pal on the phone about shitty husbands or shitty kids. I swear I've never heard middle-aged women talk about anything else. I complied and rushed up to my till, not realizing I was still holding the clipboard until I started counting up the change. When I went to scoop up a dime, it slid out of my fingertips and chinked and chimed on the floor.

"Shi—sorry." I chucked the clipboard on the countertop, shoved the sharpie in my pocket, and crouched down. I attempted to pick the coin up by scraping it into my fingernails about a thousand times until it finally gave in. "Sorry about that." I counted the customer's change as quickly as I could and then handed it over.

Asshole didn't even say thank you.

I kept a steady eye on the clock that was moving impossibly slow. I swear that stupid thing was broken. 7pm happened eventually, and I was freed at last from the confines of my holding cell of bland fluorescent lighting and 1970s food market décor. I ran to the back. Signed out. Grabbed my bag for the evening, and when I stepped outside, swarmed with the warm air of the mid-July night, I saw Danny sitting atop the driver's side of The Stang. Parked not more than five paces from the front door. His sideways grin dug deep into his cheeks until his white smile broke through.

"Good evening, Mary," Danny said, hopping off the side of the car.

And like a mad scientist, I was pleased with my lab specimen. His hair looked so good. In fact, Danny had learned so much that he'd actually tossed on a blue and white plaid too.

"Do you have your guitar?" I asked while walking towards the passenger door he now held open for me.

"What do you see in the backseat, M Dog?"

"Did you just call me M Dog?" I shot him the dirtiest The Bitch Face I could've squinched my face into, as I tossed my gym bag, sure enough, next to his brown guitar case in the backseat.

"I figured if I'm Froo Froo—the posh British poodle—you can be M Dog."

"You're retarded," I told him and he reminded me that wasn't a nice word.

Danny was annoying, like always, and pestered me about how he had been craving french fries all week since he had to sit so long basked in their greasy smell at the mall's food court. So we swung through the McDick's on Lockport and got Cokes and his damn fries that I graciously offered to pay for. He denied my offer, but I leaned over and tossed the drive-thru lady my debit card before he could reach for his wallet.

"You didn't have to pay," Danny said to me as the drive-thru lady tore the receipt from the debit machine.

"Well, I wanted to. Okay?"

Danny didn't argue. So he's learning at this point that you never argue with me because I'm always right. Even if I'm wrong. However, this didn't stop Daniel from arguing with me that Coke and Coke Zero tasted different. That shit tastes the exact same. I don't know what he's talking about.

Danny kept asking me where I was taking him, while I imitated the GPS lady's voice and directed him through the city. Further west down Lockport, we were stopped at a red light, so I used the moment to fix my convertible-swept hair in the sunvisor mirror.

He took a giant slurp of his drink and said, "Mary. Seriously. Taste this again, this literally tastes like death by aspartame."

The Coke debate raged on (that sounds much more hood than it was).

I began to say, "Danny, there's literally no difference—" when headlights beamed into the rearview mirror. Stinging my eyes. "You need to clean your frickin' mirrors." Purple and blue dots flashed in my vision.

The high-beams flashed again. My heart sank. I had a heavy hunch it was Tanner. The cut of the headlights kept flickering as the car grew in the mirror.

"What the hell?" Danny muttered, squinting in the bright glow. The car was getting so close that I thought we were going to crash. Then suddenly with squealing brakes, they veered into the lane next us. The smell of burnt rubber filled the air.

The driver revved the engine like one hundred times, and I was actually shocked to see that it was not Tanner's 2006 Chevrolet Impala, but some other similar looking piece of shit with blue rims.

"It's the bitch from the Porsche!" an anonymous voice yelped from the car. I leaned past Danny to see who the hell was grilling us. The car was full of greasy lookin' kids, and I realized it was totally those dickholes from the other night. The same squad that had tried to get me and Danny to race them.

"Come on, you faggot! Stop being such a bitch," the driver beaked at Danny and revved the Blue Rimmed Demon again. Danny didn't say anything. Another one yelled out, "I bet you're tired of two inches!" And then more unoriginal insults followed that particularly original one.

"Danny!" I jeered. He wasn't doing anything but keeping his hands on the wheel. "Danny, say something."

"Just ignore them," he replied.

"No, Danny, say something!" I shrilled. He didn't react.

The Blue Rimmed Speed Team kept revving their rickety-sounding engine, stinking up the street, and shouting the stupidest things at Danny. And, of course, we were stalled at the longest red light in the history of all red lights.

"Danny!" I shrieked and hit the dashboard. He just kept looking straight out the windshield.

The color glowing on the hoods beamed from red to green, and then The Blue Rimmed Beasts yelled something that went lost underneath the chortle of their removed muffler as they sped off.

"Danny!" I yelled. He accelerated at senior citizen speed. "Go catch up to them and say something!"

"Why?"

"Because! You can't just let people say shit to you like that."

"So? What does it matter? What would an eye for an eye solve?" He said, shifting into second.

"Yeah, Danny, I get that shit. But holy hell balls, sometimes you need to stand up for yourself!" Their tail-lights hadn't disappeared yet. "Fuck, I'll say something. Go catch up to them!"

"We're gonna miss our turn."

"GO!"

The dial of the speedometer shot up. Danny dropped his foot into the clutch—momentarily it felt as if the Mustang floated up off the ground and into the air—but then as he launched the gearshift into third while simultaneously stomping on the gas, the Mustang charged forth, splitting the wind apart.

As Danny snatched the gearshift, about to up us into fourth, he shouted, "What are you doing?" over the roaring rush.

While rummaging through all the pointless clutter in my purse, my hair whipping into my face, I looked up to see The Blue Rimmed Bitch go through a light that had just turned yellow, then fell back against the seat as Danny jostled the gearstick into fifth, blasting through the intersection, and making the end of the yellow light.

Racing in with a rubber-screeching stop, we caught even ground with the Blue Balls at the next set of red lights. I snapped off my seatbelt and stood up on the seat.

"Do you dipshits know who the hell you're messin' with?" I could see out of the bottom half of my eye that Danny was a nervous wreck. But I kept going. "Rodrigo here is the son of a COLUMBIAN COKE LORD and I'm his high-strung, coked-out,

Dominatrix. And I'm on my period and I'm bleeding like a panther. So I swear to Satan if you don't want your dicks chopped off, you better fuck off."

I yanked a red-tipped tampon out of my purse, then looking up at the Heavens, screamed: "Eat my BLOODY tampon!!" And with God's Might, whipped it at the driver.

It took the dude driving a second to realize what just hit his chest and had fallen into his lap. I've never heard a boy shriek so loud in my life.

The entire Bloody Blue Balls started freaking out right as the light flashed green.

"Mary! Sit down!"

I dropped into my seat and he raced off. Whipping around a side street, then around the back of a strip plaza, and then through another odd collection of streets until we were back on the main road, with plenty of distance between us and the Bloody Blue Balls.

"I must really like you," I said. "Tampons are expensive as shit."

"Did you actually throw a used tampon?"

"No. Of course not. Do you think I'm sick? I drew on it with a sharpie." I wiggled the red sharpie out my skinny jean pocket and showed it to him.

"You're crazy," he said.

"No. I just have balls."

He gave me a look.

"I'm kidding—I have a vagina, before you freak out. I just don't let anyone push me around. Especially not douchebags in Blue Rimmed Hondas."

13

The Chelsea Hotel

DANNY

Mary's shirt danced up her back and shimmied over her head before sliding down her arms like a waterfall. "You better not be watching!"

"Why would I do that?" I said, reminding her I was not interested in her bodacious assets. I was watching, but because—I don't know why actually—I turned away. Until I heard a zip and a snap and the ruffle of the skinny jean shuffle. Discreetly sneaking a peek over my shoulder, I got a miraculous view of Mary's nearly bare and plump bent over ass as she tugged the pants off her ankles.

And like the gentleman I am, enjoyed the show until Mary scurried off in only her bra and panties, and did a cannonball into the pool. Splashing water onto the side of my jeans.

"Crap! I was too far away!" Mary yawped as she surfaced. Her hair slicked back off her face. She even looked hot with her hair slicked. "Come on, Danny! It's your turn to strip and I'll violate you with my eyes this time!"

"I did not violate you with my eyes."

Mary just gave me a knowing look. So I turned around and started taking off my shirt.

"Nu uh!" she exclaimed. "You have to face me."

"You never gave me a frontal strip tease," I said with my back turned.

"Your nipples are free. Mine aren't."

So I turned around and unbuttoned my shirt. Mary let out a degrading holler. I threw off my Converse, snapped off my jeans, and stood on the deck of the pool in nothing but my blue boxers.

"Danny, you're packing!"

I ignored her and jumped into the pool. Swimming to the surface, I shook my hair like a dog.

"Easy there, Froo Froo," she said, so I splashed her.

"Can Froo Froo be dead already? That's like, the worst name in the book."

Mary started bubbling water with her mouth. "Sorry, Froo Froo."

I went to splash her again, but she ducked into the water. Mary started circling me like a shark about to charge, and that's when I felt her body skim my thigh, giving me an instantaneous erection.

And then, just as I was wondering how I could disguise it under the water, I felt my boxers tug against my skin and slide halfway down my butt. I plunged into the water and swam backwards, nabbing the sides and pulling them back up. Mary was laughing her head off when I bobbed to the surface.

"You realized if I did that to you, I would be jailed."

"Oh, Froo Froo." Mary swatted her hand down as if not to worry. I wanted to kill her. "I'm just having fun. Look. I'll take off mine," Mary said, and so Mary did. After slipping off her panties, she held them up.

"See?" Mary said. "Relax. No big deal." Her voice was gentle and reassuring, but I was far from reassured by anything that this anomaly of a girl did. My eyes inevitably scanned the blur of her naked legs under the water.

"Danny," she snapped.

I looked at her, but couldn't help but notice anything other than the gray panties laced around her fingertips. Dripping, drop by drop, back into the pool. "Don't be so nervous, and don't think so much. Now, before you think anything is going to happen, I'm going to put these back on."

After Mary reupholstered her underwear around her waist, we treaded water and floated on the surface and just talked. Though I couldn't focus on anything other than her naked legs and butt exposed in the water we shared.

"Are you thinking?" she asked from out of nowhere.

"Uh, no."

I scrambled the image of her naked body out of my mind.

Mary's eyelashes, wet and fanned out like the peaks of a crown, fluttered as she looked up at me, the pool-lights brightening her eyes. A half smile crossed her face as the water lapped back and forth, breaking infinitesimal waves against our bodies. Aqua blue triangles like a valley of mountains, rising and falling around us. All that could be heard was the buzzing of the forest and the soft splashes of the waves as they dispersed against the walls of the pool and then sunk back beneath the surface.

Mary's GPS instructions had led us to Winston Woods, a park in the West End of Gilmore Park. The public pool's hours were 8am-6pm, according to the sign screwed onto the post. But anyone with entry-level gymnastic capabilities could easily surmount the fence that surrounded it.

While treading the water, Mary and I entered another staring contest. Something we regularly did when the conversation stopped. When my eyes broke away from hers, I looked down through the water and noticed that under her wet bra (of course I noticed her wet bra), there were a few thin black scribbles on her ribcage. "Is that a tattoo?" I asked.

"Yeah. Wanna see?" Without waiting for my answer, she lobbed her body and raised her arms above her head so I could make out the thin handwriting scrawled along her skin.

"I can't read it. What does it say?" I asked, studying the narrow words on her body dripping with pearls of water.

"The heart will break, but broken live on," she answered.

I must admit that I'm not crazy about tattoos, but I liked Mary's. "Did you make that up?"

"Are you kidding me? Gosh no, I'm not that poetic. It was something I read on Tumblr and loved it so much I knew I had to have it inked by my tits."

"Hmm," I mumbled. "Why'd you like it so much?"

"Cuz it looks sexy," she answered, and then dove under the water. A short while later, Mary swam to the edge of the pool. "Don't look!"

Respecting her privacy (this time) I turned away, and heard Mary propel herself onto the deck by the way the water sloshed as she grunted. Afterward, I heard her rummage through her bag, followed by the snap of a towel. She then shuddered, "Eek! I'm cold! Oh, you can look now!" Her feet left behind blotchy wet footprints on the cement.

After following her lead and climbing out of the pool, Mary told me to bust out the Tillard's Estate. Then grabbing two plastic cups out of her purse, which Mary presented as "Courtesy of Wright Bros groceries," I filled both of our cups and we made cheers to the advent of aviation.

"The plastic really brings out the fullness of this one-hundred-dollar Merlot," Mary remarked as she downed her second cup. I was an impatient drinker and had already gone through round two, so Mary filled us both back up to the top. A piece of cork plopped into my cup.

The bottle was a cork-top. I'd seen Mom uncork wines enough times to know what to do, but I'd never practiced the art myself, so I ended up breaking the cork and had to scrape the rest out with my car key. Mary said that we now had no choice but to finish the entire bottle. At this point, I assumed we'd just crash for the night in my car.

"Okay," she burped. "Now you gotta bust out your gee-tar."

I swung back my fourth cup and winced. "Yeah. I was wondering what purpose my gee-tar had this evening."

"Just bust it out." Mary shooed me in the direction of my guitar case, which we'd left stacked against the fence that wrapped the perimeter of the pool. Moths whizzed around the lamppost that stretched taller then the fence, and the constant echoes of the surrounding forest erected a wall of sound beyond the confined, chlorine-steeped oasis of the Winston Wood's public swimming pool.

"I hope you're not expecting me to play anything," I said, as I walked back over. Everything was a little wobbly, but I ignored it in favor of enjoying the drunkenness. With my guitar case in hand, I turned back to Mary. "Okay, now what?"

Mary told me to take it out of the case. So I did. I still didn't know what the point of bringing and uncasing my guitar was, because I had told her several times that I was not going to play it.

So it just sat in my lap and she looked at me until she started laughing.

"You know what I said 'bout how you're supposed to envision your audience in their underwear if you're nervous?" Mary said.

I nodded.

"And you agreed that you would be able to perform if you did?"

"Not entirely, but sure."

Mary unfastened the towel from over her shoulders. "Well, you have your first underweared audience member!" She grinned and I couldn't breathe correctly. "Now perform. And if it's still not working—well, I'm pretty drunk, so I'm gonna enjoy whatever."

I was pretty sure the whole "envision-your-audience-in-their-underwear" thing was supposed to work a tad more affectively if the image was that of your chubby high school principal in tighty-whities while you struggled with your first-go at the talent show.

Not literally having the focus of all your sexual longings sitting next to you, swinging her tanned legs above the same shining water that had chlorine-crystalized her hair. Wearing nothing but a wet bra that fabulously honored her perky breasts and a wee little pair of panties you'd already seen wrapped and soaking around her fingers.

I didn't want to, and I wasn't going to, until her wandering eyes fluttered and seized the bright lamplight. And then as I watched how her chin tilting toward the midnight sky made her long and dampened hair float back behind her shoulders, I was pushed to the verge of docility. From there, all it took was one irrefutable whisper:

"Come on."

To slide through her smile for me to start strumming the chords of "Here, There, and Everywhere" by The Beatles.

I finished the song with the pluck of a single note. I was met with Mary's applause. "That was brilliant. Purely brilliant."

Mary kept clapping. I couldn't decipher sarcasm from flattery, and so took a large swig of the half-cup left of red wine, doing my best Elvis *Thank you, thank you very much* and shot the wine down the hatch.

"Wow." I winced. "I had to drink to get through my first public performance. Here comes a lifetime of rock 'n roll tragedy."

Mary laughed along with me. "Yeah? Think you're gon become famous?"

"Yeah, actually. I do. I am going to become famous. My music's *real* fucking good."

"How'd you know that you're going to become famous though?"

"I don't really have a reason. I just know it."

Mary grabbed the bottle of wine from me. "Well, not to be a bitch or anything, but what if you don't? Like, become famous?"

She tipped the bottle. A stream of the ruby colored wine poured into her cup.

"Well, that's not gonna happen because it's going to happen,"

I said, annoyed that she was protesting my dream. I watched her cup slowly fill.

"I'm not saying you're not good. You're like amazing. Like seriously, Danny. I would tell you if you sucked. But sometimes shit happens." Mary tilted the bottle back up, the stream swashed back inside the glass. "And not everyone's dreams can come true."

"I know. I'm well aware." I paused. "It doesn't come for free, you know?"

Mary swigged her wine with a gulp. "What doesn't?"

"Dreaming. Having a dream. It's not a free ride."

She shook her head. "I don't get it."

"There's a price to pay for it—pursuing it, I guess I mean to say. You've gotta sacrifice time and effort, put in a lot of hard work practicing when you could be doing different things. Like, I could have chosen to go to a different college, or university, even, to get a real job. But this is what I want to do. Play music. The price I pay in the meantime is this sort of unhappiness with everything."

"You're unhappy?"

"Well, sorta. Yeah."

"What the fuck does a rich kid like you have to be unhappy about?"

"What?"

"Nothing, Danny. Like, literally nothing. I'm just drunk. Continue speaking."

"Whatever. But, well, like, I sorta believe that, like, the only thing that will make my life turn around is this blurry vision I have of my future. If I didn't want such big things with my life, maybe like a reasonable person, I'd be happy with the small things. But, God. Sometimes I think that if I did anything else, I would be so miserable. And if things don't work out... well, I'll be paying back the time I spent trying to make it in music with regret and disappointment.

"Which is probably the same reason why Buddhists suggest 'letting go' and 'non-attachment.' You can't get hurt or disappointed when you don't want anything."

Mary stared at me with stardrunken eyes. She didn't get it.

"You should get that tattooed on you."

She then went on to show me the tattoo on her foot that read: GMFB (Get Money Fuck Bitches).

I told her that was the stupidest decision she could have ever made and that she's going to regret having that when she's old.

Mary argued that she was living fast, so she was probably gonna die young anyway. It pissed me off that Mary didn't clue in, or care, about what I had to say about my dreams. But sometimes, in favor of enjoying an attractive girl's company, you let those things go.

"It's funny," Mary then said, jumping conversations again. "My dad sort of says the same thing about dreaming."

"Oh yeah? What did your dad say?"

"He would always say to me, whenever I talked about things I thought I wanted to do, that, 'having a dream never paid the bills!' "

"That's not really what I meant…." But I was too drunk and she was too drunk for us to coherently carry on the conversation.

Then upon downing our fifth plastic cup each, in what appeared to transpire before my eyes in one smooth motion, Mary lifted herself onto her feet and dove into the water. Surfacing a few seconds later.

"Play me something."

Mary requested, and so I had to abide. And so as she floated atop the blue sky of the swimming pool, I played my guitar for her. Plucking through a progression of the most beautiful sounds I could will the guitar to conspire. A sad melody woven with minor chords, rendering the one lone major seventh a victory in the soundscape of defeat.

My fingers wrapping the fretboard attempted to emulate in song what my eyes got to see and what my heart got to feel. Praying that within each vibration, set in motion by the release of the strings off the edge of the pick, there would be an underlying reverberation of my heartfelt intentions. I hoped that my song would permeate deeper than the drum of her ear; not just ephemerally disperse there. I hoped that my music, that the passion my music was played with, would resonate deeper. Deeper like within her soul. And somehow that would make her fall in love with me.

"Can you drive me home?" Mary asked a while later, running a towel over her back. Her question stumbled over a few problems.

"Why?" I asked.

"Cuz? I want to go home? It's late?" She wrapped the towel around her waist.

"Uh, yeah…."

"What, Danny?"

"I've been drinking." Talking about drinking made me feel even drunker. The pool deck began to tilt towards me in the sudden consciousness of it.

"Yeah?"

"Yeah?" I mocked. "Mary, I've been drinking. That's illegal."

"Danny, people do it all the time."

"Well, I'm not doing it."

Mary tilted her head to the left, squeezing all the water out of her hair like a wet rag, and then fiddled it into an elastic band.

"Like, you're actually not going to drive me?"

"No."

"Christ, Danny, it's not a big deal."

"Christ, Mary, it is."

"Holy shit, I'll drive." Her thumb traced the strap of her bra, readjusting it before leaning over to pick up her bundle of clothes. Her cleavage rolled through regardless of her effort.

"So are you driving me, or what?" she asked again, looking up at me. The fullness of her breasts was unfavorably tantalizing.

"I will when I sober up."

"You're not shitting me? Danny, like—" She stopped, stood up, and searched for the words. In the end, she just shook her head and then in a demanding voice said, "I need to go home. Now."

Nothing was going to budge my refusal.

" 'Kay. Give me your phone. I'll call somebody else, I guess." She held out her hand to receive the phone. I didn't budge. "Jesus Christ, Danny. Will you let me call someone? What's the flipshit matter with you? Stop being so goddamn selfish. Seriously! Holy Christ! You're being such an asshole! You're acting like you're freaking twelve. Seriously. Danny. Wait—are those tears?"

Mary chased me to the edge of the fence, persistent in her accusation.

"I don't want to drive. Okay?"

And just when I thought she would understand, Mary asked again for my phone. I slapped it into her hand, pushed myself off the rusted chain-links, gathered my shit, hopped the fence, and then walked to my car. Once inside, I looked back at the pool. From under the moth-covered light, I watched her like an actress on stage under a spotlight, repeatedly typing on the phone and holding it to her ear as she tried several numbers. I turned the key in the ignition just enough to activate the stereo and played The Gaslight Anthem.

Watching her made me think of how actors strive to be holy liars. It boggled my mind to think of how people can be big enough lunatics to dedicate their entire lives to lying. How awful. Musicians strive to be as honest as possible.

And then, as I began nudging my head into the steering wheel, massaging out the tightness, I heard two taps on the window.

"I'm not driving."

"I know."

I turned down the volume so Mary wouldn't hear the song.

"Can I come in?" she asked; her voice deadened through the window.

With my forehead against the steering wheel, I nodded. Mary opened the door and slid in next to me. A moment passed before I turned to look at her. The curved bow of Mary's cheek took on a blue polish in the dashboard light, and whatever little brightness was saved flowed over to detail her wide-set eyes. And then the light slipped off her face all together as she laid her head on my shoulder.

"I'm sorry," she said, after a long silence. The Gaslight Anthem on the edge of inaudibility.

"Who's coming to get you?"

"I told them not to come."

"Why not?"

"Whom are we listening to?" she asked.

"The Gaslight Anthem."

"I like them."

I turned up the volume. We crawled into the backseat and pushed the front seats up as far as they could go. Transforming my vehicle from a car to a home. The sprawl of outdated digital dashboard lights put me in a spaceship. One from some seventies movie. And there, in a deserted parking lot in East-Central Jersey, we floated in outer space. Mary never officially apologized. Apologies were instead substituted for a late tender night in a cramped backseat, so uncomfortable it made the thought of having sex impossible, but still, we sat so close. The heat of her body was warmer than I could have imagined as we cuddled and listened to my favorite music. Then, with the lift of my finger, I silenced an already silent night for a lyric I needed Mary to hone in on.

"I love that," Mary said, after Leonard Cohen grumbled through the Chelsea Hotel that, "We are ugly, but we have the music."

14

Have You Ever
Seen the Rain?

MARY

The weather report called for an all-day rain. What a surprise. How very original of Gilmore Park. It always endlessly rained throughout the summer. And it was never that *pour yourself a cup of tea and snuggle up with a good book* kind of rain. It was that *infrequently spitting drizzle making a disaster of your hair, leaving everything smelling humid and gross* kind of rain. Whatevs. I'd given up on my hair a long time ago. And the downpour was still to come.

The cloud-covered light through my window dimmed the colors of my room, and the damp-smelling draft tousled the blinds, clacking them side to side against the windowpane, blowing threads of hair under and across my neck.

Squeegee Boy called on his work break to tell me that once the rain started, he'd be let off and would come straight over to get me.

Flipping through the pages of Danny's sketchbook (that he really insisted I take home after the night I slept over), amused by the little-kid doodles he almost seemed to have left intentionally intact, I saw a picture he'd drawn of two boys. Under the drawing of the smaller looking one, written in magic-marker, was the word ME, and under the other boy, CONOR. An old kindergarten pal, I guess.

Discovering Danny through his notebooks was sorta fun. Like, I felt sorry and everything for all those girls he must have pined relentlessly and embarrassingly over to write all those cheesy lyrics, but now (many broken hearts later, I'm sure) it entertained me. The greatest comedy is someone's shit luck. But as I wavered the pencil in my hand over a blank page, I couldn't help but think of those lyrics, the ones that I'd read in his notebook. The lyrics that started off with: I want to die.

A hefty gust of wind clashed the curtains against the window-pane. Dashing my startled hand across the page. Scratching the paper with the first pencil stroke that became my drawing.

My illustration started off as just a dress. Then it became a girl in a dress. Then, a few etches later, it became a girl in a dress, who I guess sort of looked like me, standing on a windy beach. Black tears, like running mascara, poured from her empty white eyes. And since I'm shit at drawing feet, I left her ankles as a single ghastly arrow. At first, I thought maybe she was a mermaid, but she turned out to be a ghost.

Then the phone rang. Danny.

"Froo Froo…" I answered, trying to be cute.

"Oh My Go—you know what? I'm not even going to say it. Because Gilmore Parkians? Are we Gilmore Parkians? Gilmorians? Whatever. Since the Gilmorians are all terrified of rain, they're driving slow as hell. Sorry for being late. I'll be there in five minutes, if Grandma Sue in front of me could drive the speed limit."

"Okay, sure. That's okay. Remember, Fisherman's—"

"Even though it's raining?"

"Yes."

"Okay, see you in like two minutes."

And he hung up before I even got a chance to tell him to say Hi to Grandma Sue for me. I started regretting my decision to hang out with Danny. I wanted to spend more time with my ghost girl. But he'd throw a fit if I ditched him again.

After *actually* playing eenie-meenie-miney-mo with myself to decide whether I was going to cancel my plans with him (I lost), I made the grand effort of removing myself from my warm, cozy bed. And just as I reached for my bedroom door, the wind wrapped its cold hands around my bare arms. Lifting the invisible hairs up my spine to my neck. Behind me, I heard the pages of the sketch-book ripple in the breeze left behind. When I turned around, I saw the sketchbook had blown open onto a blank page.

The rain began. Sitting, leaning against the screen door, lacing up my white Converse, there was only a subtle tonal difference between the gray light and the transparent shadow crossing over the sailboat painting mounted on the wall. Through the mesh screen, I watched how the rainwater ran in thin lucid lines along the bottom of the canopy, and then dropped in a stream of beads onto the floor. From an unseen distance on the road, I heard the tires of a car roll over the damp concrete and slash through the puddles. I stood up, ready to get mad at Danny, but instead, as the oncoming vehicle came into view, I saw that it was a white van coming towards my house.

I panicked.

The van crunched the loose stones as it hauled up into my drive-way. But then, to my relief, I saw that it was a *Splendid Arrangements* floral delivery van. Now, unless Jim had some secret admirer, or someone had actually thought of us, there was only one damn person in this world who would send flowers, and that meant he was beginning to spread like a contagious disease, showing up everywhere in my life. I bit down on my lower-lip, resisting my cheeks from rising, as I watched the delivery dude open the trunk and pull out a bouquet of the richest red roses I had ever seen. My palm pressed and pushed open the screen.

"Oh my gosh! Those are so pretty!" I gushed as the guy jogged through the rain up to the porch steps, holding one arm above his head. "Um. Whom might these be for?" I asked, recomposing myself, curbing my stupid girly embarrassment.

He quickly scanned the card. There was a card. And before he said anything, I just hinted, "For a Mary? Maybe?"

"Uh, yeah. Yeah, I'm pretty sure that's what the order form says."

The delivery dude handed off the roses with a smile before power-walking back to his van through the intensifying rain. Pelting louder against the porch canopy, the rapidly flashing lines zipped to the left with a swell of wind. The ignition of the van rumbled, and with a flash of the headlights onto my house, it pulled away. I lurched forward down the steps, expecting to see The Stang parked somewhere around the corner. I hated Squeegee Boy so much. But his car wasn't in sight.

I took a step back under the canopy and looked down at the bouquet in my hand. Feeling the long thornless stems through the plastic wrapping, and admiring the perfectly flourished curves of the petals; not a spot of discoloration or wilt along any of the brims. These were some hella quality roses. I removed the taped-on card, and let my inner girly-girl savor the moment, holding it dear and close to the center of my chest. Never in my life had I received flowers from anyone, let alone roses from a boy. All I could think of was how so right I must've been that the Danster was writing something about me—for me.

The wind wheezed through the crevices in the porch. My bottom teeth sunk deeper into my lip. With a surge of effort, I was able to pull the card away from my chest, peel open the sealed flap, slip the letter out, and unfold it crease by crease. I felt my heart flutter and held the roses right up to my nose and inhaled the sweetness—and then read the headline.

The letterhead was addressed to Jim. And then when my eyes

followed the trail of words to the bottom of the page, and there were no more words left to read, my eyes fell down with the letter, drifting out of my numb fingers to the floor.

DANNY

"You've just been crushing that pussy, huh?"

A random comment from Max. We were in the middle of rag folding during my first shift at the carwash in over a week. Just as I was about to accept what he'd said, to *tolerate* what he had said—writing it off as just Locker Room Talk—he then had to follow it up with: "Does Mary have a stank?"

I stopped folding. Placed two upright fists on the worktable, and stared out the window. Raindrops rolled down the glass. Slowly trickling down, occasionally merging with another, and then dropping down faster once united, sliding off the glass. I exhaled deeply through my nose, and then continued folding, ignoring Max to the point where I didn't talk to him for the rest of our shift. From time to time, from the corner of my eye, I'd gaze at him, and see him just smirking—proud of the fact that he'd been able to piss me off. I'd clock anyone who dared talk about Mary that way. The only reason why I didn't punch Max was because he was my friend.

Max had shown up to work before me, and by the time I got there, he was jumpy as all hell. Before he'd made that stupid comment, he'd gone on a talking spree since Rob wasn't hovering over us up front. So Max was yapping, as per usual, but no one was home behind his eyes. While rag folding, I saw that his pupils were dilated. Black holes devouring his irises.

Speaking of friends, Mary was my friend. Or so I convinced

myself. Our skin hadn't touched since that night in my car. And our kiss in The Alley was long-gone, forgotten. A million miles away. That kiss was just an entity of the moment. Just another grandiose example of Mary's mood swings. That kiss was just a part of her bad habit of letting whatever spontaneous emotion that rolled on through sweep her away. I was okay being a friend. Honestly.

But then—My Sweet Lord. Her panties laced around her fingers, dripping with water. Those sly, one-sided smiles. How her bottom lip pursed with the words she took the time to pronounce seductively. The beads on her skin as I read her tattoo. Her body as she swam in the pool. The sexually perplex puzzle numbed my mind. *What the hell was she?*

Outside, the branches clashed together with a loud gust. The rain swept over the parking lot.

Rob emerged from his cave in the back, and walking straight by Max and I—with no remarks made—hit the red button next to the cash register booth, closing the garage door.

"Fuck it. We're not gonna be getting any cars today," Rob said over the rumble of the garage door working to close. "You guys take off." He had hardly looked at us as he spoke. But right before he disappeared behind the car washing machinery back to his office, he said, "Don't you guys forget about the meeting tomorrow. 'Specially you, Max. Nine-am."

The last panel of the garage door locked in place against the ground. The cylindrical metal dryer continued to whirl and rattle, and the motors of the conveyor belt whined with a static buzz.

Just as I grabbed my keys off the hook, along with my jean jacket, Max asked for a ride home.

"Sorry, man, I've gotta be somewhere."

"You better be creaming in that."

I put my jacket on.

"Bro."

"What?"

"Chill, man. I'm just messin' with ya," he said and shoved my shoulder. "Lighten up! You know I'm not serious and shit."

"Yeah, man. It's cool."

"You busy later tonight? I got some friends in some high places I need to see. If I get piss drunk and shit, can ya fetch me, and I'll buy you some munchies? Ya know, like cab fare shit?"

Maybe I am just a sucker for friendship. Blocking out what Max had stupidly said earlier, I just agreed. It didn't really matter to me if he needed a ride to and from somewhere. I somehow always found myself playing taxi for him anyways.

"Brother!" I heard him call as I pushed through the side door, following me out into the rain.

"What?"

"Thanks for being real, man." Max held his fist out for a classic Danny & Max fist-bump. I tapped my knuckles against his.

"Just, like—" Max said. "Like, well, just like come through tonight, bro. Like, life chats, ya know? Stephen and those guys are dumbasses, bro, can't have good life chats. Ya know?"

I nodded. Apologies, sometimes, shine through in some-one's actions.

Mary had ditched me again. The windshield wipers scrubbed away at their song, washing back the rain as I idled at the infamous intersection. Fed up and confused because I had just spoken to her on the phone, I decided to go straight to her house. What's the worst that could happen, after all?

I dropped my foot into the clutch, shifted into first, and rolled down Seadrift, turning left onto Bayview Avenue. The windshield became a liquid screen, but when the wipers swept next, washing the aquatic mosaic away, I saw Mary. Drenched on the edge of her porch and screaming as she threw a bouquet of roses through the rain.

Without a second to think, I cranked the emergency break and dashed out of my car. My foot landed in a puddle, drenching my shoe through to the sock as I ran up the porch steps towards her.

"Mary!"

Wrapped in her arms she snapped, "I just want to be alone right now." And jerked away from me.

"What—what happened?"

Mary didn't answer me. I took a step closer to her. The water-logged wood of the porch felt like it was going to split beneath my feet. So I stood still. Trembling. Suspended in motion. I didn't know what to do. My jog through the rain had left me damp enough that when the frigid wind swelled, swarming the porch, I could feel the tiny hairs on my arms stand underneath my sleeves.

"Mary!" I said again, and took a step closer to her. Water from my wet sock overflowed between my toes as my foot landed. "Talk to me." I took another step forward. "I'm not leaving until you talk to me!"

"Danny, please. Seriously, just leave me alone."

"What happened?"

"Leave me alone!"

The stream of a thousand marbles drummed on the canopy. Feeling like a helpless idiot, I was about to surrender, but on the rim of my gaze, the brightness of the red roses lying flushed on the lawn averted my thoughts and delayed my departure. Rose petals were dismembered and scattered on the wet grass. An overwhelming deal of anger must have driven Mary to have thrown those roses hard enough so that the entire bouquet shattered. No matter how tightly bound they'd been, the impact couldn't keep them from falling apart.

The rain fell harder. The confusion brought on by the unexplained rejection left me unwittingly infuriated. I couldn't take it.

"Stop this!" I marched towards her. "Talk to me, Mary. Tell me what's going on!" Out of frustration, I slapped my hands against the siding of the house next to her head. Startling her, boxing her in.

She turned around. Looked at me. Her eyes were dry. No tears. "Mary. Come on. Don't—" But before I could finish, she wrapped her arms around my body, digging her brow into my collar.

"It's nothing," she said. "Okay, Danny? It's nothing. I'm not even upset. I'm really not. I just, just—knew it. That's all."

Standing on my toes to lay my chin on her head irritated the blisters that had concocted on my feet. Most of Mary's life was vague and misty. Nothing made sense. A part of me felt insufficient—emasculated even—because I was yet to be the someone she confided in.

The rain had settled into a monotonous patter, a dull incessant tacking on the shingles. A low rumbling thunder rolled in from behind the gray sky as the wind picked up and the rain fell harder. Bending the branches of the trees like lifeless limbs, and landing in loud, hollow plops against the metal drain.

"Mary," I said, soft and low. "Let's go."

Saying yes with the nod of her head, she stepped back from the hug I never wanted to leave. Looking down, I noticed peach blobs on my jean jacket. When I reached for her hand, she pulled away and then ran through the hard, silver falling rain to my car.

Pulling open the passenger door, she squinted through the water that streamed into her eyes and yelled, "Are you just gonna stand there, or what?"

15

September

MARY

The smoothest pop of fingers I'd ever seen grooved along the thick strings of a shiny black bass guitar.

"See, see," Danny said, leaning his shoulder into me while we sat on a curb, and pointed at Miles McJive.

A cool lanky black man with a Sam Jackson circa Pulp Fiction 'fro, sliding across a cover of Earth, Wind & Fire's "September."

"See how his bass is holding the entire song together, leading the way? He's got the perfect timing, catching the other sounds from falling off onto nothing." Danny looked up past the gates in awe. "Now that's bass playing."

Not knowing shit about actual music playing, I mumbled incoherently, agreeing with Danny. Though I must say, I did legit agree with the rain-wrinkled posters around Mansion Club advertising Miles McJive as "The Coolest Man on Planet Earth."

While weaving my clumped and clammy hair in circles around my fingers, Miles began singing the chorus in a high falsetto, and Danny pointed out how important Miles knew he was, but how laidback he kept his playing, letting the other players shine, smiling the entire time.

After having left my house, drenched from the rain, we spent the rest of the late afternoon and evening bumming around Carraway Beach for their super lame (and nearly failed due to the rain) festival. A banner slung across the promenade read: July 25th *The Height of Summer.*

Forgive me if I had earlier falsely glamorized being a Bitch From Venus. Being heartless is not what it's all cracked up to be. Despite being a wet-mess, Carraway Beach did attempt to get all festive. Even if it really was just another lame excuse to overcharge people for corndogs and crap carnival games by moving them from the empty field to the boardwalk. But it would have been nice to have a heart, and maybe enjoy it? Anyway, Dan the Man and his obsession with forced experiences wanted to indulge in the summer marvel of salty foods and horrible games, so I begrudgingly agreed to go on one condition: if he dared try to win me a stuffed bear, I would decapitate him. So, he won me an inflatable SpongeBob Squarepants instead. I hated him, I really did.

So like two wet rats hooked out of the water, we loitered around the boardwalk and bar hopped in The Alley. Watching the old people bands, listening from the curbs outside of the patios we weren't allowed in. Probably due to the fact we looked like two freaks holding an inflatable SpongeBob.

"Want to get going?" Danny suggested while looking onwards at Miles McJive. Then as all the old farts alongside The Coolest Man on Planet Earth began chanting: "Ba de ya de ya de ya," Danny joined in, singing in a high voice, trying to—and sorta succeeding in—making me laugh.

Puddles sat where the uneven pavement sank down in The Alley but were quickly evaporating with the sudden warm turn of the night. Transforming the world into a giant, humid-smelling sauna. My hair was a frizzly wet mess, and my soggy clothes were sticking to my body.

Knowing my makeup was an unsalvageable running mess,

Danny and I split ways so I could go in search of cheap mascara in one of the dinky tourist shops. By the time I got back, I had discovered that Danny had ditched me on the boardwalk. Well, not really. I'm being a tad dramatic, but it felt that way due to the nasty case of PMS I was nursing.

Being a girl is tough work, OKAY?

Being a dude must be easy-peasy. All guys had to worry about are, like, spontaneous erections and getting urinal spray splashing back on 'em. Which, well, was actually where Dan The Man had run off to—the urinal. Most likely getting pee spray on his hands. Thank God, we didn't hold hands or anything.

After I found a sizeable mirror next to a display of cheap sunglasses in a junky beachwear store and fixed my eyes, and was loitering around the boardwalk by myself holding SpongeBob, a guy came through the crowd and approached me.

I'd noticed him a moment before, in the midst of the muddled crowd walking all around. He was tall; he stood out. From across the boardwalk, we locked eyes.

"Hi," he said, walking towards me.

"Hi," I said, not looking directly at him.

"Are you waiting for someone?"

I intentionally didn't look at him. With my back to the ocean, slouching against the railing, I kept my gaze steady on the board-walk activity in front of me. I wasn't going to give him the satisfaction of eye contact, though I did, however, see out of the corner of my eye as he broadened his shoulders. I allowed myself to glance over for a better look. He was very Italian looking. I did not try to hide my now more than obvious eyeing up and down of him. He smiled at my examination. He had very straight, white teeth.

I looked back over at the crowds silhouetted against the bright lamplights and restaurant fronts.

"And if I am waiting for someone?"

I noticed the sheen of his chrome watch as he wedged his hand into his jean pocket. He had very dark arms.

"Whether you are or not, doesn't really matter, does it?"

He smirked, tilting his head ever so slightly. I reciprocated the look, matching the intensity of his stare, and then looked away, back towards the blinking colors of one of the games. The jingle of a prize being won rang somewhere behind the babbling crowd. He kept on looking down at me, smiling.

"Either way, you're too beautiful for me not to ask your name." He took a step closer.

I looked up at him. "My name?"

"Your name." He smiled.

"Mary." I smiled back.

"Mike," he said, and pulled his watch hand out of his pocket, extending his open palm. I transferred SpongeBob to my left hand and accepted the shake. My hand felt small in his. He held on for just a second longer than appropriate before pulling back.

"I can't get over how beautiful you are. You can't be from Gilmore?"

"I am."

"Crazy…" he said, his voice drifting. "My buddy's throwing a party." He made a gesture toward the street. "His uncles just purchased a new beach house. We wouldn't mind having a beautiful woman around. I'd love for you to come. If your friends are around, they can come too." This he said with his lower-lip hung, and then softened his brow to expose the vulnerability, the innocence, in his calf eyes. He then cocked his neck back, back towards his buddy somewhere in the crowd.

"We've got Goose, Patron—Palm Bays—if you're into that?"

The jingle of the carnival game rang again. Mike leaned in closer, smiling wider, just as I, over his shoulder, saw Danny.

It was then I grabbed Mike's hand.

"As impressive as your knock-off Rolex really is—" I looked over and smiled at the boy with the wet golden-brown hair swept up off his forehead. "—Here comes my man."

Mike jerked back and turned to look at Danny with a wide-open mouth. Exposing the stupidity in his dumb-looking calf eyes.

"Ooh! My boyfriend's back!" I shouted loud enough so Danny could hear me and then ran up to him, snatching his arm and kissing his cheek. Danny practically set on fire; Dan the Man was confused as hell.

Danny looked at me, then at my homie, Mike, and grunted. "Um, who's this," he asked, gesturing towards Mike, then looked back at me. "Girlfriend?"

"My homie, Mike. He invited us to go drink Palm Bays with him."

And with that, I heard my homie mutter, "bitch" under his breath as he punched his "Rolex" hand back in his pocket and stormed away.

"Uh," Danny mumbled, "should I even ask?"

"Uh, nope! Thanks for being my pretend boyfriend though." I unlatched myself from his arm and skipped ahead with SpongeBob.

I expected Danny to be behind me, but when I spun around, he was just staring, looking almost as dumb as Mike.

I could hear the murmur of the waves on the beach below, the late night tide swelling and crashing.

We entered a staring contest. Neither one of us wanted to budge. Danny eventually shrugged his shoulders and turned away to face the black ocean, leaning his forearms on the railing.

I knew this time Danny wasn't going to surrender; he wouldn't give in tonight. As I began walking towards him, holding SpongeBob by his long nose, Danny looked over and stared at me as I approached, as if paralyzed by an apparition.

"Danny," I said, stepping in front of him. Talking quietly so the conversation was only for us. "Why did you, like, first ever start talking to me?"

His eyes flickered with the jerk of his head. He took a step back. "Uh. Well, um—truthfully?"

"Yeah, tell me. Truthfully."

Danny's face went red. "I dunno. I thought you were—well. I thought you were beautiful."

"Ah."

"Ah nothing, Mary. Maybe you should ask me why I still—for whatever reason that is—talk to you?"

"Okay. Why do you keep on talking to me?" I asked.

Danny opened his mouth, but no words or sounds came out. He blushed, thinning his lips, and then turned his head away. His eyes were cast out towards the ocean as it crashed, rose and fell, inhaled and exhaled. Like this game Danny and I played with each other. A ceaseless cycle we couldn't break. A dark cloud drifting across the sky caught the moon's glow in its haze, bleeding the color like a painting dropped in water. The ubiquitous sounds of the carnival continued to jangle and spring about, and the alluring smell of sugar and cinnamon from a churro stand not too far off competed with the musky humidity. Danny was still looking off at the ocean when the cloud passed from underneath the moon, bringing back the luminance that subtly highlighted the railing.

"Danny? Why do you keep talking to me?"

"Well, because we're friends, right? You said it yourself."

"Good!" I gripped his shoulders. "You're right!"

I turned and walked away, clenching my face. Looking up at Danny's stupid barely visible stars above the aurora of light pollution, I wondered if any of those dim dots were Venus.

I turned back around once more, and yet again, saw that Squeegee Boy was refusing to behave and follow me like a puppy dog—the way all boys were supposed to behave. He was trying to be all dramatic, staring out at the ocean like he was blue-balled as all hell. I called for him. He wagged his tail over. Good boy.

Soon after, the whatever pointless dramatic episode of the teen drama show Danny had been re-enacting was over, and we were normal again, like real people on reality TV. Despite the fact that

I refused to let Danny spend any more money on my broke-ass, he stubbornly blew through a fifty-dollar bill on those shitty games and got himself a pop, and me my churro.

"You love that shit, huh?" I asked.

"We're at a carnival in the summertime. I have to drink Coca-Cola."

"You're—you, Danny."

He frowned, and then I told him it was a good thing and he lightened up. Over near the marina end of the boardwalk, we spotted ye olde hammer game (I don't know what it's called, but, y'know, that game where you pick up a giant hammer and slam it down as hard as you can?) and we decided to see who was stronger.

We both guessed at a variety of different names for it that could work: I came up with "Slam it Hard", Danny: "Hammer Time." As we walked towards Slam it Hard, Danny tossed his damn bottle of Coke like a cheerleader with her (or his) baton, and I teased him about that, reminding him he was going to have to wait, like, an hour before he can drink it.

The carnie working Slam it Hard/Hammer Time was sorta normal, other than his T-shirt tucked into his plaid shorts. He pitched us on the UNBEATABLE offer of two strikes for one dollar! Wow! So Danny paid the dude a dollar, and I picked up the hammer—which I found surprisingly heavy—and slammed it hard against the springboard. The light barely made it past red to orange. A condescending honk blasted from the built-in speaker.

Danny, upon his turn, was also shocked at the weight of the hammer as he lifted it and swung it down. He made the light jump halfway through the yellow lights, but nowhere near the set of green. A flop mocked through the speakers this time. Danny was so irked that he paid the carnie another dollar and slammed the hammer down two more times, managing to make one green light on the last swing. The machine gave him a slow-clap and a lame "woo hoo."

"Oh, come on," Danny handed the hammer back to the carnie. "You'd have to be Thor to—"

"Really, Mary? This guy?"

We both turned at the same time. I couldn't fathom a worse situation, seriously.

Standing with his arms crossed in a tank top, and propped front and center between the two guys that made up his "Crew," was Tanner.

Now, Tanner's Crew was one to see, if ever.

The Crew consisted of his two main bros: Fat Jordan and Derbie. I personally feel the names themselves are self-explanatory, but I will elaborate. Fat Jordan was a local rapper who dealt MDMA and marijuana on the side, and Derbie was just Derbie. He used to play lacrosse in high school, and now just hits on girls my age and gets in fights, typically outside the McDick's. And they all dressed alike.

Tanner stepped forward, readjusting his black ball cap.

"This is who you're with now?"

"Oh God, Tanner. Leave me alone."

I turned back around to Danny, who looked bewildered, unsure of how to react. To assure him that this was not a situation worth our time, I rolled my eyes and tipped my head towards the other side of the boardwalk, suggesting we leave.

I know most girls have these undying affections for their loser ex-boyfriends, but I really didn't. I really just hated mine. But getting away wasn't going to be that easy.

"Seriously, Mary? You left me for this vagina?" Tanner hacked and started doing that obvious fake hyena laugh, tossing insults about Danny with Derbs and Fat Jordan. "He can barely lift that thing!"

Tanner flagged his arm towards Danny, and then flounced forward and almost tripped over his own wavering feet. I realized then that they were all pretty high. Fat Jordan and Derbs just stood by, smirking, crossing their arms like they were SWAT or something.

"I did not leave you for anybody, Tanner. It's been, like, over half a year—get over it." I was matter-of-factly cold, as I had to be because dealing with Tanner was like dealing with a dog. He gets all excited to see me and then tries slobbering up in my crotch. But if you let him prance around for a while and wag his tail, while you just ignore him, he'll leave you alone.

"I'm over it you—"

"Are you, Tanner?" I snapped, cutting idiot face off. "We live in the same city. It's not very big. We're going to see each other. So stop getting a boner every single time you see me. Just. Leave. Me. Alone!" My voice cracked as I screamed and stomped my foot.

The Crew looked dumbfounded, unaware that little Mary did not take Tanner's shit.

And after the longest pause in the history of dramatic pauses, his eight whole brain cells came up with the ever so clever: "What's she even *saying*, man?"

Fat Jordan and Derbs started doing that hyena laugh as he turned around to face the Crew and waved his arms, flashing my virgin eyes with the nastiness of his dirty-blonde armpit hair.

"You're crazy! You're crazy, Mary! You're fuckin' nuts!" Tanner generously reminded me that I am, indeed, a little not right in the head.

By now our little sideshow on the boardwalk had become a collision on the highway; everyone passing by slowed down to watch. I caught eyes with a little boy mucking some cotton candy, and watched as his mother suddenly snatched his hand and hurried him along. My body cramped with embarrassment.

"Leave us alone, man," Danny said, dropping the hammer against Slam It Hard, making a loud bang as it hit the wooden-planked boardwalk; the handle scratched the chrome springboard as it slid off.

Just as Danny crouched down to place the handle back up, Tanner rounded on him. "What'd you say?"

He staggered forward, whipping his arms down, because you know, he's "throwing down," or whatever they say. Derbs and Fat Jordan closed in behind him as he stormed up to Danny, hovering over him.

"You beefin' me, bud?"

"No," Danny said, standing up. "I'm actually vegetarian." And took a step back away from Tanner.

"What'd you say, faggot? You disrespecting me?" Tanner gnarled, and moved in closer.

"I didn't mean to disrespect you, man. I just—"

"You sayin' you disrespecting me?"

"What? No? I literally just said—"

And they went on like that, and as I watched, I felt this inexplicable pang of jealousy. Why did he take Danny seriously? Why did he have to laugh right in my face? Could he not want to fight me because I was a girl? For the first time ever, I wanted to get in a fistfight like a boy.

Before Danny could get himself into another loop of pointless reasoning, I jumped in.

"Why don't you just fuck off already, Tanner? You limp-dicked bitch."

Desperately hoping he'd punch me.

But Tanner just stood straight up and hollered, "Shut up, you crazy broad!" loud enough that it sealed off the sound of the night. Behind us, people stopped in the midst of their carnival games to stare. It felt as though the entire population of the boardwalk had gone suddenly mute. I could only hear the repetitive soundtrack of the games and the surf below. All their eyes made me sick. I kept trying to tell myself I wasn't crazy. But what good was lying?

So I dropped SpongeBob, grabbed Danny's pop bottle, violently shook it as I marched up to Tanner (reminding myself that I was indeed crazy), and then stomping to a stop in front of him, getting right in his ugly face, with my thumb, I struck the cap and ripped the lid off.

The soda exploded, backfiring all over my hands. Sticky, cream-colored foam drooled from the bottle, down my hands, and leaked onto the boardwalk.

Tanner broke out a single chuckle, his breath reeking of beer.

"What the fuck were you trying to do, you stupid whore?" He smiled. "Remember, Mary, you're nothing but a stupid whore who's just as crazy as her old man. You're a piece of shit, and you'll never be anything other than an ugly piece of shit."

So I spat in his face.

DANNY

Mary spat in Tanner's face.

Then I'm not too sure what happened next. I think I heard someone in the crowd say something about calling the police. But before any of us could make a move, even take a breath, a bright white light swung onto the scene, dissolving the night. I think that the anonymous figure behind the piercing light told her to stop—but it was too late.

Mary booked it.

I could hear the tacking of her feet as she vanished into the crowd. If we're going to talk about fight or flight, I chose flight, and chased after Mary. Her trail through the crowd was made obvious by the way she displaced people as she charged through them.

Once I cleared through the crowd that had swarmed us, I could finally see Mary still running strong in front of me. I tried calling her name. But she didn't hear me, or didn't want to. Afraid that I would lose her, I ignored the limitations my jeans imposed upon me and powered up until I was beside her. Snatching her hand, Mary jumped, looking wildly over at me. I kept my face set, then led us down a nearby outlet of stairs that fled to the beach.

Our feet crashed into the sand and then we continued to run along the shore. The surf broke like a thunderstorm, and the wind brought in the rank smell of vegetation and sea-salt. Not a minute later, from beside me, I heard Mary take a weird wheezing breath. I slowed down and stopped to see that her face was bright red and lined with sweat. Through a short burst of air, Mary stammered, "C—can't breathe."

"I really—" gasping "—don't want to get into shit with that cop," I said, feeling terrible, but guilt was definitely better than what I thought would've put us in cuffs—or at least sentenced to questioning in the back of a cop car.

"Mary," I said holding my breath as she caught hers. "I know a place we can go." And without speaking, still heaving, Mary nodded.

I took advantage of our peril by grabbing her hand again, and dashed down the beach. I could feel the spray on my skin as we ran along the hard sand through the eddying tide. Foam spread and dissolved as it washed up the shore, and then simmered back to the bolt of the undertow. Our campaign led us over the cluster of rocks that sanctioned off the private beach, where the beach houses were. After a little struggle, we cleared the boulders and ran the distance of another five backyards, until we got to the beach house.

That old abandoned one.

I jarred open the gate of the fence surrounding the perimeter of the yard—where a sign read NO TRESPASSING—and then hastily unscrewed the already loose bolts of the back door and broke in.

The Old Abandoned Beach House was dark and dusty, but otherwise safe. Well, safe if you didn't take into account the caved-in floor of the veranda that still mourned the memory of the numerous hurricane beatings that rendered the place abandoned to begin with.

Mary asked where we were, and then answering through a quick inhale of breath, told her I'd explain upstairs. Initiated with the jerk of my head, we entered the long, dark hallway before us. Running along, scraping scatterings of sand against the floor, with the vacant rooms mourning in our ears, we reached the attic staircase and quickly fled up it.

Once inside the tiny wooden-paneled, slanted triangle of the attic, my heartbeat gunned. I consciously breathed in through my nose, inflating my stomach. My shirt stuck to the sweat on my back. I looked over my shoulder to Mary. Sitting on the floor with her back against the boarded wall, panting. The bundle of what I figured had to be Max's lovemaking supplies, in a bag on the ground beside her.

I thought I'd go over and rub her back or something, but thought otherwise. It was probably sweaty, and I wasn't quite sure what good rubbing her back would do. And so, in an attempt to lighten up the atmosphere, I tried laughing.

"Holy shit—I can't believe that actually—happened!" Forcing a laugh while trying to catch the last of my breath.

Mary's expression—or lack thereof—suggested otherwise.

I shallowed my breathing, making it soundless. The word on the wind was that The Old Abandoned Beach House was haunted; all who entered this place were bewitched. Anyone who bought it was sure to see it beat up again by another storm. The last time a hurricane pillaged the New Jersey Shore, the main floor flooded, causing the collapse of the veranda. Squares of plywood sheltered all the shattered windows. Only a porthole in the attic, and the window on the back door, remained intact; no other light entered the house.

I went over to the porthole and cranked the latch, opening it. A burst of bold ocean air quickly cleared out the stale attic musk. The pale-blue light of the moon shone on the rim of the window and spilled an obtuse shape onto the floor, but failed to light the entirety of the room.

Behind me, I could hear the cadence of Mary's breath flux with the breaking waves. I didn't look back at her. I thought she'd need her space. I studied the moon as I waited; it was a night away from being full. A pulsating blue halo radiated from the pale globe that I couldn't quite bring into focus, no matter how narrow I squinted. The ring of light would shoot out in crowned shafts whenever I tried to keep its image steady in my eye.

From Mary came a snort, it sounded as if she'd fought back a sob. Or perhaps she had a runny nose—the attic was rather dusty.

Finally, in the arisen silence, I turned to face her. She wasn't ready to talk, so I turned back to my moon. And as I studied my celestial orb, still trying to capture the perfect halo, I had all the time I needed to reflect on the chain of events.

Mike from the boardwalk. Being a "good friend." Tanner and his words. All I heard in my head was: *You're crazy, Mary! You're fuckin' nuts!* and, *You're crazy like your old man!*

I didn't want to know what he meant, but inevitably, as life would have it, I would find out. At that moment, however, I had no clue. Her mystery kept on compiling.

Being in Mary's company with so many questions became unbearable. My heart thumped louder than I could have imagined in the quiet, confined room. It wasn't fair. The mysteries felt almost unnatural. By now I should have been let into her world, the ignorance felt like a discourse in progression. By now, I needed to know about her—who cares if she doesn't kiss me ever again? Fuck playing it cool. I decided to put an end to all this mystery. The game was over.

"Mary!" I lashed out, my voice betraying my thoughts, she flinched as she looked up from the floor. "What the hell were you ever doing with a guy like Tanner?"

And my question, like all mine before, went unanswered.

Mary looked away to the wood-paneled wall.

"Mary!" I snapped.

"What!" she snapped back. "What do you want to know about me Danny that you don't already know?"

"Everything! Why do I drop you off at that intersection? Why can't I pull up to your house, and why did you tell me to fuck off the one time I did?" I began and couldn't stop. "What—why—the random silences? W—who, what, were those roses? Who sent them to you, Tanner?"

And as I listed off everything that had boiled underneath the surface for weeks, I became aware of her uninterested eyes, as if she knew how dumb and pointless my feelings were. I was probably whining, nah, I was definitely whining, lashing out unreservedly, but I honestly didn't care.

"Also, Mary, what the hell was up with calling me your boyfriend earlier? Who the fuck even was that random guy? Why, and well, while we're at it—why'd you kiss me that night, the night we met?"

Wishing in the second those words slipped from my lips I could take them back.

Mary stared blankly. So I concluded that treating her right was wrong.

"Do you only like guys like Tanner, is that it? Tell me. Is that what you like, guys who treat you like shit?"

And that's when Mary started crying.

I wasn't meant to win. I was never going to find a balance between my emotions as long as I knew her. There was no room for selflessness and selfishness. I was always going to have to choose one or the other.

"Mary, come on, don't cry. Can you please, *please*, just try to open up to me? I don't know what to—"

"*Stop*," Mary snapped. "Stop. Danny, just stop. You don't want me. Believe me, you only like me because I play hard to get and because I'm *not* nice to you. And, well, you said it yourself—you're only interested in me because you think I'm attractive.

"You don't know me." Her voice cracked. "You don't know my life, Danny. Believe me, if you did, you'd—you'd—"

And her sentence hung up on the end of a breath. Trembling, Mary glanced away and looked up towards some invisible entity as if that was where the words she wanted lay in wait for her to find.

The moon waxed in the sky, growing into its brilliance, pouring the entirety of its bright-pale beam into the attic. Brightening Mary, brightening her big and bewildered wayfarer's eyes. A renegade tear escaped and rolled down her face. She was so lovely. I've never seen anything so beautiful and so broken.

"I'd what?"

With the collapse of her shoulders, Mary said in a mournful voice, "Danny, please, please just—stop."

"No. I would what?"

"Danny—you're moving away soon. So, like, it's really just better if we're just friends."

"Well, just no. Not having it. Sorry!" Pacing forward to then kneel on the attic floor beside her, I curled my ring finger and caressed her cheek, stroking the tear and its trail away. "I don't care if I'm moving away soon, Mary. I am not just your friend. That's not—just no. It's too late for that! Sorry to break it to you!"

"Oh my God, Danny! Why are you so goddamn frustrating?"

"Because I like you!" I yelled, noticing the watershed scar in her makeup. "I like you a lot, Mary! And believe it or not, I like your heart!"

"Oh my God, you are the most CORNY person I have ever met!"

"Good! I don't CARE. I mean that! So tell me, why'd you kiss me that night, huh? Tell me!"

"Because I felt like it! I don't know? I just felt like it! Sorry that I don't have some deep and complex and meaningful bullshit answer that you're looking for!"

"Why do you have to be such a bitch?"

"Because I am a BITCH!"

"Well, stop being a bitch! Stop being so distant! You're driving me crazy!"

"You're driving me crazy!" she yelled.

"Tough luck!" I yelled back.

"YOU'RE SO ANNOYING!"

"YOU'RE SO ANNOYING!"

"Oh my GOD—will you just fucking kiss me already?"

"Yeah, I'll just fucking kiss you already."

So we fucking kissed each other.

The heat rushed to my face, burning my cheeks. My body raced with an instant hardening. Her thrusting hips. Her lips mashing into mine. The unreserved, unsure, placement of her hands as she searched my hair and my neck for a reign to seize control. We didn't have time to speak, to ask permission. We did what we pleased.

My lips found their way over her whole body, starting with her neck. She gasped. Dug her nails into my back. With my mouth on her skin, my attention only turned to the motion of keeping her euphoric moans from never ending. My belt slapped her shorts as she undid the buckle. Soon our clothes were drawn off. Our mouths found one another. The fullness of her lips made it all too easy to want to kiss her forever. For a moment, I even contemplated telling Mary I loved her.

And then, in the trance of lust, without a conscience thought in either of our minds, as the moonlight drowned the attic and the complexion of her skin and the tones of her eyes shone with the silver crystal quality of the stars, we, as two disciples of desire, transcended the divide between her body and my body. And then the world lost its purpose for its very being, for she became the very world.

16

Poems, Prayers, & Promises

MARY

"I never really got into comic books. They were too hard to understand," I had said, much to Danny's disappointment.

We talked as we lay down on a makeshift bed of sleeping bags and blankets that Danny had guaranteed me were all his. When I challenged him on as to why he had a Baby-Making Kit awaiting in the attic, he backtracked and said they were his and Max's. Then I further harassed him as to why he and Max were planning a romantic rendezvous in an old abandoned beach house.

"Okay, wait, so tell me. How were they too hard to understand?" Danny asked me, resuming the comic book bamboozlement.

"Like! I dunno! There were just too many bubbles, and I didn't know who was talking when, and yeah, it just got really stressful."

"I was really into the Japanese comics."

"Manga?" I asked, making circles around my eyes. "Big eyes?"

"Yes." He smiled. His face bright and blue in the moonlight that shone through the porthole. "Big eyes. I always thought it was pronounced manga, and then one day I heard monga and, I dunno, it actually put me in a funk."

"Don't they read them backwards too?"

"Yeah! I used to make comic books," he gestured with his hands to demonstrate the way the pages read. "Backwards, like that."

"Really?" I snorted. "You used to make comic books?"

"Yeah, when I was, like, twelve. I made the best monga— manga?" He quipped full of confidence for his former, and current, geeky pride.

Biting the corner of the sleeping bag, I said, "I bet you were a cool kid."

"Oh, I really was. Well, what was super cool Mary like at twelve? All badass with a paper route?"

"I did have a paper route."

"Wait, really? You were actually a paper girl?"

"Yes... What else were you doing at twelve, Danny? Other than discovering jerking off."

"Hey, hey, that was at eleven. And well, when I wasn't drawing monga—manga on the sides of my math notes, I was trying to bring my guitar to school as often as possible."

Danny's hair scrunched against the rolled sleeping bag substituting for a pillow when he turned to face me.

"Who taught you how to play guitar?"

"I taught myself."

"That's so cool."

The open porthole jerked with a stiff creak in the cool breeze that blew over us. Danny leaned up to stretch the short sleeping bag over my exposed feet.

"You know," I said as he tugged at the corners, trying to equally portion out the sleeping bag. "I think I'm over your lyrics. Next time I'm over, I want to read one of these comics instead."

"You know what?" Danny evened out his side of the cover. "They're probably a lot better anyway," he said, turning to face me as he leaned back; the sleeping bag completely slipped up off my feet. He smiled and shook his head at his short-lived effort.

"We're not going to hate each other some day, are we?"

"Um, I hope not," he said, resting his arms on his knees. "Where did that come from?"

I shrugged and sat up, covering myself. "Even if we stop doing this, we'll be friends, right?"

"This?" Danny asked.

"Whatever this is. I dunno, just, just promise me that we'll be friends. Okay? Even if you're far away in California."

His eyes took on an inward, dispirited expression.

"So, no matter what," I held up my pinky, "Friends?"

Then laughing, huffing out of his nose, Danny lay back down beside me and said, "Yeah, for sure. No matter what I'll always be there for you. Forever friends."

"Promise?"

"Promise," he echoed, extending his pinky.

I pulled my hand back. "I don't believe you."

"Oh my gosh. Yes, Mary. I promise."

Holding my hand out beside my head, I slowly squinted, staring at him. Danny mimicked me. His face looked so goofy. And then after slowly lowering my hand back down, with Danny imitating my every motion, I whipped my hand back beside my head. To my amusement, and his frustration, I taunted him, pulling my hand back in and out, until eventually, Danny swung his left arm out, grabbing my wrist, and firmly wrapped his pinky around mine. Swearing forever friends.

Act III.

17

Changing of The Guards

DANNY

The day broke with a light that I wished were that of the moon's so our night could be truly endless. Awakening to the sight of her hair rolling silkily down over the back of her shoulders, tousled in rings and waves from the rain and the humidity and the night—may have been the most perfect thing I had ever seen. And I was confident that, in that first inhale of the morning—as I held my breath to preserve all its perfection—and before the exhale of what would become the rest of our lives, that I had everything I always wanted.

I hadn't snuck out of The Old Abandoned Beach House since I was there last—four years ago. In the middle of screwing the bolts of the door back on, I realized that I had committed breaking and entering, and if I were to be caught, I could be charged with a pretty serious criminal offense. And the sunlight, blinding and bouncing off the morning tide, made it all too easy for someone to see us right now and call the cops.

> Breaking in last night / Just Mary and I,
> Like Bonnie and Clyde,

Committing some innocent crime.

Now that's one for the Lyric Book, I thought.

The only witnesses to our criminal affair were the black silhou-ettes of the seagulls, gawking and cawing overhead in the crisp blue sky streaked with faint wisps of clouds. All of which made me think that it was the perfect beach day. I nearly suggested it to Mary. When we made it to the boardwalk, already sun-beaten and hot, the smell of roasting corndogs still hung in the muggy air from the night before.

The Stang (God, did I really just refer to it as that?) woke up to her summer-self when I put the top down, exposing her leather seats to the same beating sun that I could feel on the back of my neck.

As I pulled out of the parking space, I saw the strangest thing. These two fat cats wearing suits—and not stylish ones, but the kind fat cats who have their bored wives dress them wear—get out of an Escalade with NEWCASTLE REALITY silkscreened on the door. Which was weird because didn't those guys realize that it was hot enough to break a Fahrenheit record? Shrugging it off, I pulled into traffic and completely forgot about it.

"Danny," Mary interrupted '90s Greenday on the radio to say at the red light of Lockport and Atlantic Way.

"Yeah?"

And without answering, she grabbed my face and made out with me.

We jumped at the honk of a horn; the light had turned green. So much had changed in less than twenty-four hours.

Although, other things hadn't changed all that much—such as I was still instructed to drop her off at the infamous intersection. And, unfortunately for me while we were kissing, right before she popped out of the car, I wondered if Tanner had made it any further. Was he allowed to drop Mary off at her front door? Since Mary and

I were—dating, why would a girl's parents care if she were with a sweet boy such as myself? Not only did I begin wondering if I would ever meet her parents, I wondered if last night meant Mary and I were boyfriend and girlfriend.

For my entire life, I'd been under this impression that, once I lost my virginity, I would transform into this hulking male figure of testosterone. But honestly, I felt exactly the same, which wasn't a bad thing. I didn't get what all the hype over the First Time was about. Or why there was even a division between virgins and the de-virginitized. If anything, the distress stemmed from the emotional confusion of, *Were we effing dating?*

Obviously, I was aware of every integer on the meter of my heart, but I certainly wasn't aware if, to Mary, any of the time we'd spent together was anything more than "hangouts." And then last night happened. I had to remind myself of, *Will you just fucking kiss me already?*

But, still, even that didn't provide a clear answer.

The boyfriend/girlfriend dilemma tug-of-warred inside of me until I saw Max's scrappy BMX bike tossed next to the curb by my house. Suddenly filled with impending dread, I pulled into my driveway, got out of the car, and saw Max. Sitting on the front cement steps of my house, hunched over his knees.

"Max!" I reached back into my car, where I had left my phone all night locked in the center console. "I'm so sorry, man. I never got your—" I stopped myself in the trail of my stupid words when I clicked my phone on and saw (4) missed calls from Max. I'd forgotten about his drive home.

He glared up at me. His eyes looked painfully bloodshot. "Save it, Danny. I'm sick of your shit."

"Max, it was only a ride?"

"No, no, no, my friend. It's much more than that. I was depending on you. You think walking home for three fucking hours was fun?" He stood up. "If you weren't so busy dicking around with that Mary broad—"

"Max!" I gunned back. "It was my fault."

Max began snorting, laughing through his nose as he hacked out, "No shit, man! Damn right it was your fault! Maybe if you'd pay attention to something else other than her for two fucking seconds, you'd notice what you're doing to yourself."

"Okay, Max. What is it that I'm doing to myself exactly? Please explain."

"Are you fucking kidding me, Danny? You're joking, right?"

"Well, you seem to be the expert in how I'm fucking up my life," I answered. "And since you're obviously doing so great, go on, Max. Please tell me."

"You're letting that dumb fucking broad waste all your time when there are bigger things going on, Danny."

"Dude—*what the fuck*—you just called my girlfriend a dumb fucking broad?"

"Your girlfriend?" Max laughed, rolling his eyes. "Danny, your fucking girlfriend? She's stringing ya along her fingers, buddy! You think a broad like that—the same broad who wouldn't even give you the fucking time of day until you started driving her ass around and paying for shit—actually cares? She's playing you like the dumbass you are."

"You're fucking high again. You know, maybe if you didn't smoke so much fucking weed, you'd realize that you're just jealous," I said, catching my shirt in my fists as I jammed them into my pockets; the cheap fabric irritating the scratch marks on my back.

"Maybe if you weren't such a fucking virgin, you wouldn't care about some trash broad who finally touched your tiny dick? How about that?"

"Fuck you."

Max got off the last step and marched right past me. After progressing a few paces, he turned in his tracks.

"Oh yeah, you might want this." He tossed an envelope that spun in the air towards me.

I bent over and slid the papers out. "A termination notice?"

"The meeting this morning, remember? They called us all to tell us that we're closing down. Why do you think we've gotten shit zero shifts lately? We're losing our jobs, Danny."

"The carwash has been around for forever, man. There's no way they're closing down."

"I know that that's just a job for you, Danny, but for me it's everything. That's all I had, man." Max began shaking. "What am I supposed to do for money now?"

"Dude, chill. We'll figure something out."

"Figure something out? I have no one to support me. I'm not like you, Danny. Not everyone has your life—Oh. Right! That doesn't fucking matter to you, 'cause you and mommy get to fly to California! When I turn eighteen, I'm kicked out of foster care. What the hell am I supposed to do then?"

From a deep, quiet place, I heard Max's shoe fall into the water.

I was suddenly overwhelmed with guilt. Felt it crawl up inside of me as the vision of Mary's hair, cascading over her naked shoulders, flashed in my mind. "Why wouldn't you just come talk to me about this?"

"I TRIED FUCKING TALKING TO YOU! YOU WOULDN'T LISTEN!"

"Oh—fuck off. I ran to get you that night but you decided to have a temper-tantrum over some girl who didn't want a stupid street sign."

"Fuck you, man," Max said then stomped towards his bike.

"Max! What the hell? You said all that shit about me? What even happened with Roxanne anyways? Max? Max!"

But Max just ignored me. Got on his bike, and rode away.

MARY

It was a normal afternoon in the white seaside shack with the broken railing that wrapped around the porch AKA my house. Which was a bad thing. No, not the broken railing—I'd gotten used to the fact that unless I took a brush and white paint, or a hammer and nails, that stupid porch would continue to look like shit. The bad thing was that I said it was a "normal afternoon." If I said that it was an abnormal afternoon or an unordinary afternoon, then there was hope. But when your normal is most other people's abnormal or unordinary, that's a bad thing.

So, it was a normal day, and this is how it began:

Woke up. Decided to stay in bed even though I was awake. Watched Real Housewives of Albuquerque. Showered. Poured myself a bowl of cereal. Argued with the phone company again about my phone. Watched more TV. Contemplated about changing service providers. But then decided that I was still too poor.

And then while skimming through some celebrity tabloid magazine that I had grabbed from work, Jim came home from God Knows Where. I then decided that my room needed reorganizing for the thousandth time that week, and began doing that.

I know my neat-freakness was just a side effect of my OCD, but the garbage dump of my house was enough to drive me half mental. So, the least I could do to keep myself sane was keeping my room looking somewhat nice.

But it was during the pulling out of all my old clothes from my closet, that my normal afternoon began.

"MARY!" Jim yelled from the kitchen.

"YEAH?" through my closed, thin-as-paper door, I shouted back. My house was tiny. It wasn't very hard to hear each other, so shouting was totally unnecessary on both our ends, but we did it anyway.

"Didj'you touch my work jacket?"

Like, why the hell would I have touched your work jacket?

"No, Dad."

"Alright."

Jim hadn't worked in two months since he jammed his foot on a pipeline—or something—that he'd been working on, and so was off on worker's comp. What he did with his newfound (paid for) free time, was a bigger mystery than the whole chicken or the egg debacle. At least when Jim worked the odd construction job here or there, or joined-in on some ridiculous business venture one of his drinking buddies schemed up, I could schedule my coming in's and out's a lot easier.

For all that summer, whenever I wanted to go out, I had to verify if I was "allowed." Such as that night me and Danny were supposed to go to the mall. Apparently, that night of the mall-date I looked like a whore. So I was "grounded" in order to be taught a lesson in not looking like a whore. I had no clue skinny jeans and a tank top made me look like a whore. Silly me.

Room cleaning continued with the whipping off of my bed sheets, and then the laying out of all my old clothes in a mountain of tangled pant legs and shirtsleeves, once-worn bras, and panties with dumb things like strawberries on them.

Lo and behold, Mt. Pile of Neglect!

Which actually started a downward spiral of self-judgment, regarding what had ever made me believe strawberries hugging my vag was cute. Not that the pair of panties I had on the day before were any sexier. Navy blue boyshorts that conserved too much ass for a lingerie ad, accompanied by my only good bra—yeah, looked pretty damn unflattering. But as if Danny really noticed, or cared, or better yet—would have not hooked up with me even if I had strawberries hugging my vag.

The fact that I had sex with Danny still didn't even really connect with me. As hard as I squeezed my brain, blocking the thought out, I couldn't stop thinking about It. Him. Danny. Squeegee Boy.

Danny was, well, Danny was Danny. My life up until I met him was somewhat predictable with everything under my control. I knew myself; I knew boys. I could tell myself how to react to whatever it was somebody did or said. From the minute Danny and I first really talked, I knew I liked him. As a friend.

And I was damn set on keeping it that way.

Of course I knew that he was falling in love. God—that was obvious. What I didn't know was that he was going to become such a damn interruption.

Since bitches share secrets (and I'm a bitch) I'll say it: I really wanted to have sex again. Did we have tremendously lengthy sex? No. Was it still amazing? Yes. Did I rock his world? Absolutely.

"MARY!" Jim shouted. Again, shouting is not needed in our shack. "Door," he added, and every terrible thought raced through my mind.

I left Mt. Pile Of Neglect and my hormonal urges on the bed and jolted out of my room, running to the front door.

Shaded by the black mesh of the screen, Squeegee Boy stood on the doormat.

"Danny, what are you doing here?" I demanded, pushing open the screen and mantling my arms on the frame to keep him out of Jim's sight. Which, well, was pointless. Clearly Jim knew someone was there. You know what else was pointless? That damn rusted barbecue he refused to get rid of.

Danny began saying, "I just thought—"

"Can we talk later?" I said and had to watch Danny get all tortured artist on me as the disappointment dawned on him. Squeegee Boy had mastered puppy dog eyes, but I was immune.

"Yeah, sure," he uttered.

Interruption: I'm psychic. Wanna know why? Because I had told every idiot to never come to my door.

"Mary! Get the hell back in here!" Jim blasted from the kitchen.

"Dad!" I yelled back. "Give me a second!"

I looked at Danny as he withdrew down the steps, horribly confused.

Jim's stomping shook our whole house as he stormed up and squeezed my arm.

"I want t'smell your breath!"

I tried to rip myself away, but his grip was too tight around my skinny arm as he dragged me inside. The sound of Danny's voice screaming "Hey!" clashed with the slamming screen door.

"I'm missin' the pack a smokes outta my work jacket. I want t'smell your breath," he said, an inch away from my mouth. His own breath smelled terribly dry. Meaning Jim was terribly sober.

"Dad," I jeered through my teeth. "I told you I don't—" my eyes darted to Danny still behind the screen "—smoke anymore!" Then forcing myself back with all my weight, pulled away from his grip.

The pullback shot me off balance, and while stumbling backwards, I rolled my ankle when my foot landed on the clutter of all the shoes piling on the doormat. In a desperate attempt to break my fall, I threw my arms out and nearly flat-palmed the painting of the sailboat, but fled my hand out of the way and cracked the drywall instead.

My eyes shot to Jim. He was going to be pissed. He was going to scream and blast his head off.

Awaiting the rage, I was scared to look at my wrist, as if glancing away would trigger the anger. Eventually I did. The bottom of my hand was chalky and pulsating.

"You're gonna have t'pay for that."

I looked back to where my hand had dented the wall and

couldn't help but notice the hole that the door-handle had chipped away at for years.

"So why you pullin' away, Mare? 'Fraid I'm gonna smell—" he beaked towards Danny "—that faggot on your breath, 'stead a the smokes you stole?"

Jim's chest bulged as he fled his fist to his mouth, coughed, and then glared at me. Jim's dopey stare, slouched back in his hollow sockets, didn't so much scare me as it did embarrass me.

Whenever Jim and I got in fights, he had this, talent, of always being one step ahead of me. Somehow knowing how I would react, and how I wanted, or expected, him to react in return—only to do the opposite. Such as with that door-handle thing. He was supposed to lose his shit on me. There should have been an explosion from him as he raved on about how that house belonged to his grandfather and that I'm disrespectful. But he didn't give me that. He didn't, because my disconsolation was always just a fucking game to him. So I snapped.

"Fine!" I yelled, lunging up towards him. "You want to smell my breath?"

Jim swung his hand out over my head and grabbed a fistful of hair. As he twisted and pulled me directly in front of him, I breathed in his face with the noisiest, open-mouthed exhale I could muster. And as Jim dug his nostril-flared nose into my mouth, I heard the door swing open.

"H-Hey!" Danny screamed and dashed down the hallway towards us. Jim looked up, letting go of my hair.

Turning to Danny, he readjusted his jeans higher on his waist and then cupped his hand under his jaw to crack his neck.

"You talkin' to me?" he said, as passive as ever.

Jim was a tall guy, like six foot three, and towered over Danny, who really wasn't that much taller than me.

Danny practically pissed himself responding with jittery ums and I's before Jim started his storm.

"Didj'ya hear that, Mare? We've got a little social justice warrior, a snowflake, comin' onto my land, my property." Jim glanced at me, nodding. "Our property, right, Mare? Trying t' tell me what t' do."

He loomed over Danny.

"Um, I—I'm so sorry—"

"I know all 'bout you millennials—including you, Mary. Crying, whining over everything ya don't like. All this is, you kids, is good parenting. You kids can't cry and complain about everything you don't like. You little leftist faggots need to know your place and stop steppin' outta line. Alright, son?"

Jim's thin and chapped lips gnawed the words that came out with an eerie peppiness, almost like he was playing around.

"Just like you, Mary," he added, dropping his voice and glaring at me. "Ya think cuz you're old nuff to bleed—" Jim's fist fled to his mouth for another cough. "That you can start actin' like your mother?"

"Dad—" I choked. A sense of triumph enlivened his face, attacking me where it hurt the most.

Looking from him to Danny to that dent in the wall—I closed my eyes, hardened my fists, felt my sorrow coagulate into anger, and then with an arduous acquiring of courage said: "Fuck you."

Grabbing Danny's hand, I pushed through the screen door. Overwrought by the gravity of what had just been committed, my feet stopped at the edge of the porch. But the weight of Danny's momentum dragged me down along the steps, creaking with the collapse of our feet.

"Mary! Mary! Get back here!"

Jim yelled after me as we jumped in The Stang and bolted down the street. His large body, erupting with manic gestures, shrank in the rearview mirror as we raced away.

18

We Gotta Get Out
of This Place

DANNY

We just drove. We didn't say a single word to one another; we just drove as far as the city streets could take us, and then kept on going until we met the edge of town. The humidity was so thick and sultry that it was mentally depleting. Even the winds that came from driving with the top down failed to override the heat. It was an invasive kind of heat, leaving no prisoner alive. So we put the top back up and blasted the air conditioning. I kept a steady eye on the fuel gauge, that was clocking too close to empty for my liking, as I drove us down County Line 55 to Regional Variety & Gas.

Inside the little variety store, I paid for a full tank, and for the sake of entertainment, bought barefoot Mary a knock-off pair of Crocs. Then also in the spur of the moment making the purchase, I tacked on a Slushie. For some reason. I really don't know why; I thought Mary would like a Slushie. Maybe? That was stupid.

When I stepped back outside—back into the sweltering heat that was so severe waves rippled from the concrete—I looked over at Mary sitting barefoot and still on the top of the trunk.

Walking up, dropping the knock-off Crocs next to her feet, I presented the Slushie to her. "Thought this might cheer you up."

Though her head was hung down, draping the blonde ends of her hair over her shoulders, the motion of her cheeks indicated a half-smile. Truthfully, I was expecting The Bitch Face, but she just took the cup, already sweaty with condensation, and started slurping. Against my will, my eyes turned to her feet, scuffed and red with blisters, and swaying side-to-side off the bumper.

The gas station attendant eventually came out to assist us—per New Jersey State Law that every gas attendant must pump the gas. Perhaps it keeps people employed. I should lighten up. We exchanged nods. He asked me what kind. Regular. He snatched the nozzle off the hook and inserted it into the fill spout. The dollar's rapid climb made the gallons look pathetically slow. The nozzle chnk'd as a few silent seconds sat between all of us—me, Mary, and the pump guy.

Cicadas shrieked in the overgrown grass that sprouted from the ditches alongside the endless slab of highway. Cars whipped by in fragmented processions.

Eventually, I broke the silence. "What happened?"

"What do you mean?" Mary asked, looking at me.

"Why's it just you and your dad? Where's your mom?"

She didn't say anything. She just sat still, dangling her feet, poking at the Slushie with the straw. The fuel pump made a particular clunking sound indicating that it was done. The attendant slotted the nozzle back on the pump, smiled politely, and walked away.

Mary stirred her melting cup of ice for a while. "My dad never spoke about her. Well, unless he was piss drunk and bitching about everything." Using the straw, she started puncturing the Slushie. "I never knew her. All I have is this old picture that my dad never—or well, probably forgot—to throw out.

"All I know is that she came from a broken home and that her mom was a crazy psycho bitch. But, well, that is coming from Jim.

So I don't know. Who knows?"

I looked up at the gloomy overcast sky, and my worries eased because it was starting to feel, and look like, an actual New Jersey summer's day. Humid and cloudy.

"Jim?" I asked, needing to clear the confusion.

"My dad."

While leaning on the side of my car, looking at her and waiting for her to say more, I noticed streaks of sweat under her armpits. Suddenly I became aware of my own sweaty shirt clinging to me, and took a look at my own sweat stains, feeling a little self-conscious.

"She moved in with my dad for a bit," Mary continued. "When she was young, sixteen or seventeen or something. And then, well, eventually Jim knocked her up, had a massive freak out, and then kicked her out." Mary started shaking. "And like, sometimes—" She took a gasp of air. "Sometimes thinking about it really upsets me. Like, there she must have been, seventeen, homeless, and pregnant. With me. Like, all this shit is my fault."

Mary kept her eyes fixed on the center of the plastic cup collapsing in her hands.

"Where is she now?" I asked.

"You know that day you picked me up, when it was raining?"

I nodded.

"Well..." Mary's voice trembled, and then she looked heavenwards to the low-slung, solid gray haze of sky. Mary opened her mouth again, but only noise came out, and she started shaking her head. Her chin quivered as her lips collapsed into a frown. Tears surfaced as her under-eyelids rose to resist and hold in the temptation to weep.

Of course, I had no clue what she was going to say, but from what I remembered of that day with the roses and the rain, my heart had already made vacancy for the weight of her story.

But there wasn't going to be a story. Not this time anyway.

Mary didn't look back at me. Once the billowing of tears came and passed, and her eyes were liberated to open again, she stared out towards the highway stretching along the horizon in front of us. The cars whirled by.

"Fuck," she moaned and struck her wrist under her eyes. "I told myself I wouldn't cry."

"Don't cry."

"I won't."

Throughout the whole moment, with Mary sitting on the trunk of my car against the grayness of the day, I knew I was losing her again. She was falling and I couldn't catch her. No matter how smart, or how loving, or how wise that I thought I was, there was nothing I could do and it killed me. Forcing her to talk wasn't the answer. That would only drive her to retreat even further away. And I couldn't just continue to parade on with the day, pretending that there wasn't something deep inside haunting her.

Mary lifted her head and looked at me with a horribly docile look in her eye. A dying yet hopeful glitter flickered under her grimace, as if her faith lay buried in something she waited for me to do or say. My courage failed.

She pouted, shrugged. Looked away.

And it crashed. I lost Mary.

But then prompted by one last desperate measure, I finally said, "Let's go in the store." Nodding my head toward Regional Variety & Gas.

Mary didn't argue against the suggestion. So that must have meant something. Slipping her feet into the Crocs, Mary hopped off the trunk and followed me inside.

It was one of those crummy gas station stores. Maybe not to a trucker though, they may have found paradise in there. The best was the random beach gear. I wondered if anybody actually ever stocked up on beach gear at Regional Variety & Gas.

"Here we are," I said, spotting a collection of maps on the rack by the magazines.

"Maps?"

Mary didn't get it.

For a second I doubted myself. If instead of helping her, if I were doing the wrong thing, it would only plunge Mary into further disappointment.

I picked up "Roadmap of the United States and the Southwestern United States," and when Mary asked me why, I told her it was so we could plan our escape. We stole a pack of highlighters, paid for the map, and went to the County Donuts & Coffee next door. I ordered us two bitter tasting coffees, and then we mapped our road trip across the country.

Route 306 would take us to the Garden State Parkway; agreeing that we would first go to New York City. Mary said she'd never been. When I said Frank Sinatra, she answered Jay-Z. Whatever.

My marker lines were yellow, hers pink, and together we plotted the most complicated and unconventional route throughout the country in United States history.

"If we all gon be doin' Nashville, we best swing by Texas!" I said, in my Southern Man voice. Mary stared dully at me. At first, for a second, I wasn't sure why, and then realized that that was the first time I had ever done a voice in front of her.

"Well sugah," she drawled, "we's gonna be packin' us some rifles and havin' us a gud ol' Southern Ball in the Lone Star State!"

By the time we finished our coffees, accents were flying off the map, and we were shooting up to New York City, dropping back down through Virginia, dashing to Tennessee, inconveniently looping all the way to Texas, crossing through a corner of Oklahoma to get to Colorado—Mary said she'd always wanted to see the mountains, apparently when she was a kid, she had this "weird obsession" with Denver—and then we'd be sprinting west through Utah, and from there, direct to Nevada for a wild night in Vegas. Lastly, we'd arrive in California. Our first stop, the Santa

Monica beach.

I could see it all. The deserts. The valleys. The mountains. Mary's hair blowing back in the wind, twisting and tangling like the rhymes of a Bob Dylan song as we drove for miles upon endless miles with the convertible top down. Mary would lean the seat back, exposing herself to the country sky, her skin beading with sweat as she tanned under the high-noon sun.

Then finally, after a long day of driving, the heat exhausting her to depletion, Mary would get tired and fall asleep wrapped in a blanket. I'd keep awake, I had to.

But then, just as my eyelids begin to grow heavy, Mary grabs the steering wheel and says, "It's okay, I got it. Look up." And I lift my eyes to the crystal light of the constellations woven onto the black shawl wrapping the hemispherical sky.

Eventually, like a tired little kid, she'd stumble into whichever desert motel I found with the blanket still wrapped around her shoulders and dragging on the floor.

Every night would be devoured in sex—every morning too. Once, we'd even do it behind a Denny's.

The days would start off with coffees at cheap diners with the map rolled out over the table, accumulating all the ringed coffee stains necessary to authenticate the journey that would begin all over again each sunrise.

Each state would require a new accent, a new outfit scavenged at the gas stations or the Native souvenir shops spread out along the interstate. Mary would finally get her Indian headdress.

And then finally, in the Golden State, California, we'd park our car full of belongings and, under the hot Pacific sun, sleep all day on the beach.

There we were going to be. I would be blue jeans and white tees. She, daisy dukes and rolled plaid sleeves. Together, we were to become the immortalized American Dream.

Staring down at our map, still in the desolate County Donuts & Coffee, and still on the outskirts of Jersey, Mary squeezed my arm, so I turned and kissed her.

Back in my car, I shoved our map in the glovebox, saving it for later. I drove her back to the Fisherman's Alley and Seadrift Drop intersection; Mary assured me it would be okay. Her dad apparently had the short-term memory of a goldfish.

It hit me with a hard, sudden strangeness when Mary said, "Yeah, it's too bad that you're leaving." For a long time, the move to California dominated the entirety of my thoughts, and now the actualization of moving across the country only came to me when someone brought it up. I hadn't even packed a single thing.

"Why is it, um, too bad?"

"Because you won't be around. You'll be... gone."

"Well, I, uh, don't have to be—gone."

A cold current from the air conditioning blasted against my arm. I clicked the button several times to slow down the speed of the fan.

"What do you mean, Danny? You don't have to move?"

"I don't have to—"

"Danny, Danny. No. Like, no. You're moving, it's like whatever." Mary's eyes surveyed the street through the windshield. "You're like the only person I actually know getting out of this shithole."

Getting out of this shithole. A longing I was bounded by my entire life. But, then, suddenly, I loved Gilmore Park. I never wanted to leave. I never wanted to see another day of my life without Mary in it.

19

Space Oddity

MARY

Most of what I feared came true when Jim and Danny met.

Danny didn't know about that part of my life. And Jim wouldn't like any guy I brought home. No boy had ever seen the walls of my room. But, unfortunately, Idiot had to show up at my house. Which ended up being a pointless shit-fit with me and Jim anyway.

Jim was out (probably drinkin' at Cat's or Gypsies) when Danny dropped me off after the gas station, and so I took advantage of that miraculous timing and locked myself in my room for the rest of the night. Telling myself: "To hell with the mess," as I kicked Mt. Pile of Neglect onto the floor and caught up with Tumblr until I fell asleep.

After waking up from a disturbing dream well past midnight, (I was trapped in an iron box with an open roof deep in the ground, and the rain kept falling; filling the box up until I drowned), I finally crept out of my room to grab cold chicken strips, or whatever nutritional dinner Jim would've brought home from the bar, and noticed that the house stunk like an ashtray. Curiosity got the better of me.

Why does the house smell like smoke?

I peered around the corner to the living room and saw that Jim had passed out in front of some late night cop show, with (get this) his work jacket slung over the couch. An empty carton of Newport cigarettes sat on the coffee table.

The next morning when I went to pour myself a bowl of Cheerios, Jim came in from seshing on the porch, or waking and baking as some may say, and sang: "Good morning! Good morning! All night you were snoring!"

This guy—Jim, a lot like Danny—loved a good fucking rhyme. "How's my beauty queen?" he asked.

"Good," I answered.

Jim yawned and grumbled as he dug through his pockets, pulling out a fifty-dollar bill.

"Queen Mary! As your father, King Jim the Third, I command you to go down to the mall and buy yourself something pretty. Like a nice blue dress, maybe? Or new shoes? Girls love new shoes. Right?" Then, like a fucking court jester he sang: "New shoes cure the blues!"

And with a loud smack, palmed the fifty-dollar bill on the kitchen table and hobbled towards the stairs to his basement lair.

Just as I grabbed a carton of day-old expired milk out of the fridge, telling myself I'd give my gastric durability a run for its money, Jim turned around at the top of the steps.

"Didj'ya figure things out with your boyfriend?"

"I don't have a boyfriend, Dad," I said, answering truthfully.

"No? Not that nice fellow with the hair? Daniel?"

"Danny," I accidentally corrected him.

"You met Danny at work?"

My tongue slid down my esophagus and slapped my heart with its moist pink flesh on its way to my stomach.

"H-how do you know?"

"I don't!" Jim bopped and I felt stupid. "He works at the Wright Bros?"

"Oh. Uh, no. Next door—"

"Oh! I see I see." Jim then mumbled some indiscernible gibberish to himself. "You know my buddy, Greg? He's barbecuin'. Maybe I'll bring home some steak, maybe some corn on the cob, too, if ya like that?"

"Sounds good," I said.

"Yes, Miss Mary!" he bellowed, before descending down the basement stairs, singing something about "Corn on the cob from a farmer named Bob" on his way down.

Later, as I was getting ready for work, I stripped off my shirt and felt a tight pain on my left arm. When I looked, I had five pink bruises, shaped like fingers, on my forearm.

DANNY

"What can I do for ya, Danny?" Rob asked me as I stepped into his office at the carwash. He gestured to the stool next to his faux leather chair. I took the seat. The window in his office faced the assembly line, where the carwashing machinery was hard away at work, mopping a car. The concrete block walls made his office remarkably cooler than the oppressive humidity outside. A big fat gray cloud had decided to hover over the northeast, and it didn't look like it was going anywhere anytime soon.

Rob was sorting through some papers on his desk when he looked up at me through his reading glasses.

"Have you been getting enough protein?"

"What?"

"You're looking pretty flushed," he remarked. "Have you been getting enough protein?" Then went back to his paper work. His office fan hummed.

"Uh, yeah." I cleared my throat. "Um, I talked to Max, and he told me that—we're closing down?"

Saying the words "closing down" out loud instantly acknowledged the reality of what was happening. Rob glanced up long enough from the spreadsheets and tallies he was filing to pierce me with a gaze that reminded me of being in the principal's office with Max for throwing snowballs. Rob looked back down at his paperwork.

"Yeah." He sounded pissed. "You missed the big meeting, Danny. I called. I left you a couple voicemails. I never heard back."

I damn well knew that ignoring my phone wasn't the right thing to do, and that's probably why I started feeling a hole in my stomach.

"I'm sorry."

"I wouldn't be sorry." He pressed his bottom lip out and shook his head. "You don't owe me nothin', Danny. We're just not bringing in the business we used to, so we're shutting down. Simple as that. You don't owe me nothin'."

Rob kept his eyes fixed on the papers he was shuffling in his hand. The oscillating fan gushed an unexpected cold blast onto my face.

"But what did I expect? You're movin' out to Calfornia, Rockstar. You're probably so busy thinking 'bout all the babes you're gonna be screwin' out there. You've got no time for us bricks here in Jersey."

"Well, wait. Why? What happened?"

"Danny, I already told you. When people are making money, they're spending it. When they're not, they ain't. It's pretty fucking simple," he said with a deep coarse chuckle.

Something I said had triggered Rob. This was the first time I'd ever felt like he was my boss and not a buddy. Well, former boss, I guess. I knew there were economic downturns, but I never imagined the carwash closing down because of it.

"I'm sorry, Danny," Rob said. "You're a good kid. Believe me, I wish this was different."

I was speechless.

"I've got some tips for you here," he said, reaching into the drawer of his steel desk, which was showing its age by the burnt-orange rust disintegrating the ledges, and pulled out an envelope. I didn't really care, mostly because the writing on the envelope spelled out in purple pen, *ten dollars*.

"Wait, Rob, what are you gonna do now? Where are you going to work?"

"My brother runs a little bistro over the river. He says he could use some help managing. So, I put the Porsche up for sale—that's actually why I had you detail it for me, and I'm heading out there." He started writing something, and then jolted his head up. "You interested in buying it? I know you like it. I know you took it out that night."

"I didn't take your—"

"I checked the mileage. I knew what I had, buddy. Plus Miller told me he saw you stopped at a light with some smokin' broad in the car. Believe me, Danny, I was fucking pissed, until he told me she was hot." I was about to speak up, but he kept going. "It's okay, Danny. As long as you got laid—I don't mind."

I forced myself to laugh at his remark, but couldn't help but feel exposed that my night with Mary had been intruded on. I'd thought those memories were private. But I guess nothing is private. Maybe this guilty rotten feeling was my Karma. Karma had sought, and run me down, after all.

I looked out at the now lifeless mechanical arms, buzzing patiently, anticipating the next car. Motionlessly waiting for something that wouldn't happen.

"Danny!" Rob exclaimed. "Stop looking like someone just drowned your cat. I'm not mad at ya, buddy."

I tried apologizing, but he kept telling me that it was okay. So I guess it was okay, but it wasn't. I felt like an irresponsible bag of shit, and like my first night with Mary—stargazing and dancing and beach bonfire-making—was now somehow sacrilegious.

"Best of luck to you, Danny," he said as we stood up. Nodded. Then gave each other a firm, final-farewell handshake. I walked out of his office for the last time. The heavy metal door slammed behind me. The impact echoed throughout the detail garage.

Slogging out of the garage, back into the thick afternoon air on my way to my car, I saw what I thought was a familiar dark green pickup truck idling outside on the driveway. I didn't want this person thinking I was at work, and I really didn't want to go through the process of kindly explaining to this waiting customer that I was an employee, but not working at that precise moment. And that would lead to having to explain that we were closing with a reason I didn't quite fully understand myself. But, while keeping my head down, trying to avoid all contact possible, I heard someone shout my name.

"Dan-ny!" The eerily friendly voice repeated, singing my name. I really couldn't believe what I saw when I looked up.

"Uh, hi," was all I managed to utter when I saw Jim.

"Can I have a..." his voice trailed off as he scratched his chin. "Ooh, a number three car wash, please?" He had a tendency to add a growly high-pitched inflection to the end of his sentences.

"I uh, I'm not at work."

"Wanna lift home, then?"

Jim couldn't have been any friendlier. This guy was nothing close to the sinister villain I'd come toe-to-toe with days before inside Mary's house. If it wasn't for being called a "leftist faggot" and witnessing Mary almost have a handful of hair aggressively ripped out of her scalp—and aside from having driven myself—I probably would've said Yes.

"No, I'm really quite okay. Thanks." I nodded and waved, and then picked up the pace on my power-walk to my car.

Jim pulled his truck up beside me, following as I walked. "I just wanta have a little conversation. Won't be long, Danny. Just need t' ask ya a question."

My heart started pounding. The teeter-totter started wobbling in my head. What on Earth could he possibly want to ask me?

I looked back at him. With his short messy hair and weak eyebrow bone, he almost looked like an overgrown child.

"I don't mean ya no harm. No need t'be 'fraid, right? Just a quick little conversation." His voice singsonged the words, as if the other day had just been the act of Jim's evil twin, and this was the nice twin, bopping out every vowel as he conned me into his truck. This was what I imagined a Hells Angel biker trying to sweet-talk their grandmother would sound like. I got in the truck. I guess I was the grandmother.

We drove without saying a word for probably only a minute, but it was a minute that felt like forever. The wobbling in my head didn't calm down. It only got worse. Particularly because Jim had the windows rolled up, and didn't have the air on to filter out the permanent stench of pot. Though he kept relatively steady at the wheel, I felt as though at any moment I was going to disastrously throw up.

"So," he said at last, taking an awfully long pause before continuing. "How was work?"

Did I not just tell this man that I was not at work?

"It was good," I said. I figured it didn't really matter what I told him.

He tapped the top of the steering wheel, which was worn out and partly wrapped with duct tape.

"Good. Good. That's good. Work is good." Each word bopped out with a song and the slow rocking back and forth of his torso.

"Yeah," I added. "It's a good place to work."

Good seemed to be the word of the hour.

"So," his voice smoky, light, and peppy popped. "How's Mary?"

"Uh," I mumbled. I couldn't figure out what the heck this guy was getting at, but that feeling of needing to throw up didn't leave. Especially since there was a weird combination of ashes and funk in the cup holders, and my feet were planted amongst a variety of fast-food wrappers; the smell of rotten cheeseburger rose from the floor.

"So, you like my daughter?"

"Yeah I—"

"Have ya screwed my daughter?"

"Ayee—no."

He jolted. "Danny, there's one thing I don't like." And held his index finger up. I waited for him to finish his sentence, but he just continued to hold his finger up. Like, he just left it up there.

"What's that?" I finally asked. Thought I would least find out what he didn't like.

Then brusquely, "A liar." And threw his fist to his mouth to cough. My stomach turned on its backside.

Jim then aggressively gripped the bottom of the wheel, said, "I can always tell a liar," and cranked the truck into the other lane, straight towards an oncoming car.

"What are you doing?" I yelled. Jim's eyes bulged as he started to drive faster. The approaching car started wailing on their horn. Jim gripped the wheel tighter. The car was getting closer. A crazed smile crossed his face as the lines on the road and the car warped towards us.

"Jesus Christ, what are you *doing*?"

The oncoming driver weighed down on the horn. The speedometer started firing back and forth; the engine hollered like it was about to explode.

"TURN BACK IN!" I screamed. My arms flew out beside me, holding on to the door and cup-holder, bracing myself for the high-speed crash. I swung my head all around, looking for an escape.

"YOU'RE GOING TO GET US KILLED!"

It was when we were half a second away from an engine-bursting, bloodied motor-vehicle death, that the car swerved to the right around us, nearly clipping the mirror on my side, and then raced back into their correct lane and lost it on the horn. From the rearview, I saw them stick their middle finger high out of the window.

"What the fuck?!" I cried.

Jim was hysterical. With ease, he steered the wheel, and glided back into our proper lane. "That was fun, right?" His face was all lit up.

This man is insane. This man is bat-shit, far outfield insane.

More than being on the brink of tears or of passing out, I found myself just plain incredulous. And then, I was suddenly furious at myself for giving this whole situation the chance to even happen. Why the fuck did I get in the car with this psychopath? I didn't know anything about him, except the fact that he had a tendency to be bipolar and violent. More than that, I didn't owe him anything. If all this was based on the suspicion that his nearly eighteen-year-old daughter might have had sex with her boyfriend, then this was as bullshit as anything could be.

To hell with him and the fact he was Mary's father. I was a good kid from a normal world where the adults I knew weren't mentally ill lunatics. The only responsibility I had at that moment was to my parents, the people who raised me not to get caught up in the dysfunction of somebody else's life, and to do them right by getting the fuck out of that truck.

My mind raced with how I would gently ease out of the situation. What I had to do to please this man and get the fuck as far away as possible. From the deepest recesses of my mind, I called upon Dad's voice, trying to figure out how, as a man, I should handle this dilemma, the way Dad would have.

Except, when remembering the sound of Dad's voice took longer than I'd hoped, a smirk of pity and remorse slipped onto my face.

And Jim caught that smirk from the corner of his eye. He didn't like that smirk.

"Ya think that's funny?" he deadpanned. "Ya think I'mma jokester? Ya know, sometimes there's big, scary guys. Right? Been in prison or somethin' for a while. Without a woman. Gets lonely, right? So they get carryin' 'round," Jim reached into the floor of the backseat and pulled out a tub of Vaseline. "Some a this, right? Incase they run into a cute boy like you, with pretty hair." Jim lunged his arm out and ran his hand through my hair. Then rubbing his fingers against my head, continued, "Same way you're comin' onta Mary? Right? Bein' a young guy it's all your thinkin' 'bout. Fuckin' chicks. But ya see, big guys like that protect their families, right? Don't want'ya doin' to their daughters what they're gonna do t' you."

After a light tug of my hair, Jim pulled his hand away and slapped it against the steering wheel. "Right?"

I stared out the windshield.

"Where are you driving me?" I asked.

"To the store."

"What's the store?"

"Where your girlfriend works."

"We were just beside the grocery store."

I was beyond horrified. And the horror only deepened when, out of the corner of my eye, I saw a dildo—yes, a dildo—wedged in the sun visor. What the actual fuck was that thing doing there?

With my arms braced tightly against the door and the center console, I could feel each groove and bump in the road and the truck's internal mechanics' jagged response. The brakes squealed when he slowed for a red light, and as the truck idled, the engine made a clattering sound as if the oil hadn't been changed in years.

If I ever have to say I regretted anything in my life, it was getting in that truck.

Bad judgment call there, Grandma.

Then out of the silence, Jim began saying, "I used ta drive t'where her mum worked, at the old Betty's Diner. I'm sure your folks musta known it. At the time I was driving this beautiful seventy-nine Trans Am. Oh, you shoulda seen that thing! It could rip!" Jim rambled on, absorbed in his own world.

"And her manager, where she worked, right? Would lock the door every time she'd see me pullin' up in the parkin' lot, and they'd be losing customers and she'd be screamin' out the window, '*We're gonna call the cops! We're gonna call the cops!*' And I mean, I wasn't causin' no real harm or nothin', just having fun, right? Comin' in with my buddies, ordering a couple cheeseburgs, drinking beers outta the brown bags, you know how kids used to do that, right? Waiting for Wend to get off work.

"Yeah…" Jim said with a soft sigh. Then tucking in his lips, he rocked his head slightly. "Those were the days, alright."

He looked out the windshield past where his large, swollen hand gripped the wheel. And then as another flashback of the glory days jogged his memory, he smiled to himself as if overcome by nostalgia.

I was so entranced by this psychotic dilemma I had wandered into that, when the truck jerked up over a curb, I nearly smacked my head against the roof. And when the car slammed back down to the ground, the dildo nose-dived into the cup holder and the glove box slammed open over my knees. Loose papers flopped out.

Stopped outside of Wright Bros, Jim cranked the column shifter into park, and then picked up the dildo and pointed it headfirst at me. "So, you bagged my daughter?"

The noisy whirling lash of the radiator fan loudened.

"No."

"Good!" Jim snapped his wrist, wobbling the dildo at me. "We wouldn't want any necks broken." Then grabbing the rubber phallus with both hands, Jim bent it until it tore in half. "Right?"

I unbuckled the seatbelt and jumped out of that passenger

seat. The second my feet hit the pavement, the door slammed shut behind me, and the truck roared off with black smoke pouring out of the exhaust pipe.

I stared down at the pavement, digging my fingers deep into my forehead. Then hearing the squeal of the brakes, and another car blast the horn, I watched the back-end of the truck, with the half scratched out, red lettering of CHEVROLET, whip around the corner.

The guerilla soldiers, in the incarnation of Mary's father, caught up to me and blasted thick bullet-holes through my spirit. Didn't I tell you that Gilmore Park, and all its fucking inhabitants, were waiting to break you 'til you were helpless on your knees? All that I thought I'd had with Mary was suddenly just a big joke played on me. There I had simply thought I'd met a girl who knew the difference between a Lennon and McCartney written Beatles song. But of course, the plague of that shit town would find its way into the simple friendship I had been looking for all my life.

Happiness in Gilmore Park was like sprinting with your back towards the hot Atlantic sun. No matter how hard or fast you tried, its shadow always managed to overextend beyond your feet, forever impossible to outrun. I looked up at the Wright Bros sign above the grocery store's yellow canopy, twisted open the blotched golden handle, and walked inside.

20

When Doves Cry

MARY

Stationed at my usual post, the middle checkout line of the three tills that formed trisecting lanes at the entrance of Wright Bros, I had to go pee. Like, really badly. But I decided to hold off until I was allowed to retreat from the battle in T minus fifteen minutes. I would be retreating, but the war of working for minimum wage, waged on.

There was a weird day gap of silence with Danny going on. Which was like, whatever. Not like we were boyfriend and girlfriend or anything. And I hate clingy people. I had thought for sure Squeegee Boy would turn out to be a Stage-Five.

Still, while dying of boredom at my unoccupied checkout line, I took the initiative to be productive and looked over at the flowers on display; the fancy floral arrangements from the adjacent greenhouse next door. I went fishing in my pocket for that fifty Jim gave me, thinking I'd buy Danny's mom some flowers. Thanking her for all that the "Danny's" had done for me. Just as I was wondering what would look prettier in Danny's house, Hydrangea's or Forget-Me-Not's, the devil himself walked in. As in the phrase: speaking of the devil (in this case, Danny. Not the fictional character whom I occasionally gambled with while doing my makeup).

"Who's this handsome stranger stalking me at work?" I said, suddenly wanting to touch his skin.

"Hey," was all he said back. It took a second to catch up, but then it felt like my fourth-grade crush just rejected me. I know that was immature, or whatever, but that Hey sort of hurt.

"When are you done?" he asked.

"In, like, fifteen."

Danny then said he'd wait outside for me and walked out of the store. I really started feeling the grade school blues and could not concentrate for the life of me on anything I was doing.

Ten minutes later I was off. I walked out of Wright Bros and towards The Stang parked in the furthest corner of the parking lot.

"What's up?" I asked as I got in Danny's car.

It wasn't until we were at the exit of the parking lot when he said, "Nothing," and then took a sharp turn that slung me against the seatbelt, pulling out of the driveway onto Ridgeway Avenue.

We didn't say anything. All I could hear was the moaning of the engine as it varied in speed, racing up and then slowing down behind cars as he flirted with getting in a fender bender. It wasn't normal. Something was off. Danny was horribly off. I couldn't figure out what was different until I realized that the radio wasn't on.

"Did something happen?" I asked.

Danny frowned, shook his head, then said, "Nah."

The Stang ran over a sudden pothole. My side of the car thumped down with the sound of something within the wheel-base crunching.

"Fuck," Danny grunted under his breath.

At the Ridgeway and Atlantic Way intersection, he turned right. Danny's wrist was flopped over the steering wheel, and he kept his eyes locked on the road.

"Danny?"

He glanced at me, then back to the road.

"Talk to me!" I said, pushing my open palm against his shoulder. Absently, with nothing in his eyes, he stared right through me with a disgusted and bent face that nearly made me cry. I don't know why, but I felt like bawling. He then jammed the side of his fist into the wheel, blaring the horn at a car crawling in front of us. Which, yes, was going ridiculously slow, but not to the point of justifying his extreme road rage.

"God fucking damn it, everyone drives so fucking slow in this town."

"Are you okay?"

"No." He twisted the wheel, veering down the slope of a long driveway that homed yet another pothole. The car jerked as we plunged in and out of the dip, before screeching to a stop behind the dumpy West Atlantic plaza.

Danny cranked the handbrake, slid the keys out, and fell back into his seat, crossing his arms as he let out a sigh. With the air off, the car became instantly suffocating.

"What, Danny? What the hell's the matter with you?"

"Your dad just threatened to fucking rape me."

"There's no way—" I began, hopefully, but knew all too well the very real plausibility of Jim actually threatening that.

In the following second that lacked my response, Danny lost his mind.

"Your fucking psycho dad almost got me killed in a car crash, and then went on about how if I bagged his daughter he would use Vaseline to rape me. He literally had a fucking tub of Vaseline with him. And then he started flagging this dildo at me! What the hell? What the fuck was that? Who the fuck even uses the word bagged?"

"Danny, I'm sorry! It's not like I knew my dad would do that?"

"Well, what then, Mary?" He slammed his fist down on the center console. "Did you tell him I worked at the fucking car wash?"

Vomit. I felt like vomit.

"Like, Jesus Christ!" Danny kept on raging. "I've never gone through anything like that in my life! If he wasn't your fucking dad I would've called the cops! How is that man not in prison?"

I clenched my fists in my lap, trembling, thinking of how Jim *has* been in prison. My head felt heavy and I wondered if I was hyperventilating; every breath was too fast, too shallow. The windows fogged around me, blobs smearing the glass. The guilt condensed like a heavy ball in the pit of my stomach.

"I'm… I'm sorry."

"Well, being sorry sure isn't gonna save my asshole, is it?"

"Listen to me!"

"No, Mary! How about you listen to me! First your psychotic ex-boyfriend, and now your literal lunatic of a dad? Who the hell else in your life is gonna come after me next? Your cousin? Your aunt? Your fuckin' mom—"

Pressing his lips together, Danny shut himself the fuck up. He exhaled the breath reserved for the rest of his words through his nose.

"Danny, listen—"

"No. This is bullshit, Mary."

"Dan—stop—I'm sorry!"

"Tell me you're sorry when I'm dead somewhere."

"Listen to me!" I smacked the seat.

"I don't need this crazy shit."

"Will you just—"

"I have enough bullshit going on in my own life without having to worry about some crazy man now raping and murdering me."

"God Damn It—WILL YOU JUST LISTEN TO ME?"

I barged out of the car and slammed the door.

My feet fell in circles. I was going to faint. I kept afloat to stop myself from passing out. Sauntering around behind the plaza, over the mismatched, busted-up asphalt, every time I took a breath, the humidity, the pollution, the smoke stemming from the plaza roof, brought me somewhere closer to fainting. I heard an irregular cycle of something cranking, and looked back to see Danny leaning across the front seats, rolling down the passenger window.

"Mary! Wait."

I kept walking away then snagged my shoe against a weed that had erupted through the blacktop; my toenail split with a razor pain.

"Mary!" I heard his door slam. "Get back here!" he yelled, stomping towards me.

"No, I wouldn't want anyone else in my life coming after you!" I shouted back. "I am so sorry that my life is too crazy for you! But you know, I told you. You stupid asshole."

"Shut up!" Danny yelled as he ran up towards me. Then pulling me back by the shoulders, he swung his hand out and held me tight by my arms.

"I never said you—"

"Don't touch me!"

I tried pulling away. He wouldn't let go.

"Don't fucking touch me!" I screamed.

He grasped me even tighter.

"I am going to scream help at the top of my lungs."

Danny let go and jumped back. As if putting a far distance between us would exempt him from the accusation. Standing against his car, he kept his hands behind his back. "Where are you going?" he shouted.

"You just fucking put your hands on me."

"Where are you going?" he repeated.

"Danny! You just fucking touched me! Don't talk to me!"

"Let me drive you."

"What don't you fucking get! You put your hands on me! Leave me the fuck alone! Don't ever talk to me again!"

I stormed off from the back of the plaza.

On my way, I caught a whiff of the lovely exhaust from a deep fryer. Danny screamed something again. I then heard a loud clashing bang of something striking metal. I turned and saw Danny hammering the dumpster next to his car with a scrap piece of wood.

Guys are all alike, and Danny was no exception. I should've known better. My clothes had melted onto my skin. My head was light and dizzy. The air reeked of humidity and pollution. The walk up the slope felt near impossible, the world seared around me. The humidity fell in a heavy gray haze that I could taste on my lips. From behind, I heard the rattle and rumble of his engine, and then the charging bolt as it gunned past me up the slope without braking, whipping out of the plaza.

We didn't talk for a week.

21

The Wind Cries Mary

MARY

Maybe I sort of regretted not letting Danny drive me home. I'd forgotten how crappy Gilmore Park public transit was. The idiot bus drivers were always off schedule.

Bus A was late, so Bus B had already dipped from the terminal. So I ended up waiting, like, an hour for another Bus B to come on by. Although, I guess being seated on the bus with only Homeless Josh and Matilda (she just looked like a Matilda) made sense because they were from my "world."

Matilda crocheted the entire time, even though we ran over like six hundred potholes, and Homeless Josh just kept staring at me. Not in the creepy *I'm gonna rape you* way, but as an outsider looking into a world he's never been a part of, kinda way.

Days went by without any signs of life from Danny. I hadn't seen or talked to him since that day when he'd lost it on me. It wasn't like I had a cellphone, and Danny didn't call my house phone. Which was probably a blessing in disguise, because my heart skipped not one, but two beats, every time the phone did ring because Jim didn't leave the house all week.

"What are you doing home?" I asked, surprised to see him

loafing on the couch, watching TV in the middle of Monday the following week.

He waited until whoever was on the TV to finish speaking before answering me.

"Lester had a heart attack."

It took me a minute to remember who Lester was. He was an old friend of Jim's from years ago. They didn't see each other very much, or at all, really. Lester had been to a few of the barbecues Jim would throw back in the day, and I remember going on Lester's sailboat once at Port Milford when I was a kid. That day on his sailboat had been particularly memorable because I still remember how cold I was watching a bunch of old fat people jumping into the water, and wondering if I would ever get fat and old and enjoy jumping into cold water.

"Oh," was about as much of a reaction I could muster upon the news of Lester's death.

What? I didn't actually know him. I wasn't gonna pretend like I was all bent outta shape over his heart attack. Ol' Lester had been sort of an asshole anyway, and more than likely would have tried telling me that he was my uncle if I were ever alone with him.

Jim was zoned in on the TV, and it didn't look like he was gonna get his ass up and off the sofa anytime soon. I didn't dare bring up anything Danny had told me. Instead, I kept my head down and walked down the hallway to my bedroom, and when the voices on the TV stopped again, I heard Jim say, "Yeah."

Jim, the TV, and I were soundless. I anticipated more. Then chattering cued up again on one of those afternoon talk shows that Jim usually had no interest in watching, and I continued walking down the creaking hallway to my room.

I really should get my own stall on the boardwalk as Madame Mary (no, you freak, I mean as a fortune-teller) because my prediction came true; Jim did not get up from that couch for almost a whole week. Whenever somebody he was close to died (passed away) he couldn't handle it. He couldn't even handle it when his favorite old bar from high school closed down. Hell, you'd had thought that his beloved first-born son died in a tragic accident when he had to sell his Trans-Am.

So, I guess it wasn't just death he couldn't handle; it was change. He didn't like anything changing, not that floral print couch, not that barbecue on the porch, not the cabinets in the kitchen. Nothing. He wanted everything frozen in time, exactly how he wanted to remember it.

When my grandma died (I was too little to remember living with her), Jim let his life go for so long without moving on, neglecting everything, including me, until eventually our hydro was cut. That I do remember.

It was the same thing with our house. It was a prime piece of real estate that Jim could have easily sold. He received offers on our house from eager developers all the time. Half a million dollars? Okay, Okay fine, Jim you say? How about a million dollars?

A whole fuckin' million-dollars! But, it was his parents' house, and apparently, his grandfather purchased it when Danae's Bay was a shipping port, and he didn't want to let that go. So, it wasn't really Lester dying that was devouring him; it was the fact that there was now one less person around from the past.

And that tore him up because Jim liked the past better. If I had to guess why, it was because the past was a time before there was me.

Two days later, when I was walking home from work, I felt a speckle of something moist land on my tank top exposed shoulder. A moment later, I felt more drops on my arms. When I looked down at the ground, I saw that the sidewalk was spotted with what looked like tiny gray holes. So, it could only be the sky, not somebody, spitting on me.

Earlier at work, Danny had walked in.

"Hey," he said.

"Hey."

It didn't take long after the first spit-fall for the air to smell soggy, but right then, the only thing on my mind were the few short words we had said to each other.

"What are you doing here?" I asked him.

A gust swept my hair into my mouth.

"I think we should stop."

I had to reach my finger into my mouth about three times before scooping all the hair out.

"Stop what?"

The concrete bled into a darker shade of gray with each bullet of rain that pelted against it.

"Hanging out," he said, after a slight hesitation. I repeated the phrase because I didn't quite grasp what he meant by "hanging out."

"Yeah. Hanging out," he said again. And then he mumbled something about how everything's been difficult lately or something like that. And to save him the effort of breaking up with me, I just said: "Okay."

"Okay?" he repeated.

"Yeah, okay."

"Okay," he said and left.

And then the next thing I knew, I was ringing through a customer's jug of orange juice like he'd never been there, and like, breaking up with me at my work.

Soon enough, the sidewalk was one solid shade of dark gray, like it had never been another color to begin with. The pouring rain steadily pummeled my back, and when the weight was too heavy for the leaves that caught the rainfall, they broke down on me, all at once. At first, I was angry that I was soaking and that my hair, which I had spent all morning straightening, was stringy. But like always, I got used to the rain. Once the world exhausted all of its steam, like a breath it held on too, I felt cold for the first time in weeks. It felt sorta pure. Clean. I realized I wasn't surprised that it was storming. I just should have prepared for one.

By the time I made it home it was dark; the cloudy day had cast an early night. The wet and black roads were bright with the glow of the orange streetlights. And from the bay below, the ocean sounded violent despite the momentary lull in the rain. The cold wind still came about in senseless circles, stretching over the puddles made in the depressed pavement, shredding water off the surfaces.

While passing Jim's truck and then staggering up the front steps, all I could think of was the warm shower I was so looking forward to taking after that long and drenching walk home.

Though hardly visible through the yellow porch light, I was surprised to see that the front door beyond the screen was wide open. I figured that Jim must have finally gotten up and left the house for the first time all week.

But out of the fear that he might have still been home, and desperate to evade any torment or interrogation because I was not okay, I pressed my thumb into the metal handle, and so slowly, so gently, pulled the screen door open towards me, afraid of making any noise. Afraid that something would stop me from just going straight to my room so I could cry my eyes out.

After I had crept through the door opening that was just wide enough to slip my body through, I inched the screen back into the frame with my thumb pressed deeply into the handle to avoid the clicking of the latch. The house reeked of cigarette smoke.

In the dark entryway, I tripped on Jim's construction boot laid out flat on the ground. Losing my footing, I scurried to balance myself and slammed my hand against the wall. Almost hitting the sailboat painting again.

"Who's there?" Jim called from around the corner.

"Who else would it be?"

I hung my purse on one of the coat hangers next to the front table. In the dark, I stepped on another shoe.

"Who's there?" Jim asked again as if he hadn't heard me.

"It's me, Dad," I said, kicking off my shoes, contributing to the pile of footwear.

"Who would that be?"

"Me. Mary."

I didn't know what he was up to, but whatever it was, I was seriously not in the mood for it. I took a step forward, towards the living room. The air was warm and musky with smoke.

"Mary? Who's that?" Jim asked, still masked from sight behind the wall. "What are you doing here?"

His facetiousness began to bother me. But sometimes, the only way to avoid the bullshit was to bullshit back. So I walked into the hazy living room where he was sitting on the floral couch in front of the TV.

"I am one of the two residents that occupy twenty-two Bayview Avenue," I had said, giving him the sarcastic answer he typically respected. I then turned and took a step into the hallway, determined to avoid another fight.

"No, you don't." He coughed. "My daughter does."

I froze. Then taking a step back, turned to face him. From his side profile, Jim's eyes reflected the amber light blazing from the TV. And without a flinch in his posture, he then said looking straight ahead, "And you're not my daughter."

"Who's Wendy then?" I asked. "I'm pretty sure I'm her daughter?"

The anchor on CNN went on talking about the latest presidential scandal. Jim shifted. Laughed. And then as he slowly twisted his neck to look at me, a wry grin emerged on his face. "Yeah, yeah." He turned back to the TV. "Sure, you are. But she was a whore, right? You could be Chuck McGilvery's daughter or Tommy Gurd's. She, your mother, was sleepin' with 'em both."

"Oh shit. You're right," I said, walking towards him. "How the hell would I know that? It's not like you've ever bothered talking to me about my mom."

Spoken low, with his chin dug into his chest, Jim grumbled, "Shaddup, Mary. Don't you speak to your father that way."

"Well apparently you're not even my father! Maybe I should be speaking to Chuck Mc-Gliv or whatever then?"

"Well, he was the one givin' your mother the dope that got 'er all fucked in the head. So maybe you should." Then instantly distracted by whatever claim the anchor made, Jim pointed his open hand at the TV. "I can't believe all this fake news. Makes me sick."

Angered by the blatant change of topic, I slashed my hands against the sides of my jeans. "Maybe you're the one who got her fucked in the head?"

"Whatsa matter with you?" He turned back. "Some twerp got your box busted up and now you think you can speak to me like that?"

"What's the matter with you? You think 'cause you lost your job you can sit on the couch and do nothing 'cause you're sad and miserable with your life?"

Jim howled. He was absolutely hysterical. The TV flashed with a change of footage. And then as Jim eased out of his coarse laughter, ending on a high wheezing sigh, he said, "Mary, you're fuckin' stupid. You're not 'llowed to leave the house unless its for work for the res' of the summer. Git t' bed."

"Wait. Who are you to tell me? Apparently you're not even my father? So what the hell do I do? Do I listen to you because you're my father? Or?"

"I say's shut the fuck up and get to bed."

"And I say's wasn't it my father's fucking job to tell me about my dead mom!" I yelled and dashed out of the living room toward the hallway.

"The fuck you talking 'bout?"

Scattering and tossing up all the clutter and all the shit on the front counter, scathing through the endless piles of papers, I found the rain-wrinkled letter and ran back.

"Not some letter in the mail!" I cried as I shoved the letter in his face. "Not some fucking letter in the mail!"

Jim's eyes widened as he began reading the letter and then erupted onto his feet; knocking the ashtray off the coffee table in a charcoaled cloud. "Gimme that!" he yelled, tearing the bottom half of the paper as he stripped it from my hands.

Jim's eyes reigned over the letter as he read the telling details.

"She's dead? No, no. NO. NO. Not my Bimba! Please, God, NO! NOT MY LITTLE BIMBA! SHE'S DEAD! WENDY'S DEAD! WHY IS SHE DEAD?"

"WHY DIDN'T YOU EVER FUCKING TELL ME?"

"HOW WAS I 'SPOSED TO KNOW? You—You killed her, Mary! YOU KILLED HER!"

"I DIDN'T KILL HER! YOU KILLED HER! YOU HEAR ME?? YOU KILLED HER!!"

When the black fog lifted from my head, I was on the floor and holding my face. Everything was quiet and heavy. A long, hollow moment passed before I removed my hand from over my eye. Blood ran down the inside of my palm.

"Oh my god."

Suddenly my face exploded with a hammering pain that punched through to the back of my skull.

Jim choked on a sob. I looked up. Two damp streaks ran down Jim's face as his mouth hung open. My mouth hung open. I thought he was going to cry sorry, but instead he just screamed, "GET OUT!"

Grabbing me by the wrists, Jim scraped me off the floor. "GET OUT OF MY HOUSE!" he roared, pushing me out. I tried resisting, burning my legs on the rug as he dragged me across it. "YOU'RE NOT WENDY'S DAUGHTER! GET OUT! GET

OUT!" Hauling me across the hardwood floor, my hip smacked against the corner of the living room wall. And then lifting me up by my armpits, he shoved me against the screen door, striking it open. I thought it was going to break off.

In my socks, almost slipping on the wet porch, I caught the railing before my body fell back onto the steps. The front door slammed. And with a heavy thud, I heard it lock. I jolted towards the door, whipped open the screen, and twisted and rattled the knob, trying to yank it open. It wouldn't budge.

I started banging on it. With one fist, and then both fists. Over and over and over I kept banging on that fucking door. I kept hammering it until the sides of my fists started to feel pained and bruised and throbbing.

Then dropping my shoulders, I took a few steps back until I was standing on the edge of my porch. After allowing a few seconds of silence, freezing in the wind, I ran back to the door, screaming, "FUCK YOU!" as I bashed my fists into it one last time. After a minute of nothing, it hit me that it was pointless. My knees smacked against the rain-soaked wood, skinning the flesh.

Surrendering at last, the stinging came back to my cheek and the hammering in my head was worse than before. My eyes clenched in the reflex to cry, but the pain was greater than the need to weep. The blood began to harden on my face.

Eventually I got up, seeing double, and stumbled down the front steps and off the porch. My head felt sapped, my vision flickered in and out with my consciousness. Surely I was concussed; brain-damaged even. One of the neighbors on the opposite side of the street, two houses down, stood on his doorstep with the light on behind him and stared at me. He didn't say anything, of course. He just stared.

Shivering, I walked down my street in a daze. The wind came in circles. Random and unreliable. I crossed my arms to keep warm, and then followed the pattern of the wind deep into the night.

Drifting in and out of consciousness, and feeling like nothing more than an adrift piece of wood floating in the vastness of an endless black ocean.

22

Father and Son

DANNY

I stared down at my hands—my hands—locked around the steering wheel as if cemented to it. The bulbous mounds of my knuckles were popping out and growing red with the pressure, and the cradles of my thumbs were wrinkled and white with dry skin. I hated my hands. And in my hatred for my hands, I learned about the love and fear invited by a man's hands. A Man's hands. The ability those hands hold to build and destroy, and the horror in which a woman will never really know for what means a man might use those hands.

Man, stupid man, so readily expressing his rage through his hands. I've never known myself to be so moved to use my hands. Was it nothing more than a coward's instinct to raise them only against a woman? The idea that I might have possibly been encouraged to handle Mary physically because I had unwittingly learned from her father that force was the best way to tame her behavior—absolutely sickened me.

Is my gender, renewed through each new generation, condemned to forever struggle with aggression?

Yes. Man is angry. Always will be. But, No. Man can triumph.

We have the ability to choose intelligence over instinct.

But—what to do when rage arises?

It's not so easy to subdue rage, controlling our emotions is a practice much easier said than done. Anger is a wild animal: blind and unintelligent and uncompromising. Anger will always exist; the enemies of our virtuous repose will always exist too. The agents of wrath will never die. They'll exist in bad men, and they'll exist in bad circumstance, caused by the natural or supernatural. So what to do with rage? It has to be placed somewhere. It's a painful burden that can split you from the inside out if you choose to hold on. A virulent parasite to host. But I suppose regardless of the pain, it is our evolutionary responsibility to withdraw those ancient, barbaric vestiges internally, and better to let it wreak havoc on our spirit than place that rage onto somebody else. I guess the internal damage caused by receding rage is punishment for having rage to begin with. A man should be a more dominant master of his emotions.

Men will always wrestle with their rage. A man who disagrees is a liar. But a man chooses his own hand's purpose. He is not condemned.

I remember that my Dad's hands were gentle. He never hit or grabbed Mom. Dad's hands changed my diapers. Dad's hands could find their way over the infinite combinations of notes on a piano or guitar and make beautiful music with those hands. For as long as I wrestle with rage, I'll internalize it. Save it for later. Save it for the guitar.

But, at seventeen, I didn't know any better. I was terrified with my behavior, and I didn't do a thing with that terror other than place it in a black room at the far, far back of my mind.

It started with a single hard drop of rain that shattered against my windshield. The highway wind rolled the residue up and off.

And then another hard drop fell. And then another, and another. Then with a loud crack, a showering skirt of rain rolled over the hood and pelted against the glass. The storm began.

By the time I had pulled up in my driveway, after leaving Wright Bros and spending the rest of the afternoon finding solitude on country roads that led me nowhere but back home, the world was drowned. The wet streets reflected the prematurely lit streetlights, and streams ran perpendicularly along the curbs, burbling at the sewage drains.

Mom's Jetta and a random U-Haul truck took up the driveway, forcing me to park on the street.

Okay, was all you had to say? Glad to know, Mary. Glad to know that it was meaningless to you, too.

I tugged the key out of the transmission, locking the windshield wipers mid-wipe. The rain fell mutely on the soft-top.

"Danny?" Mom called from the kitchen when she heard me come in through the front door. "Where have you been all afternoon?"

A subtle tremor of thunder broke from behind the walls. "Nowhere, Mom," I said, leaning over, spraying my hands as I stripped the wet shoelaces unlacing my Converse. Standing back up, I ran my fingers through my wet hair, lifting the patches that had stuck to my face.

As Mom walked towards me at the front door she said, "Ok, Danny. I'm trying to be patient, and I am really happy that you and Mary are friends, but you've not yet packed a single thing and I'm not going to remind you again. The movers are starting next week and if you're not going to pack, I'll go through your room and start throwing everything out."

My gaze whipped past her as I snapped, "Don't you dare."

"Watch your tone with me, Danny," Mom fiercely replied as I began walking towards the stairs. Lightning beamed in two bright rapid flashes through the window. A tumbling thunder followed.

Mom then continued to say, "When I was putting away your laundry, I saw that you haven't even touched that plastic bag full of junk. Danny, you can't leave this until the last minute like you do everything else. And have you yet decided what you're going to do with your car? It's going to cost a fortune to transport, and unless you plan on driving, we're going to have to sell it."

With my back to her, already halfway up the steps, I barked, "I'm not selling my fucking car."

"Wh-What? What did you just say to me?"

"I said I'll figure it out."

"You watch your language with me! Danny? Danny!" Mom yelled as I rounded the railing of the stairs to my room. For the rest of the night, I turned my anger to my guitar until I fell asleep.

The next morning as the sky paled from gray to a lighter shade, I awoke the world (my house) with more screams from my guitar.

Dragging my amp across the floor, maxing out all the settings, cranking that reverb exceptionally high, I channeled my rage into the stinging notes on the fretboard. Letting my fingers unfurl onto the strings all my pent-up angst in a sloppy, directionless solo.

Razor sounds lashing out. Violently constricted to the pentatonic scale. Notes raged with velocity. No silence between the sounds. Breaking down with the full-bodied crash of a chord and a raw shout from my throat. Build up. Break down. Losing myself to sound.

I was mad at Mom. I was mad at Max. And I was so mad at Mary that I tried hating her (all these fucking M's).

My middle finger zipped down the fretboard. Moving the pentatonic pattern higher.

I wanted to hate Mary. But, I couldn't help but stop and think that I was to blame. I grabbed her and I wouldn't let go.

My fingers fumbled on a difficult chord. Slap the strings down and down until the combination sounds right. Inculcate the shape to my hand. Never forget.

What—why didn't I just talk to her? I wanted to feel what I felt in that Old Abandoned Beach House again. My lust was dangerous because it stemmed from something like my hatred for her.

Telecaster hung-low; electromotive friction against my pelvis. The memory of Mary's sweat glistened breasts flattened against my chest. Erection.

But then, in the minute I wanted to love her again, the minute I wanted to nail myself with the blame and run to her and make repentance, I ripped through a barre chord, and against my will, the image of Jim's ugly face assembled in my mind. His voice resounded louder in my ears than the feedback from my amp. *"Incase they run into cute boys like you, with pretty hair."* And he had the nerve to smirk.

My fingers, leaving a wake of lightning in their motion, danced up the neck. There, I swear, is no greater transcendence of self than getting lost in a guitar solo. My fingers corrugated into the G Chord shape. Slash down.

But then striking through the strings, the G string snapped and whipped against my forearm. I went for a D chord, but my index finger fell horribly out of place on the polished surface of the fretboard; the chord sounded painfully unfulfilled.

In one flawless haul, I unslung my guitar and threw it across the room. It landed on a pile of clothes.

My butt cushioned into the mattress and then I fell back onto my bed. I looked at the pink scratch pulsating on my arm and then at my—Dad's—Telecaster lying on the floor, looking helpless, the G string sprung out like an unraveled steel intestine.

My acoustic looked rather comfortable propped on its stand, and I thought I should maybe trash the shit out of those strings too. But these weren't my guitars to abuse. Both of them were Dad's. It wasn't until then that I realized Dad had probably tried to impress Mom with that exact same guitar I attempted to impress Mary with. The thought grossed me out.

I left Dad's acoustic alone.

That was when I heard something like muffled sobbing. I didn't think Mom was home. I tried ignoring her. Her problems were her own. Although Mom's crying was like a thumping headache you couldn't suspend. It wasn't my job as the kid to go tend to her pain. She was the parent. Her tears weren't mine to wipe away. Right then, I hated her even more for being selfish and crying.

And then, like an unearthed ghost, Dad's voice, louder than that of my own thinking, scolded me. Whether from some tucked away part of my imagination, or actually right then and there, he told me to go to Mom.

I might have been the kid, but I was no longer a child.

"Mom?" I asked, in the doorway of her room, and then held my breath like I had violated the pact I made with silence.

"What Danny?" she snapped, angrily, as if she too thought I'd breached the silence oath.

I guess I reconstituted the deal because I didn't say anything back. Mom sniffed and looked up at me with red eyes. I started to form the words soundlessly on my lips as I repeated over and over in my mind what I wanted to say. But when the muted gray light breaking through the closed blinds caught the gloss on a photo-album sprawled open on her bed, I froze.

The cover of the album had a textile-pattern I didn't recognize, and the Polaroids inside had long since adopted a yellow wash on their trim. Two out of the dozen photos the laminated pages offered were missing. It was evident Mom was sizing down our entire family's history into one album, and in the process, one picture had been left out big and bold and right smack dab in the middle of her floral bedspread. It was a photo of Dad that I had never seen before in all his eighties glory.

Long dark curls of hair touched his bare shoulders, and the baddest beard that I had ever seen on a man surrounded the cigarette dangling from his lips as his fingers stretched over the keys of a piano. "Why are you crying?" I asked, unconsciously aware that I was prolonging the time I got to look at this picture of Dad. He was smiling.

"I'm not," Mom said.

"I heard you crying," I said, breaking eye contact with Dad. Mom looked up at me under her furrowed brow.

"Danny, there are certain things that kids just don't understand."

Mom was right. There are things kids don't understand. But it wasn't her accusation of my ignorance due to an age limitation that provoked me. It was "kids," and claiming, while I looked at a picture of someone who wouldn't even recognize me anymore, that I don't understand.

"What don't I understand?" I pried, mocking the condescending tone Mom had used.

"Holy shit, Danny. Losing everything!"

The wallpaper in her room was exactly the same. It was one of those strange things you inexplicably, for no good logical reason, remember from childhood. Vertical lines of tiny triangles ran against the beige backdrop. A long moment later, an "Okay?" slipped from Mom's quivering lips.

"Right." I hiccupped on a sob I fought back. "Because I'm nothing, and I didn't lose them too." I turned and pushed through the door and bolted out of the room.

Mom called my name and kept calling until she sounded angry, but I was already down the stairs and determined on charging out the front door and getting away.

Arriving at Oceanside Park, I blasted into the deserted parking lot littered with potholes of rain, and pulled my car right up to the curb. Parking in the exact same spot the night I came here with Mary. I rifled out of the car and slammed the door so hard that I thought the window would shatter.

May as well fuck up Dad's car too.

I didn't even like Oceanside Park. It was depressing and actually really dumpy once the rose-colored goggles came off.

What was so special about this shithole?

I tried to remember what had made me take Mary here. And for the life of me, tried to remember what we even talked about.

I walked through the vacant lot and saw that the carousel was closed due to the weather. All I could remember of my night here with Mary was that she was being a bitch on the rocks. And maybe that was all she ever was. Just a bitch on the rocks. I'll have one of those, Mister Bartender.

My thoughts and memories were in disarray. I didn't even know how to begin sorting and processing them. Nothing in that moment was appealing to me, not a thought, not a line of a lyric, not some sort of vista-inspired epiphany, just the stroll of depression. The complete and utter drowning of self-pitying.

Maybe if luck were on my side, a tidal wave would come crashing down and its undertow pull me away and lose me at the bottom of the sea.

The sky was stacked in various shades of gray, and the waves were a hell of a lot rougher than usual. I thought of how only the most overly ambitious surfers would be drawn to those conditions.

With my back hunched, and my hands buried deep in my pockets to protect my fingers from the numbing cold, I continued down the pier. A loud gash of wind, followed by the implosion of a murky green-brown wave crashing against the boulders, caught my attention.

I looked up and saw that a fence had been erected, blocking off the pier. I read about two sentences of the sign claiming that the New Jersey Parks and Beach Commission had declared the pier 'unsafe' before I booted the fence with everything I had—the fence jolted me back. Fence: 1. Danny: 0.

I rerouted my walk. I couldn't put up a fight.

Underdressed, and therefore, unprepared for the cold that only deepened the longer I spent outside, practically made my walk intolerable. Having then decided that the sanctuary I'd hoped for did not exist on that desolate, depressing shore, I called it quits and figured I would shortcut to the parking lot by crossing the beach.

The wet sand felt firm and looked cold beneath my feet, but at the very least, I was grateful that it wouldn't kick up in my shoes. I walked along the edge where the tides and beach met, the undercurrent ambitious in its worship of the shore, and lifted my eyes from my feet to scan the shoreline ahead.

That was when, in the distance, I saw someone sitting slumped against the back of the snack bar.

I got all worked up, angry that someone had occupied the barren scene I wanted outfitted only for me. Their presence was ruining the atmosphere that completely suited my deep, miserable thoughts.

Continuing to tread along with my head down, watching the tide creep up and almost catch my feet, a moment later, I glanced up only slightly to scope out the slumped figure against the snack bar. With each bobbing step closer, the details of their figure became clearer, and it nearly damn shocked me to death when I realized who it was.

"Mary?"

I ran towards her, yelling her name. Clumps of wet sand kicked up into my shoes. The aching in my head got worse with every pounding step. Mary sat on the beach floor cradling her knees into her chest. Everything she wore was darkened from being damp.

"Mary!" I gasped. "Oh my God! What are you doing?" I stammered between heaves as I skidded to a stop in the sand and crouched down next to her.

Tiny droplets of water dripped down the hair clinging to her face. I was confused and scared, and felt betrayed, somehow, that Mary was sunken and hiding on the beach. But the real horror— and the real anger—came about when Mary tilted her head to the right, slinging the wet hair off her face, revealing a black eye.

My knees hit the sand. The universe exploded to the farthest reaches of the cosmos, and then collapsed back into my stomach.

"Who did that?"

The wind howled, sweeping a droplet of water off Mary's face.

"Who did that?" I persisted, but Mary failed to part her lips and just answer me. "MARY! Tell me, who did that?"

The spike of anger found a release in my tightening grip around Mary's shoulder. Drenching my hand in the water squeezed out of her soaked hoodie. Shame strapped the back of my wrist and I lightened my grasp.

I asked if it was Tanner who hit her, hoping for the best. But Mary only slightly motioned her head no.

"Your dad?"

And that time she didn't flinch.

"I am going to kill him."

A sudden frenzied, murderous ambition drove me to my feet. I was certain in my mind that I was going to murder Jim. I was going to get in my car, drive to Mary's house, push through the door, and beat his face into a disfigured pulp with whatever available weapon was in my reach. Be it a chair, a golf club, a bat, the screen door. It didn't matter. In my books, he was dead.

My feet bashed into the sand as I stomped towards the parking lot, engulfed in an apoplectic haze.

Mary suddenly shrieked at the top of her lungs.

"NO! No, Danny! Don't! You've fucked things up enough for me!"

I stopped dead in my tracks, caught off guard. My anger thrown sideways.

"What?"

Mary didn't answer, so I ran back and crouched down beside her again. "What happened?"

I reached my arm out to hold her, but she hit it off.

"No, Danny!"

"What's wrong with you?" I retaliated, realizing afterward that sounded harsh.

"Great. Thanks," she said. "That's just what I needed to hear right now." She trembled and tears surfaced on her eyes.

"I didn't mean it like that, Mary."

But by then it was too late to explain myself. Mary was beyond the threshold of reason. Within her body writhed a blinding hysteria that erupted into a maniacal shaking.

"Everything's wrong with me. I mean, why am I even alive? What the fuck isn't wrong with me? You said it yourself, didn't you, Danny? My family is fucked. My life is fucked."

Using all the willpower accessible to subside my anger, I softened my voice. "Mary—please. Tell me what happened."

Hoping she would feel safe. Hoping that she would know that as long as I was at her side, there was nothing to be afraid of. Because more than the tumultuous storm of anger I'd been fighting with, I loved Mary, and I wanted nothing more than to be her hero.

"Fuck, Danny! Just FUCK!" Mary screamed into my face. "What do you want to hear? Some problem that having a dream can fix? Some fucking bullshit that this happened for a reason? I was hit and kicked out. There, are you happy? Is that what you wanted to hear? I didn't fucking think so!"

The wind whistled through the tall grass and cut through my flesh to the bone. "Mary, why wouldn't you just come to me?"

"Because."

"Because why?" I demanded.

Mary stayed silent, staring at the muddy colored waves crashing along the shore. I looked at the waves too, and then glanced back at her. Blood had dried around the swollen pocket below her eye.

"I'm here for you."

"Oh, SHUT—UP!" she screamed. "No. You're. Not!" Her eyes ripped a hole right through me. "Stop thinking you're some fucking hero! You put your hands on me too, you know! So, grow up Danny! This isn't some fairytale. This is the real fucking world, and you weren't there for me! NO ONE is ever there for you."

"Don't tell me to grow up." I backed up, but I wasn't going to give up. "I meant what I said, Mary. I promised I'll always be there for you, whether you like it or not."

"Oh, whatever."

"Okay, fine!" I slapped my hands against my thighs and stood up. "If you're going to act like a bitch, then I won't be!"

And just as I began storming away, Mary screamed, "SCREW YOU!"

I looked back around and saw her trip as she tried standing on her feet. "SCREW YOU DANNY!" Mary's voice cracked as she finally broke into tears, collapsing back down onto the sand.

"Yeah, that's right. Just walk away! Just walk away and go to California and never talk to me again." She started to tremble as tears shivered out of her black and ruined eye. "I just wish I could go back," I heard her say, before she pressed a hand to her mouth and squeezed her eyes shut.

I think she was sick of me seeing her cry. The vulnerability was killing her as much as the wreckage of her soul was. It would've been naïve of me not to recognize that her harsh words, and short-tempered vagueness, were just a part of her vain attempt at being strong. It was so devastating to stand there and watch that strength fall apart.

"Go back to what, Mary?" I asked as I paced back towards her.

All of a sudden, her faint sobbing stopped. Mary caught a breath in its momentary absence, then gasped, "I don't know." And then clawed her fingers into the sand. "I'm so cold, Danny."

"How about we go some place else then?"

Mary didn't answer me right away. She sat quietly. I felt convicted of a crime looking down at her with pity, so I looked at the meaningless graffiti tags on the wall of the snack bar instead. When I was a kid, that wall had been a mural of a cartoon beach with a stupid crab and sandcastles. Now, it was white and speckled in dirt, and collected mold and algae along the bottom.

"Where?" Mary asked, finally answering me.

"I don't know." The gray mist on the horizon blended with the distant storm clouds. "Some place better than here."

"Okay."

But as she stood, she lurched forward and said, "Oh fuck." Mary lost her balance and stumbled. "I'm seeing double."

She snatched her hair in fists, muttered another *oh fuck*, and puked yellow stomach acid.

"I'm taking you to the hospital. Now."

"Don't tell me what to—" Another burst of yellow erupted from her mouth.

"Mary, we're going!"

"NO—"

But then Mary collapsed into her puke on the ground.

———————————————————

To pass several incompetent drivers in the left lane, I had to drive on the shoulder of the 306. I gunned through a pointless red light too. My eyes scanned back and forth from the highway to Mary. She was pale and heaving nothing but air into a plastic grocery bag. She made sounds like she was choking, and her face grew whiter and her cheeks thinner. I was certain she was going to die.

I zipped into the Emergency driveway of the South Gilmore Park General, unbuckled Mary, and trudged in with her body in my arms as I held her barf bag, calling for help. Raw panic deafened my senses, but I was very aware of the faces of the other patients staring, and those of the nurses, as they rushed up towards me while I explained the story. I was also intently aware of how I was only one false accusation away from having been the one to hit her.

The waiting room smelled of disinfectant and fresh airborne disease. But that was so cliché of the hospital, I was upset. There could have been a nice lemony scent. That would have been accommodating. Fuck, shoot for the moon, they should have had coconut. That would've been luxury.

Everyone in that department of dying looked as if they'd been plucked off the street, or brought in from the downtown bus terminal. I tried not to look too long.

I then jumped in shock at the abrupt vibrating of my phone. The wait for Mary had drifted me into a near paranoid state. I slid my hand into the pocket of my jeans and whipped out my phone. Max was calling. I hit the button to mute the call. A moment later, after the vibrating ended, my phone buzzed with a text.

Lol bro did you use my shit in the beach house?

An hour after Mary was admitted, a nurse appeared around the corner, at last, calling my name. I leaped out of the teal-colored vinyl seat and rushed over.

"Does Mary have medical coverage?"

Not having a clue, I could only shrug my shoulders, and so the nurse walked away. Moments later, a man that I assumed to be the doctor, judging by his white coat and all, came up to me and explained the diagnosis. After first going through the review in a complicated medical language, the doctor told me, in his simplest terms, that Mary suffered from what was known as a "fractured trapdoor." When the doctor asked how she'd been injured and I couldn't provide an answer, he shifted ever so slightly, looking at me askance as if his suspicions were growing. Despite the doctor's wariness, he granted me the okay to go see her.

Seeing Mary in the Emergency Room was the second worst thing I had ever seen.

She was draped in a hospital gown, lying half-awake in a

medicated haze, and only separated from other patients—coughing up what sounded like death—by a thin tarp. Christ, nothing smells worse than the sick.

The light from the low ceiling kept flickering, and atop the metronomic beeping of the heart monitors, Mary's roommate kept hacking. I felt sicker with every breath I took, so I tried to breathe as little as possible.

"Mary..." I said softly, as if it were her ears that were damaged. According to the nurse, she was jacked up on an IV with a strong sedative.

Mary opened her good eye and flashed me an upside-down peace sign. The bulge under her bad eye was a terrible color of red and purple and looked like a bag full of liquid. If you touched it, it would pop.

"Are you okay?"

Mary nodded. Conversation would have been nice, but her face was once again safely saturated in color, and that was more than enough for me. Despite the scene of the Emergency Room, I got the impression that Mary was now only suffering from extreme drowsiness.

Earlier, the doctor said he needed to know—or needed me to find out what coverage Mary had before they could proceed. The question needed time to wrack within me before I asked her. Unfortunately, the only questions she answered were the ones that only required one word, and even so, most were only answered by a shrug. Mary's breathing quickly slipped back into the rhythm of sleep. The sedative was probably fucking her up more than anything.

When I went back to the doctor, I told him. He looked bitter, as if displeased with the alternate option we were now forced to make. I was only catching half of what he was saying, and then when he said, "despite the trauma, she should be fine," he sounded unconvinced, and I felt the floor slip out from under my feet. However unreasonably, I felt guilty and responsible.

More could have been done—should have been done—but the doctor assumed we couldn't afford it. I would have obviously paid for it with the Emergency Credit Card, which I had already used to pay for the initial hospital bill, including the blood thinners and painkillers. Thankfully, the medical care and drugs weren't crazy expensive. I figured Mom would understand.

After I had picked up whatever Mary was prescribed at the pharmacy, I went to check up on her, still fast asleep. The nurse informed me that, when she awoke, it was okay to go home.

"Oh, great. Thank you," I said and thought of how Mary had been kicked out of her home.

I went on to explore the hospital to pass the time. South Gilmore Park General hadn't had a facelift since the seventies, and it looked as though the medical gear hadn't been turned over since the eighties. The drop ceiling tiles had those questionable brown stains, and the white walls were streaked with black marks from either hastily delivered medical equipment, or what I had imagined at worst, violent episodes. Certain hallways had been marked off, particularly the psych ward.

Doctor, Doctor
The Savior / Accused of Theft
The Surgeons Knife,
The Thirty-Eighth Miracle / The Kiss of Death

To pass the time, I waited on a bench outside the main hospital entrance. The grooves in the damp driveway reflected the light from the gray and brooding sky; rain continued to sparingly fall. A skinny guy with a buzz cut and a larger gal in sweatpants were off on the sidewalk smoking as they argued about hospital bills.

While waiting for Mary to wake up, wishing I had my Lyric Book with me because the greatest literary insights only occur when you are nowhere near a pen and paper, a dark red van pulled up in the circular driveway. In the instant that the man driving got out of the front seat, and the woman exiting the passenger side pulled open the back door, letting a black Labrador out, a nurse emerged from the doors of the foyer, pushing a horribly disproportionate boy in a wheelchair.

"Winny! Winny!" The boy cried as the dog jumped right up onto his lap and started licking his face. "Hey—hey!" He laughed. "Oh, oh, I missed you! I love you so much! Oh, my best friend! I love you so much!" The boy wrapped his arms, as best he could, around Winny as the dog snuggled and rested his head on his lap.

The man (whom by this point I assumed was his father) fitted his arm snugly around his wife's shoulders. A high, jutted-chin grin stiffened his face as her eyes watered and she brought her hand around his.

"*Ah-ra-ra-roo!*" The boy howled, and then Winny, as if answering a dialectic greeting, howled the chorus back to him. Winny and the boy sang the chorus back and forth until Winny splayed his long tongue back over the boy's face.

The murmurs from the arguing couple off on the corner of the driveway rose when the guy with the buzz cut shouted at the gal, "Well if your daughter wasn't so fuckin' conceited, thinking the whole fucking universe owes her shit…" And then lowered to a rumbling whisper when the nurse, the boy's parents, and I looked at them. Winny and the boy couldn't be bothered, for nothing existed in the world outside the two of them.

Following a conversation between the nurse and the mother, concealed by a raised hand, the bitter-sweetness that suffused her face receded into the same high, jutted-chin grin as her husband. His hand held hers tighter.

Winny patiently, with his tail wagging, lapped about as the parents and the nurse, in a team effort, pushed the boy up the ramp that extended out of the back door. Once inside the van, Winny dutifully jumped in behind. And as the gray wind stirred and bent the palm leaves in the planters to its might, the shining wet wheels of the van sloshed over the pavement and drove away.

Then with a loud stomp on the pavement, the guy with the buzz cut scoffed, "Fuckin' bullshit," and ground the butt of his cigarette into the sidewalk with his sneaker.

I burned an oath in my spirit that if my music career ever took off, I would come back and visit the South Gilmore Park General's pediatric floor. God knows kids are the only ones who deserve it.

23

Bridge Over Troubled Water

MARY

The drug companies would make a killing if they sold whatever I was jacked up on, on the streets. Either from a deep sleep, or solid trip, I floated back to consciousness. Seriously though, by the time I fluttered my eyes open, it took me a second after recognizing the Sgt. Pepper's poster that I was in Danny's room. His bare feet stuck out from under the blanket as he slept opposite me, his face ballooning out like a baby's with his breathing. A draft tousled the blinds. I shook Danny's foot, waking him up.

He groggily recapped the entire episode for me. Only when he went through the events, play by play, did I remember. Even the beach was nothing more than a fog. Apparently, I suffered from something that I couldn't dare say, but was written on a treatment guide prescribed by the doctor: enophthalmos.

Danny was pleased with how significantly better he said I looked. When I winced in pain after jerking my head too fast, Danny busted out one of my painkillers. Yay, more drugs.

"How are you feeling?" he asked, popping open the lid of the vial and handing me the capsule clipped in his fingers.

"Well, I'm not seeing double anymore," I said, and downed the pill with a glass of water. Danny smiled and said that was good, and then we didn't say anything for a long time.

Through the half-lowered blinds, the dim overcast light threw strips of shadows across his body and the poster-wall behind him. A narrow column of light crossing over his brow pulled the hidden green coloring out of his brown eyes.

The last time I was in Danny's room, I had assumed he was just a weird guy who still had a thing for Pokémon. But understanding him better, or perhaps harboring an unrealized compassion, or perhaps now feeling I had not the right to judge him because he firsthand experienced the chaos of my life, I viewed his childhood décor from a different perspective. Pinup babes and music equipment and rock posters only stood paces in front of the video game stickers and delicate obscuring of the Toy Story figurines.

Danny's life was captured in collective evidence all around his room. Atop of old posters were plastered new ones. Books and biographies were stacked in rows on his shelves in front of graphic novels, and behind those were picture books with dinosaurs. Nothing discarded, nothing ever let go. Even the closet, which was cracked open (with Raquel's stretch-marked belly hanging out again), held stacks and rows of clothes I had never seen him wear.

The light from the lower half of the window, unconcealed by the blinds, shone earnestly on the marker drawings taped up on the far wall. Taking a closer look this time around, I saw pirate ships, spaceships, and racecars. All of them featuring cartoon characters on some sort of adventure, and realized the gallery of doodles told a story. Every page, the embodiment of a little boy's sense of imagination. The evidential baby steps to the stories that would become the lyrics to the songs he wanted to write.

"Are those marks from your kid drawings?" I asked while looking down at the multi-colored etches on the hardwood floor.

"Uh. Oh yeah," he said, following my gaze to the ground. But then the words he silently formed on his lips fell off, and his eyes took on an inward quality as he stared down at that spot on the floor for a long, long time. "We used to draw in my room all the time."

"We?"

"My brother—and I."

"Is your brother's name Connor?"

"Yeah, yeah. It is," he said. So Connor was the other boy on the family photo wall, not an old Kindergarten friend. He then asked, "How do you know?"

"You left a drawing in your sketchbook with his name," I said and left it at that. I had questions, but I did not want to pry. For I began to wonder, with everything that had happened between us, why was I in his room to begin with? The memory of his hands on me crept into my mind, but I was too weak, too desperate for the safety Danny made me feel, to let it flood my thoughts.

After a minute, Danny got up to put on a record he said I would probably like. I certainly wasn't in any position to argue. Most likely because I didn't really care what music he wanted to listen to.

He went to lift the plastic case off his turntable and replaced whatever record was on there with Untitled Album, and dropped the needle. First, it was silent, and then with a thump and the crackling grains, the first strings of a guitar sounded. Danny sat back down on the bed, opposite me, as the singer, with nothing but a lonely sounding guitar and a lonelier sounding voice, filled the space. We sat through a handful of songs without saying a word.

Danny's eyes were locked on the window. I made off and on glances at him, I wanted to see the rare green in his eyes again. Despite the welcome numbness of the painkiller, the constant movement of my eye began to make my head hurt. With his fingers curled under his lip, he looked deep in thought. I considered asking him what he was thinking. Danny had never been that quiet with me before.

Eventually, we made disjointed eye contact. My head erupted. My eye screamed. It was as if I could feel some sort of ooze from the glands slowly encrusting my eye shut. Inside, I had what felt like guilty butterflies. I just wanted to be anywhere else. He was being mean by not talking to me. I was so ashamed of myself. I hated myself.

My eye rapidly throbbed, as if it were bubbling. I felt so ugly. My appearance repulsed him. I just knew it. His bedroom was a place of peace; I didn't deserve to be there. At the end of the day, I knew what I was. And despite being crazy and ugly, as well as homeless and trash, I wasn't good enough for him. I didn't deserve him. After all, I had to con him back to me with the disease of misfortune that was my life.

And then, out of nowhere, he laughed.

For a regretful split-second, I believed everything I had felt was true and wanted to die. But then it occurred to me that I had my thumb wedged up my nostril, and I was scraping crusted snot off my nose ring. I plucked my thumb away and looked at the disgusting crud collected beneath my nail. My glance shot from my thumb to him. Danny's laugh arrived in silent heaves. I couldn't help but join him. I felt so stupid, but I didn't feel so ugly anymore.

DANNY

The rain swept over the street in hard white lines. Tattering periodically against the road as if pounded out from the base of a marching-band drum. The ceaselessly redirecting wind fluxed the trees and whipped through the leaves mourning in coarse whispers.

The weather was far from favorable, and the umbrella Mary and I sheltered behind was all too determined to blow away with every new change in the wind. But braving the storm was a challenge, and the challenge had made it fun.

If anything, I was happy to be getting along with Mary again. It began to feel like old times, and I began to miss her, even though she was right beside me. Maybe I knew then that our time together wasn't going to last forever.

Gradually, the weather receded into a gentle rainfall, and in place of the storm, we talked.

"…And that's when I realized I was the only girl without a mom." Mary sniffled, not from crying, but from the chill of the damp air. "It was the worst day of my life," she continued, unveiling the piece from her past as we walked through the misty evening.

The details of the letter that came attached with the roses were revealed to me.

From behind the metal stick of the umbrella, I caught a glimpse of her eyes fixed steadfastly on the sidewalk ahead as she talked. While I listened to Mary go on about all the pain she kept buried away, much to my own inner-disappointment, my thoughts were on her eye. I did not want to internally, let alone verbally, acknowledge that the position of her bruised eye looked a little askew, as if it were lazy. I then dismissed the thought entirely by assuring myself that once the swelling went down, the alignment of her eye would return to normal.

"If your parents never paid for singing lessons or whatever—you just didn't do those things. It sucked, Danny. Watching all the other girls get to do all these little girl things, that, like, even if I wanted to do, I couldn't."

Though her pain clawed something out from my heart, it felt like a reward; the reward for loving Mary was getting to know Mary. Getting to know her story.

A car came quickly around the corner, slashing through a puddle. Mary tugged the hood of the sweater I had lent her over her black eye.

That night, the one where Mary had wandered aimlessly alone, disoriented in spirit, fractured in body and mind, when she had left—been forced out of—her house with nothing but a T-shirt on, she had found a sweater in a tipped over shopping-cart in the parking lot of Oceanside Park. I'd thrown that ragged thing out at the hospital. I had also thrown out a pair of scissors she had with her. We never talked about the use of those scissors. Ever.

The rain had picked up again and pelted the umbrella in dull taps as we paraded through the backstreets of my neighborhood. I then caught myself pulling down my own hood, and imagined what people were thinking as they drove by Mary and I walking under the giant umbrella with our faces hidden in our hoodies. We probably looked like some goth couple, and maybe we were. Jesus Christ, those two kids were sad.

The marching-band played on though, because I guess neither of us really cared what the world driving by thought.

Later on, at some point past midnight, in the deep heart of the night, Mary turned to me in bed. By then, my eyes had long since adjusted to the darkness, and her damaged eye looked like nothing more than a black stain on the blue velvet of her midnight lit face.

Earlier that evening, I heard Mom come home, and listened to her feet pad across the hallway as she walked by to her room without stopping. We had yet to reconcile any of our words from before.

From outside the open window, I could hear water trickling off the eaves, and the air rolling into my room was cold and pure, replenished after being ravaged by the rainstorm.

Mary put her hand on my neck and began caressing my face. Running her palm against my cheek, enveloping my ear in the cradle of her thumb. Then using the short edges of her nails to stroke my scalp, a nerve-tingling warmth spread throughout my body and would have relaxed me to sleep if she hadn't pulled herself closer, and then said in a voice bearing the ache of a little girl's adolescent lust, "Kiss me."

We couldn't possibly find a way to go deeper. If a thrust driven with the right measure of passion could have entwined our bodies forever, I would have without a doubt complied.

With the momentum increasing each time our bodies clasped together, the louder the slapping of flesh on flesh became, the more and more I became annihilated by the complete enrapture of her. It was a renewing miracle each time Mary's body pushed back in a rhythm of her own against mine. The feeling of her muscles tightening beneath me. The gasps parting her lips followed by the rolling back of her eyes. The sudden replacing of arms. The bending of her knee as her leg slid across the sheet. The gown of her hair caught between our bodies beading with sweat; her fragrance arising from the heat. The frequent putter of breaths so fragile, the exhalations of pain and pleasure.

"Danny."

"Mary."

"My eye," she gasped.

"S-sorry." I immediately stopped.

"Don't stop."

So I didn't stop. Then she started crying.

"I'll stop," I said.

"No. It just hurts."

"This hurts?"

"No," she sniffed. "My eye."

Despite the hypnotic pull of the physical rhythm, the endless motion it demanded, I made sure to be gentle, so impossibly gentle. Eventually, we stopped moving altogether, but remained insepa-rable. Our chests linked together through her arms swept beneath mine. My lips grazed her earlobes, I breathed her in—an invisible memory of Beach Baby perfume. We were still in a motionless silence until my body couldn't bear the desire and nature took her course. I looked to Mary's eyes for the answer. Her reaction assured there would be no repercussions.

I love you, I thought.

"Thank you," she whispered and snuggled closer.

I had no clue what she was thanking me for, and I was disappointed that my imagination had gotten ahead of itself, but I whispered back, "You're welcome."

Mary clutched me tighter; her naked skin on mine was still warm and silky with sweat. The weight of her body made me conscious of my breathing. Other than the random thumping of pulses, the low hum from the cooling unit somewhere in my room, and the tack of the curtains, all else was quiet. And then, from out of that silence, half-spoken into the pillow, Mary whispered, "I don't want to be homeless." And looked up at me.

"You won't be," I said, before remembering that this wasn't a problem that simply having faith in a better tomorrow could fix, and so my consolation ended there.

I realized then that language had a limited effect. There weren't always going to be the divinely ordained words that would chime like golden notes in the ears of the broken. My tongue was finally at a loss. In place of speaking, I showed my affection by holding her closer. Rubbing my foot against hers beneath the blanket to soothe and keep her warm.

Mary began shivering; her convulsing body shook the bedsheet off my shoulder. She started crying meek and whispered sobs.

"I swear, Danny," she said through the weight in her throat. "I'm never going to be a shitty parent. I swear to God, I'm never going to put my kids through shit like that. I swear."

Mary then groaned in pain, it had hurt her eye to cry. And I could tell that when she realized that the expelling of pain brought on greater pain, it made her weep more.

I attempted to rely on language once again, to at the very least momentarily take her mind off the pain.

"Mary," I said, "if you are seriously kicked out, why don't you just move in here. With me."

She didn't say anything right away. A dim glow from the digital-clock glimmered behind the outline of her hair.

"Danny—you're moving to California." I felt the words vibrate from her chest as she spoke them.

"I don't have to."

"But your Mom—"

"Then come with us. We'll go together. We'll drive, like we talked about."

She didn't say anything. The cadence of her breathing was enough; I took her silence as an indicator of serious consideration. The glory I dreamed our road-trip would be lightened my thoughts.

After a few uncountable silent minutes, I asked, "Are you asleep?"

"No."

"You know what you told me about your tattoo?"

"Yeah?"

"When you first showed me, that night, in the pool, you said you had it inked by your tits. But, all that night—and now, I can't help but notice that you have it handwritten beside your heart." I gently pressed the pad of my finger along the black words on her ribs: *The heart will break, but broken live on.*

"Yes, I know," I said. "I'm sorry for being corny."

"Don't be sorry."

"I'm not."

A light gust of wind played with the curtains.

"Danny, can I ask you something?"

"Sure."

Then without saying anything, Mary rolled out from the tangle of sheets and stood up. The entirety of her naked figure exposed to me for the first time. The natural voluptuous shape of her body had me so amorously absorbed. Mary's body, untampered through neither excessive eating nor rigorous exercise, was the pure and perfect figure of a young woman. When Mary squatted before my record shelf, the contour of her hips splayed out widely beneath her and bloated her round butt. Then pulling out one of my old notebooks, she stood up and her breasts swayed with the turn of her body as she faced me with the notebook opened just below her nipples.

Mary flipped through individual pages of the book as she walked back and then sat cross-legged on the bed. The notebook sat open cover-to-cover on her thighs, against the folds of her stomach. Then dialing to the page she wanted to find, Mary spun the notebook so I could see what was written on the page.

My mind blanked. Reading what I had written so long ago. I could sense her eyes falling on a never-before seen part of me. The nakedness of my unwelcomed, forlorn mind, exposed by the voracious dashing of ink, sat between us. In a coarse voice, I read aloud what I vainly attempted to pretend was not by any means connected to my psyche.

" 'I want to die,' " I recited. " 'The ladder of life will break. The splintering shards pierced like a stake. Death will make a bitch of us all. Why even climb? You'll fall.' "

I then had to struggle to make out the rest of my hacked handwriting:

" 'Fuck. Fuck.' " It read in bold capital letters. " 'I hate this. I fucking miss you both so much. Fuck.' "

The rest of the page was covered in violent dashes and scribbles. Mary pulled the sheet up over her breasts.

"Why?"

I turned on my pillow, looking out the window. The streetlights and the clouds blinded the stars. A car outside then coughed. The sound of the rain shedding off the shingles slowly faded. I readjusted myself on the bed, discovering a new coldness on the sheets, and then looking out at the colors of midnight in my room, I drew in a deep breath.

"Mary," I said. She looked at me. "My... my Dad, and older brother, Connor—they died." I had finally said after years of holding it in. Vocalizing the events my memory blacked out.

"I think it was, um, nine? Ten? Ten years ago now? It was, uh, after a soccer game, my brother's. I remember my mom offering to go get him, since she couldn't stay for the game because she had to attend to me, or something. But my dad told her he would go. He played in a band, so he toured a lot. And this was just after his band had put out an LP, so he was rarely home. So, he wanted to surprise my brother. And, I, uh, guess, on their way home, a drunk driver crashed—into them. Head on. And, um yeah. That was it. Last time I'd ever seen them both. Yeah. Ten years ago. A decade. Wow. Yeah, wow. An entire decade.

"So, yeah. Sometimes, Mary, death doesn't seem all too bad of an idea, you know? That way I could get to see them just a little bit sooner."

I looked at Dad's guitars, the steel string on his Telecaster still springing out. "I just fucking hate it, Mary. I really fucking hate it."

And that was all I had to say, because that was all there was. Just me and ten years between us. I closed the cover of the notebook and tossed it on the floor. It slid towards my guitars.

Mary slid her fingers around my bicep and laid her head on my shoulder.

Soon, she was asleep. I had yet to join her in the realm of slumber because my mind couldn't resist replaying the past. I thought of being a kid. I thought of Dad. I thought of Connor. I thought of the nights he and I would stay up late past our bedtime, drawing on my bedroom floor. The stories we made up, the characters we shared, how I envied how much more talented he was than me. I wonder if he would have grown up to be a brilliant artist.

And then, maybe because I know how quickly the present slips into the past, how even monuments of stone fall to rubble and then return to the dust from which they came, I held Mary tighter. As if holding her tighter would hold the moment for eternity. If I let go, the sun would rise. I wanted the darkness of the night to enshroud us forever.

I kept note of how soft her breasts felt while pushed into my chest with her breathing. I counted my blessings with each of those breaths until I knew she was fast asleep and it was safe to say, "I love you," and let her rhythm soothe me to sleep.

―――――――――――――――――――――――

"Don't go any further," Mary said as we idled in my Mustang along the curb hugging the corner of Bayview Avenue. "It would only make shit worse. Believe me."

I didn't doubt Mary, and I was internally relieved.

"Do you want me to wait? What if he—you know?"

"What if my dad was serious about kicking me out?"

"Yeah."

"Then I'll gather my shit and, and, I'll figure it out."

"Will you please call me?"

"Sure."

"And will you also please consider my offer?"

"To go with you to California? Danny—that's—that's," she sighed. "Sure."

Mary tugged on the door handle, springing it open with a pop. Suddenly realizing that she was leaving, and not knowing what would happen to her, unsure of where she planned on going in the event of the worst-case scenario—and definitely without a clue for how long—I made a stupid sound that came out as nothing close to a recognizable word. I bit my tongue because I was on the verge of asking a really stupid question. Mary stared at me with impatient eyes.

"What?"

The cold air crawled in through the open door, making me

shiver. Raindrops tacked and began to build on the black vinyl door panel.

"Uh," I began, and then pushed out the following words, each with more forced jubilance than the last. "No—bye, Froo Froo?"

Mary grunted and frowned. She was clueless.

"Oh." Her voice leaped as she clued in. "Right. Ha."

But that was it. A brief smile stretched across her face before dropping back down to a straight sullen line. Mary stepped out of the car and threw back the door.

The sound of the door didn't really indicate if it had closed properly or not. So I leaned over the seats, reopened it, and slammed it again. Mary was already a house down Bayview Avenue when I propped myself back up and looked out the windshield.

Rolling down my window I yelled, "Mary!"

She stopped and looked back at me. The puddles surrounding her feet flashed with white circles. "I'll be waiting for you, okay? I'm not going to go. I'm not going to California without you."

Mary nodded and kept on walking.

I then yelled again, "I'll be waiting!" But my voice may have been lost under the shower of sound.

As I watched Mary walk down the street to her house, pulling up the baggy seams of the sweatpants to avoid dragging the ankles through the puddles, I began to wonder when the last time Mary had called me Froo Froo was. But its final utterance had long since slipped from my memory.

The downpour began to pickup, shifting the rain diagonally across the road. The saturated colors and the blended smell of sweet moisture and wet earth sent a jolt of familiarity through me.

I couldn't help but think that the director was lazy and had already used this set—Mary sunken and sore, crossing the floor of her porch on a rain-drenched afternoon. The vividity of the red roses petals dispersed on her lawn was a snapshot I could readily pull out of the gallery of my memory.

As Mary vanished behind the canvas of her front porch, to the place where untold stories unfolded, I realized something I was too ignorant to understand before. I didn't understand that Mary was doing so much more that day with the roses and the rain than I knew.

I finally realized that, after that day, that day she had to permanently close the case on her mom's life, that playfulness Mary had effortlessly carried about had just… stopped.

Sitting in my car, staring down toward the house she had disappeared into, it officially hit me that there had been no more Froo Froo's, or Snoop Dog shirts, or inappropriately timed sex jokes, or any of that, after that day. It could only have been the hope of her mom's life that kept that playful spirit alive.

Whether it was the squeak of the windshield wipers, or the pummeling of the teardrops on the city, the day provided a rhythm I could get lost to. So, like a musician in the studio who can't find a way to conclude a song, the day and the rain faded until I, the listener, became aware that the track had drifted away.

Later on that night, I had made another vile attempt at writing something in my Lyric Book. I pressed my pen to the page, but had only seemed to let the tip of the ballpoint drift away, leaving a scratched dot in its place.

I then smacked my head back against the headboard.

Allowing the weight of my skull to roll along the carved trim, my eyes landed on my phone sitting under the lamp. All its sleekness, and technological advancement, rendered utterly useless because Mary was the only teenage girl in the world who did not have a phone. She couldn't be contacted through social media because she was afraid of being found. She seemed to intentionally make things more complicated because she could, because she was Mary. That's just what she does.

Life had its way of being unethically timed. For what seemed like years, life had moved along without any rush or direct destination. Now, it felt like everything was speeding up from all directions at once. It was also inconsiderate and did not leave anything like a clue to hint at where it was guiding me—what the right choices to activate my destiny would be.

I picked up my phone, and let my finger glide over the contact list as—for the millionth time—I looked for someone to talk to. When seeing Rob's name on the list, I couldn't completely comprehend that I would never have a real reason to call him again. I called Max. There wasn't an answer.

Hey man. I miss you.

I sent in a text.

My mind refused to settle as I waited for a response I was sure I would never get. With the lights off, I kept rolling over to check my phone on the night table, stimulating my own restlessness, and it became apparent that sleeping wasn't going to be an option. So instead, I lay awake, thinking about everything. California, or not?

Coffined motionless underneath the sheets that, for the first time all summer, felt like they had a purpose, I looked out at the bright moonlight unaffected by the thin clouds drifting across. And while admiring the clarity and size of the full moon, my thoughts were an incongruent mess.

Was the last-minute change of heart ridiculous? Yes. Would backing out be abhorrently cruel to Mom? Absolutely yes. But— back when the plans to leave Gilmore Park were set, I had no clue this was the course life's vicissitudes were to take. That I would meet Mary. Fall in love with Mary. That Max would be left homeless after being emancipated from foster care. If I were to leave Gilmore Park, there would be no one to save them both from what terrible outcomes their futures might have. If a dramatic decision had to be made, it had to be made now.

The night air rolled in through the window and breathed its cool cleansing breath across my face.

Confused. Pissed off. And feeling just overall sad that I affronted my conscience with this decision, my eyes whirled around my bedroom searching for some sort of sign to guide me. The Universe isn't malicious, it's supposed to provide us omens. Correct?

A lonely sock flopped over the laundry bin. No. Not it. I am not that sock.

I checked my phone again. No response from Mary or Max. Hanging off the coat hanger was my nineties jean jacket and my Superior Carwash ball cap. Yes. Mary and Max—Max, soon to be evicted from foster care. He could, should, move in with me. Mary too. When the thought occurred to me, it actually sounded pretty awesome. I had the means. Keep the house, why Mom could certainly afford it. She could afford to move us out to California, after all.

God must have positioned me to be the protectorate of my friends. The timing was right, the realization was a part of the plan of things that Had To Be.

I was so positive that my thinking landed on a congruent track; surely there was no purer altruism than the goodness of helping my friends in need. Mom would understand.

I swung my legs off over the bed, getting up to tell Mom what I had decided. Then throwing my Lyric Book and pen aside, I looked up.

The Beatles, the four Gospels themselves, appareled in their Sgt. Pepper's costumes, stared down at me. Prince on the cover of Controversy was next. And Keith Richards just terrified me.

California was the place to fulfill my dreams. Not this dumpy one. My friend's problems weren't that catastrophic... I mean they've survived eighteen years fending for themselves without me. Max had no clue of my impending hospitality—and I've never received word from Mary that she even remotely agreed to live with me, or move out to California.

Standing, facing the door, my thinking befuddled each argument I made against myself endlessly and crashed and burned into blankness.

When Mom first asked me what my opinion was on moving, I bluntly answered:

"No."

And now, again, months later, blindly looking for the answer, the omens I requested presented themselves.

My eyes leaped all over my bedroom. To my guitars: the acoustic, the Telecaster. Both Dad's. Next, the moonlight glaring through the window. The posters. Raquel Welch; girls like her out in California worshipped boys with guitars. Back to my guitars. Both Dad's. The drawings I made with Connor.

Falling on my bed, my eyes fell to the floor.

Only then, when I had come out of my thoughts, did I feel the spinning cold draft from the fan. I kept my eyes locked on the floor in an anoetic trance for a very long time. Not a thought passed through my mind.

"Mom?" I said, minutes later, pushing open her door to see her reading yet another book on California.

She invited me in by asking, "What's wrong?"

Something inside of me, on that specific night, at that specific moment, made me want to tell Mom everything. So I got under the covers. Mom put her book down, and I told her all that had happened. Almost all that happened.

When I told Mom about Mary's black eye and taking her to the hospital, she said she already knew. The hospital had called her due to her name being listed as the primary cardholder.

As always, I felt dumbed-down by Mom's perceptiveness. Like I was forever seven, and she just went along with whatever I had to say, making me feel accomplished as I bragged about discoveries she had already unmapped.

Mom's hair flowed under my cheek as I laid my head against her shoulder. The lingering smell of shampoo and its silky texture were all too familiar and instantly brought me back to childhood, where cuddling next to Mom was something I regularly did. Resting my head on her, which I now felt was too big, and made Mom seem so much smaller, reminded me of how many years I had slept just like that.

Maybe after another half-hour, the conversation ran dry, so I told Mom I would let her finish reading.

Just as we said our ritualistic Love yous and Goodnights, I turned around in the door frame and said, "Oh, and Mom, by the way, I'm not going."

24

Daddy Please Don't Cry

MARY

"I love you," he said.

The words still rang in my ears, and like a shockwave in my heart, when I finally sat down. Danny and his mom dropped the phrase so often that its declaration had lost meaning.

Before he had said I love you, he'd also said, "I need you."

I wasn't expecting to hear that either.

He had also said, "Don't worry 'bout it."

But my eye throbbed, reminding me that it was swollen and sensitive on my face when he mumbled that. And before he'd mumbled that, I had told him: "I'm here to get my things."

The wet and muddy pant legs swayed against my ankles as I walked from Danny's car to my house. Danny had just screamed out the car window, "I'll be waiting!" But I pretended not to hear.

The rain had only napped last night, and it re-awoke that morning as the sky started to lighten. The rain tacking against the tin of the drain pipe was what had awoken me. Danny slept on through though, and unlike throughout most of the night, breathed silently. Despite the cold air slipping in through the screen, I was warm beneath his shoulder huddled over mine and with his bare arms wrapping around my body.

But out on the street, walking to my house, the rain soaked in through the sweater of his I wore, seeming to seep right through my skin, drenching my bones.

As I walked down Bayview, on the street splodged with mud and dead leaves, I kept my head down, watching my steps to avoid the worms that stretched out along the pavement. My neighborhood smelled of mud and the scent of salt from the ocean, and the crash of the surf below the bay sounded stronger than ever. As I walked by the homes of all my neighbors, I forgot about being drenched and wondered about all of their lives on this anomaly of an August day, which seemed to forecast what the oncoming autumn would feel like.

Most of the homes in Danae's Bay were built for idyllic beach life. Adorned with tall windows that served as walls, providing each room with a perfect view, and also openly exposing their lives for me to observe.

My neighbors were all huddled in for the day, cozy in their living rooms with lamps turned on to cast out the gloom of the afternoon, sipping on tea, watching the rainfall from within. All of them eager to wear the layers that summer made obsolete, and grateful, feeling deserving, for their break from the heat.

My hair mopped the back of my neck as I looked over at my favorite house from which blue smoke arose out of the chimney, floating out above the roofs, seeming to thicken the gray haze in the sky. On the lawn, birds squeaked as they played from tree to tree, shaking the rain off the leaves as they shuddered their wings and flew away. And from inside my favorite house, I heard the chime of a piano melody. I had imagined that a little blonde girl was learning how to read music on a white piano.

You see, after all those years of walking those same streets, to and from school or work, I had gotten to know my neighbors in a way they'd never gotten to know me. From the outside, I always peered in through their windows, learning about their entire lives within.

A flock of blackbirds fluttered in the treetops, rattling the leaves hung with tears.

I pulled at the ankles of the sweatpants I'd borrowed from Danny, now completely caked in mud and rain, and walked up the porch steps to my house. The doormat erupted in a mini flood, further soaking my feet. As I walked towards my front door, I could feel the blisters brewing.

Just as I pulled open the screen door, I saw Jim come hobbling from around the living room corner. Balancing his steps with a cane I wasn't quite sure of when he started using, and dangling a joint from out of his mouth. The smell of marijuana shot straight up my nose.

Jim lunged forward, limping with the wooden cane that wobbled with the weight of his body.

"I'm here to get my things," I said.

"Don't worry 'bout it." He answered. But then as Jim crossed into the gray daylight from the dimness of the hallway, standing in the doorframe, his face bent as he looked warily at me.

"Wh-What happened t'your eye?"

"Are you fuc—are you joking?"

"No, dear?" He took a careful step down on to the porch. "Your eye, sweetie. Tell me. What happened?"

"Nothing... I'm here to get my things."

"What? Why?" he said anxiously as he walked to his lawn chair. "Are you movin' out?"

"Seriously?"

Before Jim answered, he dropped the cane against the barbecue, scratching the steel as it slid off and thumped to the ground. And then while struggling to lower himself into the seat, he asked, "Still seeing... ooh? What was his name? Daniel?"

I shook my head.

"Oh. That's too bad. He seemed like a very nice boy."

On the strike of the lighter, the end-tip of the joint caught a short flame and fizzled, cupping the harsh stank of raw weed. Jim took a hard hit, and as the smoke drooled out of his mouth, he admired how fat of a joint he rolled.

Jim then went on a rant about how Danny was a Leftist and how he's a part of a group of defective snowflakes that are trying to destroy the First Amendment. And that we can't trust our neighbors anymore, and that the Left are committing crimes like not standing for our National Anthem. I stopped listening somewhere in the midst of it.

"I'm just tryin' to protect ya, Mary," he said before he began another rant about taxes, or the government, or some other conspiracy theory. Just as I nodded and pulled open the door, he said, "I just don't want what happened t'your mum, t'happen to you."

My attention averted from the cold handle.

"Ya know, your mum was young, she was your age, when she got pregnant with you, right?"

The indents of the screen door handle crushed into my palm. I didn't dare let go of my grip.

"It's just real scary t'think 'bout that happening t'ya too, Mary."

He lifted the joint to his mouth. I nodded, anticipating more.

But he only picked and chose what he wanted to reveal about my mom. We didn't say anything else. Jim vanished into a daze or a daydream, staring out towards the crevice between the close-knit properties on the east side of the street. The only view of the ocean we got.

The hinges of the screen door shrieked as I pulled it back, about to step inside.

"Mary."

I turned around. Jim's eyes were glossed over and red. Even then, I had faith they were red with tears.

"I need you," he said.

The smoke from his lips slipped into the air. The frame of the porch cringed with the rocking of the wind. Flakes of dirt wavered in the cobwebs.

"Yeah," I said. My eye throbbed.

"I couldn't handle losin' you, like how I lost your mother."

I nodded. My right shoulder muscle flexed as I opened the door wide enough to let myself inside.

"I need you," he repeated. Behind the coarseness of his leathered voice, there was a sweetness when he spoke. I looked at him through the mesh screen. I nudged my head in a nod against the steel folds of the door. My wrist began to cramp.

"I love you."

I tried to think of the name of the angle the straight lines of the door made.

"Don't you love me too?" he asked. "I've never heard you say it before, Mary."

"Yeah, Dad…" I couldn't think of the angle name. "I love you, too."

The same gust of wind that rang the chimes across the street swept drizzle onto my arm. The thin hairs stood in the sudden cold shock. I let go of the handle. The screen door slammed.

"Come over here," he said, finishing the joint. Compliantly I walked over. He softly repeated, "Come here." I inched closer to him. Jim gestured with his hands that I lean in even closer. "Here. Here."

And then, as I lowered my head in towards Jim's hovering hands that moved past my ears, his fingers combing my hair, blood rushed to my eye. He lightly pulled the back of my head closer, and eased my face towards his lips. Kissing my cheek.

Our eyes met as I slowly stood back up.

I walked back to the door, thinking there was no more, but as I pressed my thumb into the handle, he abruptly hollered, "Mare!"

I turned around.

"I need t'make a trip to the clinic," he said. "Think ya could lend me a couple hundred bucks?"

"Sure."

"Thanks."

The walls of my room spun counter-clockwise when I lifted my forehead from my knees and looked at the girl staring back at me from the mirror that rested on my dresser. What I saw was an ugly girl with an ugly black eye. An ugly girl whose lips trembled as she struggled to hold back tears she didn't want to cry. For her whole life, she told that girl she needed to be hard inside to survive, and she was just so sick of crying.

Mt. Pile of Neglect stood tall on the corner of my bed atop the halfheartedly draped sheet, pouring its remains onto the floor. A mom might have tidied that for me. A mom might have brushed out my hair until I stopped crying. A mom might have stood in the way of Jim's hand and my eye. No matter what the cost.

I reached over to my night table, opened the bottom drawer, and pulled out a photo before leaning back against my bed. I stared at the polaroid. It was an old picture of a girl named Wendy. In the fragile old photo, she was leaning against the trunk of the black Trans Am I remember Jim driving when I was a kid. Over the years, I had studied the photo well. I got my hands on it by sheer mistake.

Years ago, Jim had pulled everything off every shelf and out of every drawer one day in the late spring, adamant that he was going to sell our house and make his fortune at last.

At the bottom of a wooden fruit-crate that had been a part of a collection of boxes that housed his memories, were some old birthday cards, a tourist pamphlet for New Jersey Summer Excursions, and a loose photograph slotted between the yellowed pages of The Catcher in the Rye.

The brittle pages skimmed under my thumb until a clump of them flopped open to the page the photo had been tucked into.

The back of the white square read:

> To are many more Endless Summers.
> With LOVE—Jimbo (yur Bimbo!)

It was the first time I knew Jim could be human.

I remember delicately clipping the corner of the photo with just the edge of my fingers to flip it over. Intuitively knowing its importance. At first, I thought maybe it was from a magazine or something because the girl in the photograph was too gorgeous to be real. But there was the note on the back, and Jim's football jersey rolled up over the girl's narrow belly just above her high-waisted jeans.

The thought started off small, but in a matter of seconds, in a surging wave it amassed over my head and crashed down on me. I knew that she had to be my mom. The girl just had to be. The similarities terrified me. Although it took years of withstanding the shouting to hear the stories that only spilled out with the encouragement of alcohol passing his lips, I never found out much about her. Other than that, in Jim's words, she was a "whore." There were too many times I had stood there, taking the abuse, hoping to hear something more.

Eventually, the clutter that had scattered throughout the house went back in unkempt piles in drawers. The memories went back, locked away in the basement, never to be acknowledged as important until the moment of disposal came about those boxes again. But I kept my photo.

I kept it hidden. The polaroid with its crusted trim felt older than it had when I first found it. So did the hairstyle, maybe the makeup too, I don't know.

Mom's face had lost all its detail, either through the subpar quality of the film, or being taken on a dinky Polaroid camera, but I could imagine what she looked like. Maybe what she sounded like. The things she liked: Jim's jerseys, hoop earrings, grunge rock, maybe pop. She danced, definitely. Mom dreamed of getting out of Jersey and going to New York City. Being a Rockette, a backup on Broadway; howling the blues as a lounge-singer, wearing a red dress that matched her long red nails. Jim showed her off to the guys at the dingy local boardwalk dives where she spent countless nights dancing up a storm. She was so vibrant, so natural, so untouchable. Even the band played off time because Mom made her own rhythm. She danced to her own beat. Guys would try, oh boy would they try! She heard every pickup line imaginable—twice—in one night. But every night she only went home with one man. Her hero. This macho Bad Boy who stood broad by the bar, only because he was secretly intimidated by the dance floor his girlfriend owned. When not with her, he would tear his Trans Am through the circuit, putting other racers to shame. To the kids who weren't old enough for the bars and dickered around outside The Alley, he was something of an idol. He was the Leader Of The Pack, a residential Rebel Without A Cause; taking the heat from the cops who dared stop a race (though it almost always ended in a brawl). Street cred meant everything.

Mom would occasionally join in on these diesel-fueled runs under the midnight sun, cheering him on from the passenger seat, shoving his arm and calling him "Jimbo the Bimbo!" A convoy of chrome, driven at dangerously illegal speeds, soared through the night. She would eventually fall asleep on his arm to the hum of the highway.

But then again, maybe not?

Maybe she was just another stupid bitch. Stupid enough to fall in love with someone who would eventually hit and hospitalize her daughter. And she was damn cruel enough to leave me alone with him.

There was so much I wanted to, but would never, like ever, find out. What color were her eyes? What did her voice sound like; was it high or low? Was it raspy like mine? How tall was she? At what age did she have to start buying tampons? Did she lose her virginity to Jim? Could she even fucking dance?

I collapsed my head into my hands. A sharp striking pain rippled through my face.

Would she have stepped in between my eye and Jim's hand? Would she have been strong and run away with me, despite the odds, so we would have been safe?

Teardrops fell, one and then another, onto the photograph.

"Why did you leave me?"

But as always, my question went unheard by the long-forgotten photograph. I heaved, bursting out a sob. But then quickly rolled my lips in and clasped my hand over my mouth so Jim wouldn't hear. My chest palpitated as if I were disciplining a laugh. But the longer I kept it all bottled up, the more the core of my chest rotted to black.

There I was, as I'd been my entire life. Waiting for someone who only existed in photographs. Wishing that somehow (some impossible way how) my mom would push open that bedroom door and come sit next to me on my bed and cry with me. And that somehow, she would find a way to be strong. Mom's voice would sound fragile, on the verge of cracking, yet she would remind me that everything would be okay as she brushed back my hair. Even if she didn't believe that—she would have told me anyway.

I cried for a while into my hands. Not daring to look up. Partly believing that if I were just sad enough—she would be standing there. Waiting at that opened bedroom door to come to me. To avoid being crushed, I remained facedown in my hands. Eventually, after the tears retired and I could breathe again, I steeled myself for the disappointment. But no matter how stupid and childish I knew that hope was, no matter how hard I tried to stay unbroken, a part of my heart still died when I looked up and saw that the bedroom door was still closed.

Act IV.

25

The Sound of Silence

MARY

"You look very pretty today," Nenita, my squat Hispanic co-worker, said to me. Though it sounded more like, *Yew luke var-ee prittee too-day.*

That was sweet. Sure. But I did not think that the patchy concealer rolled around with dried scabs, so it looked as if I had mold mushrooming on my face, was what I would've considered pretty. Nenita appeared fairly harmless though, so I smiled and said, "Thanks."

It was when my break came up at work, and I went out to the back of Wright Bros to munch on a sad-excuse for a sandwich, that Nenita bombarded me. Yes, Nenita was out back first muckin' on some funky stew-looking thing out of a Tupperware container, mind you. But still, she intruded on me.

I started using my fingers as a comb, channeling my emo days, to brush my hair over to the right side of my face in an attempt to curtain my black eye. Earlier that afternoon while getting ready for work I had this wondertastic (cuz wonderful and fantastic should sometimes be one word) idea to apply a gross amount of concealer to my eye, thinking that would make the bruise disappear. Instead, I got what looked like a blotchy surface of skin-colored makeup miserably disguising a scab. At least the purple had begun embrowning into a more delightful mustard-yellow color. An entire week had now gone by since I had a normal looking face.

It was slowly getting dark out, and between the blue clouds, strips of orange and pink filled out the sky. The color variety was impressive. Though thinking that way immediately made me feel sick with myself. A few weeks earlier, on some evening leaving Danny's house, he was so stupidly amazed at the most generic looking sky I'd ever seen. I hated him for it.

Out of the corner of my (good) eye, I noticed Nenita taking nervous little peeks at me. Which was mega weird. Then, after a few more bites of the funky stew, and a few more double-takes of me, she asked, "Do you have—boyfriend?" Nenita twisted the knife and then sprinkled salt in the wound. I shook my head and told her no.

"You're so pretty though!" Nenita squeaked and then giggled, covering her mouth with her hand. She went on to tell me: "You should have boyfriend."

Yew shude have boy-frend.

I hacked out the most forced laugh of my life, answered her romantic inquiries with "Maybe," and then broke eye-contact to further attend to my sandwich of white bread wonder.

No matter how softly I attempted to chew, it still sounded disgustingly loud. Ever since bearing witness to Danny's obnoxious, loud, open-mouthed, typical boy chomping, I had become incredibly self-conscious of making sure my own chewing was at least bearable. I hated eating with him. I missed him.

Still half concealed in the saran-wrap, I hauled that flavorless sandwich into the dumpster. It clanged when it hit the vacant steel bottom. Nenita shot a glance at the dumpster, and then back at me, looking stricken with betrayal as if she'd had a personal soft spot for that sandwich.

Fuck off, I thought as Nenita looked back at me.

I was certainly in RBF (Resting Bitch Face), and in response, she broke out into another squeamish giggle.

Now, it wasn't like discovering fondness for a mischievous child, cuz, y'know, some kids can be cute and stuff. But something about Nenita, whether it be her jet-black hair tugged into a ponytail bound with a bright blue scrunchie, or her orange Aeropostale T-shirt—which reminded me of McDonald's with Danny—made her grow on me like an adorably smug puppy.

"What are your plans tonight, Nenita?" I asked when my curiosity about this strange woman ignited. Nenita continued giggling and fanned her hand over her mouth again.

What is up with this woman? I thought. *Is she, like, nervous to talk to me?*

"I'm going to—next job," she said.

"You work two jobs?"

Nenita murmured with a nod, and then put up four fingers. "Four kids," she said and flicked her eyebrows.

"Do you have a husband?"

Her giggle went into turbo-mode as she shook her head. Everything she did was done with a hint of giggle behind it. My bafflement made me curious at the same time.

Was her nonexistent husband, like, funny?

The realization crept up on me that perhaps Nenita hid her mouth behind her hand, the same way I hid my eye behind my hair. For the rest of our conversation, I tried to see if there was something wrong with her dental work, but she had mastered a way of talking without ever showing her teeth.

Conversation ran to a sudden stop as Nenita and I had little to talk about, let alone the ability to communicate fluently in the same language. Nenita's phone started to ring and she reached into one of the plastic shopping bags by her feet and whipped out a silver flip-phone. Her tongue began rapid-firing a strange language that did not sound remotely close to what I recalled from ninth grade Spanish. Perplexed as hell, I tried to pick out the sounds that sounded Asian with a flamboyant enthusiasm that exaggerated the vowels.

Then pulling up in a deep heave of exhaust, the 6:30pm bus came to a stop across the street. Nenita said something in the phone that I assumed was Bye, then bent down to pick up her shopping bags that were tearing at the seams. Just as she began to hurry away, I said, "Nenita, you're not Spanish, are you?"

Giggling, looking down to hide her mouth because her hands were full, Nenita flicked her eyebrows, said, "Filipino" and continued her rush to the bus.

Nenita did a better job of concealing her mouth than I did my eye. And that was why I began to wonder, as I watched her bus pull up and watched Nenita waddle away, that if it was because of my eye that, for the first time ever, Nenita had decided to talk to me and call me prittee.

I continued to watch as Nenita struggled to scoot through the doors with her full plastic bags, and embark upon that empty-seated bus.

As the bus sighed and pulled away, I thought of an endless amount of questions I wanted to ask Nenita: What happened to her husband? Did he just pick up one day and leave without a trace? Did he die? Did Nenita, while chopping vegetables within the gray cinder-block walls of the storage room, also feel like she was in a timeless void?

I wish I had asked her what her second job was. With her half-broken, Filipino accented English, I doubted it was anything remotely glamorous.

If I quit Wright Bros tomorrow and went a week, two weeks, or even a month without work, life would obviously be shitty because I wouldn't have any of my own money of course. But I could still eat the crap Jim brought home. As long as I didn't ask about my mom, my eyes would remain intact.

I realized that if Nenita quit one of her jobs, for even just a day, her children would go hungry.

What I hated, absolutely hated about this messed up world, was that nobody really gave no shits 'bout whether or not you's gots a big heart or cared about your kids. It seemed to come down to: Are you attractive enough? Or, could your provided intelligence financially benefit me? For what was undoubtedly an overworked, and what brazenly appeared to be an unrewarding life, was it even possible for Nenita to ever go through a day without pertaining to the responsibilities of her employers or children? What if she wanted to go out on Friday nights, and go on dates, and feel loved and romanced and sexed like the rest of us?

"Have a nice day," I said, back up at my till after my break, and forcing a smile for the sake of the old lady buying her groceries. Avoiding The Bitch Voice at all costs.

"You too," she croaked and then grabbed the green plastic bag containing her margarine, small jar of Patterson Family apricot fruit jam, and baloney.

I watched her, out of utter fascination, as she shuffled out of Wright Bros. God, I never want to get old.

My inner philosopher came out (for some reason it always did when I was at work and bored AF, never when it really mattered) and I thought about how I had my useless high school diploma, at least, and if anything, I could speak good English. What did Nenita have? Aside from a big heart and clearly, an endless devotion to the four kids she worked every day for. Even if I got fired from Wright Bros, someone would give me another sort of decent job because—nail me to the cross—I'm pretty and white.

A bell—well, more like an electronic sensor—rang when I swung open the glass door of Ashley's 7/11. The bright lights in the store stung my fragile little eyes. It had been a week since I'd spoken to Nenita, and two since I had last seen Danny. And, oh, speaking of eyes—the bruise around mine had officially been reduced to a faint shade of yellow easily painted over. The scabbing had fallen off, leaving a pink patch of flesh in its place. Forever would I need concealer.

Hunched over at the counter, cradling her phone below her waist, Ashley was mid-text before she lifted her head and saw me.

"MARY!"

"Hey, Ash." I produced a smile.

"Where've you been?" she asked, before tacking on a series of questions that I answered with jagged half-truths and totally made up on the spot stories. Lester's cottage (God rest his soul), taking double-shifts at Wright Bros, a changed cellphone plan, and a ruse about apartment hunting in Atlantic City.

"Uh, yeah—might get a job at the, uh, one of the casino bars there. Good tips." My voice finally trailed off along with my God-awful story.

"You've been seeing someone?" Ash asked in a way that pried for the telling of my kisses.

"Yeah. Sort of."

"Sort of?"

Out of loyalty to girly habits, I almost leaned closer over the plastic countertop to tell Ashley everything. But then looking down at the smudges smeared above the lottery tickets, I thought better of it. Ashley didn't seem to mind socializing her forearms with the oiled fingerprints.

Story-time was postponed, however, when the electronic beeping went off and a customer limped through the door.

"I'm off in like five minutes—"

"Okay, we'll talk then."

"Okay! Let me just wait for Alan to get here. You know Alan, with the ponytail?"

I shook my head No, and then excused myself from the front of the empty line to let Ashley assist the limping dude looking to buy the "cheapest carton of cigarettes." I was impressed with Ashley's immediate recital: brand name and price, down to the tax.

I had already known Ashley knew her smokes. But it was the way she navigated the selection of cancer-sticks and variety items that got me. Despite her flighty nature, she even sounded unexpectedly responsible at her job. Which was a good thing. Ashley, patiently and, like, professionally, waited with a smile as the man scrounged around in his worn gray shorts for all the loose-change his pockets could possibly carry, and then kindly reminded him of the total when he asked.

Sitting on the curb outside of the 7/11, the blackened globs of gum that bespeckled the sidewalk kept my attention until the headlights of a green car pulled up. Out of the car came a flustered man draped in the same polyester 7/11 uniform Ashley wore, who sure enough, was rocking a ponytail. He marched straight past me, grumbling something under his breath, and barged into the store. Ashley came flying out about ten seconds later.

"Sorry, Alan was late," she said, hurling off her golf shirt.

"Oh. That's okay."

For a second, I was totally jealous of Ashley, until I assured myself it was a double pushup.

"So, Mary," she said, yanking a white tank from her bag and slipping it over her head. "I want to see you and, like, catch up and stuff, but—"

Distracted, Ashley broke off as she began rummaging through her purse. "I'm going to this bush party—" she popped out a cigarette, "—Do you have a light?"

Out of habit, I reached for my right pocket. I hadn't carried a lighter in weeks. Ash looked inconvenienced, and without a word, she spun back inside the 7/11 and purchased a small sized Bic. Sliding back out, ringing the sensor again, she recovered from her frustration with the lighting and inhaling of her first drag.

"So, Mary," she said again, with an outburst of smoke. "I obviously want to see you, but yeah, I'm going to that Winston party. Unless you wanna tag along?"

Moths hovered around the light above us.

"Yeah, I'll go," I said, watching them zip in and out of the light.

"You'll go?"

"Yeah."

("Bush Parties," for y'all not from Gilmore Park, are parties attended in the deep of the forest. Voila: a bush, and a party.)

"Okay." Ashley's smile was huge as she gleefully burst out, "I'm so excited to get you drunk!"

Honestly, I was excited to get myself drunk. Back in my prime, I had my alcohol tolerance calculated down to how many nights I had already drank that week. Now I had no clue. The last time I'd had anything to drink was, well, with Danny at the Winston Woods swimming pool.

Not before long, Ash began her bitchfest about her mom. According to legend, Ashley's mom, Diane, had come barging in her room earlier that day, bitching at Ashley for no reason. Making claims that Ashley didn't contribute to the household, which eventually tumbled into Diane blaming Ashley for why her life had ended up in "complete shit." The usual. I was tempted to interrupt and tell Ashley she should be thankful that she had a mom, but then Ashley would turn around and tell me to be thankful that I had a dad. So, we both sucked.

After the bitchfest, she asked again about the "guy I had a thing with," and once again, I nearly told her everything about my summer.

Right before I could, though, she asked, "Want a drag?" and held the smoke out (incredibly less sexier than I would have).

Danny had always strongly hinted that he did not like smoking, and once, even dared to list off every possible health risk smoking possessed. So for his sake, I just—stopped smoking.

But Danny wasn't in my life anymore.

"Sure," I said, and clipped my sexy fingers around the cigarette, put it to my lips, and coughed my life away. With my lungs on the verge of exploding, I passed the cigarette back to Ashley, who found this whole hack-attack hilarious.

Picking up on the obvious hint that I hadn't smoked in weeks, Ashley eased all my worries away when she told me, "You'll get used to it again," and pushed her palm out to imply that I should keep the smoke. The filter was ringed with Ashley's pink lip-gloss, but whatever. When the smoke rolled into my lungs for the second time, I did not cough. Voila: I was a born again smoker. Re-inviting cancer back on the list of "Possible Ways Mary is Going to Die."

When I finished Ashley's cigarette, it felt as though a new distance had just been placed between Danny and I. It was still kind of hard to believe that it had really been two weeks since I'd seen him last.

The ball was in my court. I know. I know. I was supposed to contact him; it was safer that way. And I had not forgotten his offer. It wasn't a bluff, and that's what made it scary. Him scary. Yes, I would be lying if I said I hadn't considered it for more than once. But, no. He had his life, I had mine, and they were to take separate paths. Give it a few more weeks, and out in California, living and enjoying his new life, Danny will have completely forgotten about me and be glad he didn't bring me. Never are we aware of the weight of the promises we make. But, whatever it was that we had, was over.

So, it wasn't until I took that cigarette, behaving in a way that didn't take his feelings into consideration, that I felt as if I had cut the invisible tie that still had us bound.

Even though it pissed me off because Ashley and Bass Player were still together, and we weren't, I was thankful that Bass Player and his boys showed up outside the store to get us, because, somehow, Ashley and I had run out of things to talk about. Over the summer, she had changed.

Although dealing with the whole lot of 'em at once was annoying as balls, they took me out of my thoughts and the sudden sinking in my chest I now felt every time I thought of Danny.

One of Bass Player's buddies was driving. I took the passenger seat; Bass Player and Ash took the back. He bothered her for a dart, and once again, Ashley reluctantly caved in, despite her claims of being "seriously out of money."

When I'd left my house earlier, looking for something to do, I had no intentions of going out. I just needed an out. And being out of the social media loop, I wasn't even slightly aware that there was a bush party going on.

After an exhausting minute of all Bass Player's buddies bantering back and forth about how "dickered" is a fucking stupid way of saying you're gonna get sloshed/shit faced/blitzed/wrecked/etc., the weak one who brought up dickered said to the guy driving, "Yo, do you know where…" he then looked down at his phone. "Nine-hundred and five Facer Street is?"

"How the fuck am I s'posed to know where fucking nine-hundred and five Facer Street is?"

"Fucking chill your nuts, bro. GPS it or some shit."

Ashley then piped up, "It's like, sorta by the West Atlantic plaza." Already having found the location on her phone.

Dickered Kid then said, "This kid's such a fuckin' tool. He just started trapping and doesn't even like properly scale his shit."

"What's he selling for?" Bass Player asked and then took a drag of Ashley's charity cigarette.

"I can get like, half an O off this kid for like a hundred bucks," Dickered Kid answered. "And if I burn with him, he won't even charge me shit."

Soon after (and after more arguing on directions) they pulled up at nine-hundred and five Facer Street.

"He says to meet him in the lot beside."

So they rolled up in the vacant lot beside. "I think he's coming." Dickered Kid said, and then a second later I heard the back door slide open.

"Mary?"

I turned around.

"Max?" I was dead-assed shocked. He looked absolutely terrible. His skinny ass had probably lost ten pounds since I'd seen him last, and he had deep pink bags under his eyes.

"What the fuck are you doing here? Shouldn't you be with California celebrating his birthday or some shit?" Max then turned to Dickered Kid. "So what you sayin'?"

"You just trappin' that chron?"

"Nah, fam. I got 'em Scooby snacks."

"Lit, bro."

Max and the Dickered Kid left the van to quickly make the exchange and then returned soon after.

"Mary," Max said, mantling his arms above the open door. "Give California a kiss for me."

"Wait, Max. Like, today is actually his birthday?"

"You betcha!" Max slapped his hand against the roof of the van. "Wait, how the hell do you not know? Is he not leaving tomorrow?"

"Tomorrow? What? Actually?" Out of the corner of my eye, I saw that everyone in the van looked askance. Jerking my head toward the window, I said, "Come here."

Bass Player grumbled under his breath, "Who the fuck they talking about?"

"I dunno," Ashley answered.

Rolling down the window as Max approached my side of the van, I said, "I thought Danny wasn't going to California?"

Max began snickering and then leaned his forearms on the door.

"What the hell do you mean he's not going to California?" Then as the thought crossed his mind, he said amusedly, "What? You two decided to play house and move in together?"

"He told you?"

Max backed off from the door. Looked away. Sneered. And then shaking his head said, "He didn't have to," and bolted towards his shitty BMX bike. Lifting the handles that were bent up against the ground, he hopped on, and then popped a wheelie before riding away.

"I told you guys," Dickered Kid said. "Kid's such a fucking tool."

26

Band on the Run

DANNY

The weeks that followed after I had last seen Mary were sparse in design. And the days of those weeks were surprisingly pleasant; a solid mask of blue draped the sky and a northerly wind rolled over the East Coast, winnowing the hazy gray humidity out from the atmosphere, keeping each day just on the knife's edge of cool. August's heat wave had crested and had begun to decline; September was about to descend upon Gilmore Park and its unsuspecting inhabitants. Including me. Although those weeks possessed a satirical sense of irony because I couldn't enjoy the blue skies I begged for all summer—because I spent those weeks hopelessly waiting for the phone to ring with her call.

The majority of my quiet hours those weeks were consumed with my hand poised atop the blue lines of my Lyric Book, waiting for the right words to spur endless scribbles of poetry across the page—and avoiding Mom at all costs.

Needless to say, Mom did not take to my decision all that well...

"What? Danny, what? What do you mean you're not going?"
"I told you what I said, Mom. I am not going to California."

"Danny—stop. No. We're not going through this again. You're already enrolled at LACM, *it's paid for*. I just finished finalizing the paperwork to secure my new job—no. Just, no. We are not doing this again."

"I had already called and revoked my acceptance, and we're getting refunded on nearly everything except the registration fees."

"Which were over five-hundred dollars."

"I'll pay you back—I have a lot saved up from the carwash."

"Danny—it's not about the money. I mean, my God! I'm not just getting a job at Wal-Mart. I'm moving into a salary position! We're planned to move—we're moving. That's it. I'll take not a word more of this bullshit."

"Ok, well, then as I was saying this entire time. You move!"

"How can you be doing this to me, Danny? You can't be doing this to me."

"Mom, I can't leave my friends! So I'm not going!"

"Danny! I know you care about your friends, but, like, I've begun listing our house!"

"WHAT? No! No you're not! Not this house!"

"We've talked about this!"

"I'm not letting you list this house! I'm not moving! I'm not leaving my friends. I'm not leaving this house. I'm going to be a legal adult and I want to stay here!"

"You're being so unfair to me and so insensitive. I can't even believe you."

"You're being insensitive!" I yelled back and then spun around to storm out of her room. Grabbing the edge of her door, determined on slamming it. But then realizing what I was about to succumb to, that taunting rage dwelling inside of me, my hand turned light as air and I let go. Channeling my anger into a guitar solo instead.

Mom and I had several discussions—arguments—such as that over the next few days. Two enormous hands took hold of my conscience and pulled me apart. I was terribly in the wrong by how I treated Mom. Of course I was being indubitably cruel, backing out at the eleventh hour. But, I couldn't leave Mary. Couldn't leave not knowing the outcome of her disposition.

Not a word of anything lyrically worthwhile came to me. But I somehow had invented an abundance of episodic titles like:

The Doomed and the Defeated, Ballad of the Broken Hearts, The Saints that Looked Like Sinners—and other titles in the same vein. I knew they were melodramatic—and yet no drama could compare.

Moving trucks came all week, taking only half of what was primordially set to leave. But the majority of boxes that had been piled up along the corridor of our house for months were now suddenly gone. Our cousins from Pittsburgh came that Sunday afternoon to pick up Mom's Jetta. It was weird.

There were mournful hugs and goodbyes—though we hardly ever saw them—and jokes made about how—now that'd I be on my own—I could bring back girls without troubling Mom, which only made me painfully think of Mary, but reaffirmed my stance.

They gave me a birthday card with a crisp twenty-dollar bill, which was nice enough, I guess, and then left soon after, happy to be in their new car.

After the Jetta had turned around the corner, off Eneleda Crescent, Mom glared at me with a piercing look of disproval. The jokes about my new bachelor pad angered her. And it was the worst kind of anger—the silent anger.

"Let's go get lunch," Mom finally said.

We went to a little panini restaurant downtown Gilmore that, in any major city, would've been packed on a summer's afternoon. Mom had gotten to know the owner through regular visits. The Italian momma that served us had opened the joint last spring with her husband, hoping the governor's alteration to the tax plan, and the Gilmore Park Gladiators fans pouring in there after games, would guarantee them some success.

But the city refused them parking space, and ever since, they've been involved in year-long negotiations with lawyers and were forced to close on afternoons they spent in court.

"Eggplant parmigiana," the Italian Momma said, placing a plate down in front of Mom. "Chicken pesto." Clinking my plate against the table before me. The emboldened afternoon sunlight permeated the large glass window we sat next to, working me up to an uncomfortable sweat as I ate the hot panini.

Nibbling most of our lunch in silence, Mom, after every few bites, would glance at me. It was not until our coffees arrived after our meal that we made any conversation.

Beginning with Mom asking me, "Is it really because of your friends?" Then took a cautious sip of her coffee, steam rising out of the flat brown surface. With my attention zoned in on the crumbs on my plate, not answering her, Mom continued. "Okay. This isn't one of your mood swings, is it?"

"No, Mom. I don't want to move."

"You are being very tenacious... so okay. Let's have a serious conversation then. How do you plan on earning an income?"

"What?"

"Well, I cannot afford to own two homes, Danny. You're going to be a homeowner, living on your own. So, just tell me, how do you plan to pay your taxes? Your utilities? You know? Hydro, gas, internet, phone bill—well, I suppose you don't need a landline, but your cellphone bill will be an additional expense. Oh! Can't forget about groceries. You'll go broke eating out every night."

I grunted and looked at Mom with a wry discomfort.

"And there's our home insurance plan. I mean, that could always be canceled, but Heaven Forbid the damages if we get hit with another hurricane.

"Danny, I'm not trying to patronize you. I'm treating your decision very seriously because, as you said, you're a legal adult now, so I'm not insouciant about this. Let's figure out how you're going to live. Perhaps you can teach guitar at the Gilmore Park Conservatory of Music."

Mom was obviously trying to push all the right buttons to persuade me out of staying home. She lifted her coffee and took a hearty sip, staring at me past the porcelain brim.

"Mom, I'm—I'm just not ready."

"Because of your friends?"

"Well—yes. Mom, I just can't leave. Not, not yet."

Mom turned to the window when the shrilling beeps of a construction truck going in reverse, carrying a mound of gravel in its crane, caught her attention. "Danny." She took another sip of her coffee. "As much as I like Mary, I don't know her well enough. Hence I am going to refrain from passing any judgment. But, yes, I'm worried about Max, too. Your main concern, Danny, should be him." A thought crossed Mom's mind. "Max hasn't been over all summer. When was the last time you saw him?"

"A... a few weeks ago."

"Explain?"

"Well, he's been a dick about things with me and Mary. And we fought. And I think he's been taking a lot of drugs."

Deadpanned. "You haven't."

"No, no. Of course not, Mom," I said defending myself, but really only deepened her concern.

Mom's jaw stiffened as she turned to look out the window. Her eyes began to lightly water.

I reached my hand out across the table and held hers.

"Mom?" She turned and met my eyes. "What if—what if I just stay home until I know he's alright?"

"And then what? You'll come to California... when?"

"After Thanksgiving? Christmas? I'm not sure, Mom. I don't

have to be in school, a lot of kids take a year off after high school. Just, I'm really in a position to make a difference."

"Danny, I know—I know kids move out. It's what happens. It was bound to happen. But… but to be so far and…" her voice thinned to silence.

Mom's fingernails scratched against the table as she clenched her hands into fists, resuming her composure. "Okay. I'll agree. But only if you promise that this is strictly to help Max and not to try to solve Mary's life. I'm sorry if I'm sounding harsh. But Danny, I don't think Mary's life—if her father's as mean as you told me—then I don't think her life is something that your intervention will fix."

"I know."

"So, I am to cancel your plane ticket?"

"You haven't done that yet?"

"Of course not," Mom said and laughed with tears. "If you were being thick-headed for any other reason than staying behind to help Max, my hot Latina/Italian blood would have smacked a dough-roller over your head and dragged you onto the airplane. But if this is—something—you need to do, in that case, start today, and it's imperative that you go to Max's and make amends. Even if you disagree with him. Invite him over for your birthday dinner. Maybe I'll get through to him."

When the Italian Momma came back with our bill, she informed us that the coffees were on the house.

But it was when Mom looked up and gave the Italian Momma a truly appreciative Thank You, I recognized her fortitude and realized all the sacrifices, both big and small, Mom had made for me. How throughout the years, she had to embody the roles of both Mom and Dad. Teaching me how to drive stick shift and shave, while also making sure that my little tummy was always full. Perhaps it's wrong to say, because unconditional love is something presumed between children and parents, but when I realized how remarkably strong my mother was, it had made me love her even more.

We had decided not to indulge in a dramatic goodbye before she was to depart for California, and I told her that I did not need anything extra or over the top for my eighteenth birthday. I told her I didn't even want a cake. Just chips and guacamole, our favorite movie—Before Sunrise—no tears, no nostalgia, just a mother and her son on an ordinary night, as if everything in our lives wasn't about to be uprooted. That was all I wanted.

The shadows lengthened on the pavement with the descent of the sun as I drove through Gilmore Park on my way to see Max.

With my hands hooked around the bottom of the steering wheel and my foot planted on the gas, I could feel the aching power of the engine thrum within the body of the car as I glided through the city that was my home. Its former pride, perhaps, still lived on in the bolstered ads running on the local news-stations. But as I panoramically surveyed the streets I drove down, all I saw around me was a dump of a community whose glory days had come and gone.

A busted-up orange and white construction sign lay toppled sideways on the shoulder of the road. And hanging off the sign by the few nails that left it intact, was a piece of plywood advertising the road's closure date: **APRIL 20-22.** Weatherworn litter and other assortments of trash were scattered in the ditches overgrown with weeds. And even the grass lining the broken-in concrete of the sidewalks was dug up in mounds, destroyed by the previous winter and untouched since.

A man with a prominent mustache, driving an electric scooter with his plaid shirt unbuttoned to expose his hairy potbelly, passed me in the bike lane before I crossed over the Delaware Road Bridge.

Hating my hometown for being my hometown wasn't enough. On top of Gilmore Park being that place where you had to watch the faces of familiar strangers grow old, there was a ubiquitous air of discomfort. Blaming it on hate was too easy. All you needed to do was look around. Driving by, I realized living in that dumpy town made me feel so angry because all around me was the omnipresence of degradation. It was a city of ruins that beamed neglect from every street corner to every crack. Worst of all, the people didn't seem to notice, be bothered by it, or even really give a shit.

A group of young people—because a certain sloppiness made their ages indiscernible—wearing pajama bottoms at the bus stop stared at me as I waited for a pedestrian traffic light. A barefoot girl with frazzled, red-dyed hair, caught my attention before I went through the green light and turned the corner to Max's. From top to bottom, she looked like a mess. It was obvious by her appearance that her life had been nothing but a wreck.

I was suddenly struck with a certain shallow realization about myself. Nothing in this world would have made me spin my car around, pull over, and give half a fuck if she needed a ride home.

Typical of my self-deprecating ways, I began to question my own morality. *Did I only care about Mary and her wreck of a life because I found her attractive?*

As my car rolled over the half-decayed and crumbled asphalt of the speed bump anchoring the entrance to Max's subdivision, I got funny looks from the neighbors.

Sitting in complete silence in their front yards in rickety lawn chairs, wearing MAKE AMERICA GREAT AGAIN baseball hats; equipped with a cigarette, or a can of beer, or both; they were ringing in an early Labor Day.

I felt like an entirely out-of-place asshole in my roofless car as I drove by. Thinking of how with my posture and windswept hair, and my skin glistening with the sun-tanned beauty teenagers adopt in the summertime, I might as well have been a visitor from another planet.

The doomed and the defeated, I thought, looking around.

But unlike the short stories of Greasers and Spanish harp

players and forgotten hometown heroes I wrote about, nothing significant, nothing special, had ever happened to these people. Lost jobs. Alcoholism. Drug addictions. The shards of a broken home cut too deeply in their souls. I don't need to apologize when I say their problems weren't special. They were tragedies told in tearful strides every night, everywhere, all over the world. A life of struggle had sunken all of their faces to look the same.

A dog barked to interrupt the silence. Maybe the only one brave enough to admit his dislike for the visitor they all had the right to hate. I was surprisingly nervous, feeling like a trespasser for trying to reach out to Max. I was stepping out of bounds.

When I got to Max's, his foster-parent, Lucille, answered.

"Not home."

I noticed a fresh scratch on the door when it slammed in my face. For a second, I thought about knocking again, but the chain of events that led to the End of the World had already been set in motion.

In the sky beyond the cars waiting at a red light, a limb of orange stretched through the clouds that were growing navy with night's ascent. To keep a tally of my losses, I looked at the clock on my dashboard. 8:05PM. The days were getting shorter.

While clicking my thumbs in a rhythm against the steering wheel, waiting for the light to change—and noticing the clock now read 8:06PM—a bro in a bright orange tank top across the intersection caught my attention. One too many bros like that took home in the state of New Jersey. There was a one-hundred percent likeliness that his tanktop had been purchased at some Carraway Beach T-shirt shop, and a one-hundred percent likeliness of also having something douchey written on it.

But next to the bro—I noticed the profile of a really hot girl in the passenger seat. And, for the first time in weeks, feeling like I now had the permission, I guess, to check a girl out, fucking depressed me. I wanted to feel guilty for looking at anyone other than her. But the sight of this girl excited me, as even in her ambiguity she totally looked my type. And so until she turned, so I could get a full look at her face, I unapologetically stared, checking her out.

Then the light turned green. And as I passed the car encasing my hot mystery girl, she finally looked forward. A lightning bolt blasted through me.

Mary.

Through the tint of the window, I could clearly see it was her. At first, I was stupefied with shock and excitement. Having forgotten how happy seeing her made me feel. But a sudden implosion of mind-warping jealousy wholly eclipsed my initial reaction when I put the equation together. Mary was with douche bro.

A deep-seated anger roused in me and strapped my mind into a one-tracked thought: *Mary is mine.*

My foot smashed the pedal to the floor gunning through the intersection.

I then raced alongside the median of the road—which lasted forever, until the hood of my car touched the end and I careened around it in a tire-burning U-turn, and charged down the road after them.

A minute later, I'd caught up three cars behind the van, and followed wherever it was going.

The wheel crushed beneath my grip. And though my head pounded with rage, my stomach felt hollow. In my gut was a deep uprooting of sadness.

Mary couldn't call me, but she could call up that douche?

Memories flashed in my mind. Replaying all the times I'd had with her. But the sum of it all was that I was the one who'd been there for her when she cried. Not that guy.

27

Smells Like Teen Spirit

MARY

Ashley gave me a Coors Light from some guy she had to hit on to obtain. I really, truly, did appreciate her soliciting her girly charms for a warm can of beer. The burn of tobacco on my tongue made the warm beer more enjoyable with every sip.

Ashley and Bass Player, who I had since remembered was named Cody, ran off to the woods to hookup.

So, sitting alone like a loser, a few drunk girls came up to me telling me how pretty they'd always thought I was, and asked if I'd take selfies and shots with them. When one of them (I didn't have a clue who any of them were) told me that, "This shit will seriously get you so fucked up," and spun the bottle, presenting the label for me to read—Birthday Cake Vodka—the stupid thought of stupid Danny, and how he was probably celebrating his birthday at home alone with his mom, entered my mind.

I gladly accepted the offer. So, like bitches, we snapped a few selfies, tongues out, duck lips, and all, and then downed that shit. I mean, free alcohol is free alcohol, right? Plus, I needed to forget him. Birthday Cake Vodka tasted as terrible as it sounds, inarguably worse than the warm Coors, but needless to say, after a few shots of that shit, I was drunk.

After parting from my new squad of girlfriends, Simon Jenkins, my ninth-grade ex, spotted me and flagged me over to him. He was ripping bong with a group of people over at a picnic table. We met in a weird one-arm-around-me-and-one-arm-holding-the-bong hug. He offered me a hit (I declined), but then, after realizing the thought had crossed my mind to call a cab and go to Danny's to say happy birthday or something gay, I accepted. My mind cleared out into a blissful smoky haven, and I started laughing my head off.

"That's some cream shit, eh?" Simon smirked, and then wrapped his arm around my legs and started rubbing my thigh. Putting my hands on him, trying to push myself away, I made sure to charm a cigarette out of his front pocket before I left.

I walked back to my picnic table and sat by myself. Holding the cigarette that I whored my upper thigh out to get, I patted down my pockets and checked my purse for a lighter. Remembering that, because of Stupid Danny (in my completely blitzed state of mind, Stupid Danny was all I would refer to him as), I didn't smoke. Telling myself that Stupid Danny had ruined my life, I got up to search for Ashley to use her lighter. Anyone that I saw holding an orange burning ember in front of their face could've sufficed, but I was convinced only Ashley had a lighter. I was sure that Cody came fast anyways.

Wandering, getting dizzy just looking through the crowd, I decided that I wasn't high enough. So, when I smelled the dank aroma of marijuana, I completely forgot about needing Ashley. The source of the scent was easy to find thanks to the nearby circle of guys all passing a joint.

Hmm, that's funny, I thought, *That guy with his 2004 styled baggy shorts and Devils jersey looks a lot like Tanner.*

And little to my surprise, and much to my disappointment, it was Tanner. Standing loyally by his side were Fat Jordan and Derbs, but there was a chick wrapped under Tanner's arm that I didn't recognize. My first reaction was to feel really sorry for her; she must have had a few screws missing to be with that guy. Did people feel that way about me when I was with him? Probably.

No matter how bad my itch for more weed was, no weed from Tanner was worth it. Telling myself that I was invisible, I avoided being recognized at all costs. I mean, the last time I'd seen the fucker I spat in his face.

As I spun in the opposite direction, back to my solo picnic table, deciding that another lighter would do just fine, I heard Fat Jordan grumble behind me. "Yo, man, is that Mary?"

The long wet grass slid across my ankles as I skidded, freezing into a standstill. In a sober state of mind, I would have just kept walking, but drunk and high Mary thought that if she froze they wouldn't notice her. But it was too late. I heard Tanner and Fat Jordan mumble something, and then Tanner said:

"Where's your queer boyfriend?"

Now, I get it. One would think that in the presence of a new girl-friend (side-hoe, hookup, whatever), you would leave your ex alone. Especially if the new hoe was a major downgrade. Like, bitches be crazy, right? You'd think she'd start punching his chest when he even dared to look at me.

"Huh, Mary?" Tanner said, and then his voice took on a sudden threatening tone. "I've been meaning to fuck that kid up."

All three of them, much taller than me, stared down as though I were the one they were about to beat up. Derbs, the only true tough one in the Crew, standing next to Tanner like a pillar, flexed his long arms locked at the elbows.

The Crew had been a nuisance in my life since the tenth grade. Always causing more shit than they were worth, always too friendly to make enemies with anyone they could. Derbie picking fights with kids from different high schools (for no reason), resulting in a season of someone getting hurt, someone's windows getting smashed, so the Impala getting keyed. One battle after another. From fifteen to nineteen, and easy to bet that well into and after their twenties, these guys would not change.

"I told you, Tanner, not to talk to me."

"I don't want to talk to your retarded ass. I just have a big wad of spit for your face."

"And I'll call the police."

"How was sleeping with some rich kid for money?" Tanner said, making the Crew laugh. In his high, slimy voice, Fat Jordan mumbled, "The rich bitch."

Tanner then continued, "You thought you were all top shit, huh? Now where is he? He got what he wanted and dumped your slutty ass? Serves you right for being a gold-digging whore."

In the younger days of one born with female genitalia, promiscuous accusations may be one of the most shocking and upsetting things you can hear. Then, you grow up and realize that men are actually just too dumb to think of anything else to say.

Tanner then abruptly broke away from the Crew and stomped up right in front of me. I then lunged out to the left, trying to get away, but he bolted to stand in my way, not allowing it. Every time I dashed to break away he continued to block my path, all the while reprehending me.

"Remember, Mary, no matter what you do in life, you're trash. Worthless trash, and you'll always be trash, like your fucked up family. I can't tell you how happy I am for getting the fuck away from your life. Go admit yourself and your dad to the same mental ward, you lunatic."

My neck muscles stiffened as I looked up and stared him right in the face. An overwhelming strength that could only have come from a determined drunk mind weighed any tears down. Tanner's face flickered with a hint of weakness. Maybe even he realized that any and all emotional power he'd once held over me was gone. His habit of provoking me via my family was getting old. He wasn't deserving of my spit in his face. I would never enable him to spit back at me, no matter how badly he wanted to.

Staring him deep in the eyes, giving him nothing; not a parcel of any emotion other than deep indifference, I lifted my hand up from my waist, softly landed my fingers on his chest, and then with a gentle force, pushed him aside. Compliantly stepping back, Tanner moved out of my way, and I walked forward. A self-satisfying glory pumped through me. No one, nothing, would ever break me again. It felt good knowing that somewhere along the way I had matured; I was stronger than before.

But then while marching away, from behind me, I heard his new girlfriend sneer.

"Mary?"

I spun around. Tanner had fallen back next to Fat Jordan and Derbs, and she had walked towards me, taking it into her hands now to confront me.

"Nice eye, bitch."

Now, this hoe was hardly a threat, but that took things too far. My cool drunken confidence began to wane, stifled by a hot rising fury inside of me. I had thought my eye was now unnoticeable. How could she even tell something was wrong with my eye? What was still wrong with my eye? On the edge of either crying or going crazy, I began to tremble with a rising of hysteria. Ready to explode.

If there was any benefit of having a father who terribly insulted me from time to time, it was that I had adopted a cruel ability to scope out the hidden insecurities of just about anyone, and then shamelessly bludgeon them to tears with their ugly truth.

"You're not gonna say anything, bitch?" she said with her face cocked, prepared to counter my insulting response.

A smile turned my lips, amused with my savagery, but then my wobbling drunk eyes steadied the image of this girl, and I saw her for more than her physical misfortunes, and saw her for who she was. Another broken girl with a broken life.

With the pudge of her mid-drift hanging out of her unflattering

T-shirt, and the grease in her thin, highlighted purple hair gleaming, it was clear that she was an uncanny basketcase.

And judging by her crooked nose and the scar cutting through her eyebrow, she looked as though she was no stranger to abuse.

So it made me sick with myself that her beaten-looking face was the source of humiliation I wanted to inflict upon her. That was hell, and I refused to use the fact that she had been on the receiving end of a brute hand against her.

Deciding that I would not give her the satisfaction of making any comeback at all, I walked away. Name-calling and taunting erupted behind me. Derbs might have even said, "Go kill yourself."

I didn't give them the satisfaction of turning back around.

Seconds later, I spotted Ashley at last. When she saw me walking towards her, she waved a finger up to Cody as if to say *one second*, and then stumbled a bit on her way toward me.

"Mary, what just happened with Tanner?"

"Nothing," I said, suppressing the muck of emotion in my gut. Waiting for the vodka to drown it out.

"You know, Tanner really wants to get back with you. Cody was telling me that you're all he talks about."

"That's great."

Ashley didn't seem recognize my indifference—or disgust, for that matter.

"Yeah, everyone was wondering where've you been all summer?"

Stupid Danny and his stupid ugly face came back to me as I nodded. "Just working a lot. Really. Nothing special."

"That's good Mary…" I could hear in her voice that her thoughts were really not all that concerned with where I'd been. "Okay, I've got to tell you something, but you have to promise you won't tell anyone."

Ashley usually had something she had to tell me that I couldn't tell anyone. This was really nothing new.

"Yeah, sure. What's up, Ash?"

I assumed she'd cheated on Cody. Cheating on boyfriends was also nothing new for Ashley. She looked left then right, before leaning in close to me. "I'm three weeks late."

The meaning and impact of the sentence had taken a three solid seconds before I registered what it meant.

"Oh my God... do you think you're—"

"I don't know." She looked down to the ground. Somewhere in the close distance some guys started chanting, "Drink! Drink! Drink!"

Ashley managed to say, "Just—" before her voice trembled and then took on an irritating whine. "Just I've been so busy and tight on money and, like, I don't even know why I said anything. It's probably nothing." She reached for a cigarette and lit it. "So, yeah, just forget I said anything."

I asked to borrow the lighter and Ashley handed it over. Just as I lit the cigarette, ready to discuss the dilemma further, someone shouted her name. She turned to me, saying, "Can you hold this for me?" Pressing a pint of vodka into my hands. "I'll be right back." And ran off.

DANNY

My spot-on prediction came true, unfortunately; the van turned down the side street that dipped into the Winston Woods Park. Undoubtedly, Mary was going to attend some variation of a Bush Party. I cringed at the idea.

To double make sure that I wasn't just following Mary and a group of strangers into the woods, I checked my newsfeed. All my suspicions were verified:

@_____TotsMichael
gonna get fucking bucked tn! Everyone cum to winnys wood

@itssSsarah_xx
aha @ _____TotsMichael ur such an idiot #cum

I parked my Mustang in the farthest, most secluded corner of the parking lot, mainly to separate myself from the potential misfortune of having some drunk jackass piss on the soft top. Sitting in my car with the engine off, an old familiar type of social anxiety kept me from letting go of my tight grip on the wheel. What did I even hope to see? Getting out of the car was sending my heart on a suicide mission. Finally, my restless curiosity got the better of me, and when I finally wandered out of the car, I was shocked to see that beyond the front gates of the park, it was pitch black.

Isn't it too early in the night for the swimming pool lights to be off?

Further down the mud and gravel lot, loitering by the green sign with Winston Woods mounted on in gold lettering, I saw some kids I recognized from high school doing God only knows what. Apparently, anything that could be associated with clear thinking did not have a parking spot that night; rationality must have kept on rolling down the highway because I decided to ask these bums, smoking or snorting or something, how to get to the bush party.

I had never before attended a Winston Woods bush party, believe it or not. Those frolics in the woods late at night, fueled by the stimulation of drugs and alcohol, were the epicenter of fun for the majority of kids that went to high school in Gilmore Park—other than the action at the McDonald's, of course.

So, I asked those bums how to get to the party, and none of them were intellectually adequate enough to give me a solid answer.

"You wanna go to your vagina."

"Then take a left at the dog park, and then go back right, and then go back left, and then go back right and then up the butt. Take the stairs."

The whole squadron of comedians laughed. Ah, boys. Good chuckles we had once shared, but your stupidity just made me hate you all that much more. I might be able to appreciate a good roast or some clever trolling, but that didn't make any sense.

So I nodded, thanking them, and followed the noise and the smell of campfire into the forest. From the path I chose to follow, I got a good solid view of the pool. The tall fence had been taken down, and a mountain of dirt filled the base of what was once my chlorine-steeped oasis. They were digging the pool out. Later I learned that the city could no longer afford to run it.

The path that the pioneers of woodland partying before me had carved was impossibly rigid and nonsensical; I almost had my eyes clawed out by a vicious low-hanging branch, and stubbed my toes more than once on an unsuspected burst of root.

Jared Piotrowski and Danielle Hartmann, the high school sweethearts, happened to be roving through the same path and let me tag along on their trek through the dense shrubbery.

Jared and Danielle first started inboxing each other in seventh grade and started dating in eighth. They attended every formal, junior prom, and senior prom together. It was nauseating.

Jared Piotrowski and I talked a bit as we walked; he and Danielle were both enrolled at Gilmore Park Community College. He was taking sports management, Danielle nursing. At last, we made it to the core of the party, said Bye, and parted ways.

I found myself standing in a small outlet in the forest, the gap in the trees just wide enough to host a bunch of drunks.

The cacophony of a hundred voices completely drowned out the crackling of the trashcan-raging fire in the center of the clearing, which had become the focal point for socializing. And other than the trashcan fire, the only other light came from the random bright flashes of cellphones, which almost always went accompanied with the high-pitched squealing of a girl as she recognized somebody she knew.

Come on, Becky, seeing Sarah isn't that exciting.

I waded through the dark clusters of people passing all around me. Every face either concealed by the night, or illuminated by the flickering orange flames, looking for Mary among them. Mindy Coleman meekly muttered, "Hey," when she turned around after my excited, but false, Mary recognition. It would've been easier if Mary had pink hair or something. A few feet away from me, a group began chanting as some jackass did a keg-stand or something else that apparently demanded the praise of united singsong like that.

Sauntering into clumps of people, intentionally goofy-footed to pass off my intrusions as drunkness, I kept my eyes open for Mary. Kids younger than me gave me looks that heavily implied, "Danny? That freak who wore band-tees and played guitar by himself outside the cafeteria? What's he doing here?"

With each step I lost some height. Over the summer with Mary I'd grown so tall.

Everyone was having fun. Everyone was drunk, if not stoned too. All I felt, though, was that I was being dragged back to a time I never wanted to go back to. Back to high school. Back to being all by myself. I had assumed the whole point of graduating was so I never had to see these stupid people ever again.

Cue the record scratch:

Wait… what? What am I even bothered about? I'm onstage—yeah—at the Troubadour at 9081 N Santa Monica Blvd in West Hollywood, California. Playing lead guitar for, the, um, the Electric Soul Revue, strumming a funk-inspired rift along the treble strings as the three-piece horn section lifts their instruments to shine in the stage-lights, responding to my music. Big Bobby Lewie suddenly steals the show to beat out a bongo-drum solo. The crowd goes wild.

Next, my bandmates, my friends, and I are out after having drinks, raving about how we killed the set. Some girls recognize me and say Hi. All three of them walk away with my number. The lights in the valley cascade up the hills and touch the night. Everyone is a dreamer. Everyone is an artist. Everyone came from a town full of losers. And even if you never hit the big-time stride, knowing, just knowing, that your night's unfolding on a street that a song has been written about, knowing that that bold, cut-out lettered sign—Hollywood—is peaking out somewhere, just obscured from your sight by the hills, means that you won. You won because you got out of your shitty small town called Gilmore Park or whatever place first came to your mind.

So what was I doing being bogged down and depressed by the lowbrow losers of New Jersey?

But wait! I thought. I have nothing to fear. I'm here, drunk, and I'm actually having a lot of fun. I smoked weed too, and I'm numb and out of my mind. I'm stumbling from one group to another, and everyone's really excited to see me.

Hey, Danny! Where have you been all summer, man?

I started spinning my head around on my neck, making myself dizzy, making myself so high. And—like I'd been doing my entire life—I found myself hiding my insecurity behind my imagination.

An incredibly hot blast of air made me look up. Wrapped up in my make-belief parade, I'd wandered a little too closely to the fire. Any closer and my face would've melted off. The underside of the branches glowed in the firelight and the bark of the trees took on an orange tone. My eyes followed the shadows striking intermittently against the tree-trunks until they fell off permanently into the glade.

Deciding that this was probably a total lost cause, that Mary at any given moment might be off getting taken advantage of in the woods, or, in the act of unorchestrated timing, she had left and we'd missed each other, I took a seat at a vacant picnic table next to the motionless body of Mitch Jergens lying on the grass.

I then watched as some guy I didn't recognize stumbled out of his huddle, spin the cap off a bottle, chug the whole thing, and then, without any hesitation, without any thoughts in his mind, whip the empty bottle into the thick of the woods.

And that was it for me.

What the hell am I doing?

I flat-palmed a mosquito that'd begun making love to my arm. I flicked the little bugger's corpse off of me and decided to leave the party.

This isn't my life, my world, anymore. I have California to go to. California. Mom. Oh shit. Mom! What was I thinking? What have I done? Was I throwing my future away for some girl who wants this to be her life? I offered Mary California. She didn't want to go, Danny. Accept that. Okay? She doesn't want what you want. Accept that and move on. But, No. I love Mary. And my house. Can't we keep the house? Can't we move, but keep the house? Come back and visit when we need to? Need to.

Walking away from the center of the party, with my head down between my hands, my wrists crushing the sides of my scalp, I looked up for a second to watch where I was going and saw Mary. Standing by herself.

"Mary!" I unthinkingly hollered her name and then staggered, about to run, but then stopped myself.

Mary looked over at me.

Her eyes then widened in that way they did when they were so bright they pushed back the night. "Danny!" she cried and then ran to meet me. Throwing her arms around me, Mary gushed, "Oh my God! You're here! You're here! I'm so happy that you're here! Happy birthday!"

A startled shock rang through my body. In the second Mary hugged me, I was mistrusting. If I touched her back, the spell would break. But then I felt the softness of her cheek against my neck, and breathed in the smell of her Beach Baby perfume. Irritation over what else she smelled like quickly came and went. Gentle acceptance besieged me. I was too happy to be holding her again. My hands fell uncertainly against her back, trying to remember how to hold her right.

"I've missed you," she whispered, the wetness of her lips moved on my ears.

My palm ran up across her shoulders, rolling over the straps of her tanktop, and then found a resting place on the back of her neck. I closed my eyes, and the world shut out. In a realm absent of sight, we were alone. A white aura blanketed us. Things were finally back to the way they ought to be, her and me. That was the last time, for a very long time to come, that the world felt right.

I peeked my eyes open and looked at the triangles of my elbows pointing out. The lightness of Mary's body fell suddenly heavy, requiring an energy I didn't have to hold her up. From over by the black mass of bodies, the flames of the trashcan-fire licked up high over the brim as the douche in the orange tanktop splashed kerosene in. *That's right. She came with him.* The waves of revelations pushed our bodies apart. We stared at each other. Not in a contest, no. Trying to figure out what had changed.

Not a word. Not a gesture. Nothing. Nothing but her lips bending to a frown, the quivering before crying.

Mary then reached into her purse and pulled out a bottle of vodka, taking a long, guzzling swig. And then ripping the bottle from her mouth, she pursed her wet lips, wincing as the taste barreled through her. A sudden paranoia crept over me, *Does she only care I'm here because she's drunk?*

I asked her, "How much have you drank?"

"I duntno?" she said irritably. "What do you care?"

"I am asking because I care?"

Then in a gesture of pure spite, Mary tipped the bottom of the bottle skyward again and chugged back an even larger amount. "Oh fuck," she groaned, wrapping her hands around her waist. I lunged back as her face twisted in a sour expression fighting back the impulse to vomit. She recovered a second later, and then looked up at me. "Stop judging the way I live my life. You've always judged me. You tried to change me so much, Danny."

"I never tried to change shit? Live however you want to."

"You always take shit so seriously. If I want to drink and have a cigarette now and then, it's not a big fucking deal. Stop acting like you're so perfect." Mary chugged back even more of the bottle.

"I'm not acting like—what? You're being an idiot. You know what—fine. Do whatever you want. To me, this isn't even you. You were different with me."

I had only spun around and took half a step away before Mary started again.

"See! You fucking liar, you don't care about me. You never cared about me. You fucking hurt me!"

"Jesus Christ, Mary! What the hell do you want me to say? If all the time with me you were secretly just wishing to drink and get fucking high and smoke cigarettes, that's fine with me! Okay? Sorry for wasting your summer."

"I'm not saying that's what I wanted."

"Then what the hell are you trying to say?"

"That you fucking put your hands on me! You almost hit me! Remember that? Stop acting so fucking righteous. Ever wonder why I never called you?"

"What? I never almost hit you? My God. I'm sorry for grabbing you, but, almost hit you? That's just bullshit."

But before Mary had a chance to reply, a sudden piercing scream cut off our argument.

"Max!" a girl cried. "Get the fuck away from me. We don't have anything."

Jolting my head towards the direction of the scream, I saw

Max frantically scuttling around the girl we'd stolen the street sign for. Roxanne.

"But I got that street sign for you! Like you wanted!"

"Max!" I shouted. "Hey, Max!" I then looked at Mary. The tone of her eyes changed, as if understanding. Kicking back my feet, I dashed toward him, closing the gap between us. Hoping to distract Max before he caused a scene that to an onlooker would have certainly looked like sexual harassment.

Running, I yelled, "Let her go!" and grabbed him by the arm. His drawstring backpack swung around his body, hitting my thigh as I struggled to hold him back.

"You're a slut, Roxanne! A stupid slut!" he screamed, and then shoved his free fingers under my grip to wrench himself away.

Whipping my other hand around I trapped his arms at his sides. "Max! Calm the fuck down!" As I forcibly held Max from behind, Roxanne and I caught eyes; her expression was petrified, as if she were afraid of me too. I was swamped with embarrassment. Here we were, two losers who had grown up to be bigger losers, desperately pleading after uninterested girls at the same party.

"Get your fucking hands off me, Danny!" Max snapped, throwing his weight forward and breaking away. The six-pack of beer hooked in his fingers swung around. "What do you even care? You're with her." He jerked his head in Mary's direction. "Why would you care about anything else?" Spit shot from his lips as he continued to yell. "I was there for you for years and then she comes along, and that's enough to leave me homeless and move her in with you?"

"Move her in? How—what are you talking about?"

"Oh, don't fuck with me, Danny. You've got this big empty house all to yourself, and you're going to move in some fucking broad and not me, your brother?"

"Max, I don't know what the hell you're talking about."

"Shut the fuck up, Danny. You have the fucking nerve to use my shit in the beach house and leave your white fucking cum stains everywhere, and can't even help me out?"

Lowering my voice, I did my best to sound calm. "Max, don't start." Knowing he was out of his mind. We were a couple of outsiders dragging our drama into a party meant for everyone else, all of who still seemed to be having fun, oblivious to the rising feud between myself and the two people who mattered the most to me. Coming from Mary's direction, I felt a penetrating beam of tension. Knowing she was standing still, momentarily suspended from our argument. I worried that if the battle with Max dragged on too long, I would lose her.

"Why?" Max then shouted in my face, clearly having no intention of matching the tone I'd set. He staggered so close toward me that his forehead grazed mine.

Quickly stealing a glance at Mary, I said to Max, "Let's talk about this someplace else." And took a step back.

"Is it 'cause Mary's here?" He lurched back in my face. "She's gonna be moving in with you, so why does that matter? Can't she see you be a bitch?"

The circling of Max's torso seemed to wrap and bind my ability to think. The veins under his wrists thickened as his fists grew red.

Irritated by my lack of response, Max said, "Huh, Danny? Come on, do something about this."

And slapped my face, cutting my mouth on my teeth.

"Come on, Danny, care a little bit!" He then hit me again and again.

From the background, Mary came charging up, pushing her arms between us as she yelled, "Max! Stop!"

Max then spun around and drove his hands into Mary's chest, screaming "SHUT UP SLUT!" as she splashed onto the ground.

The commotion from the rest of the party instantly died. Our outsider affair became public. We were fully clothed, yet naked under the stares of a hundred pairs of eyes; exposed to a thousand soundless judgments. Slowly, the crowd retreated further away. The air around us was infected.

Sliding back her arms to lean up on her elbows, Mary stared at me from the ground.

Right away I knew any redemption between us was dead; Max's hands may as well should have been mine. And aside from the death of our relationship, Mary certainly wasn't looking to be ostracized by her peers as one of us outsiders. But she would recover.

Max, on the other hand, looked mortified. With his jaw dropped open, it was easy for me to see what was racing through his mind. Throughout high school, he'd made vain clutches at popularity in the hopes of being widely accepted. Though, for whatever reason, be it the details of his home life that had leaked out, or the transparency of his degraded, second-hand clothes, it never happened. He never got the girls he liked, never properly belonged to any group of friends, or went to anyone's house without their parents wondering where he came from. So, all in that silent second, that had lasted only a heartbeat before murmurs arose, I could see in Max's face that he believed he'd lost it all.

Dropping the case of beer Max ran into the forest. I screamed after him. But it was Mary who yelled, "Danny! Go!"

Flinching, then following her advice, I sprinted off into the thick of the forest after Max. I tore through the trees after him and ran full-on into the ravine that opened beneath me like a chasm into the underworld.

The night transformed the forest into an unforgiving, thorn-ridden slaughterhouse. Neither of us were ever the athletic type, but I was gaining ground. Focusing my attention on how Max maneuvered through the shapeless woods, I didn't notice the massive root about to collide with my foot.

Tumbling towards the ground, I flung my forearms before my face and scraped through the undergrowth and got plastered in mud. The muck overflowed between my fingers as I forced the ground back, then getting up on my feet, I regained my stride. Max wasn't much further ahead.

Immediately almost falling again, I saved myself by latching onto, and ripping my hands through, the thorny stems of the thicket. Then in my bouncing, jagged sight, I watched Max brutally wipeout and heard the terrible crack of the fallen branches snapping beneath his weight. He howled in great pain and then got up and kept running.

I could only barely see the outline of the trees and thorn bushes ahead before I dashed between them. Having to decide in split-seconds how to wrap myself around the limbs that twisted from the dark earth. My chest burned. My breaths drew in shallower. But I couldn't stop because Max wasn't slowing down.

We came upon another decline of the ravine. Ahead, I watched Max plummet onto the leaf-shrouded floor and slide down the slope, caking his jeans in mud. I shimmied my steps, fighting to keep my balance, but then the broad side of my foot rolled beneath my ankle on a plot of mud. I cried in pain. Max got up after sliding down the hill on his butt, and charged on. And so I kept on running after him, terrified for my ankle with every step.

The ravine ended abruptly in a deep ditch with a running stream that I watched Max leap. Save his fall by latching onto a thin tree. And then propel himself upwards to begin climbing the opposite slope. Following the same strategy, I leaped over the ditch and started the climb.

Back on the flat ground, the forest gave way to a chalky surface that housed a railway bed of gray and white stones, surrounding a set of train tracks cutting a tunnel through the woods.

I then watched as Max jammed his foot into a half-hollowed block of wood, fall face first, and then skid across the gray and white stones. Out from his backpack a black object struck through the air and landed just a few feet in front of him on the bronzed tracks.

Mid-sprint, I slid to a sudden stop. My breath came out in bursts. Max pushed himself up and jumped onto the tracks to nab the black object that I, in one split-second saw, and determined to be a gun.

"Max!" I wheezed, horror dawning on me. "What's that?"

He shoved the gun back into his bag. "I hate you, Danny," he said. His forearms chalky and bleeding.

"Why do you have a gun?" I yelled. I could have collapsed. I didn't know the thumping in my head from the grumble of the approaching train. "MAX! Why do you have a gun?"

First, he twitched, and it seemed as if he was going to refuse to answer, but then, unpredictably, he snapped.

"You have everything so perfect!" He screamed, dropping his posture on the outburst. "You have—" he stomped his foot. "—No idea what I'm going through!"

"Everyone has shit they have to go through."

"What could you possibly have to go through that's so bad?" Max shouted.

"Stop."

"Huh?" He lunged towards me. "Tell me, Danny!" He shoved me. I staggered backwards.

"I wasn't born with a future," he said, shoving me again. "I'm not going to school—" He pushed me once more. "I have no job—no money!" Then wounding his arms up, Max screamed, "No family!" as he drove his hands into me with the entire weight of his body. My legs kicked in the fight against gravity, but then I landed the ball of my foot on a hard stone and fell back. I threw my arms behind me to take the impact of the landing.

"Do you have any idea what it's like not having a family?"

"DO YOU HAVE ANY IDEA WHAT IT'S LIKE LOSING ONE?"

Only my faint echo answered my words. Soon, everything was silent, except for the muted rumble of the forthcoming train. "Okay, man?" I said, cutting the stillness. "I'm trying. I'm really fucking trying."

The stones beneath our feet started shivering.

"Then how do you always have your shit together?" Max's aggression retreated to a desperate inquisition. The stones shook like we were moments from an earthquake.

"Because," I began, "I was sad and lonely, for way too long." I dropped my arms. "And crying doesn't change a thing."

The lights from the train began washing Max out. We were too close to the tracks.

"Move," I said, and took a step aside, assuming he would follow my lead. Instead, he stepped inside of the track, straddling the rail.

"No," he answered.

"Max, you're going to get fucking hit. Max! Move!"

He smirked.

"MAX! MOVE!"

I couldn't see anything but the blackness of his pupils. The train blasted its horn in a haunting clamorous mourn as it roared towards us. Max closed his eyes.

In just one second, the world perished into a white washing light and a boy standing on the tracks and the scream of a train and the blink of an eye between life and death. Without thinking, I dashed forward and tackled him to the ground, away from the tracks.

A jagged stone pierced my leg as we rolled atop the railway bed. And before coming to a stop, I had to throw my elbow out of the way of Max's stomach, crashing it against the ground with an impact that shattered through my arm.

Fighting through the jackhammering in my elbow, I kept Max pinned down to the rocks. The force of the charging train racked the air. I cowered my head into my chest in fear. Not believing that those tracks could contain such vehemence.

A moment later, the train passed, leaving a trail of absence behind. The crickets were loud again.

I crawled backward off of Max. I reached for where I was certain the stone had cut through my jeans. No blood, thankfully. Back on my feet, I watched Max lift himself up. Coming to sit on his knees, he rested his hands on his thighs, and then spread his bloodied and mottled forearms apart.

With his head hung, Max said, "God damn. I wish I could've pushed you into that train, Danny."

Through a heavy breath, I asked, "Would've that made everything better?" He didn't respond. "Tell me, Max," I gasped. "Would have that made everything better?

Still no response.

"Yeah? Max? Yeah? When I'm the one trying to fucking help you? Just push me into a fucking train? Would've that made you happy?" I continued lashing out. "I'm sick of always trying to fucking help you through your shit! I was gonna stay behind and not go to California for you! But figure your own shit out for now on! Alright, Max? Then that way you won't have to blame me anymore! Okay, Max? C'mon answer me. Okay, Max? OKAY MAX?"

He stood up.

"SHUT UP! Shut up! Shut up! SHUT UP!" he yelled, scraping the top of his lungs, sobering my hot temper cold.

Then like a child in a tantrum, Max yanked off his shoe and threw it. Making a thud upon hitting the ground. Saliva slung out from the sides of his mouth as he turned and then screamed into the black.

After, he collapsed to the ground, landing on his knees. The tears streaming from his eyes cut through the dried mud on his face.

I stood there and stared at the once charismatic and energetic kid I'd grown up with, and felt sunk as I looked piteously upon the broken, deeply troubled, and lost orphan I now saw before me. I walked in the direction of Max's shoe, trying to figure out what was worse: having a widowed parent, an abusive parent, or no parents at all. I saw the shoe in the grass. Knelt down to pick it up. And then walked back towards him.

"Come on," I said, crouching down beside him, holding my hand out. "The ground's cold. Come on."

28

Telephone Line

DANNY

Max and I walked in silence back along the tracks, taking the longer, but actually established path through the forest this time. Groaning as our injuries caught up to us. The walk instantly made me think of all our childhood exploits—making fires and blowing up hairspray bottles, or the time we were certain we were going to build a full-on log cabin in the forest. We had the first four straps of plywood nailed together, but then construction stopped when girls became more important, I think. It seemed like our friendship was built in the forest.

By the time we made it all the way back around to the entrance of Winston Woods, the flock of cars had left. Only my Mustang sat in the far corner, and when inspected, it did not appear to be vandalized.

"Who'd you come here with?" Max asked.

"Myself," I said, unlocking the doors. "You?"

"Same."

We drove in silence. Grotesque shadows cast from the orange streetlights leaped across my car. Between Max's legs sat his backpack. His gun. I felt like a felon. A splitting, gut-wrenching nausea leaked from the pit of my stomach. My fear of getting caught was so loud inside of me that I was convinced anyone with a sharp sense of intuition could feel it radiating through the shock-waves of my pulse.

While sitting at one of the many, many traffic lights Gilmore Park hosted, a black police car pulled up behind us. I looked over at Max's bag. The cop stayed behind us for several more lights until, as if on cue—guess my fear really was being broadcast to the world—the whirling array of police lights beamed in my mirrors. Max and I looked at each other; the dried sweat on his skin took on a purple glow in the collision of red and blue lights. "Bro, bro. Cops need a warrant to check shit. If he asks to search your car, say no."

I immediately pulled over, hoping that my obedience would obliterate any of the cop's suspicions.

"License and registration," the cop said as he approached my window. He then took a closer look at me. "Why is your head bleeding?"

My eyes shot to the rearview mirror. The cop was right. I had a nice gash of blood running down from my forehead to the side of my nose. Behind me, Max feverishly grinded his teeth.

"I, uh—" I stumbled to answer. All my years of make-believe and storytelling had been put on the spot. The test was now. "Family party. My younger, baby cousin, um, was very aggressive. You know kids, right?"

I grinned larger than my face. The cop didn't seem to buy it. Firm-mouthed and menacing, he looked at Max for confirmation. He then looked back at me. Max was drunk and had a gun (and yup, a shit ton of drugs). The cop proceeded to ask us more questions, starting with how we were related. Max began to say, "We're broth—" at the same time I blurted, "Friends."

"License and registration." He didn't so much ask but had commanded. I leaned over to the glove box, over Max's gun-filled bag, pushed through the papers, shoving back Mary and I's road trip map, and pulled out my registration. Digging out my license from my wallet, I handed both to the officer.

"Whose vehicle is this?" he asked.

"My dad's, sir."

Which wasn't technically the correct answer. It was under Mom's name. The cop took my paperwork and returned to his vehicle. Max and I sat without looking at each other. The embarrassing exaggeration of the cop lights still spun behind us. I wished he'd turn them off. By the time he returned to my car for further interrogation, he had got a call on his radio, and so simply handed me back my license and registration, and drove off.

Not long after, we were on the poor side of town and rolling over the speed bump into Max's townhouse complex. Then idling in the parking space beside the dumpster next to his house, the radio on low, the headlights bounced off the wooden fence back into the car. The engine rumbled. Both of us looking for some sort of truce, but neither of us spoke. As I inched the radio knob, trying to find something tolerable to listen to, landing on U2's "Stuck in a Moment You Can't Get Out Of," Max spoke up.

"Danny, promise me you'll go to California."

"What?" I asked, silencing the volume. "Where's this coming from?"

"What you said, bro. 'Bout not going. Just promise me you'll get outta here. I know how much you hate this place. Okay? Don't stay behind for me or Mary. Just get the fuck out of this shit town. What did you always used to say? You were gonna Eric Button it outta here?"

"Eric Burdon it outta here." Correcting him. "But Max—I don't want to go. Not yet, anyways."

"Danny, why the fuck don't you want to go to California?"

"Man, I've been trying to call you about it. I've been trying to tell you to move in with me. My mom wants you to as well."

Max's mouth twitched in and out of a smile as he said, "W-wait—what? Seriously, bro? Like, you're not fucking with me?"

"Wh—*Why*—Max, why would I be fucking with you?"

"But, I thought—Mary said that you asked her to move in with you?"

"When'd you talk to Mary?"

"I, um ah, earlier. At the party."

"Well, yeah, bro. Like, if both of you could, then that'd be cool. But it's like, whatever about her. I just—just—care about making sure you're alright." I said, and then looking over, I noticed Max was sweating profusely.

I don't know a lot about drugs. I've only tried weed twice. The first time I didn't even get high, and the second, I tried listening to Jimi Hendrix's *Are You Experienced* and fell asleep during "Hey Joe" with my hand buried deep in an empty bag of Tostito's. But from what I knew of hard drugs—Max was on 'em.

I then drew in a breath in anticipation for what I had to say next. "Now, I'm going to take that gun—"

Max's eyes grew wild as he clutched the backpack to his chest, like a child guarding a toy he refused to share. "No."

"Max—"

"It's a friend's. I gotta give it back." We made eye contact for the first time since the train tracks. The up-close clarity of the reflecting headlights exposed the indented pink swoop carved out beneath his eyes. Red veins clawed through the glossed-over whites. The deprivation of his eyes spoke to my own drowsiness, and suddenly I wanted to sleep to cure us both of our sick, sick tiredness.

Endowing my trust into Max, not wanting to argue anymore, I said, "Okay. I trust you." And sincerely hoped I believed it. "Tonight's been a little too much for me. I'll see you tomorrow and we'll figure out how you're gonna move in with me. Alright?"

His largely dilated pupils honed in on the windshield. The

brightness illuminated the thin hazel rings his irises had become. And then, without warning, Max's hand shot inside the bag. I feared for my life. Though it wasn't the gun he pulled out.

Max cracked the lid on a vial and a rush of white pills poured into his palm before he collapsed his hand over his mouth.

"MAX!"

Several pills tumbled out from the sides of his mouth, falling onto his lap and then onto the floor. Max then dove his hand back into his bag, withdrew a bottle of whiskey, ripped the cap off, and started chugging. Washing down the drugs.

"Hey! Hey! Max! What the hell are you doing?"

I swatted my hands at him to get the bottle. Max dodged out of reach by tilting his head back, pounding down the liquor. Waves swashed back and forth inside the glass bottle as it drained into his mouth in loud gurgles. Jolting my body over the seats, I swung my hands at him, but once again, he twisted out of the way.

"Max, fucking stop!"

With the rear of the bottle facing the corner of the seatbelt, the alcohol gushed out over his lips, over his chin, and onto the seat.

Slashing out my forearm, I struck his chest, knocking the bottle away from his mouth. Whiskey erupted and splashed out all over his shirt. Max whipped the bottle back to his lips and drained what was left. Max then squeezed his face tightly in his hands and hunched over. Groaning painfully like a fist had landed deep and hard in his gut.

With his lips peeling up off his gums, Max looked at me.

"What the fuck was that? What the fuck was that? What fucking drugs did you just take?"

Hiccupping, he then said, "It was just melatonin, bro. I want, ah, fuckin—" Max started stuttering. "I— j—us' need tew fuc-gin' sleep, maann. I jus' need tew sleep. You—You're aye, ah good fr— end an' shit. You c—are, man. You actually fucking care. So thanks."

"You swear that was just fucking melatonin?"

"Yeeahh maann."

Max then belched. Shaking his head as the roar of alcohol hit him once again. Then grabbing his bag, he bolted open the door, and stumbled out of my car. Slinging his backpack around his shoulders, Max fell forward in the momentum, caught himself on his knees, and then moaned again as he straightened.

"Max. Wait."

I got out of the car. He looked at me, his face bent in pain. I rounded the car, my body eclipsing the dual-sphered glow of each headlight as I crossed them, and then stopping in front of Max, digging my gaze deep within his eyes, I hugged him.

At first, he stayed stiff. But as I held him tighter, not letting him go, the tension strapping his body eased, and then he wrapped his arms around mine. Then we were both holding onto each other tight. When we finally let go, he smiled, and I smiled.

The clacking from the overheating engine grew louder from behind me as I supervised Max's drunken stagger to his townhouse. With his knees spontaneously collapsing and then straightening in his stupor, and hiccupping rapidly, wheezing in air, I kept an eye on my drunken friend until his hand wrapped the railing, and he dragged his feet up the steep concrete steps.

Upon reaching the door, Max tipped his forehead against the screen and moaned, "*Ugh*, I'm so fuh—fucking drunk."

I couldn't help but laugh. But once assured he was all right, I turned around and walked back through the weightless night to my car. Sighing on the impact of the door, I thanked God for getting me through the evening.

Through the passenger window, I saw that Max was still leaning against the screen. Figuring I'd wait until he went inside, I spun the volume back up on the radio to ELO's "Telephone Line."

Out of the corner of my eye, I saw one of his sleeping pills on the seat.

I looked back out the window.

Max's ribcage was rapidly expanding and collapsing.

Curious, I clipped the pill between my fingers. Held it up. Brought it into the light. And then read the word inscribed in the white coating. Xanax.

That's not how you spell melatonin.

I bolted out of the car.

"MAX!"

"DANNY!" He wailed. "It hurts so much! My head hurts so much!"

He lifted the gun from below his waist and rested the barrel directly against his temple.

"Max—Max! Just drop the gun. Just drop the gun and come here." Terrified to get close, that a sudden erratic action might just end my life.

Desperately wheezing in a breath, he then blubbered in the terrible way in which grown men cry, "Make it go away, Danny!" He cried harder. "Make it go away. Make it go away Danny! *Make it go away!*"

Max fought for a breath then his head crashed into the screen. Throwing his arms out against the door, trying to save himself, he tipped over and his jutted elbow smacked against the brick wall, setting the gun off, and then falling backwards onto the steps, his skull thumped down each concrete block before his body landed and skidded out onto the road.

29

Any Old Kind of Day

DANNY

It started with a horrifying scream. Then there were people and then there were sirens. And then there were people, sirens, and lights. Then there was a woman crying. Then there were children crying. Then there was vomit. Then Lucille collapsed in hysteria. Then there was a stretcher. Then Max and I were thirteen and riding our bikes and exploring the forest. Then we were talking about girls. Then there was blood-soaked linen. Then we were deep in the forest and nailing together our log cabin. Then there was the smell of diesel. Then there were more sirens. Then we got into a fight over trading cards. Then there was a hand on my shoulder and words spoken to me. I nodded. The crying continued. Then we made up from that fight over trading cards. The crying stopped. I kept on nodding. We then began high school together. Then the crowd left and then the people went inside. I was tired. Then Mom was taking pictures of us at grad. Then there was my parked car. Then what was, wasn't anymore. I was exhausted. There was nothing left but the night. Then the black gave way to navy, and navy gave way to blue, and blue gave way to the sun.

Then I was driving home and passing people driving to work.

And then the rest of the world woke up and went on like it did any other day.

Then I parked in my driveway.

Then I opened the front door.

And then I saw my birthday cake encircled with eighteen unlit candles.

Then I realized Mom had left.

Then what was, wasn't anymore.

Then I gushed with tears.

Then I begged to a God I hoped existed that I would stop feeling. I prayed I had died too.

Then God reminded me that we only prayed when we needed something, and turned his back.

When I eventually collected myself up off the floor, I was certain that had all been a nightmare. Although, I wished that the delirium after emerging from the blackout lasted a little longer upon waking than it had, because the tsunami of reality broke me back down. Tragedy punished its disbelievers.

I didn't know when I'd gotten home, or how long I'd slept for, but judging by the light shining through the windows like illuminated mosaics in a church, highlighting the dust hovering around— I determined that it had to be some point in the late afternoon. On the counter by the front door, I saw my phone. Exactly one hundred missed calls from Mom. I walked into the kitchen, and it looked too familiar.

The windows should've borne scars of shattered glass, and the cabinets broken and left in wooden scatterings on the floor. The world should have been engulfed in flames, been destroyed, torn apart by war.

But no. Everything looked as if it could've been any old kind of day:

"Danny!" Mom would call out from the living room. "Max is at the door!" I would run to the front door, too excited to only be greeting a friend.

"Yo, Max!"

"Hey, Danny."

"Let me go grab my bike. I'll be like two seconds." I would turn my head in the direction of the living room and shout: "OKAY, MOM, I'm going out now!"

Mom would shout back: "You boys better wear helmets!"

But we never wore our helmets because we couldn't die.

My eyes scanned the kitchen. All too easily I could envision it. How effortlessly my legs could collapse so I would fall headfirst into the gloriously pointed edge of the kitchen table. Jabbing deep into my temple. Relieving me from this exhaustion.

I noticed a note on the table:

Danny,

I guess you got caught up with your friends last night. That's okay!

I understand!! I'd already arranged to have Tracey Young and her husband from down the street drive me to the airport anyways. I'll call you when I land in California. I love you, Danny! xox

PS. YOU BETTER PICK UP YOUR PHONE WHEN I CALL, YOU BRAT!

PSS. I did some research and there's an organization by the name Age-Out Angels. They help kids transition out of foster care. I want you and Max to look into it.

I reached for my phone and called Mom. It went straight to her voicemail. I wanted to—no, I needed to talk to someone. Anyone. But as I'd told Mary, I only talk to three—two—people, and one of them wasn't answering. The other couldn't. That was when it hit me. I was alone.

The clouds and the sun took turns sharing the afternoon sky. I sat on the front steps of my house, clutching Mom's letter in my hands, watching the clouds and their corresponding shadows drift by. Looking up, I saw the leaves flutter in the wind; struggling valiantly to hold onto their hue, but summer's green was already giving way to autumn's gold. Somehow I found the strength to move and went back inside.

On my walk up the stairs, I took a moment to stop and stare at Connor's picture on the wall. Looking at him with his big brown eyes and closed-mouth smile, I missed my older brother all over again with a renewed and deepened sadness I didn't know was possible. He couldn't have been any older than nine years old in that photo. And yet, somehow, now I was older than him. It crashed in my head. It didn't make sense. It couldn't make sense. He wouldn't even recognize me anymore. Connor kept his eyes locked with mine. His beautiful, childlike expression of innocence transformed to one of scorn. He was disappointed with me; I'd let him down.

Plagued with regret, I walked up the rest of the stairs.

And then, as I pushed open my bedroom door, I saw it, lying flat on my bed. The photo album Mom had been working on before she left. The plastic cover creaked as I lifted it open. Written in cursive in the center of the first blank page, Mom had penned an inscription.

Nothing Will Take My Sons,
My Sunshines Away.

And here I thought I was the family poet. What family?

Sinking to the floor, I flipped the pages and laughed while I cried. There was a picture of me and Connor in front of the TV as I sat on a training-potty in, yes, a cowboy hat. What was I doing wearing that thing? I laughed, not at my innocence but with it— Goddamn I missed that little kid in the cowboy hat. I missed him so much; I was jealous of him. And then after peeling back a couple more pages, I saw Dad holding me and lost it. I hadn't cried so much since they'd died. I was sick of losing people to photographs.

Once my eyes lightened after losing the weight of all the tears, I lifted my head and looked around my bedroom. So much of my life I kept embodied in the past. The marker etches on the floor, the posters on my walls. Even my record collection only housed the names of the departed:

John Lennon. Michael Jackson. Harry Chapin. George Harrison. Elvis Presley. Jimi Hendrix. Jim Croce. Jim Morrison. David Bowie. Whitney Houston. Johnny Cash. Prince. Glenn Frey. Chuck Berry. Nat King Cole. Clarence Clemons. Bob Marley. Roy Orbison. Marvin Gaye. Miles Davis. Kurt Cobain. John Denver. Frank Sinatra. Joey Ramone. Leonard Cohen. Barry White. Andy, Robin, and Maurice Gibb of the Bee Gees. James Brown. Pete Seeger. Mary Travers. Lou Reed. Freddy Mercury. Ben E. King of The Drifters. Maurice White. George Michael. Jeff Buckley. Tom Petty.

And the uncountable rest whose names and credits were scribed on the sleeves of the albums. Looking over at the Biggie record Mary had never taken home with her, I thought of how even he and Tupac were dead.

Those musicians, those artists, those poets, they were the ones, who, through their music and their words, had taught me how to live and how to feel. They were all outsiders, all a little strange; all had been scoffed at and ridiculed on their way to reaching their dreams. Their stories, through biography or song, gave me hope. Now they were all dead. My record collection was a memorial.

A yellow shaft from the late afternoon sun slanted across my room before my eyes. Spreading the elongated shadow of my torso across my record shelf. What would I do? Sit there—stuck—crippled by nostalgia, waiting for time to claim the names of whoever was left?

I got up from the floor and dropped the needle on my dad's LP, Insight Job, on the record player; still unchanged from that time Mary and I listened to it all those weeks ago. I sat back down on the floor and listened to my dad's music. Then, closing my eyes, I tried to imagine the expression on his face as he sang, "Someday I'll catch myself a southwest breeze and land in paradise."

And couldn't help but wonder, Did it look like mine?

30

Only the Lonely

DANNY

My guitar cases and gym bag slid right in place in the backseat of Dad's Mustang, easy to pack with the top down. A sunken sun shone through the breaks in the clouded sky. With the twist of a key, the lock of the front door fell into place with a thud. With another twist of another key, my car ignited. And as I grabbed the gearshift, I couldn't help but think: *Dad was supposed to teach me how to drive.*

I was getting tired of having to change the story each time someone went away. It wasn't what I necessarily wanted, but the only way.

In the height of summer, I didn't really need to think twice about running out the door, jumping into my car, and driving off anywhere my heart oh-so-wanted to go. The cold tinge in the infancy of the evening air reminded me that we were all too subjected to the never-ending pull of the Earth on its axis. Physically, we were further away from the sun than we'd been before. Darkness fell onto the world evidently earlier than it did back in June. And until the depth of winter, each and every day would just get shorter and shorter. Darker and darker. I knew I could catch the sun if I were to run. Because somewhere, the sun wasn't yet setting on people. Somewhere it was bright and beautiful and tanning the bodies of those who bathed in it.

> We were Children of the Sun / Take my hand, Mary
> We can make it if we run.

I kept my mind preoccupied trying to roll that one lyric into an entire song as I drove down all the familiar streets. The South End swept away when I looked out the side of my car. One after another, the houses stretched into blurred lines that whizzed by and eventually disappeared.

And then, accelerating to merge with the 306, my car crashed against the atmosphere. Forcing the still air into a dashing wind that tousled my hair in a dance above my head. Above, a dark gray cloud hovered through the sky like an abandoned continent adrift at sea, receding eastwards, allowing the golden light from the sinking sun to prevail across the world. The magnificent light, so immaculate and golden that it must have broke from Heaven, stood in deep contrast with that dark cloud wrapping the lower half of the hemisphere.

The division of the globe was a near perfect masterpiece. An excellent telling for the duality of life. The rarity of which such phenomenon occurs undoubtedly would convince anybody that the creator of the world had illustrative intentions in mind.

The wind skimmed the hood of my Mustang, cycling through a flapping sound like a waving flag. That rebel one nailed to my back.

There's not a single stretch of paved road in this country that doesn't connect to every other. Highway, freeway, backstreet, dead-end, a street winding around in a crescent, the Nevadan Interstate; any two lanes will do just fine. They're all connected. Inviting anyone with the will, and an adventurous soul, to chase a rising or setting sun. All you have to do is drive.

Most boys will grow up to be men who will only ever set their sights on the pavement that takes them to school, their mother's house, the rounded driveway of the church hall on their wedding day, through the factory gates, to only U-turn back to the same church and hitch the only free ride life ever gives you to the grave.

So, as my car obeyed the turns of the 306, a vision of my future-self as a Gilmore Park working man filled my eyes. How the rubber of his daddy's car will burn against those same tracks on that same highway until that Mustang's driven into the ground. And on that same highway, the dial will turn up on those same songs he listened to since he was sixteen to get him through the night. To save his spirit from completely breaking. Every beat of his heart, a beat closer to death. The body he'd been blessed with rotting away in the slums of Gilmore Park, New Jersey.

By the time my car braked at the Fisherman's Alley stop sign, the last rays of the setting sun were threading through the intersecting branches. Cutting deep black shadows where the light had failed to reach. Out from the side of the open roof, as I watched the rows of houses in Danae's Bay slip away one after another, the space of a vacant lot provided a little vista from which I could see the ocean. The geography of the bay and the roof peaks prevented me from seeing the sun itself, but the pink and blue sea guarded by the dark cloud honorably mirrored its expression.

My heart battered at the cage of my body as I turned down Bayview. No doubt in a desperate attempt to escape and save itself from the inevitable wounds to come. I could always just drive on; transform my intentions, and therefore myself, into just another car on the road passing by. But despite all the internal alarms, blaring on high alert, my mind was set in a stone heavy determination.

As my front tires straddled the curb three houses down, the long frilly leaves draped from the massive heights of the willow trees swayed lazily to and fro. Beyond the vegetated curtain, I saw a tiny playground I had never noticed before on Bayview. The playground held only a pinkish, sun-faded slide, and next to it, a two-seated swing set. The cloth of the caved-in seats had long since been worn down, and the steel had rusted where the beams conjoined and the chains were browned with age.

And in that second I saw it all: Mary as a toddler, chubby-cheeked and curly-haired, struggling with the mechanics of flight. The scrawny and hungry kid, only nine years of age, camping out after another night of her father's drunken rage. She was also there as a heartbroken fifteen-year-old, blanketing herself with the invisibility of a hoodie. Maybe the day was cold and wet with April's rain.

The willows and the scenes I imagined quickly fled out of sight. An uncertain purple glow from the sky descended upon the evening. In the lull afterward, I slid my key out of the ignition and listened to the distant waves of the Atlantic crashing along the shore. And as the birds sang to each other, Roy Orbison over the stereo sang "Only the Lonely" to me.

From down on the street, I looked up at her house. The dirty floor of the porch. The rain-beaten shingles. All of the splinters mottling the wood. Jim's burnt-out Chevy pickup in the driveway. The back of my neck cracked as I glanced up to the treetops one last time. I then popped open the glovebox, pulling out our map. Fear stilled my hand as I grabbed the door handle, but courage pushed it open. Cutting the running battery off, Roy Orbison sang no more. My Converse crunched against a scattering of loose gravel as I stepped out of my car.

Above those three rickety steps of the front porch, I heard the front door unlock. The pulse in my head gunned. The screen door pushed open and then slammed back as Mary ran onto the porch. Her white sweater, falling down long like a dress, swayed with the stride of her feet. Mary stopped and gazed down at me from the porch's edge. Three more steps were all that it would take.

"Danny."

Mary's long hair lapped against her shoulders as she stepped to the side and grabbed the railing.

Just walk down those three steps.

"I heard about Max—I am *so sorry*."

The wind sighed through the trees. "I… I can't even think about—*that*—right now." I fell back against my car. "Can we talk?"

Mary let go of the railing and then backed away to grab the screen door handle. "I can't. I'm sorry, Danny. I can't. I have to go."

"No, Mary, please! Don't run back inside. Please, Mary. Don't run back inside."

She hesitated, but slowly, reluctantly, returned to the porch's edge; one foot away from those three steps.

"What if my dad sees you?"

"I don't know," I answered. "Are you just going to put up with his bullshit for the rest of your life?"

Mary stared at me. Her lips trembled, resisting the urge to settle into a frown. I stole a glance at the concrete beneath my feet. And then as my gaze lifted over the weeds that shot out from the lawn, and went past the dark scars splintering the paint, and landed on her face, studying the expression I hoped was remorse, I noticed something was off. Horribly off. It only took me a second to realize what it was—and what it was killed me.

That slight obscuring of her eye had skewed the alignment of her entire face. Mary was still beautiful—nothing, no force in this world, could ever alter that. But Mary was never going to be as beautiful as she had once been when the arrangement of her face inspired perfect harmony. How each of her features flawlessly spiraled in with the rest, leaving not a single disruption in the current of the admirer's eye. Her face at seventeen was gone forever.

In that lack of her response, I said, "You're better than that." Shattering the silence.

Mary started shaking her head. "Well. What am I supposed to do, Danny?"

"Come with me, like we talked about."

"Where? Like, actually go to California?"

"Yes! There. Somewhere. Anywhere. God." Tears blurred the corners of my eyes. "I just know there has to be some place better than here."

Mary wavered in her stance. It was only when the porch light flashed on that I realized the sun had set.

"How do you know?" she asked. Behind me, a pair of evening larks began to sing.

"Because... because we promised each other in the old abandoned—"

"Oh my God. Danny, don't do this."

"Okay. I'm sorry. That was stupid of me. That was stupid and childish. And I should grow up. I know, Mary."

She stopped moving. I swallowed through a lump in my throat.

"That's not even it, Danny."

"Then what, Mary?"

"Danny, I've had a lot of time to think about it. And, like, you— you grabbed me, that day. You got mean, angry. Aggressive, with me, Danny. Like you bruised my arm." With her palm facing her, Mary bent her arm up as to emphasize the veracity.

Mary continued saying, "I don't think I know you, well enough. As well as I thought."

"Mary! My God! I'm sorry! It was once, and it was a mistake. Let me prove to you that it will never happen again and—and that, that wasn't me!"

Mary fell silent. She then took a deep breath, looked up to the sky, and then sighed as she said, "But, Danny, it was you. Maybe it's not who you are every day, but that was you who grabbed me."

"Mary, please. I'm so sorry. It will never happen again."

"I don't...trust...that. I've been—too many times, in my life. I don't trust you." Mary started stepping back toward the door. "I don't know you."

"Mary, please! I hate myself so much!"

"Don't," she said, stopping. "Danny, you're the last person who should hate themselves. You're an amazing person. Maybe the most amazing person I have ever met. The way you see the world. Your dreams. It's all beautiful. Don't ever stop. But that's not for me, I can't see things the way you do. I didn't grow up like that." She gestured helplessly toward her house. "I want to. I thought I did. But...I can't. I can't trust you, anymore. Please go now."

"But—but, Mary!" I whipped our map out of my pocket and fumbled to unfold it. "I have our map! What about all the places we talked about seeing? Colorado! You can finally see Denver! The mountains! The desert, California—"

"Danny. I just told you—those aren't my dreams. I thought they were. But they're not."

"Mary, come on. You can't be serious—"

"I am, Danny. Please, please, forget about me. Just go," she said, retreating further, pulling open the screen door.

"But Mary! No, wait! I love you—"

But by then, the screen door had already slammed back behind her after she went inside.

31

A Case of You

MARY

It wasn't intentional. The moon was right and the night had settled with a late August chill.

When Danny went running after Max, he didn't come back. The instant the boys had cleared for the woods, the onlookers had shrugged, another day another drama, and then immediately went back to their keg-standing and yapping. I couldn't quite do the same; far too much of my life had just been exposed. Not far from me, I saw Tanner's huddle, all with their backs turned, and heard Fat Jordan mumble something about "the rich bitch," as he turned to jeer at me.

But no matter how drunk or embarrassed I was, I waited for him.

Ashley tried coaxing me into getting a ride home with Tanner, who apparently wasn't drinking and "weed doesn't make a difference," and who, somewhere along the way, had become friends with Cody. But no amount of persuading, even as I continuously drank and smoked, blitzing my mind, would ever tear my pride down that low. I told Ashley I had a ride and waited at the forest's edge. I didn't want to leave without Danny.

By the time the night had dwindled into the single digits of the morning, the bulk of kids cleared out—only a few all-night partiers stayed behind. The fire in the trashcan shrank into a flat glowing light that glared off the inner steel brim.

The last drop of Ashley's vodka drained down my throat. Throughout the rest of the night, I would drift back and forth from the edge of the forest to a huddle of stoners sitting at a picnic bench back in the main clearing. I'd con a shot, a hit of a joint, or two, and then return to the edge, watch for Danny, and then go back. And so on. It was just as the trashcan fire died that Sean approached me.

My head fell into his chest when he staggered up behind me. I had to look up to see his eyes. He asked me if I had a smoke. Together we found one of the party's leftovers, and without any trouble, Sean got cigarettes for us. The flame jumped out of the darkness as he touched the tip of my cigarette to his lighter. An orange ring glowed in his eyes. He called me beautiful and grabbed my hand.

The next thing I knew, I was in Sean's car and he was driving me home. I told him I didn't want to go. He asked me if there was anywhere else I wanted to go. I said no.

We parked on his street, and he led me by the hand through his back door. When we reached the bottom of the basement stairs, he grabbed me by the shoulders and kissed me and I locked my hands around his head.

We fell on the bed. Thrusting his hard erection through his pants onto me. Then, God, I couldn't slip my jeans off fast enough, and he was touching me. His fingers were so long. I grabbed his face and pressed my lips into his. Our faces seemed to mash. He snatched the lace of my panties and stripped them from my waist, tearing them off my ankles.

And then I was down on my knees, giving him head, and then we were fucking. The biggest I've had. It was amazing and I was drunk and I needed him. I loved him.

"Can I fuck you in the ass?"

"Sure."

Then it fucking hurt. And I went from feeling like an angel to a whore, and he didn't stop. With my face continuously crashing down into the mattress, my eye exploded with pain. I howled, trying to tell him to stop, but it didn't sound any different than an orgasm. The tears stung where the flesh was still raw, and every time he submitted me into the mattress, the ache burst all over again. I never told him to stop. I never wanted him to stop. He finished when and where he pleased and then crashed into the mattress. Snoring.

My panties had disappeared in the dark. So I slipped on my jeans, pulling the inside-out leg back out, and by the wits of my bygone drunken mind, somehow found my way out of his basement apartment. The pain shooting from my eye throbbed from my temples to my chin.

When I got to the intersection closest to his house, I saw that I was on Penelope Street, just west of the boardwalk. After ten more minutes of walking, the road hit Atlantic Way. I continued past downtown Carraway Beach and The Alley, staggering along the curb closest to the boardwalk. There wasn't a soul in sight. It was weird seeing the Old Abandoned Beach House from the street.

In the end, it turned out Danny was right. The walk to 22 Bayview Avenue from Atlantic Way did take about two hours. By the time I got to Danae's Bay, the blue of the morning was lifting against the night sky, and early birds were chirping as I pushed through the screen door. Coming home.

So, it was the guilt that killed me.

As I leaned against the back of the front door, after slamming it in Danny's face, I hated myself.

I heard grumbling from the kitchen and the limping stagger of Jim's footsteps. Guilt and anxiety stretched and split open my stomach. What was he going to say now? Would I be in trouble because Danny showed up? When he limped around the wall, leaning on his cane with a joint tucked in his lips, he had a self-satisfying look on his face.

"I'm glad'ya told that cuck ta finally leave ya 'lone." He hummed.

"Yeah."

Only later did it occur to me that he'd been listening in on our entire conversation. I could just see him sitting there—grinning at Danny's desperation. Finding some sort of amusement in our drama, like our feelings were just a part of a game meant to entertain him.

"See, I toldj'ya, Mare, that he was no good. Right?" He straightened his hunched spine in order to start preaching. "You know, they come in all sortsa shapes and sizes. The terrorists, right? Young kids ya wouldn't 'spect are trying to enforce the Islam, spread the Sharie Law. Startin' up revolts 'gainst our government, trying t' shut down free speech. Calling President Trump, Hitler. Can ya believe that? Hitler?" Jim recited what any conspiracy vlogger would say. "It's a scary, scary world."

I just kept rocking.

"See. I know ya think I'm the bad guy, but I'm just tryin' to protect you. You can't trust no one, right? If there's one thing I've learned—it's that," he said with the pointing of his finger.

Jim kept looming around, just waiting to get some reaction from me that I was not going to give him.

" 'Kay. I get it. Be mad at me because I shooed your boyfriend 'way." The tremor of Jim's voice picked up with a steady incline of fanaticism that seemed tied to the staccato snapping of his open hand. "Jus' don't come cryin' ta me when after you two've been t'gether for a while, and you're both sicka each other and start bangin' other people and he ends up leavin' ya 'cause he knocked up some broad."

The long muscle of his forearm popped out as he drove his weight into the cane.

"Mare, it's just—it's a nasty world. A nasty, nasty, nasty world. I've seen that happen too many times, right? Ya know, Mare, itta happened to your Mum, right?"

"What? What happened to my mom?"

Jim then stopped. Taking his time to look inward, inward on the past. "Come outside," he said, taking a step in the direction of the door.

Settling down into his favorite lawn chair on the porch, he rolled the leg of his shorts over his right knee, revealing several scars, and began extending the joint as best he could.

"Physician told me today that what's been actin' my knee up is a wearin' down of the cartlidge. Said it's most likely the osto-thritis caused by tearin' my ACL when I was a kid. Y'know I blew it playin' all that football, right? So ya see, Mare," Jim kicked his knee out. "I only gotta 'bout a fifteen to twenty degree extension in the knee. Gonna try t' get one of those medical marijuana cards. Lawyer says I might get outta jail time if I present it in court. Six fuckin' months for havin' a roach in the cup'older. Retarded, right?"

"Yeah. That is pretty retarded." Genuinely agreeing with him. "But, um, Dad, you were saying something about… my mom."

His smoker's yellow fingernail dug into the worn plastic mesh of the lawn chair. Clicking away at the plastic flakes.

"Dad?"

"Yeah?" His eyes down at the chair.

"Wendy… she is my mom, right?"

"Yeah." He sighed. "Yes, Mary. Wendy is your mum."

"Okay. Then what happened to my mom? Why did she leave?"

Jim scraped out a large plastic flake from the arm of the chair that fell to the ground.

"Dunno. Guess she liked the dope more than us."

"No, Dad. No. Tell me everything. I need to know"

"Well," he said, then looked up to the street. "When she got pregnant with you, her mother, the Snake Lady, kicked her out. So bein' my girlfriend and all, I couldn't jus' leave 'er on the streets or somethin'. Ya know? Good-lookin' girl, right? Woulda been dangerous. So I told Wend, your mum, just t' move in with me. Told 'er to quit workin', that I would provide. But that's a lot for a young guy, right? Movin' in with a girl, providing for a family. So, ya know how young guys are, right? I started sleeping with an old flame a mine. Nothin' serious, right? I was just young and dumb. Leavin' Wend alone lot in the house.

"Your mum after findin' out was pissed off and started hangin' 'round with this jerk, Chuck McGilvery, and he started 'er on the dope. I was upset, right? That your mother, pregnant with you, was doing dope. Came in 'er room one night an' saw syringes and burnt spoons and tubes and shit all hidden in the closet."

Jim started shaking his head.

"Fuck. I was so fuckin' pissed. I struggled 'lot to get her off the shit. Tried gettin' her to go t' rehab and get help, but she was hooked. And then, when Chuck found out I was tryin' to get her straight, he started filling her head with all these crazy ideas, tellin' her that he would marry 'er and adopt the baby. You.

"So one night, after getting home from drinkin' with my buddies at Cat's, I found out that Wend had packed her bags and ran away. I tried searchin' for her. Shit. Tried everything. But she wasn't anywhere. Found out later she birthed you without tellin' me. Somehow the hospital got 'holda my number and called Johnston Construction, where I was workin' at the time, right? And, and— God. God I was so excited, so relieved. I was so excited that I ran off the jobsite hollerin' at the foreman 'I gotta go see my kid!' and jumped in my truck and raced to the hospital."

Jim swatted his hand and caught a mosquito that was whining about. The crumpled body of the insect lay in the middle of his palm when he opened his hand. He flicked his wrist, throwing the mosquito away.

"But, well, when—when I got there, the nurses told me she had the post-partum and had run away. Sayin' that it was very normal. That a lot of women with the post-partum run off, right? Sayin' they've seen it 'fore, and that the mothers always return. Tol' me that either I could leave you in the care of the 'aternity ward, or I could take ya home. And, well, I thought that Wend would return. She was in love with the idea of havin' a baby, right? I knew she oughta come back. She had too."

"Did you le-leave me there?" I asked.

Jim leaned back in his seat and scowled. "Are you kidding me? Of course I didn't leave ya there. I mean, I had no freakin' clue what t'do, but of course I wouldn't leave ya?" Jim looked away and shook his head, dismissing the ridiculousness of my question.

"Like my mum, I thought Wend would do all the baby and girly stuff. Can you believe it? I bought all this boy stuff, a lil football, and Lester gave me some his kids' old trucks and toys, thinkin' that you were gonna be a boy!

"Back home, I rocked you t' sleep and read my dad's Bible. I pulled outta highlighter, tryin' to find a good name, but my mum stopped and told me that if I marked up the Bible it would affend the Lord. So I picked out the first name I read. Mary. So, I sang 'Mare-ee had a lit-tle lamb' to lullaby you. Since you didn't have little girl things, I used t' try to play trucks with you. That was stupid of me. I was in my twenties, right? I was still doing the video games. The PlayStation, right? I didn't want to look gay buying dolls and shit. My dad never did that kid shit, y'know, buyin' toys, right? But for you, Mary, guess I should've."

"It's okay, Dad."

"I never stopped looking for your mum. Every day since, I've tried t' track 'er down. Sometimes at work, right? I would get thinkin' 'bout it, all pissed off and shit, and just leave to go check the streets. The bars. Try to see 'er old friends. Thought maybe she was dead. So I'd go by the cemeteries and read the stones. Took fuckin' years, but finally the city got back t' me, and well, that's when they woulda mailed that letter you read, right? So that's why, Mary, that's why I coulda never told ya that your mum was dead, because I—I didn't know.

"And who knows, Mare. What did that fuckin' letter say? Health complications? Drug overdose. Suicide. I don't know. She ran away from me and t' this day I'll never understan' why. I made mistakes, sure. But I was good to her?"

His memories and the circumstances didn't make sense to him. "I was *good* to her." He reassured himself. "I was."

Jim's eyes automatically went to where the ocean was visible from our porch. But by then in the evening the streetlights masqueraded the sight.

"I'm gonna start bein' a better dad," Jim said. "I'm sorry for everything. Wish I woulda played dolls with you when ya asked me to. But I was waiting for your mum to come home and do that. Want to go down to that Toys R Us? Buy you Barbies or somethin'? We can play?"

When Jim turned to look at me, I now looked out for the ocean. The streetlights were aglow in a long necklace down the road. But above, the colors of dusk caught my attention. The feathery undersides of the clouds facing the west radiated in a vermillion flare against their larger, dark blue bodies. I turned back to Jim.

"It's okay, Dad."

He nodded.

Just then, Jim's stupid, dizzy-sounding ringtone went off, and he started blabbing away.

I went to my room. His loud obnoxious voice only muted when I closed my bedroom door. Mt. Pile-Of-Neglect stared at me. I stared back. I wanted to kick it. But I didn't. Not long after, I heard what sounded like a baseball bat break the living room lamp.

The last of the evening light entered my room when I made my first attempt to sleep. But since my body refuses to do shit-all for itself, for the life of me, sleeping was impossible. Desperate to forget the day and just deal with tomorrow, I tried it all. Lying on my back. Lying on my stomach. Lying in fetal position. Cuddling a pillow. Sheets off. Sheets on. The cold side of the pillow. The other pillow. The cold side of the other pillow. I even tried counting sheep. But let's be honest, that shit never worked. When I decided that I was just wasting my time with my eyes closed, I rolled over and looked at my clock. Total darkness encased the night but it was not very late. So instead, I lay awake. Engulfed in a mystery, plagued with the biggest question of them all:

What was I going to do with my life?

My future felt imminent. The beginning of the rest of my life would begin tomorrow. Why, I don't know, but whatever was left of my teenage life would be gone by dawn.

My wide and awake eyes scanned the matted midnight-blue spectrum of my room. Searching for a clue. I had completely given up on righting the wrong that was the impossible mess of the place. My jeans draped over my sad excuse for a desk chair looked inaccurately large for my waist. Maybe I was fatter than I thought. I don't know. Whatever. But that was when I spotted it. And it bothered me. A lot.

My Saint Maria Goretti grad hoodie flung on my dresser and wrapped around itself in a sloppy mess.

I ceased to be a bystander of such atrocious disorganization. Whipping off the pale pink sheet, I propelled myself out of bed and began folding my old grad hoodie. Funny word choice, Mary.

Old.

It felt old. A measly two months ago, I was still in high school. And now, a measly two months later, like ceasing to be a bystander of disorganization, high school ceased to matter. Any of it. None of it. All of it. The good, the bad, and the ugly (regrettable colors of hair, acne, raccoon eyeliner, etc.,).

After folding the sleeves in half and flattening the fabric with my palms, I flipped the folded square over and looked down at the embroidered letters: SMG written right-smack-dab in the sweater's chest. Underneath the acronym, written in a smaller-cased font: SAINT MARIA GORETTI CATHOLIC HIGH SCHOOL; complete with my last name and graduating year written bad-assily on the hood

My mind replayed and raced through the memories of the day I received my grad hoodie.

It was early in October (a lil audacious of Saint Maria Goretti's to assume I would graduate), Tanner picked me up at lunch and I skipped the rest of the afternoon. And truthfully, it was one of those rare occasions in which Tanner could actually be pretty sweet, most likely in an attempt to make silent amends for cheating on me.

We got high by Lake Heely, sat on one of the concrete ledges surrounding the dock, dangling our legs above the water, and talked about life. Making a promise that if he and I were ever to break up, that we would remain friends. That if we ever saw each other somewhere, such as the grocery store, when we were forty, we could say Hi, and catch each other up on the outcome of our lives.

After smoking by the lake, we took advantage of the all-day breakfast at Betty's Diner. Tanner proved his masculinity by finishing their Hungry Man's challenge; the munchies aiding in the accomplishment.

That night, getting in late from being out with Tanner, it took Jim only to hear the rusted hinges of the screen door to start yelling at me for "breaching my curfew." And then once he saw me in my grad hoodie, he made fun of me for it. Telling me I was too stupid to graduate high school. The battle led all the way to my room, where he ended up smacking the lid of my laptop down hard enough that the screen shattered. Leaving me to type out my assignments for the rest of senior year on my phone.

And then I met Danny.

And, well, Danny was always pretty sweet. And, on a rare occasion, he got impatient and angry. And then him and I swore to each other in the Old Abandoned Beach House forever friends, even if he were living out in California. And then my dad hit me and kicked me out of the house.

And then a haunting stillness occupied my room. And then my thumbs caressed the fabric of the sweater as I stared at my written name

And then, that was to be the endless cycle of my life. The wheel of fate that would forever spin until I am old and die. And such as it were to be with everyone else I knew. Nothing but the places, the faces, and the reasons would ever change; the causes and results would relentlessly remain the same. It astonished me that most of humanity was so blind to the patterns that dominate their lives. How miserably we all fail to see the operations at work that command our personal laws of attraction.

The thread connecting Jim, Tanner, and Danny became so crystal clear.

Just because of who I am, just because of how I think, how I feel; because of the biases and judgments I pertain to, and because of how my broken past shattered the lens in which I saw the world, subconsciously, I would forever engender similar men into my life. Men who could be so giving and so kind. And men who could be so ruthless and so inviolably cruel.

Jim will die missing the past and aggressively standing in the way of that which suggests the future.

And my next boyfriend, well, he'll be a boy better than the rest. Whether it be his affiliation for weed and souping up the Impala, or for rock 'n roll and unrealistic dreams, his individuality will impress me. He'll know how to outwit me, pretending to be a fiercer intellect than he really is. And when I start giving him too much of my shit, he won't take it. And that will regrettably turn me on, making me fall harder in love with him.

And that next boy will drive me down those same streets of that same small town in a car that emblemizes his personality; all while

I try to forget those same drives with his predecessors. Inevitably, the dysfunction of my life will arise. And unknowingly, I'll guilt him into carrying their weight. And no doubt, that just like Danny and Tanner, only in the balance in which sweetness and rage are dealt will differ. Someway, somehow, his hands will find their way on me.

But I'll make him, too, promise to never leave me.

Imperceptibly, each time the wheel of the story comes around, with each new rotation reaching its apex, the stakes and the causes will proliferate. Crashing down in more cataclysmic consequences than before.

Once the pattern of my fate collated in my mind, it was impossible not to see. Because of my history, because of the way the lives of my family played out before me, I was bound to the vortex. Hell, I was born into it. The wheel of my life will keep on spinning. Maybe next time it's a fiancé; there's a kid involved. Jim dies and leaves with nothing but unfulfilled vows "to change." Forever to spin. Spin and spin and reel faster and faster with greater velocity until it becomes an inextricable whirling hurricane of chaos that I can no longer escape.

There will be no salvation in the moments between the relapses. Mary, just another fucking small-town tragedy.

What even is Destiny? Does it even exist? Do the destinies of the damned possess some hidden altruistic purpose that exists only in the celestial plain beyond human reach? Or can I, using all my might, charge a wedge deep in the spokes of fate and stop the predetermined course of my life from consummating?

Through the thinness that was the architecture of my house, I heard an undeniable crackle, the thunderous roar of an engine. A car engine.

No. It's too late for thinking like that.

But the roar grew unforgivably louder.

He's already long gone.

I kept repeating the phrase: *He's gone, he's gone, he's gone,* but then he grinded the engine outside like a racer anticipating the final run.

You stupid boy, I told you to leave! Leave! Leave! Leave!

I dashed out of my room with my grad hoodie still clenched in my fists. Accepting that the rickety floor would betray the flight of my feet, I threw caution to the wind and ran down the hallway. Then avoiding the shards of broken glass from the destroyed lamp, and plowing through the scattering of shoes on the mat, I snapped and slid back the bolt. Cranked the knob. And with a hard push, palming open the screen door, I skidded to a halt on the porch.

And just like the girl I had drawn who turned out to be a ghost, as was he. No car. No Danny. No intervention of destiny. Just an empty street. That roar came from elsewhere, possibly across the shore. That thunder was meant for someone else.

Resurrecting my long dead imagination, I tried to assemble the features of his beautiful face and see him in that roofless Mustang. Sitting, waiting for me in the halo of yellow porch-light cast out on the street. Scanning through my memories, I replayed all the times his face had stood out in my mind. How handsome he looked with his hair brushed casually off his forehead, like that first night I noticed, with his nineties jean jacket on the carousel.

But already Danny was slipping out of my memory. Every time I thought my mind was on the verge of constructing his features just right—a hazy memory plastered on a blank mannequin—it slipped entirely from me. I struggled to remember his face. I couldn't. I couldn't. Oh my God no, no, Danny no.

The screen door then slammed and snapped in place behind me. "Mary!"

Jim roared my name from deep inside the house. With a loud crash, the porch started sporadically shaking as he attempted to run with his limp. Looking through the mesh at his gray figure getting bigger down the hallway, and then looking back to make sure Danny really wasn't on the street, my eye throbbed, as if anticipating another hit. And in the shock of the realization, the realization of how badly I had been scarred, I dropped my grad hoodie like a rag at my feet.

Jim screamed my name again. The boards of the porch shook with a great force on the pounding of his every step.

And that was when I did it. When I made one of those choices you can't take back; the kind that changes lives forever.

"MARY!"

Jim continued to scream after me, but by then, I was already away, running down the street. Only looking back for a second when I heard the snap and the bang of the screen door breaking off its hinges.

Running above the pools of orange streetlights, passing all the old houses, I heard him from all the way down the road, cursing my name every way he knew how. And I felt sorry for Jim. And then in that instant, it felt as though everything I'd held within—the frustration and the anger and the hate buried deep inside—expelled with each smack of my bare heels on the concrete. And from then on, my flight felt loose. Free.

I forgave my dad.

Up until then—God—I thought he hated me. The epiphany hit as a dusting of loose pebbles crushed into my feet. Some people, maybe, can't love. Can't love us the way we want them to. Dad feared losing me.

The shallow road rushed up into an intersection shaped like a T.

Two houses down to my right, the earth dipped into the sea. And in front of me, the lamppost leaned to the left, so I followed its lead. When I escaped the entangled streets of Danae's Bay, the roads got wider, and the stretches of darkness between the streetlights longer.

Life resurrected on Lockport Road. People were out and cars raced by. In my adrenaline-rushed and hollowed mind, the world around me spun in a transfixing daze. The bright lights. The shock of every stranger's perplexed gaze. The commotion of the traffic. I was overwhelmed. For a stunned second, I completely forgot about my destination. The gas station.

The gas station. The gas station. The gas station.

It was an improbable gamble, but if I knew Danny at all, I knew he would stay true to his word and begin his drive with our planned rendezvous in mind.

While pitching my sob story to another waiting patron of the midnight bus, hoping to use it in exchange for the fare, I didn't even consider the unlikeliness of catching him in time. But I knew I would catch Danny. I had to. God, it was the ambition fueling my fate.

Was it my fate to be born to Dad? That was noble of him. It really was. A young guy, adopting the baby girl birthed by his dead-beat, drug-addicted girlfriend. He didn't have to, and he tried his best. He loved me, I realized. It broke my heart to think of how differently things could have been if he'd only known how to love me.

The guy I begged two dollars and fifty cents off of might have thought I was strung out, crazy, and homeless—and was probably terrified by the frantically shivering, and barefooted girl, crying about her life. When he fended me off by giving me the money, my eyes welled with tears and I thanked him repeatedly for his benevolence like he was a saint.

The irrevocable consequences of my decision only caught up to me when I had a moment to breathe on the bus. While holding onto the steel railing, feeling the bus shake as it rolled over the bumps in the road, I started bawling.

I'm sorry, Dad.

I remembered what Danny had said to me: it doesn't come for free. For the rest of my life, I would pay the price by living with the knowledge that I had robbed Dad of the last thing he had. Me. But I was so terribly hurt, and I had tried so hard to love him, but this was my life—and unlike him, I knew that he would never change and that Mom wasn't coming back.

I'm so sorry, Dad. I hope someday you'll forgive me.

The bus wheezed to a halt at its last stop on County Line 55.

Regional Variety & Gas, a million miles away and glowing in the dark, desolate countryside. Danny's red Mustang was parked out front.

The bus driver unfolded the doors and I leaped off the steps, almost wiping out on the road. As I started sprinting to the gas station, Max suddenly came to my mind.

I wish I could have talked to him. It made me sad to think that I'd never gotten the chance to know him very well. We would have gotten along. Maybe even more than Danny and I. Did he choose to die? If so, when did he just decide that was it? That he was going to end all the insurmountable sadness with one swift click. Bang. What invisible thing needs to break for someone to make that choice, the choice to kill themselves? And why hadn't it broken me?

If Max did kill himself, I'll never be convinced that makes him a terrible person. Choosing to die. Life is hard, and it appears some are born solely to suffer through it. As the Queen sings, we are Born To Die. So why not bring our inevitable oblivion closer, and experience life's antithesis? If Hell is indeed here on Earth, then why chastise those longing to return to Heaven? Why, if I would've grabbed his gun, I might have just shot myself that night.

Regional Variety & Gas got closer with each thudding slap of my feet against the road. My right side started to cramp, I felt winded, but I kept running. The bright luminance of the lone canopy light brought out the red in Danny's car. My thighs begged me to stop. I kept on going. I rehearsed my speech in my head. How I would tell him, *I want to run away with you.* And I imagined that, as I ran up, chest heaving, out of breath, he would roll down the window and look at me with his dark eyes.

Standing at his window, I would tell him everything. How I felt. How I was sorry for hurting him. How I chose to cower behind the one thing he did wrong and use it as an excuse to turn him away.

"Danny, I don't care where we go. Let's follow our map. I don't care, so as long as we are together. My future isn't so scary when I'm with you."

He would push open the car door and stand over me; his brown eyes, with the rare green shining through, would look into mine. My hand would lower into his palm. His hand feeling so rough as it held and protected mine. I then get in the car. The engine rumbling with life. And his foot will floor the clutch, and then he'll shift into gear, and then we will be driving, following the highlighted route we had made. And finally, we will be free.

I ran harder, closing the gap. A hundred feet. Fifty, thirty, ten. Five. When I reached the driver's window, the plush blue dice dangling from the rearview mirror confused me. I thought that was a strange aesthetic choice for Danny's road trip. My fingers smudged the glass as I peered in. Then it dawned on me. That wasn't Danny's car.

"There's a better reflection in the pisser," a brusque voice from behind me grumbled, followed by a stiff laugh. I spun around. Some old guy sporting a tucked-in plaid shirt and nursing a styrofoam coffee cup walked up behind me.

"Was there another car just here? Like, this one?" I choked on the words.

"Sorry, girly. Couldn't tell ya," he said, and then mumbled something while inspecting the smudges I made on his window, mentioning something about loading up and out. Before whirling around and dashing into the gas station, I noticed that his car lacked the horsey symbol. That wasn't even a Mustang.

Pulling open the gas station door, I shouted, "Was there another red car here earlier? A red Mustang? Old, like, uh, from the eighties old, with a black racing stripe?"

The attendant behind the counter stroked his beard in thought. "Yes, yes. The young guy. Pump four. He has the brown hair? Yeah?"

"When?" I died.

"Oh, probably… five minutes? He was waiting around all night, yeah?"

"Is there a phone?" I demanded, sprinting up to the counter. "There has to be a phone I could use."

"Payphone in the front."

"Please, please, please can you lend me some change?"

Opening the till, the attendant pulled out three quarters and dropped them in my palm. I darted out the door.

"Shit, shit." I fumbled to deposit the quarters into the change slot. Then unhinging the phone, cradling it between my shoulder and neck, I went to hit Danny's cell number.

"Eight-four-eight." Clicking in the area code. "Six. Eight. Uh. Fuck."

For the life of me, I couldn't remember. Was it 848 687? Or 848 688? And what in God's Name were those last four digits?

I jammed my finger into the 8 button and then typed in a random four digits. My fingers clicked all over the number pad until I started swapping my hand down repeatedly over the buttons. A high-pitched tone blared from the receiver, letting me know that my call could not be complete. About to slap my hand down over the buttons again, the pad of my middle finger hooked onto the ledge of the 2 button. Suspended. I froze. Pulling my finger down until it plucked off.

While staring at the black, worn-out buttons on the number pad, the dial tone droned helplessly in my ear.

I then let the phone fall from my shoulder. It jerked up on its suspension, and then recoiled and spun in aimless circles, dangling by the chord. The receiver shrilled dimly below.

Sauntering back into the gas station, the walls tilting and slowly pulling away from me as I waded into the void, all I could think of was, *Five minutes. Five fucking minutes.*

"Thanks." I handed the attendant back the lone quarter. He then asked if he could be of any help. Sounding sincere enough.

But then a look of wry realization came into his eyes, and he stared at me strangely. Suddenly aware of my cold nipples cutting through my nightie, I crossed my arms over my chest and shook my head No.

My feet peeled away from the sticky floor as I walked out.

Five minutes.

The door made a double beep after I pulled, and then pushed it open, and then found myself a seat on the curb. While rubbing the bottom of my feet against my ankles, scraping off the pebbles that had tacked themselves into my skin, I got lost in a staring contest with the ground. I eroded from the inside out. Crumbling. I started crying. My tears landed in dark rings beside my dirty feet. Realizing that all I was veiled in from the unsympathetic gas station light was my nightie, I began praying to Saint Maria Goretti for protection.

"You hear that?"

He would've said, acknowledging the singing crickets. "Listen to how they envy the songs in the sky."

I started laughing through my tears.

I never even got the chance to tell Danny I loved him.

My ass felt boney sitting on the curb for so long. So maybe I wasn't as fat as my draped jeans had made me believe. God, I don't know. What did that matter? I started laughing silently again.

After sitting in the dark for a long while, there was one thing I noticed. And that was that the gas station light couldn't outshine the moon. And as I continued to stare up at the black sky, trying to find my faith entangled somewhere in the stars, I realized that all I held my faith in was gone.

But—I didn't need Danny for my dreams.

While sitting there on that cold hard curb. Dispossessed. Examining my chipped nails and muddy feet, with the gas station light throwing my dark shadow in front of me, I remembered what Danny had pointed out what was not inked beside my tits, but in fact, handwritten next to my heart: *the heart will break, but broken live on.*

Epilogue.

32

My Back Pages

I made it to California in three days. As the wise men say: sleep is for the weak.

Mom nearly had a heart attack when she opened the front door and saw me standing on the other side. She went from shocked to worried, and asked me why and how I was there, as I had not answered a single one of her many, many phone calls while on my drive. I collapsed into her and started bawling. She cried because I was crying, and then we went inside and sat on the couch, and I cried some more. Once I could catch a breath, I told her everything.

Mom broke down into a sobbing mess, and together, we were dragged back into the undertow of tears I thought California's shores would surface us from. Exhaustion flooded me and I cried until I blacked out.

I woke up some hours later; it was dark out. When I looked at the clock, it read ǀ ǀ:23PM. I collapsed into the couch and fell back asleep.

When I woke up again, it was light out. My head still felt groggy, so I forced myself back into more sleep.

When I woke up the third time, it was late in the morning and Mom was at the kitchen table making phone calls. Max's funeral was to be held on Saturday. Today was Friday.

For a second, I tried to comprehend the reality. But I was unable to. I was in a silent asylum of my own. I couldn't think or feel anything. There was just a hollow beating somewhere in my chest. Something that reminded me that I was alive, and somehow this must be real because everybody was playing along. Somehow—this became my life.

Mom and I took a red-eye back to New Jersey late that night. I pressed my forehead against the cold window of the airplane and temporarily enjoyed the child-like amusement of watching the world shrink into a play-set as the plane took off.

Not long after, we were above the clouds. The moon shone an otherworldly light on the sea of rolling white mountains. I tried to think of all the poetry to describe the moonlight's glow—but all I could think about was how this was where I wanted to be for the rest of my life. Above the clouds in the otherworldly moonlight. I could lie down on the bed of clouds, sleep, and float away forever.

Max's funeral was painfully barren. No one except a few teachers and the principal from our high school, and some kids I didn't recognize, attended the service. For a second, I thought I would see Mary, but she wasn't there. Fucking Stephen Belanger didn't even show.

For obvious reasons, the casket was closed. Just beneath the sanded oak of the coffin lay the lifeless and pale, and now horribly disfigured, face of my best friend. Touching the surface of the casket discharged a twisted guilt from my heart. I felt like I sinned for trying to bridge the worlds of the living and the dead.

You are alive. They—or better yet in this case—Max, is the dead. The dead cannot feel your touch, Max cannot feel my touch, so do not mock the dead by touching Max's tomb like he'll be able to feel me apologize. But I dispelled my own feelings and placed my whole hand on the casket and let the acidic agony burn through me all over again.

I deserved to feel this. I could have charged up those steps and forcefully grabbed the gun. How could have I just sat there as he downed those drugs? I could have kept an eye on him that night.

"Hey, Max, man! Listen to me! Seriously, dude! Calm down. Okay? You're my brother, man. I've got your back. Stay with me, at my house, tonight."

But I never said anything like that.

I tried to think of some sort of eulogy. But the *what if's* and *should have's* ate away at my conscience like termites in my soul. I didn't deserve to speak at his funeral like I had been a good friend.

And so, my friend Max joined the rows of the dead. Such as we are all one day to join too. And the gravestones in those rows were of all different designs. Some were etched with a picture of the departed; a Cross or an angel guarded others. The Chinese had their own way of protecting the resting place of the dead. Most of the plaques declared the finest achievements of those who were buried: A loving grandfather. A beloved wife and daughter. A Dreamer, A Visionary, A Father.

Max would never even get to fulfill one of those average achievements. He wasn't even granted the right to die with the most effortless legacy of them all, someone's beloved son. Yes, he was someone's child, but he had died as no one's son. And I hated his parents. That wherever they were, somewhere out there in the world, they were not aware that their son had died and that they were going to live a longer life than he had. Max would leave nothing but a slab of limestone behind.

Mom and I went out for dinner after the funeral and stayed the night at the house. It was weird being back because it didn't feel like our home anymore. It also made my final farewell to this place when I drove off feel anticlimactic. Maybe it had been too soon to say goodbye to Mary. Maybe if I had given it a week, or a couple of days, she wouldn't have just cut me off so cold.

Mom asked if I still planned on staying around for Mary. I told her I didn't know.

The following morning, I took the rental car and drove to the North End. Stopped at the Fisherman's Alley stop sign, turned right onto Seadrift Drop, and then drove down Bayview Avenue. Even though I was undercover in the rental, I still felt as though one of them would look out their window, right into the car, and see me. But even before I got to the house, I realized something was different.

Slapped over the giant realtor sign in the middle of the front lawn, was a big and bright, and bold label that read: SOLD.

I cranked the car into park and ran out and up the porch steps. Peering into the front window of their house, I saw that the living room was all cleared out, and only a few lights were left on. Something had changed. Transformed. Then taking a step back from the window, I looked around at the house, thinking that the porch might have been repainted, but then I realized the transformation was that the barbecue was gone. They were gone. Mary was gone.

I reached for my phone before remembering that Mary didn't have a phone—but, maybe she had gotten that old number reactivated. I clicked my screen open and scrolled through my contacts to M.

Mary, Max, Mom—all in a row.

Tapping Mary's name, I let it ring for a second until the automated woman's voice recited: "The number you have dialed is no longer in service. This is a recording."

My thumbs raced to search her up on all versions of social media, but then I remembered that Mary didn't have an account on anything.

When I got home later that day I began another search. It took me a while to find her, but I finally found Mary's blonde friend, Ashley, online.

At 1:47pm, I sent her a message:

Hey,

My names Danny. Mary was a friend of mine. I know this probably seems really random but I was wondering if you knew where she moved? As I'm sure you know she doesn't have a phone, or any form of social media, so she's making it pretty impossible to get a hold of her ahaha. Please let me know if you know how I can get in contact with her, thanks!

For a good solid minute, I stared at my page, waiting for the little inbox icon to light up and make a pop sound with a notification. At this point, I still didn't really know if anyone in Mary's life even knew who I was. Eventually deciding that sitting, waiting, looking at my phone all day was going to drive me mental, I took the afternoon off watch duty to spend time with Mom.

We drove to the Gagliardi's house; Mom was having coffee with the Mrs. My thumbs dwindled over my phone as I was forced to listen to another painful recount of why we were back home, spoken in hushed tones in the opposite room. I didn't think Mom realized I could hear every word.

Later, after leaving the Gagliardi's, Mom asked if I wanted to go out for dinner or stay in. I reminded her that everything sucked around Gilmore Park, so we agreed on staying in to eat. When driving down Ridgeway Avenue on the way home, we passed the boarded-up version of Superior Carwash. Next to it, Wright Bros looked lonely. It missed her too.

Later that evening, as Mom was preparing food she had picked up from the grocery store—telling me that we were going to make a second attempt at celebrating my birthday—I was in the living room, escaping myself through the piano, when I felt my pocket vibrate.

Ashley had finally replied.

Hey danny

yeah I sort of no who you are. Mary mentioned you. But no sorry I havent heard from Mary since I saw her 2 weeks ago. But she does this tho she disappears for a bit and then comes back. Ill messge you if I hear from her

Ashley's inbox did not make anything better. It only opened up another foggy chasm of questions.

If Ashley doesn't know where she is, then where the hell is she? Is she safe? Did she move by herself? Or with her dad? Is she dead?

I played through every scenario in my head, trying in vain to piece together what were only imaginary clues. Where was she? How, how? I had stood there with my open heart bleeding, pleading for her to believe in me. Had Mary already been planning on running away, even then?

Holding my phone above the white piano keys, staring into the bright screen, I searched my thoughts for the right questions to message Ashley back with. Anything that might evoke a simple detail to help unravel the mystery.

Then I heard Mom through the closed glass doors on a quiet phone call explaining to one of her California colleagues about the spontaneous departure.

"My son's friend—he died—we flew back to attend the funeral…."

My spirit had been hanging on to denial as a means of defending itself the entire time. On my drive out to California, I wasn't even myself. My identity had been forfeited into a car on the road. Without a past or a home, only a destination to go.

And up until that very instant of sitting in front of the piano, staring at my phone, all the tears I had cried had been welled from a deep and painful place of exhaustion. It was the delirium that had made me sensitive; just the word for word of the story was enough to make me sad. They were just sad words strung together. No different than reacting to a heavyhearted headline on the news. At the funeral, I had still been afloat in the esoteric world of the rolling sea of clouds. Denial had time-trapped my heart. My heart froze when the gun went off. And hadn't even so much flinched as it received each new wound.

But then, at that very moment, the time-trapped timer reached zero. The metal chain of the spell snapped—and I felt the entirety of the tragedy all at once.

I slammed my hands down into the piano.

Storming out of the living room, up the stairs, passing all the photographs of Dad, Connor, my family, my childhood. All that was, that wasn't anymore. All that was gone and never, ever coming back. I barged into my old bedroom and strode across the magic-marker etches on the hardwood floor. The plastic bag holding my Tiny Tigers tea-ball mitt was still where I'd left it all those weeks ago.

I took a seat on the corner of my messy and unmade bed. That bed, that very same bed where Mary had combed her fingers through my hair. That same bed I held her in as she cried late into the storm-ridden night after we had sex so tender and slow. That same bed Dad used to sing me to sleep in.

First my legs slipped, and then my butt crashed down to the floor. The pain riveted through my body. I slapped my hands down hard, clawing my fingers over the magic-marker strokes that had slipped off the paper in my shaky, five-year-old hands.

In the darkness behind my tightly closed eyes, I desperately brought forth the scene: me and Connor, making up stories, drawing characters; Dad walking in and telling us to go to bed. Don't worry, Dad. We went to bed. We grew up. Those boys are asleep.

"Danny!" Mom yelled as she pushed through the door and saw me on the floor. Hurrying over, she sat next to me and held me. "What's wrong—why are you crying?"

"I fucking miss them, Mom! I fucking miss everyone! Why'd they have to die? Why does everyone die! God—"

My voice cracked as I bawled into my hands. An amount of tears that I did know possible for the human body to possess leaked through the cracks in my fingers. Then removing my hands from my face, I started slapping the floor, repeating: "Why Why Why Why Why Why?"

I screamed and then bawled harder into my hands than before.

Mom rubbed circles against my back until I could catch a breath. The anger subdued into a steady stream of weak sadness. A corner of my heart was still full of hate for myself. How could I have gone so far as to being completely alone and self-sufficient for three sleepless nights on the road, but then, yet, here I was, at eighteen years old, after having convinced the gentle hand on my back that I was emotionally secure enough to live on my own, on the ground of my childhood bedroom wailing like a baby.

"Mom," I finally said, croaking through the raw patch in my throat. "When we leave, when we're gone, who's going to remember them? Where will we be? Who's going to be here to look at the marker on the floor and remember them? That marker on the floor, that blue one, that was him! That's him, Mom! Connor! Who's going to guard him? I want to remember him and protect him. I can't leave him. This, this—it's the only physical thing left, like, his hand actually drew that! I can't leave him, Mom. I can't leave that mark."

Mom started crying. We sat on the floor holding hands and cried together for a long time.

But all things pass. And in the space of that passing, all things resume. The night picked up where we had left it. Mom and I attempted the Danny Birthday Dinner 2.0.

First, we were silent. The only sounds were the seconds ticking by on the clock, but then, one of us made a joke, and conversation resumed.

Mom had gotten another cake. *Happy Birthday (again) My Handsome Son*, the blue icing on the chocolate cake read. And from her many magic hiding spots, she gave me my presents. A new phone and a brand-new Mahogany, hollow-bodied, Fender Telecaster.

The high-quality wood felt amazing beneath my hands as I discovered quickly how I would hold it. My face must have been glowing with an embarrassing amount of joy, because when I looked up at Mom, there were tears above her smile.

Somehow, happiness still found its way through the cracks. Even though sitting in the kitchen felt like deja vu. Two actors, now much older, brought back for the anniversary episode. It was a slight reminder that life will go on. Although a grave shadow stretched over us, it was still possible to be happy. It occurred to me that it didn't need to be that kitchen table, or that particular dining room set; a family could relocate anywhere. You can make anywhere feel like Home.

Once the evening had settled, Mom asked: "Danny, has there ever been a single day where you haven't thought about Connor?"

I shook my head.

"Then has he really gone anywhere?"

But how about those who did not die? Such as that girl I used to know. The rest of Mary's story? I'll never know. No, really. I never saw or heard from her ever again. The questions I asked Ashley were hardly answered. Eventually I did follow her, only to see that her timeline was dedicated to promoting her upcoming baby.

Some further investigation, however, did get me a nudge closer.

22 Bayview Avenue was demolished in order to make room for another Jersey mansion. And speaking of demolishing, my old friend Max, that mystic he was, turned out to be correct about Gilmore Park's future. Pretty soon after moving, I learned that downtown Carraway Beach was flattened. The natural elevation of The Alley was brought down to be level with the sea. The condo development that went over-budget, and then eventually bankrupt, shut down. Leaving a flat field of dug-up dirt and makeshift rocks in its place. The Alley and her endless summertime riots, the screaming guitar solos and the clashing drums that raised Rock 'n Roll Hell from the chambers of her bars, eventually became no more than another New Jersey Myth.

I don't need to fill the rest of these pages telling you about my broken heart. In the end, like always, time mended it. The agony indeed toppled me many days, and many more lonelier nights (the nighttime always made missing them worse). But there came a day, when, well, I realized that I didn't think of either them once the day before.

Max stayed with me for a very long time, but Mary was soon only remembered after having realized that she was forgotten. Although, the harshest of realizations came to me about three months to the day I'd seen her last:

I was established in my new life—if only so rudimentarily—out in California. I wasn't quite yet tearing through guitar solos at the Troubadour, but that's coming.

One afternoon a girl caught my attention. The first girl my eyes had allowed me to see since New Jersey. Believe it or not, I had begun practicing yoga with much heavy pushing from Mom, and from the woman she had arranged for me weekly to talk to. Other than the embarrassment, and the pain I experienced the following day after the first class, I liked it.

I was waiting in line at a smoothie bar in the plaza of the yoga studio, when I couldn't help but find myself very attracted to a strawberry blonde behind me.

Somewhere inside of me, my old naïve confidence sparked to life:

"Excuse me," I said, catching her attention. "Just so you're aware, I am going to take an incredibly long time to order."

Her smile spread across her face like wings. "If you can actually hold up the line longer than that guy," she gestured forward. "I'll submit you for a World Record."

"Will you, please? I'm looking for a quick shot to fame."

"Well, hold on a minute," she said urgently. Her lower lip then dipped, completely collapsing the serious face she was trying to make. "Will I get to make some sort of royalty off this? You know, since I'll be the one who discovered the guy who took the longest ever in smoothie-order line history?"

"Of course, I'm a team player. I'll need your name, though."

The pink gemstone bracelet spun around her wrist as she presented her hand.

"Gabby."

"Danny."

We joked back and forth until my turn came to order. After I had placed my order as fast as possible, I said, "Oh, and I'm covering whatever she's getting too."

As we parted at the door, I reminded her that the Guinness World Records people would need a number to get in contact with her.

Two days later, we were to meet at Urth Caffé on Melrose Avenue in West Hollywood for a dinner date. Arriving a little early (or perhaps Gabby a little late), I waited at one of the sidewalk tables watching all the soon-to-be Walk of Famer's passing by. When overhearing—listening in on—a conversation about a script that just couldn't be passed up, through the crowds on the sidewalk, I watched as Gabby looking immaculately arrived. Wearing a sand colored, open-shouldered romper tied by the waist with a belt, and heels with straps that ran up the shins, finished with a thin gold piece of jewelry strung across her collar, she was breathtaking.

"Danny! Hey!" She spotted me. Gabby had mastered a way of keeping the amorous strutting of her hips contained enough to preserve respect.

While talking over dinner, her ability to fluently communicate impressed me. She was working in LA as a model.

"Well, model slash actress," she said, needing to humble herself.

Gabby was shy to admit that her budding career was being funded by the bank of Mom and Dad back home in New York City. My neighbor on the opposite side of the Hudson.

"…And those were my main influences, but I'm totally a 1960s guy," I told her when the tide of conversation turned my way, asking me about what I do, getting us talking about music.

"You know, I find liking Bob Dylan has become a total cliché when anyone gets talking about folk," I continued. "Like, there are so many other greats from that era that are totally underappreciated, but Bobby's lyrics are still great. Um, I also dig anything British Invasion. But, I must say, The Beatles were the only band that had ever really mattered." My long-winded answer dwindled away with a strange tone. Gabby didn't seem to notice the soft dip of my inflection and told me that she wholeheartedly agreed.

She then went on to say how she loved the unsuspecting bella figura of Europe's 1960s avant-garde artists. A genre that had been long deprived of authenticity, and was now a baseless drape for anything the modern LA art world declared abstract, she said, before shifting the conversation to her idols. Brigitte Bardot, she told me, was her spirit animal. And the tribulations of Serge Gainsbourg's numerous affairs were repulsive and inviting to her all at the same time.

"But I'm stupidly hopeless romantic, and am still waiting for my Marcello Mastroianni to come wading through the Trevi Fountain to kiss me. But my dreams of being Anita Ekberg will have to be put on hold because guys in LA are so not romantic."

It was also the films by director Vittorio Di Sica that inspired her to get into acting.

My whole understanding of what I'd thought had been an expansive knowledge of 1960s pop culture dwarfed into nothing. I was absolutely clueless.

Only later—when in the bathroom—did I have a chance to Google on my phone who and what the hell she was talking about.

I picked up the bill at the end of the evening, even though Gabby insisted that she pay for her half. Afterward informing me that the next one was on her.

We parted with a kiss on the steps of her apartment on North Spaulding Avenue just off of Fairfax. The kiss felt more than good; it felt great. Gabby was a well-spoken, beautiful, ambitious, culturally and artistically sophisticated, high-class girl who made it worth your while to roll out the red carpet of chivalry for. Her personality had been left unaffected by her superficial surroundings. Things with Gabby were off to an amazing start, the way romantic connections between men and women were supposed to go.

As I left her front steps, from behind me, I heard the metal gate shut, and walked back to my Mustang parked on the street with the biggest smirk smacked across my face. The crisp California night prompted me, by force of habit, to flip up the collar of my jacket. It was late in November, after all. But it was only when I felt the roughness of the material beneath my fingers, did I realize I was wearing my jean jacket. It hadn't even crossed my mind.

The ridges of the key vibrated through my hand as I slotted it through the ignition. But somewhere in the motion, my wrist lost the strength to push through the resistance to start the engine, only turning the battery on for the radio to play.

Sitting in my car with the roof down, resting my elbow on the door, I clenched my hand into a fist and leaned my head against it. The razor-thin wind cut across my face, blowing my hair down onto my forehead. I'd let it grow out since the summer.

Sitting there, shifting through the unfamiliar LA radio-stations, I got thinking and finally acknowledged the underlying truth: I wasn't talking to Gabby. I knew that. Who was I kidding? I wasn't in that restaurant once all night. I wasn't on her doorstep on North Spaulding Avenue; it was another's lips that I felt on mine. Hell, I wasn't even there in that smoothie line. And even then, sitting in silence with the radio as my only companion, I wasn't even in that car under the glowing-cone of the Los Angeles street light. I was sitting in that car, but on some early July night all the way back in Jersey.

That entire night, I was trying to talk to Mary.

As Gabby spoke, it was only under a near-invisible layer of my conscious that I knew I was sorting through what she said. Finding the pieces of her that reminded me of Mary. Trying to find a way to reintroduce myself, to reinvent the way she got to know me. Saying practically the same words and sharing the same ideas. Hoping that if Mary got to meet the new me—the mature me—things would have played out differently. Since she left me that day, so suddenly, so unceremoniously, without a proper goodbye, without a "*Thank you, thank you for that summer. I'll never forget you*", and with Max's death the pivotal point of all my sadness, I didn't even really get the chance to be heartbroken over Mary. The ranges of my heart had been overloaded with too many other tragedies.

It was with the anger that roused when I realized Mary had been forgotten about, that I regained the strength to turn the key in the ignition. And like always, my engine had to rattle a bit, making me question its mechanical proficiency, before roaring to life with so much confidence it rocked the car left then right.

The streets of Los Angeles are suspiciously vacant at night. Where did all those millions of cars that delayed the day's traffic go? With the wide streets and the multiple lanes to crisscross aimlessly through, it was easy to get lost in thought and just drive.

The music on the radio seemed to push the car forward through the night. The tempo of the song—one I did not recognize—a perfect complement to my speed.

While driving, I lamented over the empirical injustice of chance. The cruelty of the genetic lottery. Involuntarily, I compared the lives of those two girls. Growing up only fifty miles and the Hudson River apart, yet, completely unaware of one another, and with grossly disproportionate advantages in life. Gabby was a mirror to what Mary should have been had fate's dealing been scrupulous.

Sixteen sweet years from booster-seat to driver's seat. First, I had to obtain that taunting beginner's license, and then, I had to ace parallel parking in my first shot on the exam, all for the greater safety of others on the road. Other than getting laid, what requirements does it take to make and raise a child? The irresponsibility happens far too often. The power lies with the parents to decide what irreversible effects they choose to impart on their children. Yes, it is inevitable. Everyone will screw their kid up. Even the best parent in the world will. And, Yes. It is up to the individual to sequester the damage and heal. God, that's what makes us individuals, after all. But, unfortunately, those with the odds stacked against them, don't always make it out on the winning side.

It doesn't matter what money or privilege you're born into. What matters is the love from the family you're born into.

I'm getting sick of witnessing all of these families generationally bequeathing their dysfunction onto the next.

How in Hell was a girl like Mary supposed to get ahead in life while entrenched in the eye of her life's storm? Her impasse the spawn of her parent's selfishness. Mary never once, I believe, lived even one day reprieved from her hurricane.

Gabby, on the other hand, was born into a propitious pedigree. Cherished and liberated to think without restrain and have thoughts that were listened to and discussed. She was free to discover things like sixties actresses and bougie French words to articulate her opinion of art. Gabby probably—no, definitely, got to do all those little girl things Mary told me she never got to do. Other than maybe having shorter legs, Mary was unquestionably more beautiful. She could have been in Gabby's place, pursuing whatever her dreams called her to do out in LA, if that was what she wanted. But I don't even recall Mary having any real dreams. Mary was a victim of circumstance, and that's the worst kind of victim any of us could be.

On the drive back to Pasadena from LA, Ventura Highway (ironic for a guy like me) took you up and around a mountain ridge. The lanes of the highway were dark, and right out the passenger window, the lights on the endless hills sparkle like moonlit crystals on a black sea. It was a sight I always wished Mary could have seen every time I made that drive home. On the loneliest of nights, when I turned to catch a glimpse of the picturesque landscape scrolling out before my eyes, I would try to see her. How her head would lean back. How the wind would blow back her hair. But I had a hard time remembering how she would have sat.

Resolution is hard to achieve without closure. Letters with all my confessions and questions were penned without a mailing address. I'd have to live with my unanswered questions. Still, all I really wanted to know was if she, even for a second, in the deepest heart of our most soul-filled night, had loved me too.

And then there was the discarding of her memorabilia as

well. Hardly a whisper of Beach Baby perfume still lingered on that Rolling Stones sleeping tee. When I held it up to my nose, it escaped out of my senses forever the second I could no longer differentiate the smell from any other. Another time, I was driving and discovered a woven thread of long brown hair, dyed blonde at the bottom, in the sleeve of my sweater. I pulled it out and watched it wave in the wind. What was I going to do? Keep it? I let it go with the breeze.

I dreamt of her many times. How she would surprise me at the door of my Pasadena home, telling me in a beautifully worded confession that she was sorry and that she loved me. But nope. Unlike all of her vanishing acts before, that time she had disappeared for good.

So Mary, wherever you are, if someday you ever read the words of this book, I really hope one of those sly, one-sided smiles, sneaks onto your face when you remember who you were at seventeen.

And just know that I don't cry for you anymore. I've gotten over you, many times.

But I won't lie. Sometimes, when the radio plays those songs we listened to on those summer nights when our walls came down, I go back. I'm seventeen. And I remember you. And I miss you.

I can't write the rest of your story because I never knew. I did my best to remember, the rest I had to fill in with what I made up given what I knew of the circumstances surrounding your life. But the writing of the rest of your story is now up to you, Mary. I've spent a lot of time patching up and repairing the past. Reassembling the memories and their reasons to fit the story I need to believe. I hope you've done the same. Your life wasn't easy. And I'm sorry. If I could have done more to help, I would have. It was beyond my limits.

I'll pass the pen on to your hands now—under one condition. Whatever your story is, make sure its ending is a goddamn happy one. Got it, Froo Froo?

33

Thunder Road

The desert highway rolled into an intersection. I wasn't quite sure how to get to where I wanted to go. My expedition to see the Mojave Desert wasn't quite what I had expected it to be. Gas was running low, and I thought for sure that I was either going to get mugged or die. Which I thought was an awful shame considering I had made it this far. Now, I know better—I was somewhere outside of Twentynine Palms—but at that moment, I was convinced I was in the Middle Of Nowhere. So at that intersection I rolled up upon, looking like a giant concrete cross in the middle of the desert, I waved down a truck transporting bales of hay.

" 'Scuse me."

"Ya?"

"Um, where's tha I-10 and tha closest fillin' station?" I tried to talk Southwestern for these folk.

The truck driver stopped for a second, weighing the route in his head.

"Ya see that road up 'head there on tha left?" The mustache-wielding man pointed out the window towards a long stretch that ran into the mountains. I nodded.

"That there is Thun'ner Road. You'll wants ta follow that and it'll take ya where yer lookin' t'go."

"Thank ya, sir."

I could tell he appreciated being called sir.

He nodded. I nodded. He drove on by.

I looked down at the infinite gray line that ripped through the canvas of ivory sand on both sides. The desert was beautiful. The sun was hot and the air was dry, and it wasn't quite the past and it wasn't quite the future—you couldn't tell what it was—it was just now. It was me and that car, and the road in front of me and the road behind me. And in the hazy blue distance, the mountains stood tall and grand like the ancient edifices of time that they are. Solemnly listening in on all of history's stories as we ephemerally drift on through. Undoubtedly set to outlive us all.

Standing there, staring out at the vastness of the desert, at the magnificent white clouds sweeping boundlessly across the blue sky, and feeling the heat of the sun beating on my skin, I got thinking of you, Max. I got thinking of all of our adventures as kids, and wished you were there on this adventure with me. You would love the desert. Open, soundless. Free.

So getting back in my car, which was like a little piece of home, I followed the trucker's direction and sure enough that street sign read:

Thunder Road

And not long after, I found my fillin' station, shared a smile with the gap-toothed woman working the cash, and embarked upon that endless drive. It was long, it took a long time, it took until the sun set beyond the mountainous horizon line. But that didn't matter. Because my faith in that long stretch of asphalt known as Thunder Road took me at last to that place I wanted to go. Home.

Acknowledgments

The story of *Some Place Better Than Here* has gone through many transformations throughout its lifespan. The names listed below collate the story of the story:

First, I would like to thank Miss Hotte for sending me down to the principal's office in the ninth-grade because I was looking out the window and daydreaming. I would like to thank high school principal, Mr. Simpson, who thought my reason for being sent down to the office was stupid, so instead sent me to go around the local neighborhood to drop off pamphlets in the mailboxes that warned of a rising graffiti epidemic. I would like to thank Bruce Springsteen for the song that came on my iPod Mini's shuffle while dropping off those pamphlets.

I want to thank my friends in high school for not only supporting, but also participating, in my grandiose independent film projects; those endless summer nights attempting to capture those perfect shots taught me that imagination channeled through hard physical work produces results. Next, I want to thank the high school faculty that was so fed up with me by twelfth grade that they ACTUALLY gave me a credit for writing the screenplay of SPBTH.

I would like to thank that psychic in the Mojave Desert for saying about my screenplay, "Yes. That one. That's what you need to do."

I want to thank Laura Matley, G-Loco, Talia Yousef, Vincent Atallah, Kylie Robbins, Jarek Uchmanowicz, Kevin Teng, Vanessa Popoli, Rory Vanderbrink, Karlene Coffel, Kelly Pickett, Ana Lara, and the hundreds of girls who auditioned for Mary. Without you all, this dream would never have been pushed to the extent that it has.

I would like to thank Bruce Springsteen, again, for taking the time to approach me in the lobby bar of the Hyatt after the *Wrecking Ball* concert in Rochester, New York (most likely due to my ridiculous excitement during the show). And for when I told him I had written a screenplay inspired by his music, putting his hands on my shoulders and saying, "That sounds great! Keep it up." I took that VERY seriously…

I would like to thank Fatmir Doga for taking an interest in my screenplay and for providing me the opportunity to (almost) have it produced by a legitimate production company; hence if not for that opportunity, I would had never written the "novelization companion piece."

I would like to thank Massoud Abbasi for being a mentor and for introducing me to Aman Chatha, who I would like to thank for advising me throughout my early career. And if not for Aman, who casually said one day: "I've got a buddy who works for this company, Wattpad. Ever heard of it? You should upload your book on there and see how it does."

I would like to thank the Wattpad community for believing in my work and giving me the encouragement required to finish writing the novel. I am very indebted to each and every one of you Wattpad readers who reached out to me, reminding me I wasn't absolutely crazy for believing in this story for so long. Thank you.

I would like to thank Sari Ruda for handing off a TIFF party invitation to me. I would like to thank Don Ziraldo who helped me get into that party when my name wasn't on the guest list. I would like to thank an individual I met there for introducing me to Caitlin Krahn. Caitlin, you've been an amazing friend, an adhere supporter of SPBTH throughout these years, and if it wasn't for your editing, my book would probably be a catastrophic disaster (such as this acknowledgements page most likely is).

I would like to thank the team at Friesen Press, Jamie Ollivier, Judith Hewlett, Warren, and Dahlia for overseeing the production of my novel. I want to thank Meg Sethi and the team at Evolution PR for helping my book find its home with readers.

I would like to thank Matt Taylor for teaching me everything about the guitar and what it means to live and die for your art. You can listen to his band "The Natrolites," pretty much anywhere on the internet where you can find music. (They may or may not be the real-life version of Danny's favorite local band, "The Broken Lyre.")

I would like to thank my buddy Brian and my buddy Tim for getting me through those dreary winter days. I would like to thank my partner in crime, Aiden Booth, for being the best guy around to talk about dreams with.

I need to thank my beautiful little baby, Sheba, for being the best dog in the whole wide world ♥

I would like to thank my older brother, Skyler Wakil, because, God, if it wasn't for you I probably would have turned out to be a sports kid or somethin'.

I would like to thank my younger brother, Seager Wakil, for keeping my teenage references somewhat relevant and because I love you.

I would like thank my Mother, Marie, for continuously believing in me and being the first person to tell me "Land, you would make a very good writer."

I would like to thank my father, June, for everything. For teaching me all the right lessons regarding what it requires to be a strong and gentle man in this world. And for blasting the Psychedelic Sunday radio program, forcing my young developing ears to be inclined to screaming guitars and crashing drums, and for introducing me to all of those great songs that we live our lives through.

And... Mary, wherever you are, I want to thank you too.

CPSIA information can be obtained
at www.ICGtesting.com
Printed in the USA
LVHW091829080319
610000LV00005B/74/P

9 781525 506093